Also by Robert French

Passion of Shadows

The Diary of Nellie Mill

Lynch

Sigurdsen

Josephine Littletree

Robert French

Josephine Littletree

First Edition

978-0-9952671-6-9
978-0-9952671-8-3 (KDP MOBI)
978-0-9952671-7-6 (EPUB)

Cover design by Caligraphics.net
Formatting by Polgarus Studio

Questions, comments, contact: afterwords@shaw.ca

Contents

Preface

The publication of these manuscripts has long been a wish of mine. I have not done so before now because of a promise made decades ago and the intensely private nature of some of the material. But not publishing them would be silencing Josephine Littletree in her journey through a world that has disappeared and yet is very much with us. The facts have changed but the prejudices have assumed different forms.

I have provided minimal background material in my introduction and textual notes, resisting the urge, always present in academics, to provide footnotes. That would reduce Josie to history, and to a kind of respectable and mouldy irrelevance. Writers worth reading are those whose words live, and by that test she deserves to be heard. Her voice speaks for her people, and for the rest of us.

My personal recollections at the beginning attempt to set the scene. They provide another example of coincidences that sometimes seem almost predestined but are in truth additional proofs of the inscrutability of happenstance. All this is not to slight Sam, without whose appearance in Josie's life her story would not have been as wide-ranging. He provided a larger world. She makes it part of hers, seeing the links that make all worlds the same.

Richard Kendrick
Wharton Hall

Introduction

Sam McLendon turned 108 a few months ago. That wouldn't mean anything to many people now. I hadn't seen him for over thirty years and had assumed he was dead until I saw the story in the newspaper. He's living in a government-subsidized waterfront apartment and he's not only its oldest resident, he's the oldest person in the city. He finally got some attention after all, and I'm sure he didn't want it. He was a writer but never published anything and didn't care. That's why I remember him, and because his stories were good.

I first met Sam McLendon when I was a kid. He was living in a shack on pilings on an inlet stretch of waterfront below a three hundred foot bluff covered in trees and brush. There were a lot of shacks in that area then, and between them and the bluff ran the main line of the Canadian Pacific. The people in the shacks were squatters and in the late Fifties were cleared out. The railway police had already begun to treat everyone who went down there as trespassers. But when I went there in the mid Fifties I never saw the police and people crossed the tracks freely. There was a path through the forest and a flight of wooden steps down to the tracks. In rainy weather the steps were slippery and you had to hold onto the handrail. After school I would watch from the bluff as steam locomotives hauled boxcars and tank cars, or a snub-nosed diesel raced by pulling the steel-bright streamlined transcontinental. At twilight the locomotive smokestack seemed a black Roman candle bursting with sparks of orange and red stars, and through rectangles of yellow light in the day coaches of the transcontinental you could glimpse passengers sitting as they whizzed past. The best part was before. The silence teased with a rumour of sound far off and you didn't know if a train was coming or not but your excitement said it wasn't the wind in the trees behind you or the water in the inlet below. When you knew you knew something wonderful, waiting for the crescendo of noise to swallow everything in a passing roar. And after so much longed-for significance, as if all the world was there in the jabbing madness of pistons and grinding screeching wheels, an emptiness like a loss. I'd scramble down the bluff to that impossibly narrow track and touch the warm rails. Somewhere in the blue dimness off to the east and hidden by a curving shoreline was where you wanted to go.

But that going and that place were far off, the rush of lights and echoing noise taking the promise away along the silk-smooth rails. On the other side of those rails was a more immediate life. The shacks were strung out along the shoreline, some almost next to each other and others more than fifty yards apart. They were in the sandy stretches of beach, between the sections with heaps of boulders and driftwood. Many shacks were little more than one-room unpainted cabins on pilings. I would scramble down the weedy embankment, getting a first whiff of the briny smell of the beach mixed with the odour of tangled kelp strewn above the line of the tide like rust-coloured ribbons with frilly edges and rubbery bullwhips swollen at one end to the shape of an onion bulb. Miniature crabs the size of a watch dial scuttled everywhere among the kelp and rocks, and along the sand were the spout holes of clams. Clinging to rocks were pink and red starfish, a surface of hard goosebumps to your touch, and spiny sea urchins lived in tidal pools. Almost always there was a breeze off the water, bringing the cold salty broth to your nostrils. The ritual refrain of the waves and the lip-edged frothy surf burbling among rocks and hissing along the sand crested and ebbed in the blood repeating what no words can say, you hearing without listening as your shoes slipped on water-polished boulders and scrunched across gritty shelving sand.

Sam's shack was larger than most of the others, had two rooms, and there was a back porch on the north side, facing the inlet. The shack was sturdy, with pilings like logs, and the entrance and porch doors and window frames bore traces of white paint. The entrance door was on the side facing east and a flight of steps went up alongside to a small landing. Nearby and high up on the beach were Sam's rowboats, an old leaky one with an empty coffee can for bailing and a much better boat painted white, with red oarlocks, which he'd let older kids take out if he could trust them to avoid the eddies and riptides of the inlet. I was seven when I first went there and nine the last time I saw the place, so the only rides I got were with other kids, taken out by an older teenager who wasn't sure if he wanted to show off to us more than he wanted to be rid of us. I wanted a chance to row but the oars seemed too long and thick for my small hands and skinny wrists. We'd go out when there wasn't a tide running, the sky usually overcast and the grey water a heavy smooth silence close to the sides and getting deeper as the shore slipped away. An occasional wave from a passing freighter brought the heaving grey mass nearer as we lifted and sank. We never went far out on those calm days or risked the trickier parts, with deadheads and shoals, and the only danger was a drifting log that had escaped from a boom at one of the sawmills on the North Shore. I remember most the sensation of floating on something immensely powerful that could never be entirely trusted and demanded your respect.

You never visited Sam. You walked in after school, on weekends or during the summer holidays and looked around for other kids, and in fine weather went out onto the porch to see who was sitting in a deck chair, feet on the railing, or was trolling for fish. I never saw anything but sprats or dogfish caught there, and once a gumboot, but kids kept trying. Sam was usually in his combination living room and kitchen, next to the porch and taking up most of the shack. Everybody assumed the other room, at the front, was his bedroom. The door was always locked. If he wasn't smoking a pipeful of Old Chum on his overstuffed and battered sofa as he was fooling with a concertina, which he didn't play well, he was sitting and writing at a small oak table near the bed. On a corner of the table sat an old black Underwood looking like a model of a medieval castle, flight of round keys leading to the ramparts. He never used the typewriter. I figured somebody picked it up somewhere and gave it to him. He used pencils, which he kept in an old tobacco tin, and wrote in exercise books schoolchildren use for lessons, with lined pages and a coil binding. I never knew what he was writing until years later, after his shack had been demolished. None of us paid much attention to him and he hardly noticed us. We had the run of the place and that's what we wanted, our own waterfront shack. Only it wasn't ours and that made it better because someone else took care of it. Friends of his would drop in, some from the other shacks and some from the city. They would bring food in shopping bags, cans of beans and tins of corned beef and sometimes cartons of eggs and packages of side bacon. The only thing I ever saw him cook were pancakes, which he called "flapjacks." A blackened skillet hung on a nail above a small cast-iron stove, next to the porch door. He would use dried and cut driftwood from a box beside the stove, starting a fire with newspapers or cedar kindling. He'd strike a wooden match against his thumbnail. He could have struck it against the stovetop but that wouldn't have been Sam. Something about the quick way he did it told you he took a small pleasure in that simple dexterity. He'd dump ingredients into a mixing bowl, give them a few stirs, then pour enough batter in the skillet for a pancake and wait and flip it neatly once and onto a plate, and so on until he had a stack. He'd clean a place on his writing table and set the stack down and plates and forks and get butter from an icebox on the porch. Sometimes there was also a can of corn syrup, and once I saw a bottle of maple syrup. Sam would brew a pot of tea, using water from a galvanized bucket he'd filled that day from a pipe beside the bottom of the steps leading from the bluff.

None of us kids were offered any food. Neither Sam nor his friends got too close. There was none of that too friendly stare of a pederast, no odd appraisals or lingering touches or gifts with strings attached. The morality squad would have fallen asleep at Sam's as he and his friends talked international politics while they ate and later as they smoked and we climbed all over the shack and rambled along the shoreline digging up pails of clams to take home. That was before the clams and other bottom feeders in inlet waters had become tainted with sewage and poisons from passing freighters and tankers and pleasure boats.

Sometimes I think the Fifties down there were the last part of a short dream and the shacks and the Depression castoffs who lived in them and the easy unsuspicious friendliness of life among them and the clean waters never existed. But to me Sam is still real, ruddy face almost round, grey hair topped by a blue cap with a visor, and his heavy frame in ribbed woollen sweater and blue jeans and gumboots with the tops turned down, and the way he had of always thinking about something other than what he was doing. Sam's friends are still real too, especially Josie, an aboriginal woman who came to see him a couple of times when I began going there. She had red hair, a small mouth and straight nose, and her skin had a coppery tint. I thought she was beautiful and was desperately in love with her for a whole year after she smiled at me. Josie would occasionally kick Sam softly in the shins when they sat at the table drinking tea. I wondered about that and figured it was because she was a woman, and that was as far as I got. He seemed not to notice her doing it, and I didn't know if that was good manners or a bum leg. He grinned a lot when she was there. They talked quietly and I didn't hear what they said but I guessed it wasn't about politics. Most of his friends in the other shacks were eccentrics and neurotics of various kinds and degrees. There was a guy who had gotten out of military service during the War by remaining mute until the army psychiatrist declared him mentally unfit. He had been an orphan and raised by the Christian Brothers in St. John's. From what he said about that, you could understand why being mute would be easy for him. His short stay had been in the artillery and sometimes he wore his army beret, with a bronze-coloured badge pinned to it. He left the beret on the table once and I sneaked a peek at it. Under a crown and between scrolls with a motto in Latin across them was a muzzle-loading cannon, above it, *Ubique,* and underneath, *quo fas et gloria ducunt.* A guy named Eddy kept a goat called Gertie in his shack. Captain Billy had fished commercially on both coasts and had skippered an ore carrier on the Great Lakes and a banana boat in Central or South America. An old prospector who had been in the Yukon during the gold rush talked about the Klondike. On weekends obvious political types, socialists, communists, anarchists, anarcho-syndicalists, came from the city and could be heard from outside the shack. Some wore suits and were union organizers. Others were less professionally doctrinaire, leftovers from the Depression who were trying to patch up their beliefs in a postwar world of consumer demand and nuclear weapons. They kept the faith because they couldn't do anything else.

This social flotsam and jetsam gathering at Sam's place on the inlet kept a kind of community going for a while. They were a glimpse into the recent past. On a strip of shoreline those shacks and those outcasts were a precariously odd defiance, the tracks on one side and silky cold riptides on the other, and in back and rising above everything the wooded bluff, behind which society went on with its proclaimed and boring necessities. Deep smells, kerosene lanterns burning with a wisp of black smoke above a flattened flame, briny buffeting wind off the water picking up the decay of stranded kelp scattered across crushed shells and sand, tarry creosote oil staining ties embedded in grey pea gravel, damp cedar and hemlock in drizzle on the way home. And behind, a last heard seagull's cry on the wind.

After two years I didn't go down there any more. I don't know why or if there was a reason. It simply stopped being a place to go. Other things replaced it but what they were I can't remember.

In 1957 the National Harbours Board, which had jurisdiction over the coastline, decided to evict the squatters, and they were relocated in government-subsidized housing in Vancouver. That shoreline community, known as Crabtown, had been established as early as 1912 by sawmill workers and would reach its peak in the 1930s, when the Depression drove many homeless to seek accommodation wherever they could find it. Accounts of that time mention families with children living in painted and well-kept houses with porch gardens. A boardwalk offered driftwood art for sale. I saw no families when I went there, only an aging population of single men. By my reckoning there were about 100 structures of various kinds, including sheds and boathouses, and all looking badly weathered, needing repainting and repairs. Sam's shack was in a better state of repair than the rest. The decline would have begun with the War, families and able-bodied single men leaving to take advantage of an improved economy.

When I heard the shacks had been torn down, I felt a vague regret. I didn't see Sam for twenty-five years, until a Saturday in 1981. I was driving along Powell Street and saw him picking oranges from a box under the awning outside of a market. He'd aged so little it seemed he'd come into the city to buy provisions for his shack. Still the cap with visor and the sweater and jeans but a pair of white sneakers now. I wanted to know what the end was like for him and the others. I parked around the corner and went and introduced myself. He didn't remember me, said he never paid attention to the kids that came around. We stood talking for a few minutes as shoppers darted between us, our backs to the noise of traffic on Powell. I told him I was an English professor. I mentioned the exercise books and he said he would let me have a look, said he lived in an apartment nearby. He paid for the oranges and as we walked to his place he told me the prospector and the man discharged from the army as unfit were dead, the guy with the goat had disappeared and that Captain Billy had moved to one of the Gulf Islands and died there. He mentioned two other squatters, a guy who had joined the army and fought in Europe as a tank driver and a neurotic who thought megadoses of vitamins induced mystical states of consciousness. He didn't know what happened to them. Of the political types he said one had become president of a civic workers' union. Most of the rest he'd lost track of, except for two who still came to talk politics. He didn't mention Josie.

His apartment building was on Alexander Street, four blocks from the market. It had been built a couple of years earlier and was tenanted mostly by pensioners and welfare cases, all male. He had a one-bedroom suite on the fourth floor at the front. There was a view of the waterfront from his living room window but it wasn't the one I'd seen from his shack further up the inlet, blue mountain forests across the water, stark summits of bladed stone wintering in white drifts. And the green summer evenings with sun sparkles on the water burning like a welder's torch as the evening breeze blew cool along the inlet. And the band of low morning mist on the North Shore in autumn, and the winter days when you couldn't see the mountains but a grey blankness out there beyond the heavy waves of flexing steel sheen. And the mud flats at low tide, a smell of sea sewage and wriggling with stranded life. And the tide rushing in cold and salty, clear and froth-edged onto your feet, bubbles of saliva from spinning eddies and the undertow. Sam's view now was a congestion of piers and wharves and sheds and loading cranes on rails and offices of stevedoring companies. The mountains were further away, further than distance could take them. Suburbs were burrowing tics spreading up their scarred sides for an expensive view of an inlet now an oil-smeared canal for metal tubs and a public toilet. All this in little more than a hundred years of progress, and the politicians and real estate developers and the other legions of the aesthetically blind and the spiritually retarded were having a fine time showing Mother Nature who was boss.

I turned from the window and looked around the apartment as Sam prepared the tea. I saw a photograph, a five by eight black and white in a gilt metal frame propped up on an end table beside the sofa. Not the woman I had seen but a younger Josie. Slim and looking in her late teens, she was standing in front of a wooden house in what appeared to be a rural setting. He came in from the kitchen holding a couple of ceramic mugs and handed one to me. I sat on the sofa and he sat in the same chair and at the same table I'd seen in his shack. The old tobacco tin was on it, pencils arrayed around the open top like wooden spears. He took a couple of sips and began talking, guessing the first question I would have asked.

"The federals knocked on our doors one morning. Notice to vacate, relocate. Said they'd help put us in low-rental housing. Thought we were jungle hobos, bindle stiffs, loganberry lancers, canned heaters."

"They give you a reason?"

"Didn't have to. Some took it better than others. Captain Billy was gone in two days. He knew people in the Gulf Islands who'd let him stay in a cabin on their place. Been there already. Lots went into low-rental places. Others back East. Don't know where they all went. Couple of guys turned up years later. Told me where some ended up, who died. Never saw the others again."

"What did you do?"

"Lifted. Drifted. Grifted. Sifted. Wasn't ready for the bureaucrats."

"The years don't seem to have done you any harm."

"That's something I owe my relatives. They live long slow lives."

"How did you come to live in a shack on the inlet?"

"Came out here in the Thirties. I was a carpenter. Couldn't get work. Relief camps had closed. I was tired of bumming around. Saw the shacks in the False Creek flats and knocked one together for myself. Torn down by the cops at the beginning of the War. I'd heard about the inlet shacks. Met two guys with the same idea I had and the three of us went out there and built a good one. One guy took off after a year. The other was an alkie who went nuts and drowned."

"Have a hard time finding lumber?"

"It was there if you knew where to find it."

"I've never liked the idea of the Harbours Board evicting

you guys. That was part of the coastline. But you weren't doing any harm. You should've had something like squatters' rights."

"Should've. Could've. Would've. Had've. Sortof. No government in this country, from the feds on down, has listened or ever will listen to anybody but the corporations. It started with the deal the railway made with the federals to build the first transcontinental line. They got so much land on either side of the track. Sweet deal. Made millions from real estate in all the big cities. This country has been run by corporation lawyers from the beginning. It's a business, not a nation. Land of the apology for being big, fat and happy, and the stock exchange is our politics. Don't kid yourself, most of your fellow citizens like it that way. Get in, get yours."

"What about your radical friends?"

"Those jokers. Poor cranks, most of them. Didn't know their theories were nineteenth-century fairy tales. The smart ones were idealists on the make. Could twist anything, justify anything. If I had to choose between them and the corporate cons, I'd pick the cons. They'll cheat you but won't shoot you for calling them phonies."

"Your shack always seemed full of people. Sometimes you'd be writing at that desk when everyone else was arguing or eating."

"It was a free-for-all and that's the way I wanted it. Never liked too much order in my life."

I glanced at the photograph of Josie. Sam saw me look.

"Not everybody fits. Those that don't shouldn't try.

There's room for everybody but not in the same place. Have to pick your own."

I nodded at the photograph.

"I remember her. She was nice."

He turned to the table and pulled open a drawer. I'd forgotten it had one, if I had ever noticed. He took out a couple of exercise books and leaned towards me and tossed them in my direction without a word. I caught them with my free hand and put the mug on the end table. There was nothing on the buff covers except the name of the stationery company, how many pages a book contained and that the pages were ruled. I opened the top book. His name was on the first page. It was the first time I'd seen or heard his surname. His handwriting was large and awkward and tilted backwards like a child's. I turned the page and saw the beginning of a short story. There was no title. His handwriting dominated the blue lines, rising above or sinking below them. There were obvious erasures, smudged lead written over, or paper tinted pink from eraser residue. In some places he'd rubbed so hard the paper was transparent. I mention all this because of my ingrained academic fascination with the look of a manuscript, and especially a handwritten one. It's the writer's personality in front of you, the struggle to find the right word. What I saw was unhurried patient labour, a dialogue between author and story as one worked to fix the other, fix in two senses.

I read the story. It was about a hobo during the Depression. A man who walked ten miles to a convent to get a headcheese sandwich. Saw only the white hand of the nun raising the wooden panel in the window and sliding out a paper bag. Who left the family farm and walked fifty miles to the nearest town to hop a freight. Who had walked in prairie heat and cold, found shelter from rain and snow. Walked for ten years across the country, until the War came and he got a job. The unspoken theme haunted the pages, those awkwardly written words. The man was everybody who had walked through those years. Walking for no reason except there was nothing else to do or anywhere to go. You walked as if that was the one thing no one could take away from you in the vast land, your right to go anywhere. Movement was freedom, and finally illusory, using up hope and energy until it exhausted them. Working during the harvest and the farm women watching their young daughters carefully as the women brought the food to the hired hands at a trestle table. Chewing on sunflower seeds in a workers' hall and listening to radicals. Getting a free meal and a night in jail out of the weather, courtesy of a judge who expected you to be out of town the next day. ("You had to hope for a bit of luck, like the local beak getting a piece of tail from his wife the night before.") Handouts at the back doors of farmhouses. What could be spared. Don't look like a bum. Wear a suit and tie. You're a tradesman out of work. You're trying to get something to help you on your way. Thousands of gallons of milk poured away, food spoiling in warehouses. Eggs a nickel a dozen. Few customers. Vagrants everywhere.

Sam had been one of the vagrants, crossing the stretching miles, smelling roadside dust in July on tufted clinging weeds. It was in the grey lead trailing across empty spaces, leaving the gritty convolutions of vanished souls. He remembered the facts, changed nothing, and through them had written a memorial for himself and others like him. And like all good memorials it was simple. I was impressed and told him so. He looked as if I had told him it was going to rain tomorrow. I realized I didn't understand Sam McLendon. His stories had not been published. Why not, if the rest were as good as this one? He'd been writing as far back as the Fifties, maybe longer, and yet all his efforts amounted to were handwritten stories in some exercise books.

"Ever try to get published?"

He scratched his chin with that thumbnail I'd seen strike a lot of wooden matches.

"In the Forties one of the guys who used to come to the shack tried. Leo Peters. His people were Russian. The family name had been changed by an immigration officer too dumb to spell it right. He was a radical but the only one I ever met with a sense of humour. He inherited his politics from his father. I think he believed that stuff because of his old man. He read some of my stories and said I should send them out to the magazines. He said he'd get the addresses and mail them out. Use his address as mine. So I used that Underwood that Old Percy had dropped off—Old Percy had gone somewhere by the time you came around. He was a tramp who rummaged around the east end. Had a bicycle with a sidecar to put things in. I typed a couple, gave them to Leo. Never heard anything for a while and forgot about them. When he showed up, he handed me one of the stories back with a note attached to it by a paper clip. The note was from a magazine and said something like my story wasn't suitable. Hadn't heard anything about the other one. Said he'd let me know when he got anything back. That was the last time I saw him. He went up the coast."

"I could try to get them published."

"It's not important to me. Ever look up at the stars on a clear night? Nothing but space and time. When I found out how long it takes starlight to get here, I figured nothing we do is really important. It wouldn't change much of anything if people read my stories."

"The one I looked at is good. I think some people would enjoy them."

"Maybe. And maybe they'll find something else they'd like. Doesn't make any difference to me. In the long run nothing matters except the life you live. Trying to impress someone else is a waste of time."

I couldn't budge him. I handed back the exercise books. He put them into the drawer. We had another cup of tea and talked more about the inlet. I mentioned eating the salmonberries that grew high up along the face of the bluff, and the tire hanging from a branch of vine maple on a rope we'd use to swing across a gully with a small runoff creek that emptied out up there. He said the aboriginal peoples liked salmonberries, but looked as if he was thinking about something else. A few minutes later as I was leaving he left me at the door and went back to the desk and opened the drawer and took out seven exercise books bound together with string and said he would give them to me if I promised not to publish the story in them. I told him I wouldn't. As I walked along Alexander Street in the twilight I loosened the string enough so I could read the first few pages. It was about Sam and Josie. Something told me it would be. When I decided to publish his manuscript, along with Josie's, I wrote him to get his consent. After all this time I didn't think that publishing them would be a violation of my promise. I have a hunch he expected me to do so. My letter seeking his permission returned with an "OK" and under it his signature. His story is probably the one piece of writing he would want to be remembered by, if he wanted to be remembered at all. The manuscript, printed here complete and unedited, has no title.

Sam McLendon's Manuscript

Let's play poker. I don't like cards. No, like this. I'll be Gertie. You be Eddy. Poker was two words to her. We kidded about it. Stud, play the hole card. Or draw, draw to a flush. Stand. Know why I come here? Yeah. Oh, you. You're not so good at it, you know. So I'm no good and you still come.

She would touch me when I said anything like that. Kick me in the shins with her foot. Pinch my arm. In my family you didn't touch, ever. If you forgot yourself and did, you pretended it was an accident. My childhood was an apology. It was Sunday all the time. Take your hands out of your pockets. Keep them away from your face. Where are your manners? Did you wash your face before dinner? Sit up straight. You haven't cleaned your plate. Your shoelace is untied. Don't run off. Ask to be excused from the table. Behave like a little gentleman.

I didn't want a life working in the family hardware store in small-town southern Ontario. Church faces, Sunday manners. Too many ties and wing collars, petticoats and high-button shoes. Too much lace and whispering. But I stood it for years. Got engaged. She smelled like talcum powder and Dr. Dennison's Nerve Tonic. I sampled it once. Quite a kick to that stuff. It smelled like cough syrup and tasted of something hundred-proof. Whitewash skin, pimples under her jaw. Pale eyes staring, stupefied. Narrow body, bloodless hands in her lap. Like dead white mice. Why are you so restless, Sam? Keep your hands to yourself. Try at least to be a gentleman, will you, please? She was already dead and I was waiting to die. And everybody cluck-clucking about how perfect a couple we were. I could see every step ahead to the end of it. Walk out of church a groom, be carried out in a casket.

One Sunday night after a boiled dinner I was summoned into the front parlour and had to answer to her mother. Everything in the room was waxed, polished or covered with antimacassars. All the furniture had fat legs. I sat on the bloated sofa. She parked herself in a chair upholstered in red velvet. I always had a hard time breathing in that room. There's no inquisitor like a prospective in-law.

"I think we should have a little talk, Sam, about Lenore. She's not getting any younger. And neither are you. What do you plan on doing?"

"About what?"

"Are you going to fritter your life away? And hers? That's not fair to her. She's a bright young thing."

Bright—hardly.

Young—technically.

Thing—things don't breathe, she did. Barely.

"We're engaged, aren't we?"

"It's been almost three years. When are you going to set the date?"

A noose tightened around my neck, handcuffs squeezed my wrists, manacles pinched my ankles. Love shouldn't feel like that. Neither should marriage, in theory. In practice, from what I've seen marriage is getting used to saying yes and fighting for the occasional no, or taking a walk, and that means lawyers.

"Sam?"

"Three years isn't that long when you're thinking about the rest of your life. What I mean is, I'd like to be able to provide properly for her. I'm still a junior clerk. I don't make that much."

"I've spoken with your father. From what he says, you'll soon be the assistant manager."

Going behind my back to speak with my father and he went along with it. Wasn't anybody on my side. Like watching from behind bars as a lynch mob gathers. Justice was a ring around my finger or rope around my neck.

"Even as assistant manager I won't be making that much. She's used to having lots of things."

"Some day you're going to be the manager and owner of the only hardware store in Airdrie. That's quite a prospect. Lenore is mindful of that. She's willing to wait."

A life of waiting for both of us. More lace and talcum powder and nerve tonic. I'd end up on the nerve tonic. Or something stronger. If there was. The respectably pickled.

I'd seen that. Small-town life. No parole from that prison. Respectable is a life sentence.

"Sam?"

"Look, Mrs. Whittaker, I need more time to put some money in the bank so I'll be able to provide for her. I've got plans, things I'd like to do."

"Like what?"

"I'd like to see Toronto." (Lie.)

"You have to learn to put personal things aside when you're married. You've got to think for the two of you from now on."

She had it all planned.

"You could stop off at Toronto on your way to Niagara Falls for your honeymoon, a double treat for someone from Airdrie. Quite a few of us have made that trip over the years. A lifetime of memories. Some go back for their fiftieth anniversary. Those that God grants such mercy to."

I could see the postcards. Having a wonderful time. Wish you were here. All of you bastards. Lenore will be coming back in a box a bit smaller than the one she lived in. Fell overboard from the Maid of the Mist in an unguarded moment. Wet deck near the Falls. She was going to run off with a defrocked missionary. Tibet was far enough. But I wasn't sure he'd keep his word. I'm crossing ice floes in the Arctic. Hope to get to Siberia. Regards from slippery Sam.

"Sam?"

"What?"

"Upcoming church picnic would be a great time to announce the date. Right after the three-legged race, say, or the egg rolling. Before they dish out the potato salad and slice the ham. You two could stand together and Reverend Cambie could announce it. I get gooseflesh thinking about it, don't you?"

"I may not get to the picnic."

"Whyever not?"

"I've got lots to do. What with the store and finishing that cabinet for my dad."

Large enough to hide in. Get it shipped to Faraway Places. Pack a light lunch, some brochures. Get out in Bali. Beautiful girls with skin that's seen the sun. Eyes flashing with the right kind of danger. Swim naked, don't they? Water so clear you can see everything. Dancing in the moonlight. Gestures that speak volumes—not a cliché when you're raised in Airdrie. Work on my tan. Set myself up in a grass shack on the beach with a willing maiden. Forget it. With my luck it would be Sudbury.

"Sam?"

"What?"

"I know you wouldn't leave poor Lenore high and dry."

She was already high most of the time. That covered dry too.

"No, not really, intentionally on purpose, but a guy has to think carefully about such an important step in his life. I been thinking I might not make her a good enough husband."

"That's nervous jitters, last-minute stuff. Lots of betrothed couples feel that way. Don't you worry, you're perfect for each other. The other day Minnie and I were saying how suited you were. I think your next step should be seeing Reverend Cambie. He'll calm your fears, Lenore's too. She should go along with you. Why don't I arrange that?"

It was a conspiracy. They were all in on it, including Minnie, the mayor's wife. Public knowledge. No privacy. So many eyes were staring my way. Don't make a mistake, young man, or you'll regret it. There was a threat behind it, that if you didn't follow the timetable of their crummy lives you'd miss out, and in case you felt you weren't missing anything they'd make you pay for the rest of your ungrateful life. No thanks.

Our town was on a spur line. Train twice a week. Once on the way to work I saw a man get out of an empty boxcar near the station, cross the tracks and go to the back door of the Haslam house. Mrs. Haslam put a sandwich and a pear into a paper bag and gave it to him. Found out later from a salesman the hobo left Airdrie that night, hitched a ride with him. I left a month later in a boxcar. They didn't miss me. There was another free plot in the cemetery. You can waste your time but don't waste your life.

It was 1929 and I was twenty-three. I timed it right, eight months before the Wall Street crash. Hired out on construction in southern Ontario before things got serious. When I was a kid I'd picked up a bit of carpentry from a couple of uncles of mine. Used to help them during school vacation and earn a bit. My bourgeois shopkeeper family didn't like me doing what they called manual labour but they liked the money. I wanted to apprentice with my uncles but the family said no. So I used to sneak in time with them, became as good as a journeyman. Made cabinets, liked working with hardwood, the feel of the grain. Had a set of tools. Took some with me and sold them over the years, picked up others later on. As Josie said, we borrow, we don't take. I bummed around for years before I got out to the West Coast. Right away I knew it was the place. A saying going around was, "Vancouver is the only place in the country where you can starve to death before you freeze to death." I flopped in the parks that first summer. Somebody would stand me to a meal. But I got the itch and took off again, living in hobo jungles and relief camps, hopping freights and riding the rods. And riding the blinds, which was better because you were out of the wind and had some protection in cold weather. I'd get into the blinds at the front of the mail car, between it and the tender. Nobody would bother me around the station because I always wore a suit and tie. The important thing was not to look like a tramp. I'd hop up there when the conductor wasn't looking in my direction. You had to stay on your feet. Rode hundreds of miles that way. Did it once for two days to do it, that's all. Would smoke my pipe, the closest friend I had as the years rolled by.

On my way out west in the spring of Thirty-four I stopped in Winnipeg. Red Winnipeg some called it, for all the communists and other radicals of various stripes who passed through or called it home. You might think the city was nothing but revolutionaries from that, but most of the leftists lived in the North End. It had a large working-class population of Ukrainians. The rest of the city was as conservative as any other except for Toronto, which prided itself on being the scourge of the left. I wasn't a communist but was open to lots of different ideas. I attended meetings and rallies of parties on the left, the right offering nothing I could see to guys like me. Two groups got my attention. The communists and the ILP, the Independent Labour Party, an offshoot of the British Labour Party, and most of whose membership was British. The difference? They didn't preach worldwide revolution and the end of capitalism. Their brand of reform: better wages for workers, no wage cuts, no company or police strikebreakers, free health care for the poor, low streetcar and bus fares. These two "friends of the workers" weren't friendly to each other. Social outlaws to many, I saw these competitors as in-laws, and there's nothing like in-laws for enemies. They'd send hecklers to each other's meetings. That's how I met Tatiana. I was attending a public meeting in a draughty hall sometime in late March or early April, listening to speakers on the platform extolling the ILP's program, when a young woman stood up and interrupted the latest speaker's recitation of the party's aims.

"You're in bed with the mayor and business."

Somebody in the audience shouted back at her.

"I wouldn't mind being in bed with you."

When the laughter died down she answered, speaking with a Russian accent.

"You have a fat chance of that."

As the chairman called for order I looked at the heckler,

standing three rows in front of me and to the left. That's a bad joke but I'll leave it. She was wearing a fur hat and a quilted jacket. Round face, large eyes, dark hair, very pretty.

"We are for the workers," she shouted, handing out leaflets as she left the hall. I locked eyes with her when she looked in my direction but she gave a leaflet to the man sitting beside me. The girl of your dreams, the poster girl, the pinup girl, the girl who can't be had. I followed her out of the hall. Nobody else did. Make any difference? Not to her. She was too busy counting the leaflets she still had as she walked along the chilly street. I kept following. "The meeting is at seven o'clock," she said, finally looking at me. "Here." I got a leaflet. She could have told me where the meeting was and saved herself some paper. She crossed the street and was gone. The leaflet was revolution red, the print in black block letters.

It was one o'clock. I spent the rest of the afternoon in the public library. At five I got a meal in a mission and at seven I was in another draughty meeting hall, this one decorated with Soviet flags. Like the other meeting, this was attended by the usual party hacks, the curious, the bored, and maybe an RCMP spy in an old coat and trying to look hungry as he surveyed the gathering with policeman's eyes. Communist notables were shadowed by the Mounties and suspected it but I never heard the ILP complain, so I guess they didn't rate the coverage. Something about being British, I suppose. She was sitting in the front row, minus the fur hat. I could see her hair was braided into a large coil at the back of her head. On the platform were four men in suits sitting behind a table, all with appropriately messianic looks. That meant they couldn't be British. The next two hours turned out to be a series of speeches reflecting the party line, including references to the coming revolution. There were calls for better unemployment relief, raising taxes on the rich, lowering them on workers, replacing slum housing, and for support of the May Day parade. She didn't move an inch, her eyes focused on each speaker in turn. Things got emotional when a speaker referred to recent police attacks with batons and tear gas against the unemployed at demonstrations. The meeting ended with audience and speakers standing and singing the Internationale. I stood but didn't sing. Afterwards I went to the front to talk with her. She was having a conversation with one of the speakers. With the same idea I had, he'd stepped down from the platform. I could see they knew each other. I hung around close enough and long enough so they'd notice. She did, swivelling around on one foot to face me.

"So, did you see?"

See what? I grinned and nodded. All I could see were her eyes, pale grey and soft. What did they see? I hoped they saw me.

"I told you so. We are for the workers."

I grinned and nodded again. It seemed to work.

"You are here to offer support. If you come tomorrow to party headquarters, I will speak with you."

With that, she swivelled away.

I didn't plan on becoming a communist stooge but I wanted to see her again. After a night in a mission bed I showed up next morning at party headquarters. It was a storefront in the North End, a room facing the street used as an office and a much larger one at the back for meetings. A door separated them. Propaganda posters with idealized profiles of industrial workers and peasants and calls for revolution and working-class solidarity were tacked up on the office walls. The hammer and sickle was emblazoned on the posters and a Soviet flag was nailed to the wall behind the only desk in the office. She wasn't there. Hangers-on sat in three beat-up chairs held together with wire. More lounged on the windowsill. A party hack sitting behind the desk was talking on a phone. I had to wait till he received his orders from Moscow. Where was she? He didn't know. She was busy with plans for the upcoming May Day parade. He stared at me. Why did I want to know? I told him she invited me to meet her there. When was that? At the meeting last night. I could see suspicion worming its way behind those apparatchik's eyes. Was I a police informer? An RCMP undercover agent?

"Come on, Benny. Tatiana's always inviting guys here. Picks 'em up like stray dogs. You know that."

One of the hangers-on, leaning against the windowsill, had spoken up. Work shirt, overalls, cap, denim jacket and chewing on a toothpick.

No accent. Benny had one. Russian. Probably accounted for the interrogation. He didn't like Toothpick's attitude. No respect for the party, meaning Benny's authority. But never forget worker solidarity. He grinned the grin of a man who hates to grin.

"She'll be here this evening."

I got into a conversation with Toothpick on our way to a mission dinner. He was a prairie farmer on the bum because of drought and low prices. He left his father and the rest of the family staring into a dusty wind knocking over withering stalks of wheat. A relief camp would be his next stop. After a while he got around to Tatiana.

"Most of the guys are crazy about her. She's the party mascot. She's a hard-liner, though. About everything."

He poked me hard in the ribs with his elbow. He liked her too.

I went back to headquarters at seven and Tatiana was there. Busy. Always busy. The revolution couldn't go on without her. She'd never get excited about anything else. I knew that the guy she would finally pair up with would have to share that passion. It wasn't going to be me and I knew that too. I hung around anyway.

She was talking over with Rosenheim (that was Benny's last name) the making of the party banners for the parade and what slogans would be best and how to make sure enough communists turned out to make their contingent the largest. They didn't think there would be much trouble with the cops or counter demonstrators. Leftists usually weren't bothered on May Day. "Outside of the Chamber of Commerce, who would demonstrate against the left in Red Winnipeg?" I said. She went into high gear.

"Have you never heard of the Canadian Nationalists? Nazis who wear brown shirts with swastikas and beaver emblems. No, you are not in Berlin, you are in Winnipeg. Does that shock you?"

I looked properly shocked. It was a surprise. I knew the country was basically conservative. I wouldn't have recognized it otherwise. But Nazis?

"I suppose they're German."

"Many members are Mennonites. There are some Ukrainians. The leaders are British army veterans. They put out an anti-Semitic newspaper and they are anti-Bolshevik, believe Bolshevik leaders are Jews."

"You'll be telling me next the Klu Klux Klan is in Winnipeg."

"No, on the West Coast. Their headquarters is a mansion in Vancouver. In Shaughnessy Heights, a wealthy suburb. In the university out there the eugenics movement has support from both faculty and students."

That shut me up. Know your own country. I didn't. The promised land had been promised to somebody else behind my back. Tatiana got my respect after that. She could see she had impressed me. We left together after she had finished sorting out the parade details with Rosenheim. He didn't like us leaving together. To hell with him. As we walked to her place, I asked where she was born.

"Novgorod. The old capital of Russia."

"So you're not Ukrainian."

"I am proudly Russian. I say it with no disparaging of other friendly workers and farmers. We must unite against our capitalist oppressors. We share the same struggle."

"Do you ever take time off being a party member?"

She stopped and stared at me in the circle cast by a streetlight. She thought about saying something but changed her mind and walked on.

"Do you want to help us, or are you content to be a nomad wanting to wander over the world, accomplishing nothing?"

I stopped under the next streetlight and looked at her. I noticed she wasn't wearing any makeup. She wouldn't. She looked better without it, I decided with the usual male arrogance.

"Maybe I'm looking for something or someone. I don't think I'll find it in doctrine. Especially doctrine from another land. I don't believe there's one answer to everything or for everybody. That makes as much sense to me as your political stuff does to you."

We had reached a street of workers' apartment blocks, tenements smelling of dingy hallways and cabbage soup. She halted in front of one and we could hear a baby crying and a couple arguing.

"I am staying here. For the time of being."

We laughed quietly, small sounds lost in an empty street. She nodded at me.

"Goodnight. I will see you again."

She opened the door to her building, its red paint peeling off the weathered wood. Too many winters in Winnipeg. That wasn't going to be my fate. But I hung around for a while, chewing on sunflower seeds like the other tramps to keep away the hunger pangs. There wasn't much going on except the usual wrangling at City Hall. The communist and socialist minority on council used the meetings as a platform for their respective agendas and kept asking for help for the poor and unemployed. The mayor and the rest were middle class conservative business types. Lots of rhetoric from both sides from little guys caught up in something they couldn't figure out themselves and who needed to borrow from pamphleteers or newspaper editors. At communist headquarters we tramps kept ourselves busy doing stupid things. We'd sit against the walls of the meeting room. Whenever we saw somebody crossing the floor we'd stamp our shoes and boots in a steady rhythm and the person would begin to march. Women were the preferred targets. Never failed, except with Tatiana. She knew the game and would manage to keep her stride. It was close to a march, anyway.

The May Day parade was the special event of the year for the left. Guys wore suits and ties, caps or fedoras. Women wore their best dresses, hats and coats. Everything had been cleaned, stitched, mended or darned to keep it from looking shabby. They marched in a solid line blocks long, four or five abreast, with banners. "Fight for Noncontributing Unemployment Insurance." "We Demand Work or Full Maintenance." "Join the Young Communists." I saw Tatiana holding up a sign on a stick. "Overthrow the Capitalist System." As usual, it was a mostly silent affair. But I remember one—I forget whether it was in Vancouver, Regina or Winnipeg—with a brass band of cornets, tubas and trombones blaring out the Internationale.

I was one of the crowd watching from the sidewalk. Along with deep desperation stemming from poverty there was a religious zeal about it, and as usual with zealots you got a one-sided view. But I had no political home, no steady job and no place to go, and at least they were dressed as poorly as I was. The country club set weren't my cup of tea, but I never believed they were completely responsible for the ills of society. Society covers a lot of ground and no group has ever had a patent on responsibility for which way it goes.

I didn't see Tatiana much during that time. I think she gave up converting me. I still went to the headquarters for something to do. I was waiting for warmer weather before hopping a freight west to find some work. One day in early June I was in the meeting room when a guy ran in shouting.

"Those Nationalists bastards are attacking our people in Market Square, right outside City Hall."

All the guys jumped up and headed for the door. I had a peculiar feeling and shouted at the guy who had run in.

"Where's Tatiana?"

"Where the hell do you think?"

I joined the rest. We grabbed a streetcar to Market Square. It was a battleground of Nazis, communists and cops, everybody yelling, punching or swinging something. There were many more communists than Nazis but the brownshirts had knuckledusters, blackjacks and police batons they'd taken from inside their shirts. The communists had gone through the market and were fighting back with sticks and two-by-fours they'd pulled from crates and stalls. The cops were whacking everybody they could get their hands on. It took a while to spot Tatiana. She was wielding a two-by-four against some brownshirt's head. He was doing his best to poleaxe her with a baton. With fists and elbows, I battered my way to her, getting a knock on the head. From which side, I couldn't tell. I grabbed the brownshirt from behind, arm around his neck, and threw him down. One of his pals missed my head by inches with a baton and Tatiana walloped him and he went down, out cold. She gave me a look I'll never forget. Her eyes were on fire.

"Go and get yourself a long stick. Keeps them away and you can hit them."

"I want to get you out of here. The cops are going to be making arrests."

The brownshirt I threw down was getting up. I picked up his baton and sent him to dreamland.

"Come on, Tatiana, before it's too late. You don't want to have to go through a stay in jail and a trial."

She nodded and we held hands as I pushed and punched my way through the melee, managing to avoid the cops. A big sedan drove up to the edge of the square and four brownshirts got out and then a man with stone-grey hair, who looked around quickly. The Nationalists were getting the worst of it. Bloodstains on those brown shirts. Many of their wearers had bloody faces. The man with grey hair ducked back into the car and drove away, leaving the four stranded. Tatiana was triumphant.

"He's their leader. Deserting his bodyguard. The fascist pig. He could see we are winning."

A couple of blocks away and we were out of the mess. She let go of my hand. We didn't say anything for a while. I knew she was thinking about something, figured it was regret at abandoning her comrades.

"As a journeyman carpenter I can say you're pretty good with a two-by-four."

"I am going back to Russia. That is why I left with you. I don't want to delay my return. I would never have abandoned my comrades if not for that."

I got the feeling a guy gets when a woman says something he's afraid she'll say.

"Why are you going back?"

"I can't do any good here. I can help build socialism there. Socialism at home, then abroad. One before the other."

"You're going to disappoint a lot of people."

"You mean men?"

"Yeah."

"Is that important?"

"It is to them."

"Are you speaking for them?"

"For me too."

"You don't attend many of our meetings. You go to as many labour party meetings. We know about such things. I asked you months ago if you wanted to work for us. You do nothing but hang around. When you want to. We need more."

"Always the party."

"I am a communist."

We had been headed that way. I had kidded myself off and on about maybe something different. There couldn't be. That didn't make me feel any better.

"When are you leaving?"

"The end of June."

I nodded.

"Good luck."

"Good luck to you. I hope you find what you want."

"Don't you ever want anything else?"

"I know my duty. I want nothing unless it can be part of that. You are like a boy. You want what you can't have because you can't have it."

"In this country we still think we can have what we want. It helps with the hard realities."

"Come to my country if you want to see hard realities."

"Is that an invitation?"

"Yes."

"I may take you up on it."

"You are too comfortable in your boy's world."

"Don't be too sure."

"I am sure of one thing."

"I'm sure of nothing except the right not to be sure."

She shook her head. Time to get serious.

"I am going to headquarters."

I went with her. Rosenheim was on the phone. He was jabbering away with Jake Cohen, the party lawyer. Cohen was on a nominal retainer, provided legal aid to party members and represented them in court. The word I got was he was a secret party member. Rosenheim told Cohen we had arrived. He handed the phone to Tatiana. She gave Cohen an account of the fracas. Apparently the communists were holding a demonstration when the Nationalists showed up. They'd planned to hold one of their own. A shouting match began, the Nationalists waded into the communists and the battle was on. Something Cohen said made Tatiana grin and she hung up.

"He's going to the police station. He will be there when they bring in our people."

She looked at me.

"He said you did the right thing getting me away."

Tatiana left three weeks later. The night before her departure she was given a send-off at headquarters. Party faithful, hangers-on and stiffs like me who knew her gathered in the meeting room. She was seated with the party top brass at a table at the front. Toothpick and I were at the back, our chairs against the wall. As a concession to capitalist decadence several bottles of wine were opened. It was Ontario loganberry wine. I was against Prohibition on principle. Drinking is part of civilized life. It's barbarous to ban it. But if anyone wanted to ban loganberry wine, I'd be hard pressed to say no. I'd had a brush with that stuff. Coffee mugs, drinking glasses and teacups of it were passed around. I stood up and raised my teacup in a toast proposed by one of the local bigwigs to Tatiana and passed it to Toothpick. He had drunk his shot in one gulp. Ignoring the toaster, who had begun a party-approved litany of Tatiana's virtues, Toothpick polished off my shot. We sat down and he tilted his head, looking at me.

"She's one fine girl. Pick of the crop. Going to be lots of broken hearts. Including yours, huh?"

I didn't say anything.

"I'm right, huh? Thought so. Smiling on the outside,

crying on the inside. Can't blame you. Our loss, Russia's gain."

"Cut it out."

"You're hurting."

"You'll be hurting if you don't shut up."

"I touched a nerve, huh? She's another piece of tail you're not going to get, that's all. You'll get over it. Too bad she's not Ukrainian. Those broads give it away."

"I thought you were talking about hearts."

"We both know what I'm talking about. Hearts and flowers and the old whatchamacallit."

"Is it the loganberry speaking or has that prairie dust got into your brain?"

"My brain is OK. My brain is fine."

"Your brain is barely functioning. You're a moron."

He shoved me and I shoved back and we threw punches and fell to the floor, rolling around among fallen chairs and cigarette butts. I hurt my hand hitting a chair leg and he howled when I stepped on his foot. I was trying to get up and it was unintentional, sort of. I felt Toothpick's arms go slack as he was being pulled away from me. I grabbed something to pull myself up. It felt like a woman's leg. I looked. It was a woman's leg. I glanced up and saw Tatiana scowling. I stood up. Everybody in the room had gathered around to watch the fight.

"Sorry. Guess I ruined your send-off."

I could hear Toothpick behind me.

"He called me a moron."

I didn't bother turning around.

"You are."

Tatiana shook her head. Rosenheim was standing beside her. He had to stick his oar in. It was to show off to her. He had as much chance of impressing her as catching a butterfly with a pair of tongs.

"You guys are a disgrace, ruining our tribute to Tatiana. This is civilized behaviour?"

Toothpick snarled at him.

"What do you know about it, Jew boy? Put your pencil back in your pants."

That brought in Cohen, who in a rare appearance at a meeting, had come to Tatiana's farewell. He was thickset, with a quiet voice.

"We can do without your racism, sir. I think you should leave."

"Fuck all you Jews. The Nationalists are right. Bolshie Jews are at the bottom of everything. You caused the crash. You talk revolution so you can grab everybody's money and control everything so the rest of us end up your slaves. All you want to do is ruin this country, turning us against each other. You should all be deported back where you came from."

Toothpick snatched his cap off the floor, jammed it on his head and left, slamming both doors on his way out. Cohen broke the silence afterwards.

"Let's not allow an ignorant and unhappy man to ruin Tatiana's night."

The crowd broke up and drifted back to the front. The rest of the loganberry was poured out and that seemed to lighten the atmosphere. Tatiana and I stayed at the back. She made a face.

"This is goodbye."

"You could stay."

"You could come."

"No chance of that. Or the other, I guess."

She shook her head.

"Either you would be unhappy or I would."

"So we let the big things run our little lives."

"We have no choice."

"I think we have."

"Such a boy you are."

"That again."

A voice at the front called her and she shrugged.

"I have to go."

We said goodbye and I watched her walk to the front with that swinging stride of hers. I never saw her again.

After a trip to the coast that summer I went back to the prairies for the harvest but didn't want to spend the winter there. If you want to know how bad a prairie winter can get, stand on the corner of Portage and Main in Winnipeg in January. The wind stabs you with daggers of ice. Exposed skin goes numb before you know it. If you're lucky a girl will spot frostbite, grab some snow and rub it on your nose. It's a variation of an Inuit kiss, all in the name of public spiritedness. I never got that lucky.

That fall I returned to the coast and signed up at a government employment office in Vancouver for a relief camp. If you were a single male between sixteen and twenty-five you had to go to a camp to get government assistance. Me, I was tired of city life and roaming around, wanted a break, bunk and three squares. The government clerk perked up when I said I was a carpenter. "You're a skilled tradesman." The communists had set up an office at 52½ W. Cordova where they recruited guys heading for the camps. They established a union for them, the Relief Camp Workers' Union. I heard from some of those that went to their office that they would try to get them to smuggle propaganda leaflets into camp. I was sent to Camp 210, in Hope. It looked military, with rows of wood-frame bunkhouses finished outside with tarpaper. Inside unfinished fir walls and floors, with rows of double bunks and a pot-bellied stove. The barracks look was deliberate, the camps being run by the Department of Defence. We weren't treated like soldiers, more like inmates at a minimum-security prison you could leave any time you wanted to walk the miles to the nearest town. You'd get thrown out if you disagreed with anything, and the authorities didn't want to see petitions. We were paid twenty cents a day, worked a forty-four hour week and were given breakfast, lunch and dinner and work clothes. Relief camp workers had taken to calling themselves the Royal Twenty Centres, the Royal obvious irony, but the low pay was a bad joke. The government thought it would discourage us from becoming dependent upon government help. We weren't driven hard but the work would have been easier and quicker if we had been allowed to use machines. But the government wanted to keep us all busy and save money on gas and equipment repairs. So it was picks and shovels and saws for us. At that camp we did some road building but mostly woodcutting.

Al Jessop ran the camp. He was a war veteran and easygoing as long as you weren't a troublemaker. Before I got there some communists had been thrown out for organizing protests and calling for a strike to change conditions. They concentrated on three grievances: poor food quality, not enough bathrooms and the low pay. Behind much of the unrest was the isolation. There was nowhere to go on weekends because the camps had deliberately been set up away from densely populated areas, another misguided government decision. With no women and no society but their own, most guys weren't happy, no matter how many books, magazines and decks of cards charities sent. And there was always that miserably low pay.

I worked on roads and cut wood but sometimes I did repairs on the bunkhouses. Steps, doors, door frames and roofs. There was no shortage of wood. Everything was kept in first class condition. Kept me busy.

I'd been there a few weeks when the RCWU circulated a list of grievances. No surprises on the list. I wouldn't sign it. The next night two apparatchiks came by my bunkhouse and wanted to know why.

"The food isn't bad. I've eaten a lot worse and been glad to get it."

"Is that your only objection to the list?"

"It'll do."

"You're betraying your brothers."

"Since when are we brothers?"

"We are all engaged in a common struggle against fascism."

"This country isn't fascist."

"It's capitalist. The same."

"By your definition, not mine."

"Your fellow workers have signed."

"That's their right, as it's mine not to. I don't believe they've all signed."

"Most have."

"So you've been making the rounds and putting pressure on the rest of us."

"We're trying to present a solid front to the government. The more who protest, the more chance we have of changing things."

"Not with this government. Do what you will, they're not going to budge an inch, especially to communist agitators. You're out for propaganda. You're doing this for your own reasons and they're not mine. No sale."

"You're a skilled tradesman. You should be getting more than a labourer."

"I thought we were all brothers. I'm not a master carpenter. I'm a journeyman. I'm not kicking. And if you think the government is going to increase wages for anybody, you're dreaming."

"If you don't sign, you won't be popular with your fellow workers. They might think you're a spy."

"For saying the food isn't bad? In June I fought Nazis in Market Square in Winnipeg. Check with the party back there. I worked on farms this fall. I'm as much a workingman as anybody here."

Everybody in the bunkhouse was listening and one of the guys in a nearby bunk spoke up.

"Ah, leave Sam alone. He's got a right to his opinions."

The apparatchiks left and one of the guys came over.

"I heard about that ruckus in Winnipeg. What was it like?"

"I got involved to help a woman."

"What was she like?"

"Beautiful."

"So what happened?"

"She went back to Russia."

Some of the guys laughed and started talking.

"Women."

"They'll do it every time."

"You can't count on them."

"Leave you with your tongue hanging out."

"Not the ones I've known."

"You going to tell us your fantasies again?"

"Not fantasies."

"Sure. You're as hungry as the rest of us."

"That's the kind of food we need."

"Shut up, you guys. I got to get some sleep tonight."

"Yeah, for twenty goddam cents a day."

The apparatchiks presented their petition and Jessop threw them out. Before they left they came around to say goodbye and shake hands, ignoring me. They'd expected to be thrown out. It was part of their martyrdom. They were building up to a general strike in the camps throughout the country. I wasn't against protesting the conditions, especially the low pay, but I didn't want them representing me. The truth was, there was nobody else representing the workers. The bigger truth was nobody, including them or the government, knew what to do, and all they were doing was pushing the party. It was a world crisis and another one would solve it. I knew something would happen but not what it would be.

After the apparatchiks left, Squealer Pete, also known as Cuckoo Pete, came to see me. He was the camp snitch. He'd listen in on conversations or pretend to be a friend so you'd tell him something he could use against you. He'd run and tell Jessop. No one took him seriously. He walked around as if his arms and legs were about to fall off. He'd keep touching his face with an invisible rag and would grab a pick or shovel handle as if he was blind. He'd gotten shell shock in the War, was supposed to be an assistant to Jessop, who hired him to give him something to do. It was either that or an asylum. He'd sidle up to you, arms and legs jerking and voice jumpy.

"Didn't sign, Sam? That's what I heard. Don't get me wrong. I'm for the worker. But those guys. Yeah. You know. You know what. What I mean. Don't have to tell you. You didn't sign. You fought for the commies, I heard. Winnipeg. Took their side. Don't get me wrong. Stand together. I'm for that. You bet. We're all workers. So it's true, is it? About you back in June in Winnipeg?"

"Hey, Pete. The sky is falling."

"What?"

"The sky is falling."

"How can the sky fall?"

"Look up, you'll see. I thought you should be the first to know, seeing as you're the one who's always on the lookout for trouble."

He looked up.

"I don't see anything. No. I don't. No, I don't. You're kidding me."

"There's cracks in it. Look carefully, you'll see. It's airplanes flying all over the place. Sound waves from the engines are damaging the stratosphere and propellers are chopping it up. All these radios with their frequencies are no good either. Radio waves are bouncing off the ionosphere, picking it to pieces."

He grinned at me as his hand scampered around his face with that invisible rag.

"I don't believe you."

"Have you noticed the dust is falling in larger particles lately? Have a look at the sunlight through a window and you'll see. It's like a curtain. The light is having a tougher time getting through the dust. And those particles are going to get bigger and bigger. Pretty soon they're going to be coming down in chunks. People won't be able to walk in the streets any more. They'll have to wear helmets and armour. They'll be running to get into streetcars and trains. Finally the chunks are going to get as big as buildings. We'll all be buried under that."

"What can we do?"

"Don't get on a plane. Turn off your radio."

"People going to do that?"

"You know how people are. They don't listen until it's too late. Then everyone runs around hollering for help. Won't be anybody to help."

He looked up again, squinting.

"Don't know. Maybe you're right. What you're talking about. Yeah. I can't see like before. Things are darker. Holy shit, yeah, they are. They are."

"You a religious man?"

"Guess so."

"You could always pray."

He scurried away, eyes darting up at the sky, and told Jessop. Jessop saw me later as I was repairing some steps.

"That was the best laugh I've had since the camp started. Pete's gone to pray."

There was one way to get Pete to stop yapping. Yell "attention" and he would stand at attention, stiff and silent, and when you said "dismissed" he'd walk away without another word. One time somebody had had enough and didn't say "dismissed," leaving him standing for hours behind a bunkhouse in the snow. Jessop found him shaking with the cold, snow on his head and pee running down his legs.

In the spring of 1935 I left the camp. The big moment for the communists came several weeks later. The RCWU organized a strike in camps on the coast and boxcar loads of strikers headed east in the On-to-Ottawa Trek. The idea was to present their grievances directly to the federal government. It was pure propaganda but the trek got a lot of public support because many were dissatisfied with the government's halfhearted measures. The train got as far as Regina before the government halted all freights headed east. It tried to defuse the situation by agreeing to meet with the leaders but the encounter ended in a shouting match. In Regina a crowd of trekkers and sympathizers gathered on July 1st. RCMP and police attacked the crowd and there was a riot. The strikers accepted the Saskatchewan government's offer of a ride back to the coast. There was an election, a new government and the camps were closed in 1936. It came down to a bunch of manoeuvring by both sides and a change of party hats, with the unemployed caught in the middle. I remember something Cuckoo Pete had said. "We're all for the workers. So who's against them?"

When the camps closed a lot of RCWU members went to Spain. Unemployment was still high and by 1936 the big topic among leftists was helping the Spanish Republic against a fascist insurrection. The fascists were getting help from Nazi Germany and fascist Italy, but no government except the Soviet Union was helping the republic. Taking their cue, communist parties on both sides of the Atlantic were sending volunteers, which became known as the international brigades. The Soviet aid was a Trojan horse. Moscow had decided to kill off the republic because it wasn't and would never be Stalinist, and there was a chance it might become a social democracy. Stalinists in Spain spent most of their time rounding up and shooting other leftists. The international brigades were eventually sent home and the republic died. I thought it was ironic that three years after the unprotected Spanish town of Guernica was bombed to rubble in broad daylight by the Condor Legion, Paris was occupied by the Wehrmacht and London was the target of German bombers. Those fates have a habit of getting around to evening up things sooner or later.

The international blindness, cynicism, self-interest and fanatical obedience that killed the Spanish Republic did it for me. I had thought about going to Spain to fight for the republic. But the communists wouldn't have accepted me and I couldn't have paid my own way. When I found out why things ended the way they did, I wasn't sorry I didn't go. I lost faith in any kind of politics. I would listen to discussions and sometimes offer criticism but no opinions of my own. I became even more determined to live apart from society. I decided I would quit the hobo life and stay out on the West Coast.

After some trips back East I built a shack in the east end of Vancouver on city property, part of the Raymur Avenue dump, west of Glen Drive, where shacks had been thrown up since the early days of the Depression. It smelled bad on hot summer nights. People in the houses around there closed their windows and doors. If we squatters had a window or door we closed it. There were at least a dozen shacks already there when I arrived, made from sheets of tin taken from the dump. You'd lay a piece of flat tin on top of a dirt floor and fit the corrugated stuff together for the walls and roof. Outside you'd use corrugated pieces as gutters to carry rainwater away. It would run into a creek that fed a small lake, which went from the dump up to and beside the railway stations on Main. It froze up in the winter and you could skate on it. It was deep enough. One winter a Japanese guy went for a skate on thin ice and drowned. Everybody had a stove, with a stovepipe through the roof and some asbestos around the hole where the roof touched the pipe. You'd use an old coffee can to brew coffee or make tea in and you'd put up shelves for your goods. Plenty of fuel around for a fire. Cardboard boxes and wooden crates in the dump and coal along the tracks in the CNR and Great Northern yards. We were all on the bum, making do. I remember a guy who'd lather up with face soap and shave with a piece of sharpened glass. There was enough food about. Mushrooms grew in the sooty soil under the railway bridge at the eastern end of the yards. You could scout around in the refuse in the boxes at the back of nearby warehouses for fruit and vegetables that weren't too spoiled. One guy would make plum jam—he called it that—from the stuff he picked up there.

You didn't have to depend on the dump for food. The missions over on skid row were always good for a meal. Every Wednesday the Sally Ann on Hastings sold a bowl of pork and beans for a penny. One bowl to a customer. Some restaurants were good for a handout. An Italian place on Main would give you leftover spaghetti and meatballs. If you had any money you could go to a Chinese restaurant on Pender for chow mein or liver and onions. If you didn't want to panhandle, you had the option of washing dishes in a restaurant to pay for your meal. Tell the manager you were broke. The next stop was the kitchen.

The more socially minded, and there were a few,

gathered at the White Lunch on Hastings, same block as the Sally Ann but on the north side. We'd meet guys in from all over the country, hobos that hopped a freight into the city. And there were others, who had jobs and wanted to talk ideas. We'd sit around and yak for hours. We'd chip in for a "coffee an'," which meant a coffee and a piece of pastry, but we'd get a pot of tea, more economical. The management was pretty good. They'd let you go back and fill the teapot with hot water to stretch the tea. During the summer we'd walk through Stanley Park the rest of the night talking philosophy. On those midnight walks under the stars you felt you were discussing the fate of the world. We'd been shaken out of the social mix for a decade but it wasn't lost time, it was time to look at what happened. Some got carried away, prophesying revolution and already counting the decapitated bodies of capitalists. I've never believed in any kind of holus-bolus philosophy that turns people into political ideas. There's more blood and dead bodies on that road than any other. There were lots of wild notions floating around. The wildest was, come the revolution the working stiff would be free of the capitalist yoke and would turn in his leisure, after sharing equally in the profits of a proletarian economy, to studying the great works of western culture. Read only the great books, discuss philosophy. No more Hollywood trash or tabloids, pulp fiction or potboilers, no comic strips, called the funny papers. Radio only for symphony concerts and serious drama. Nobody ever kids you as much as you kid yourself. If you're aiming to get rid of the system, you dream up a new one that ignores the same human nature that created the first. Among the tramps I knew there were those who'd have thrown every classical music score onto a bonfire rather than miss one issue of the funny papers. None were any threat to storm the public library's section on philosophy. The common man is common, the regular monkey. Cannon fodder, lynch mobs, believers, fans. More important than anything else, our greatest dream and we never spoke about it, we lived in a big beautiful country blessedly innocent of the bloodletting of many other societies, a land that dwarfed and awed us and defused our words of any real rancour.

Doc Jenkins was a Welshman and leader of the White Lunch get-togethers. He'd been a ship's carpenter and was a socialist who liked philosophizing. He never got excited. To him all of us whatever the political stripe were soldiers in a good cause. He'd always sit near the window, his back to the street, thin face of an ascetic, hair almost down to his shirt collar, dark blue suit and maroon tie and a cup of strong black tea in front of him. He lived for discussion, searching for some kind of truth in the palaver coming from all parties. He was on the left because he was a workingman and the right was bankrupt, but he hated theory without humanity and he thought any government was in danger of forgetting that. Tall, lanky Rod Stowe was a lawyer, book smart and a good debater who never pushed an opponent to the wall once he'd got the advantage of him unless he wasn't a leftist of some kind. E. A. Hammond, known as "E. A.," and never without his pince-nez, was a poet who had founded the city's poetry society, mostly a bunch of women who thought poetry was somewhere between religion and romance. From what I saw of their stuff they wrote a lot about unspoken love and were silent about the real article. Jack Egan was a railway brakeman who sat in to listen and learn something. Other working stiffs dropped in, guys who lived in rooming houses in the area, and there was me and two others from the shacks. George Ousby was dirty from head to darkened toes sticking out of his shoes. You could see the ring of dirt around his neck. He smelled high, like rotten fish, but nobody said anything out of respect for sweated labour. George never sweated at anything but that was beside the point. And Bill Telford kept talking about his high school education. "The Lady of the Lake got me ready for the breadline." Hammond looked a little hurt behind the pince-nez.

In Thirty-eight Henry Brownell was MP for city centre, and old-line party all the buttoned-down way. Private school, corporation lawyer, grandfather had been federal Attorney General and wife brought him a fortune. But he was caught with one hand in the public till and the other up a Sunday schoolteacher's dress, took a drunken swing at a traffic cop who had the nerve to stop him and passed out in church with liquor on his breath, so he had to resign "for reasons of ill health." In the by-election the old line party put up a hack, a canvasser and bagman. The socialists were going to run Ernie Phipps but he had been caught twice in Stanley Park by park police as he was peeping at girls undressing in the bathhouses. He was literally caught with his pants down. Years later this had blown over and he was elected as MP for the east end, but it was too fresh at the time. So the nomination went to Doc Jenkins. The papers played it up, with editorials saying that if he won the country was sure to go red. He was about as red as maple syrup but the newspaper hacks had been given orders to lambaste him. They didn't want an intelligent man elected who would speak the truth. A nincompoop like Ernie Phipps, who was on relief and was looking for a steady paycheque in return for a few socialist platitudes, was safe. They didn't have to worry. The election wasn't even close. During the War Doc ran again, this time in a provincial general election, and came to within twenty-five votes of winning. Later on Rod Stowe won in a wartime federal by-election, with a big boost from the servicemen's vote, and he went back East and did what Doc would have done. He told the smug bastards off and a cabinet minister challenged him to a fistfight. In the general election a year later they poured in money and beat him. And that was the last election for any of the gang. By then Doc was dead. I'd moved from the city and hadn't gone to the get-togethers for years, and from what I heard it wasn't the same after he died. He was the leader because he was more than a politician, he was a man who thought about politics and only ran because he thought it was a citizen's duty to run if there wasn't anybody better. There wasn't. Next to him they were all small fry and I didn't have any use for them, though I listened to their yakking. They were citizens too, I kept telling myself.

All that talk at the White Lunch seems one long conversation now, except for my last time. We had heard the news about the Nazi-Soviet Nonaggression Pact. It was August, Thirty-nine, and everybody knew a war was coming but nobody expected the dictators would cosy up to each other. A decade of high-flying theory and low-flying fact should have prepared us for it. Party members around the White Lunch table looked uncomfortably certain that evening and fellow travellers started washing their political hands with amnesia. Doc couldn't resist a dig at the faithful.

"Strange bedfellows. I wonder which is the big bad wolf?"

"Not our Little Red Riding Hood," Rod said. "She'll have a surprise in her basket of goodies when it's time to go to grandma's house to reckon with the wolf. A steaming bowl of borscht. There'll be sour cream all over his mustache."

Rod crossed his long legs and leaned back and laughed, his Adam's apple bobbing over the tie he always knotted tight as a piece of string.

"They're peddling something," Doc said, "and there's going to be lot of backpedalling now too. You go far enough right or left and you meet the other gang coming. The toughest balancing act is in the middle. That's politics."

Rod leaned over and said to me, "We're all believers here."

"Pleasant company excluded," I said.

Hammond quoted something from an anti-war poem written during the First World War. Jack Egan wondered how soon and how the draft would be worked. Doc said war would mean more socialist legislation because the servicemen would vote for a change. And the colonial empires would disappear because the subject peoples wouldn't fight for the survival of the democracies and not demand their own freedom. He said the Depression would finally be over. After a while nobody spoke. It was as if something died right in front of our eyes. History had turned on its fulcrum, the past suddenly far away.

A couple of days after the War began I came back from a day's work at North Star Fish Packers, where the foreman every morning picked that day's workers from the crowd of hopeful guys who waited outside the entrance. I had been working on and off there for months. When I returned to the dump, I saw the shacks had been torn down. Where mine had stood was a flattened jumble of junk. The stove was on its side and the stovepipe crushed. Bill Telford came a while later. He said cops on horseback had knocked down the shacks with billy clubs and soldiers had rounded up everybody they could find and put them into an army truck and taken them to the barracks on south Granville to enlist. He'd been released because he was deaf in one ear. We helped each other find what we could of our stuff. I found the few tools I had left. I slept on park benches for a couple of weeks, thinking about what to do. The weather was turning cool and I didn't want to spend the winter sleeping in windy alleys and doorways under a pile of newspapers. The city was home now, I didn't want to leave. I met two hobos who had recently come in on a freight, and Dick Ives and Ray Kelso were sniffing the same breeze I was. We decided to put up a shack on the south shore of Burrard Inlet, outside the city limits, where I'd heard there were lots of shacks already. It was a late summer day in September when we set out for the inlet. All we took with us were two bags that held cooking utensils and my tools.

It was a different world before the War. No one will ever see it again. Plenty of room for everybody. No crime to speak of, not a lot of running around buying up things. Not a lot of strangers trying to make a city out of cars and highways, using up land and air, trees and water as if they mean nothing. Out where we went, when you looked across the inlet to the north you saw mountains covered in trees. The water was clean and boats few. If a shack was empty you moved in, fixed the place up. There wasn't anything good available, so we built our own right on a nice bit of beach. For pilings we used boom logs that had escaped and drifted ashore. Sinking them was tough. Making sure they were solid. The rest was easy. We worked at it steady. Slept on the beach at night. People helped us find lumber. Two months and it was finished. At first we got along. But Ray drank too much. He'd go crazy and start to tear everything apart and we'd have to grab him. He'd drink anything he could get his hands on—homemade wine, canned heat, aftershave. He'd see devils, try to fight them off. One night he tore a hole in the roof and we had to pull him back in. He was a big farmer from the prairies, hard to handle, even for two guys. Dick was a tough little Yorkshireman, except rats got on his nerves. The ones down there were the size of humpy cats and had tails like whips. Sometimes they'd get into the shack and he'd go nuts. Run around with a hammer. Hit one once and there was blood and mangled guts all over the floor. Packed up his things one night and left. I couldn't handle Ray alone. He was on dandelion wine. Somebody in another shack gave him a bleach gallon jug of it. He went berserk and tried to kill me. Said I was the Evil One. Red-eyed skookum farmer, he came at me waving a crowbar. I dodged him and he ran out and down the stairs and into the water and disappeared. The police found his body a few days later when it washed up on the other side. The rip current carried it two miles east from where he stepped into the water. After that it was quiet.

The War was the only news now. I got on at the shipyards, where they hired anybody. With many guys in the armed forces, labour was scarce. Government contracts, lots of war work. I bought a couple of rowboats, some furniture. Dressed better and got out a bit, mostly to pubs. They were called beer parlours. Captain Billy cut war maps out of newspapers and magazines and pinned them up in his shack. After D-Day there were bulges indicating battle lines and wide arrows like cut ribbons with points showing the direction of Allied armies getting closer to Germany. Sugar, meat, alcohol and gas were rationed. You'd see old biddies in the liquor store. They had probably never touched a drink but didn't want to miss out on their liquor ration. There was a black market in gas ration coupons stolen from the offices of ice and coal delivery companies and transfer outfits. Any business with a fleet of trucks was a prime target. If people wanted to say something was good they would say it was pre-War. For a long time afterwards that meant quality. It still does to me but not in their way.

What you remember. Don Richards was a communist,

got it from his people. We used to argue. He was one of the "comicals," the zigzaggers who spouted whatever party line came out of Moscow. One Sunday morning in June of 1941 he came into the shack, said he heard over his radio that the Germans had invaded the Soviet Union. The Nazi-Soviet pact was conveniently forgotten and he could be a patriot. In December the Japanese bombed Pearl Harbour. There was a scare that the West Coast would be invaded. As defence the army put an artillery piece in a pillbox in Stanley Park, on top of the cliff near Siwash Rock. A few rounds from a single cannon wouldn't have made any difference, but fixed gun emplacements were part of the mentality then. Copying the Americans, the federal government interned all Japanese, including those who were citizens, and most of the public supported the order. Notices posted on telephone poles and in the newspapers told them to take their cars and trucks to Hastings Park to be auctioned off. The internees were held in barns there until they were sent away to camps in the interior or on the prairies, and some ended up back East. Families were put in stalls used for livestock during the yearly autumn agricultural fair and had only pot-bellied stoves against the winter damp and cold. Their property, including houses, businesses and fishing boats, was picked up cheap. Nothing like patriotism to turn a profit. German and Italian aliens were interned but they could be released if an employer vouched for them.

One Saturday night a week before Christmas in Forty-one I was in the Brompton down on Powell Street and Victoria Drive. Used to go there because it was closer than the other east end pubs. Walk along the tracks and up past the crossing gate and you could see the back of it on the northeast corner. I was sitting with the Captain that night and talking about what was going to happen overseas. We agreed the Germans would stage a new offensive against the Russians in the spring and the war there would be a long hard slog. It was snowing outside. I thought about how cold it was going to be in the shack when I got back. As usual on a Saturday night there were lots of people making lots of noise. That night the loudest was coming from a corner near the back, by the toilets. A woman and a man who both looked to be Indian were sitting with two working guys. The Indian man and the other men were hollering at each other. The woman's eyes went from one to the other but she didn't say much. She looked about twenty-three. The manager told them to leave. They got up, still hollering, and left by the back way. I don't know why but I got up and followed. I pushed the exit door open and could make out their dark shapes through the heavy snowfall. There was a small area paved with asphalt at the back and some garbage cans by the service entrance, twenty feet from the exit, and ten feet away was a flimsy wooden fence made of thin slats bound with wire, and beyond it the tracks. In the distance a streetlight with a faded yellow halo glowed through the snow. They were near the fence. I could hear swearing ("half-breed horseshit"). I saw an arm make a quick thrusting movement and a body fall and two men run to a truck parked on the corner and drive off.

I went back inside and told the waiter to call an

ambulance. When I went outside again, the woman was kneeling beside the body and crying softly. I could see blood on the snow, as if somebody spilled a bottle of ink. I went over and said an ambulance was coming but she didn't look up. When it got there, he was already dead. One of the paramedics said he had been stabbed in the neck. The cops came and I could see better now because of the headlights on the squad car. She told the cops the dead man was her brother, down from a reserve in the interior. They had met the men that night, when they came over and sat down at the table. Wanting to buy her for the night, they'd argued with her brother. When she said no, they thought she was holding out for a higher price. The cops, two big guys with sandy hair and pink faces and whose parents had probably been British immigrants, looked at each other and grinned. "You got anywhere to stay?" one of them said to her. I stepped up and said, "She's been staying with me, officer." "Who are you?" "I'm a friend." "What's your name?" "Sam McLendon." One of them shone a flashlight on my pink face and that was it. Didn't ask for my address. Put their notebooks away and no mention of an investigation, an inquest or notifying her of anything. As they walked away I could hear, "Another one bites the dust."

The ambulance and squad car left. She started walking along Powell and I went after her. She turned on me and in the streetlight I could see wet tear marks on her face. "White men only want to fuck squaws." "I got a shack on the waterfront and you can stay till you feel better. I don't have much but you're welcome to share it." She began walking again but slowed down and I stayed beside her. The snowfall blotted out the street, our voices sounding like intimate echoes through the silence. "I think I'll kill myself." "You're not going to do that, not as long as I'm here, and I'm not leaving you." I meant it, possessed by the feeling we were important to each other in the cold whiteness of desolation blurring our shapes. She stopped, stared at me. I guess her eyes saw something in mine. "I'm tired." I took her gently by the elbow, more carefully than I'd ever touched anyone in my life, and steered her back.

The Captain was waiting outside the Brompton. He wished her a Merry Christmas. Merry Christmas? Her brother had been murdered. He was embarrassed around women, didn't know what to say. But he was gallant in his own way and took off his heavy wool overcoat and draped it around her shoulders. I took off my cap and put it on her head. It was Christmas, the real Christmas, as we headed through the snowflakes. The lights on the switches alongside the tracks glowed like decorations. Then it hit me what she must be going through.

After giving her a glass of rum I put her in my bed in the kitchen and piled the blankets on her and took off her shoes. She was shivering, from what had happened as much as from the weather, I guessed. I got a fire going in the stove, put some blankets on the floor and slept there. I had a couch but it was lumpy. Before I lay down I looked at her and could see the rum had knocked her out. Saw her face clearly for the first time. It was a beautiful face, skin like a golden sunset, a small straight nose and little mouth with a pout to it. Her eyes were greenish hazel. She had red hair with a lovely curl to it. She slept curled up and I liked that, and made no sound, and I liked that too. I felt peculiar, having been without a woman for so long. I didn't think of her as mine but it was good having her there. She made the place seem different, warmer. I didn't want to think about what was going to happen, in case things didn't turn out. And it didn't seem right to think about myself when she'd gone through so much. If she took off on me, so be it, I hadn't any rights to her. I lay down, hoping she would stay for a while.

I woke up first, a little after nine. I made myself porridge because I figured she'd be sleeping in late. She slept till noon. She yawned and I stopped reading a week-old newspaper I'd picked up on a bench a few days ago and looked over at her from the couch. I could see her remembering. She shut her eyes, opened them and looked at me. "Want something to eat?" She nodded, staring at me. I fried some bacon and eggs. She got up and looked around. "If you've got anything to take care of, it's outside and up a ways." I pointed to the west. Near a municipal sewer outfall we'd built an enclosed one-holer with door, planks leading out to it, and others were welcome to use it. Many living down there had more informal arrangements. When she came back she washed her hands with water from the bucket beside the stove and sat at my writing desk. I used it as a dining table. She finished everything on her plate, even the toast I burnt in the skillet. I'd have done a few more but I'd run out of bread. I told her that from the couch and she nodded. I made us a pot of tea. I had some cookies in a tin somebody brought a month ago and I put the tin in front of her and told her to help herself. I put the teapot and a couple of mugs down and sat there as she was prying the lid off the tin. She gave me a quick look when I did that. She ate all the cookies. I could tell she didn't like the tea, sipping it for the heat and inhaling the steam. After a while she looked around the shack, eyeing everything carefully. I knew she was going to stay, but she still couldn't figure me out.

"You going to sleep on the floor all the time?"

"I don't mind it."

"Give your bed to a squaw?"

"If you need it."

"You're not like a white man."

"What's a white man like?"

"He spits on Indians and fucks their women."

"Not all of us."

"All I've met."

"You met me."

"You're tricky."

"So are you."

"So is everybody."

"That's right."

We grinned. We drank tea and she asked about her brother, what would happen to his body? She'd given his name and location of the reserve to those officers. I said he probably would be buried in the city cemetery in an unmarked grave. Police and local officials didn't bother about Indians who came to the city from reserves, and probably wouldn't even notify his people. She wasn't angry or even surprised by what I said but she wanted to know where he was buried so she could visit his grave. I said the coroner's office kept records and maybe could help her. I figured her relatives wouldn't have money to come here, claim the body and ship it back. I asked her how she was going to let them know and she said write a letter because she didn't have money to go home. And she didn't want to hitchhike because too many guys would proposition her, expecting her to sleep with them in exchange for a lift. "They see us and expect it, even if they're fat or ugly or drunk or beat us up or cut us or do anything they want with us—we're like cows and mares to them and they think we're always ready." She spoke without anger, used to this attitude and expecting nothing else. I thought about myself and whether I was really any different from the others, only slower and a few years older than most of them. I wanted her too, but to me she was important, not for a few blind hours in bed but for I couldn't guess how long. She didn't trust the colour of my skin and she had the best reason, the need to hold onto her dignity. She didn't want to be some back alley boy's snatch on the road to manhood, a crotch for a stranger's quick fun. She wasn't a no-face thing to be made drunk and used and thrown away, and maybe she had a hunch I would never treat her that way.

A week later she said, "Why don't you sleep here?" And that was it. Without benefit of clergy. I'd almost forgotten how smoothly soft a woman's body is. But you never do. Christmas was special that year. Right away she started using my galvanized washtub for a bathtub and so did I. Lots of exercise carrying the buckets of water across the tracks. Lots of firewood heating up pans of water on the stove. I hung a piece of wire across the room for our laundry. In spring I nailed two-by-fours at the far corners of the porch and strung a wire between. She did the laundry and we shared the cooking and cleaning up. The guys in the shacks and most of the ones who came from the city on weekends to talk politics accepted her. She was quiet but she had a habit of staring right through you if she thought you were lying or too full of yourself. Some of the city politicos got antsy in front of her. She was bored with all of the politicos, thought they were full of horseshit. The Captain doted on her. He was getting on even then and she became like a granddaughter to him. And she acted and looked younger once she settled in. She told me she was twenty-one. When he came over she'd sit with her legs crossed on the bed, next to the desk. He'd sit on the couch, beside the stove, feet crossed and stretched out in front of him and smoke his pipe and drink his glass of rum. I kept a bottle of dark rum especially for him. He'd spin yarns about going up the Orinoco and earthquakes in Lima and headhunters, jaguars and boa constrictors in the Amazon and fishing for blue marlin off the Florida Keys and looking for buried pirate treasure in the Dry Tortugas. I didn't know how much was true. I never asked Josie how much she believed. She liked listening to him talk. And I think she never forgot him putting his overcoat on her that first night. She said he looked like Santa Claus. He could have been hired as one by a department store. He had a round face and red cheeks and a big white mustache and whiskers. But he had a sailor's walk and wouldn't have known a reindeer from a dog. "My dear," he said to her, "I've seen things you don't want to know about. I tell you the stuff that's fit for your pretty ears. Or you wouldn't be able to sleep. And I'd have a bad conscience about the nightmares you'd be getting." He'd solemnly wink an eye at her. That would make her laugh. Sometimes he would have more than a glass and need help with the stairs. I'd walk back with him to his shack as he tottered along, to make sure he didn't fall down or wander off.

One Saturday morning in March, three months after I'd met Josie, I could hear the Captain hurrying up the steps before he tapped on the door, letting himself in after waiting the usual few seconds to make sure we were decent. I was lighting a fire in the stove.

"Blow coming, Sam. Batten down the hatches."

"Big, Captain?"

"Biggest yet."

You didn't ask the Captain how he knew. That would've been like asking a carpenter if he knew what a finishing nail was. It had been windy. There was a high tide.

"What's the worst?"

"Doors blown in. Porches torn off. Everything knocked sideways. Chance of being blown apart."

"What about mine?"

"It'll take it."

"When's it going to hit?"

"Early evening, on towards supper time."

"Better get knocking on doors. I'll go east, work my way

back. Anybody's welcome to sit it out here. You start at the other end. I'll meet you partway."

I looked over at Josie. It was early. She had been sleeping and the Captain's arrival had woken her up. She yawned and quickly covered her mouth, as if she didn't want us to think she was making light of things. "I'll go with you," she said to him, throwing one of my sweaters on. It would be hard for him to climb up and down all those stairs to the shacks. Some didn't have stairs. There was a chance he'd slip going down the bank or on slimy rocks or wet seaweed.

I got lots of different responses as I worked my way along the shacks. "I'll stick it out here." "Won't be all that bad." "The Captain's wrong." "Been here ten years. Seen it before." "Thanks for the word." Two said they'd think about coming but didn't show up. Josie had better luck. She convinced Myrtle and Harold Bunyard to sit out the storm with us, along with the Captain. The Bunyards were the oldest residents down there. She brought her knitting and he accepted a pipeful of Old Chum. They talked about moving away from the inlet. They took turns when they talked, Myrtle first. She never missed a stitch.

"We got a little money put by. Thinking of buying a house that's for sale up on McGill. It's a cosy place at the back of the lot. Room enough for us."

"Dampness gets in your bones here. Coughing pretty near all winter."

"Smoking didn't help it."

"We're the only couple, except for you two."

"Mind your own business, Harold."

"I was telling Josie something she mightn't know."

"Why would she be interested?"

"She'll be the only woman."

"That's none of your business, Harold."

As we waited Myrtle talked, the Captain slept, Harold took another pipeful and Josie lay back on the bed, eyes open as she listened.

"Mrs. Tweedie is moving in with her daughter up on Dundas and that's why her house on McGill is for sale. She was a servant back in Scotland. Used to wait on Queen Victoria when she stayed at Balmoral Castle. Got a special spoon given to her by the Queen for that. That's something to treasure."

"Be worth a bit," Harold said, checking the draw on his pipe after tamping down the tobacco with his little finger.

"Not in your way, Harold."

"Still and all, she should keep it in a safe place. Worth something soon enough."

Not missing a stitch, Myrtle gave him a look before continuing.

"Inlet's changing, what with the War. Most all the families here because of the Depression have gone. Some had kids going to school. That was the best time. When nobody's got anything, everybody has something."

Harold lit his pipe.

"Remember that artist fella and his girlfriend? Used to paint pictures of the North Shore mountains and the shacks. Sold 'em on the boardwalk. People came down and bought 'em. Oh boy, were they the merry couple. Always drinking and fighting and making up after. Lots of noise, no matter what."

"None of your concern, Harold."

Wind came down the inlet in gusts, giant sledgehammers slamming in turn into the shack, rain pelting the walls like lead shot. The only window was in the room facing the bluff and shielded from storms by the bank. At the height of the storm the blast hit without a stop. Beams and joists creaked and strained as if the shack was about to fly apart. Waves surged onto the porch and around the pilings, heaving against the floorboards and water began to seep through and form puddles. Something heavy, probably a log, thudded against and shook the pilings. Towards morning the wind let up and with dawn the sun came through the last of the storm clouds and I went outside and surveyed the damage. None to the shack. Logs and driftwood washed ashore lay in tangled heaps, some logs sticking up like masts, and among the piles broken branches, small trees and an uprooted stump. I walked east and doubled back to the western end. The worst was a porch blown away and shingles off some of the roofs. A few residents were out. Quiet pride, and a hint of sarcasm. It was part of living down there and not anything personal.

"Slept right through it." "Got rid of the cobwebs." "Porch wanted rebuilding." "No washing the floor now." "Nothing to fix. How'd you make out, Sam?" "Seen worse. How's the Captain?"

Along the inlet the Captain's stock went down after that. He didn't seem to notice. The Captain didn't notice much.

Except the weather. I helped rebuild the porch and replace the shingles. Neighbourly stuff. The Bunyards left. Josie and I were the only couple.

Thanks to my work at the North Shore shipyards in the late summer and fall, I'd had money enough to fix up the shack with some odds and ends and bought an icebox, a couple of good blankets, pots and crockery. Up to then I'd cooked everything in a skillet and eaten from it with a big spoon. Besides the kitchen, which I used as a living room as well, there was a smaller room. Ray and Dick used it as a bedroom and I'd slept in the kitchen on a cot. After they were gone I turned the other room into a storeroom. I gave the cot away and made a bed, extra wide, and a good thing I did. Everything came in handy after Josie moved in, though after a while she wanted curtains on the windows and pillows for the couch and bed.

When spring came I gave her bus fare to go and see her people. I took the streetcar with her to the bus station to see her off. A couple of old biddies stared at us when we kissed goodbye. The driver wasn't too friendly when she boarded and it was my turn to stare. I waved when the bus pulled out and she waved back and said something I couldn't hear because of the noise. I followed the bus to the exit, watched it get smaller and something got smaller inside me. On the way back I stopped off at the Captain's, stayed till it was late.

Josie came back two weeks later looking better and worse. I could see she had lost weight and was tired. Any little thing irritated her. She didn't want to stay, seemed to be waiting for a chance to leave. I figured something happened on the reserve. The first day I made us some flapjacks and poured maple syrup on them, thinking she'd like that, and she called it white man's food. I said it was anybody's food, and didn't her people make something like them? She laughed and said I didn't know anything about her people or any of the other nations. She wanted to fight. And that was why she looked better, too. Her eyes were sharper than I ever saw them, fierce and fearless. She was taking out her anger on me. I was getting her so she didn't know what she felt. She couldn't hate clear and sharp, the way she wanted. She stood up, dumped her flapjacks onto my plate and started yelling and ran out.

I followed her down the stairs and over the embankment and onto the tracks, where she turned and began throwing punches. I held her by the wrists and she struggled to free herself. From the bend up ahead came a noise that's never anything else. She and I knew. Only a minute away. A whistle. They saw. "Josie, I love you." "I hate you, Sam McLendon." "I'll die here then, without you." "Sam, you son of a bitch." I lifted her by the waist. "You want me to die?" "Yes." A scream. The scream and a second blast from the steam whistle came together, her mouth open, head back. We were possessed by something. The noise was hurtling towards us. My legs shook with the vibration of the ties and I could feel everything sweep me away. But I had enough left to throw her clear, and as I did those fearing and fearless eyes locked onto mine for the shortest time in my life and I knew and felt something I never knew before or since. And she snapped her leg out as she fell back and her foot caught me in the stomach, shoved me away and I fell out of the way of the locomotive and lay there on the gravel beside the tracks.

I froze, didn't know where my hands were but knew if I moved I'd risk losing something. A blur of black enamel piston housing followed by the huge drive wheels in a rushing whirl of steel spokes and jabbing rods and shafts and I felt a warm drop of water or wisp of steam on my face. Endless square shapes of the journal boxes and sharp step edges of the coaches blipping by inches away and the click-clack of wheels across the rail joints. I shrank within myself, praying for it all to pass because now I wanted to stay alive. Suddenly it was over, the end of the maroon parlour car with its railed vestibule and cream canvas awning turning into a dot far down the tracks and the silent sky with its few white popcorn clouds so open and blue. I scrambled to my feet looking for Josie and saw her on the other side of the tracks on her knees and looking for me. I guessed she must have fallen further than I did and maybe rolled because there was dirt on her face but she didn't seem to be hurt. We met in the middle of the tracks and touched each other as if we didn't believe it but looked both ways and didn't stay there long. As we walked to the shack she laughed. "Oh boy, are we nuts." "Absolutely." I only ever loved one person and it was all crazy but she was the right one.

That night she told me about being sent off the reserve to a residential school. "The boys had to wear the same pants and shirts. The girls had to wear the same dresses. They were made of cheap stuff, hung like a sack and had a floppy collar.

They separated the boys and girls, so when my brother was sent there I didn't see him. They said, 'Don't talk Indian, talk white.' You got slapped if you didn't. We were supposed to forget our language and our customs. We wouldn't be Indians any more and we'd never be white. So what the hell were we? They made us nothing. Not welcome in our own land. We were supposed to change into something we didn't want to be and couldn't be. We got to hate ourselves and the white man got ready with the liquor and jails and said you could never civilize those savages."

Her mother married a prospector named John MacCammon, who was killed in an accident in the backcountry. She died of tuberculosis when Josie was two years old and she had been raised on a reserve by her maternal grandmother. Josie's sister, who was a year older, died from tuberculosis too. Of the three children it was Josie who bore the strongest resemblance to her father. Her red curls set her off from the other children on the reserve and she was teased. Her brother turned her name against her, calling her "Scrub Brush." He was two years younger, so she won all the early fights. Her face was different too, like a white's. That brought the attention of white men when she left the reserve. She learned there was a different moral code for Indian women. But she had learned self-respect from her grandmother, who told her never to sell herself short or think whites were superior. She ignored those invitations to "have a drink, honey" or "go for a ride." She didn't say anything about her boyfriends except they had no chance. Like her, when they left the reserve they entered a larger prison. It was take your choice, put up with segregation or face contempt when you didn't.

She came to the city with her brother. She had a few dollars, their only money. They lived in a skid row hotel until her money ran out. They slept in alleyways afterwards. She wanted to go back to their reserve and tried to convince him to return with her. He wanted money for drink, had a plan. They wouldn't have to panhandle or to sleep in alleys any more. She could make money by selling herself. She refused at first but he kept after her until she agreed. She knew he'd be dead in a few months if she left him alone. The night I saw her in the pub he was bargaining with her first customers. She was making things difficult because she didn't want to go through with it. When her brother struck a deal with the fishermen, she wouldn't agree. She could see they wanted her badly. That made her hate them more, and more eager to get away. She asked for more than she knew they would pay. She didn't know how everything would end and finally she didn't care.

"I was tired and hungry, watching them bargain over me. I thought, why should I care about myself when nobody else does? Jimmy John was going pretty good at them but it wasn't really about me, it was about who was going to get the best deal. He said I was a princess, a virgin. 'Look at her,' he said, 'you can see she's not a squaw.' The manager said we were making too much noise and would have to leave. I didn't want to go out the back way but Jimmy John said to, so I followed. When he got mad, you couldn't tell him a thing. It all happened so quick I didn't see the knife, I saw him fall and the blood going all down his shirt. Don't remember the rest. Cops standing there, that's all. You began talking to me and I was so worn out I felt like falling down and sleeping in the snow. The next morning I didn't know what to think. I'd never been with a white man. But you didn't act like any other white man I ever met. They'd undo their zippers or fly buttons as soon as they started talking to you. You could have had me the first night. I was too tired and woozy with the rum to stop you. When you didn't I decided to stay. But I didn't want to make it easy for you. When I went back to my band I saw how poor they live, my cousins and everybody else. My grandmother's getting old now and she's sick. Nobody's been close to me like her. I want to help her but all I can do is watch her die. I'm not happy on the reserve because of what I see. The city is tough. Where can I go? What can I do? People stare at me. She's a half-breed. Not a person, a dirty klootch. Sometimes I go crazy. I want to hurt somebody. I know if I start drinking I'll go crazier and die sooner. Maybe that would be a good thing. Or maybe I'll go back, pick the slower way to die. At least I can hold my grandmother's hand for a while. Maybe that's best. For her. And for me."

"Stay here with me. What's mine is yours, Josie, always will be."

"How long will it last?"

"How long does anything last?"

"I'll be Sam's squaw."

"You'll be who you want to be."

"I'd still be Sam's squaw."

"Say that once more and I'll take you over my knee and spank you."

"I might like it if you didn't hit too hard."

"I could never hit you hard."

"You'll get tired of me."

"Not unless you phony up on me, get some manners and start talking like a white bitch."

"You like us savages."

"I like you."

"You said love out there."

"I meant it. I'd have stayed on those tracks."

"You got some way of showing love."

"I only had a few seconds."

"I had less to save you."

After that we settled down, though she would still go funny every so often and I'd give her money to go see her people. Sometimes that worked and other times she came back worse, talking about the problems her people had and how she felt frustrated about helping them. The war news was unreal to her. Continental Europe was under Nazi control yet but Britain was getting more than lend-lease from the Americans now, becoming a launching pad for an invasion. The ferocious fighting in the Soviet Union continued, with enormous casualties on both sides. Later in the year I would get weekend work at the cannery sometimes and having two jobs helped with the groceries. I was able to give Josie money for medicine for her grandmother. Her grandmother had rheumatoid arthritis. We didn't have to eat as much clam chowder, though she got more tired of it than I did. She liked salmon, and I was able to bring some from work in my lunch pail. Most of the guys there hid nice pieces to take home. There were more jobs now and more money around, and it struck me as strange that it took a war to end the Depression. The politicos who came to the shack used to talk about that and second-guess everything going on. They'd been doing that since the beginning of the Thirties. When the Germans invaded the Soviet Union in Forty-one the communists were relieved, could play up the fight against tyranny, ignoring the brand they'd bought. For such hard-liners it was their religion. I used to kid them. "How are things in the workers' paradise? I hear the commissar of truth has been sent to a labour camp to be re-educated because he forgot himself and actually told it." They'd never touch a drink, only tea, strong and black, lots of sugar, no milk. Sometimes I'd hold up a can of condensed milk and say, "You'd better have a drop of the milk of human kindness." "This isn't the land of milk and honey, not yet," the politicos would answer. Josie couldn't stand much of this stuff. She'd go out on the porch or lie down and close her eyes during the winter months. She'd get mad once in a while, and you'd always know by the way she'd toss her curls back something was coming. "You're here in the land of my people and all you're interested in are the troubles of the rest of the world." Nobody ever answered.

The main politicos? There was "Red Willie" MacKay, a bandy-legged Scotsman from Glasgow who loved kippered herring and hated monarchies. Leo Peters, a union organizer whose people were Russian and who unlike the rest of his kind read more than propaganda from Moscow. Seedy Ralph, always eating sunflower seeds, hanging around union halls and getting up petitions and attending protest rallies. Norman Sirinov won every game of checkers he ever played, all over the prairies and on the coast. Wes Bygate, born and raised a Nonconformist in Manchester, had memorized and would quote long passages from the main communist works and "liked a bit of bird." Sid Kamenski, another union organizer, was one of the gimlet gang, believed in boring from within capitalist institutions to destroy the system. Don Richards' people were from Sevastopol, in the Crimea, and he a Moscow-directed agitprop opportunist who infiltrated the labour and socialist movements. He recruited fellow travellers, especially writers and teachers, and was always ready to give them that helpful nudge towards the promised land. He had the best line of bullshit in the business.

I've seen all kinds come and go, riding high, full of piss and vinegar. Think the world was invented for them. In their twenties nothing's too big, they're conquerors. In their thirties women get most of them. In their forties they're full of opinions. In their fifties they're full of booze. After that they crawl along the earth like crippled bugs, and one day it's over. When I first knew these guys in the dark days they were so sure of the fall of capitalism and the coming workers' revolution. Now some were starting to look for careers in a better economy. They had to me an incredible ability to see things one way, and it didn't matter what happened, they never gave up that one-way view. Even when peace came they made money in a capitalist economy and talked communism, as if somewhere up ahead in the mist the revolution was still coming. They refused to see they were obsolete, tramps and working stiffs that were taught or grabbed at a fairy tale that made them feel better. They weren't the only ones. Better educated people fell into the trap and never managed or wanted to climb out. Most people, if you can get them young enough or at a critical time, can be made to believe something they'll never give up no matter what. I was never a believer, and that's no small handicap when you're trying to change the world. So many tell you who you are, and if you believe them they have you. You can't let others tell you what they don't know. Look up into the sky at night. Who am I? There is no answer and that's the answer. Some give themselves the right to hand out name tags. Lots accept what they're told. It's all systems telling you who and what, as if you don't have the right or the brains to figure things out. And those wanting a new system usually cause more trouble than those they replace. They are the true believers. The human animal can be interesting but every so often you need a drink.

Don Richards was the slickest of the bunch. I didn't know how slick until I found out the hard way. Horn-rimmed glasses and always a suit and tie. He had what some people would take to be an intelligent look, a cross between a schoolteacher and an encyclopedia salesman. He wouldn't fool the more knowing, especially after hearing him. He had a way of agreeing with you as he was trying to make a monkey out of you. Once you caught on you knew he had contempt for everyone, including fellow travellers and party faithful. He was a born apparatchik, always out for the main chance. Ideas didn't mean anything to him except as something to show he was smarter than the other guy. He'd argue fine points like a matador taunting a bull and he had the sword ready behind his red cape for the final lunge. Always the slight grin and the cool words. I could guess what he really thought of Willie fulminating against the British monarchy for not paying its fair share of taxes, or Kamenski the party hack, or a camp follower like Seedy Ralph, or Norm and his checkers, or Bygate's recitations and Leo's reading bourgeois novels.

The others were victims of the times, small men who couldn't see a way out except by believing in something unshakeable. Don Richards only believed in himself. We never got along, before or after he brought the news about the invasion of the Soviet Union, but he began coming earlier on weekends. He got friendlier with Josie, asking about her relations, and especially her sick grandmother. She started talking to him and he forgot the usual political palaver. I'd leave them alone sometimes to solve the problems of aboriginals around the world. One Sunday morning I went to do some work for the Captain. All the steps to his shack were rotten and needed to be replaced and I told Josie I wouldn't be back till late. The job went faster than I expected and when I got back she was putting clothes into a couple of shopping bags. I could see she was angry I'd come back so soon. I already knew the answer to my question but I had to ask it.

"Where you going?"

"We're not married."

"You're going to see that phony son of a bitch."

"Leave me alone."

She hurried out and I heard her quick footsteps on the stairs. It was like somebody took the guts out of me. I felt hollow inside and couldn't move. I sat staring for hours. Nobody came around that afternoon and I was glad because I couldn't have talked anyway. Late that night I heard her footsteps, light and rushed. She came in and threw her shopping bags into a corner, took off her coat and sat down on the bed. Her face was dark and she was breathing heavy, trying to catch her breath. She wiped a hand across her face, as if she'd been crying. When she spoke, the words poured out.

"He said he was going to help me. We were going to do something about the problems on the reserves. It was a shame what was happening and he knew big shots who'd change things. He had connections, friends. He knew the right way."

She stopped, took a deep breath before continuing.

"I met him at the Brompton. In the lobby. We were supposed to take a streetcar to the ferry dock to go to the Island to see some politicians he knew. All of a sudden he remembered it was Sunday and the politicians we were going to see wouldn't be in their offices till Monday. He said he wanted to get some tobacco. We went to the cigar store across the street and he bought a pack of cigarette paper and a package of tobacco. He rolled and lit a cigarette and looked at me through the flame. 'I'll get a room for us. We'll take us up some booze. Have a nice powwow.' I left him standing there. He called after me once. I didn't look back. My name in his mouth sounded like shit."

I went over and pulled her up by the wrist and over to my chair and put her over my knee. I yanked up her dress and took down her panties. I smacked her twice. The quivering of her backside, a deeper sunset colour in the places I hit, got to me. I turned her and held her, kissing her. "The door," she said. I pushed our bureau in front of it. She smelled like sourdough and buttermilk that night.

"If you ever do anything like that again, we're finished," I said the next morning.

"Where's my wedding ring?"

The next I heard of Don Richards he'd left town on a train to escape the draft. A couple of the gang had gone down to the CN station to see him off. They came by and said he'd refused to try an old trick, drink a bottle of Worcestershire sauce and go without sleep for a night. When you got examined by the army doctor your blood pressure would be sky high and you wouldn't be crossing the Atlantic any time soon. Years later I heard he became head of a large union local back East. I realized that Josie taking off was partly my fault. She wanted to get married and I didn't, couldn't see any future for her with a tramp like me. And I guess I wanted to live the way I'd gotten used to and hoped she would too. Neither of us said anything right afterwards because we were happy things worked out. That time was like another honeymoon for us.

The rest of the wartime years were quiet. I stayed on at North Shore shipyards till the end. There was enough money for Josie to make regular trips up country. I told her to go whenever she wanted to see her grandmother. After her grandmother died I made a point of telling her to go any time. Sometimes she wasn't moody when she came back. She'd try to accept our life. One day the Captain said, "She's all of a piece." I knew what he meant. Most women are made up of parts. Most of the parts are locked up except on certain occasions, and some make you pick the locks and some give the keys for the right price. A few aren't divided, are the entire woman all the time, and she was one. When you saw her you saw everything, even the secret darkness. It was on her skin like a fine oil, a warm gloss, and in the sheen of her eyes, in the flexing of her back, the way she had of turning and dipping her shoulders to look at you and the way she stood with right knee slightly bent and resting on the ball of her foot. I used to watch her dig for clams, bare feet in wet sand, blue jeans cut up to her thighs, one of my old work shirts too big for her and hanging outside, tortoiseshell barrettes almost lost in her windy curls. Every so often she'd stand up and look around for a while. She'd grin at something I couldn't see, up in a squint of sun or out among the spooling sockets of currents. Something was speaking through her, in the glint and tumble of her hair, in the quivering rise and fall of her breasts, in the ecstatic spread of her fingers, in the open thighs and the knots in her calves and the clenching of her rump. That picture of her standing golden on the shoreline during those wonderful days has become my favourite memory of her, the glorious goodbye to all the years. The sun, the genius of paint, tinted her ochre and auburn, russet and leaf tan, even the wavering hint of green in her hazel eyes. Tramps like me float by as invisible dust but she was the colours of autumn.

Life along the inlet after the War stagnated. The turnover in the shacks was slow, few moving out and fewer moving in or knocking one together, and nobody around now but older guys. A few of the politicos drifted away. Leo Peters still came by. He'd bring books from the city library and when I'd finished them I'd take them back. After a while I thought it would be less trouble for him if I got a card. But I wasn't living in the city, was in an adjacent municipality and didn't have an address. He said to use his address. One Saturday morning in 1945 I went with Josie to the old library downtown. She wasn't too hot on the idea. Leo Peters came out anyway, so why not have him keep bringing the books? I told her I wanted to be able to take out anything I wanted at any time. It was cold, even for the last week of November. We got to Main around eleven and hurried inside to the information desk, on the first floor. A duffer in some kind of conductor's uniform told us library cards were issued on the second floor at the checkout desk. That's where the books were, aisle on aisle of bookshelves, many volumes morocco bound, and tables where readers sat quietly, some in overcoats even though the radiators along the walls were doing a good job of keeping the place warm. Very quiet, except for the odd sniffle or a book being closed. The linoleum was khaki coloured and warped and creaked a little, very little, but you could hear it in that silence. Near the staircase was the checkout, a high counter with rubber stamps on waterdrop handles, ink pads in opened tin boxes, piles of books and a line of patrons getting due dates whacked onto stiff pieces of paper which were inserted into envelopes inside the front covers. When the patrons had left, one whacker remained behind the desk and I went over and said I wanted a card. Hair in a tight bun at the back, she was skinny, wore round wirerimmed glasses and had a long nose for smelling out dirty books. I had known lots of her type in my hometown. Her eyes inspected us. Josie had the wrong complexion and I showed bad taste in companions. What could she do about it? Nothing except make us uncomfortable.

"What is your address?"

I gave her Leo's address.

"Do you have any identification? Birth certificate, driver's licence."

"I told you where I live."

"We can check the telephone book, the city directory, you know."

"Check all you want. I want a card."

She scurried to an office at the back, her backside stiff as a mannequin's, and returned with a bald guy in a tight suit of superiority, a colonial aping an English upper crust accent and sounding like a snotty butler.

"We require some identification, sir."

"I didn't bring any."

"I suggest you get some."

"All I want is a card. What do you think I'm going to do, steal the library?"

"We will be happy to issue one when you bring documentation."

Josie stepped up.

"I want a card too."

"What is your nationality? We don't make a practice of issuing cards to resident aliens unless they submit the appropriate documents."

I couldn't figure out if he was deliberately trying to insult Josie or was blind and was as stupid as he looked. As a leftover bit of imperialism, Canadian citizens were considered British subjects, but Status Indians hadn't even been made citizens yet. Two years later, in 1947, Canadian citizenship became separate from British nationality but Status Indians had to wait till 1956 to be citizens. Josie took two steps back and raised her hand to the level of her cheek, her palm flat and towards him.

"How. Me ride here on back of chinook salmon, me Princess Wannascratchee, daughter of Big Chief, bring greetings to place of many eyes, no sight."

"Please keep your voice down and try to act civilized."

So he did know. When I stepped closer to the counter he moved back. The tips of his fingers touched the oak top as if it was burning. Never know what these tramps will do, and especially one consorting with a savage. Funny thing. I never heard myself speak. The words seemed to come from somebody else. But I remember every one of them.

"Your kind has been here a hundred years and you think you own the place. Her people were citizens here when yours were painting themselves blue with woad and living in wattle houses on an unknown island. You brought gunboats and a colonial tea culture, parasols and remittance men, and you think you're civilized. Moral outcasts and sweepings of the slums. Trash who call others trash. Over half the books in this library condemn what you said to this woman. Or doesn't that mean anything to you? Or what the country you live in helped fight for in Europe and the Pacific?"

His face reddened—wrong colour, old boy—and he turned to his waiting underling. "Miss Halliwell." She understood. Call the police. She hurried to the office.

I'd said what I wanted and nothing was going to change. Rows of faces, all white, stared at us from the tables. Complete silence. I of no respectably-fixed address and she of no respectable nationality were social outcasts. Strangers in our own country, unwanted reminders that there were other ways and other kinds. People like the great ideas of liberty and equality as long as they remain in books, where they look nice and can be read out to schoolkids. The minute they become too much of a reality most people back away fast. Even radicals and revolutionaries will go berserk for a while on too much freedom they don't want anyway except to get power for themselves, and proceed to go back to the old tried ways of managing others by using colour and class, power and police. So I couldn't expect anything from librarians who thought they had a safely monotonous job stocking shelves and readers happy to be out of the cold, all of them probably thinking they were looking at a couple of subversive smelly lunatics. Synchronized in our thoughts we left together without exchanging a look. As soon as we began to walk down the winding staircase the hubbub started. It must have been enshrined as one of the highlights of the bookwhackers' stuffy lives, to be stamped, for gossip only. Out in the street the air smelled cold and clean. I breathed deeply a few times, figuring we had better move off in case any cops arrived.

"People make me sick sometimes. I need a drink bad."

We walked north towards skid row and the nearby waterfront. The hotels there weren't as bad as they got later on. There were a couple that had pubs where you had to watch for flying glasses. Best thing to do was pick a table so you could sit with your back against the wall and see anything coming. Most times things were quiet. The end of the month, payday for most, could be a problem. The pubs weren't open on Sundays then, so Saturdays were a bad time too, general weekend rowdiness packed into a few hours. Most customers were merchant seamen in port, the navy on shore leave, loggers and relief stiffs, and a floating population of boosters and hookers and their pimps. The lighting was dim, the talking low, and lots of eyes watching without seeming to. The waiters had gambler's eyes. As the night came on and the crowd got drunker the heads on the beer got bigger. Every so often there'd be a ruckus and a prowl car would siren up and take away a couple of guys who'd given a pint to each other instead of the Red Cross and sometimes an ambulance would pick up a dead body, either from the floor of the pub or a room upstairs. A few minutes later you'd never know anything had happened. I knew a guy named Eddy Stirk, who cleaned up the Clarendon on Saturdays after it closed. He said the gobs of spit, the puke and piss and shit on the bathroom floor was something you wouldn't believe and would mix with stale smoke and rancid sweat, and the stink got into your clothes and no matter how much you washed up later your skin and hair still smelled of it.

It was an end of the month Saturday and we went to the Highland. On Cordova near Carrall, like most of the other hotel pubs the building was narrow, made of red brick and had a flat roof. Its cornice stuck out over the street. And like the others the hotel was an excuse for the pub, the moneymaker. We got there about a quarter to twelve, went in through the "ladies and escorts" side, where couples sat, the other entrance being for "gentlemen." Half full, dim lighting, buzzy sound of talking, clinking glasses, that sour smell of beer and cigarette smoke all pubs had. Small round tables, leather chairs with curved backs and padded armrests, and talking together at the bar but with their eyes on the room all the time a thin waiter in shirtsleeves, collar open, and behind the bar the bartender in a pinstriped shirt and on his silk tie a hula dancer wearing a grass skirt and lei. There was an empty table next to a side wall and we took it. We kept our coats on till the warmth got into us. I signalled the waiter and he brought the beer, with the colour the right shade of gold and the heads still small. I'd picked the Highland for a reason. They didn't serve New Westminster beer, that green liquid soap some other pubs did. Sipping the beer, I thought about all those books four blocks away. A world so different from this one, but they met where everyone shared the dark. Only some had more words to describe it, and their words were gathered where they could get them easily and take comfort from them. But here in daylight dimness words were the picks and shovels of daily life, grunts and cries. And getting drunk was easier than trying to figure things out.

I looked at Josie. She was rubbing those small hands of hers, the palms narrow and the fingers slender. The Captain was right, fineness of spirit and fineness of flesh. She hadn't said much since the library, was in one of her thoughtful moods, quiet, almost dreamy, and you never knew what was behind it. I looked outside, saw it was clouding over. Cold enough to snow. Thinking about catching a streetcar and getting back, I finished my beer. She hadn't touched hers, didn't want any. I drank hers and ordered another for myself, drank it and had to pee. I headed for the washrooms, at the back. I thought I saw someone move towards our table in the dimness behind me but wasn't sure. I opened the washroom door and saw a short corridor lit by a dim ceiling bulb, two doors halfway along and facing each other and both shut. The doorknob on the one for guys was dented and hung loose and as I shoved it open I felt a hard push and went headlong into space, my knees and elbows landing hard on a cold tile floor smelling of cigarette butts and piss. What's going to happen now, I remember thinking, as if I was watching everything. It must have been only a few seconds, though I seemed to have time to figure I should crawl away from whoever was trying to hurt me. I felt another push, on my shoulder to keep me down, as something pointed pierced my shirt and scraped my back like a needle. Then the sharp thing was gone and I heard choking and a thump and shoes scraping and sliding on the tile behind. Before I realized what was happening I thought stupidly that something had turned against itself. Instead of crawling away I turned my head and saw two forms locked onto each other and moving into the toilet cubicle. One form forced the other's head into the toilet bowl. Whining air squeezing itself out of a mouth, repeated cracks of bone against the bowl, forcing down into filthy water, a gurgle, water bubbles boiling, arms banging the cubicle sides, legs twisting, shoes kicking, followed by silence and a smell. I heard quick steps leaving, got up and went over. Back humped inside a jacket, arms relaxed, legs splayed, blood smearing the bowl, a ball of hair jammed under a ring of dark slime. Somebody calling into his forever in the bloodied mouth of the bowl. I heard Josie's voice. "Sam, get out of there." She was in the corridor and holding my coat, handed it to me and we hurried out through the rear exit.

After we ran through the alley, I put on my coat and felt a stinging pain low on the right side of my back. Josie looked and said there was a cut and some blood. We went to Woodward's and I took a leak in the washroom and rinsed the blood off my shirt and my back. The cut was a deep scrape about three inches long. Hungry and in need of a rest, we went to the cafeteria in the basement. She asked about my back. I said it was all right but I better keep the coat on in the store in case the tear in the shirt looked suspicious. The waitress brought our ham sandwiches and coffee and we sat on stools at the counter and ate and drank and spoke in low voices. "Who was he?" "Someone I know." "From the reserve?" "He's a cousin. He came to the table when you left and said, 'Is he your man?'" "He killed that guy." "Don't talk about it. We should go." We didn't talk on the way back.

The next time she returned from the reserve she was quieter than usual, with a defeated look. Lying beside me in bed a couple of nights later she spoke, more to herself than to me, though she knew I was awake. "I did it." "Did what?" "I got rid of it." "Rid of what?" "Never mind." She didn't talk like that again and I didn't ever ask her what she meant. I should have. I know that now. But I thought it wasn't important, only a mood of hers. She began to eat more and get a bit sloppy but not so I noticed it much. We're comfortable. That's what I thought. When I tried to get her to read something she'd get huffy, say I was trying to make her as stupid as the political gang. Doesn't have to be politics, I told her. Read anything you want, there's plenty of stuff out there. Not for me, she'd say. She'd have a look I knew meant shut up or else. After a while I gave up, except for leaving a book or magazine lying around where I knew she would see it. She picked up one book I'd left on the bed and smacked the top of my head with it before dumping it into my bowl of porridge. I've never forced anyone to do anything. But there was something inside of me upset because she had made it an attack on me, as if books and reading weren't the issue at all. All I wanted was to help educate the woman a bit so she'd understand better the world she was living in.

By now it was the Fifties and our routine was established. I'd put aside enough so she could go to the reserve every couple of months. She'd usually stay two weeks before returning. She began to stay longer. I missed her but didn't say anything. Once or twice I thought of going up to the reserve but didn't know where it was or how to get there. I hadn't even asked her the name of her people. So I would wait. She would return, involved in her moods, sometimes all right and sometimes that silent way of hers. It seemed she was living two lives that were moving further apart. She never mentioned any more what happened during her time up there. After the first time she stayed away for a month I said maybe it would be a good idea to give me a place to write to so I could ask about her, find out if she had gotten sick. She was sitting cross-legged in her underwear on the bed and I was at the writing desk and using a penknife to scrape carbon from my pipe. It was getting dark outside. I struck a match and lit the lamp and saw her distant unconcerned eyes.

"If I'm sick, my people will help me."

"I'd like to know, anyway, so I could do something."

"Somebody would send word."

"How, by smoke signal?"

"Some of us can actually write but you don't even have a real address, so anything written to you would end up in the dead letter office."

"Give me your address and I'll give you Leo's and you can write there. He'll bring me your letters."

"No."

"You stubborn little brat."

"You live with rats on the water. So shut up about helping anybody."

"Rats have got nothing to do with this."

"Neither have you."

"I'd worry about you if you were sick. Doesn't that mean anything to you?"

"I'm tired from the trip. Don't talk. I want to sleep. Turn down the flame."

"You're getting more tired each time."

"Let me get some sleep."

She fell backwards onto the pillow and a sleepy hand searched out the blanket and pulled it over her legs before falling on top with curled fingers. For a while I watched her sleep, her slightly parted lips still breathing the need for rest.

A year later, in the spring of Fifty-six, she hadn't returned after four and a half months and I didn't know what to do. I packed a bag a couple of times. Remembering what she said, I made myself wait. Besides missing her now, I was afraid something had happened to her. I drank more but it didn't help, and pretending didn't work either. I waited. Nothing else meant anything.

He showed up one Sunday morning in April. We'd had an early spring that year. The maples and alders that mixed in with hemlock, cedar and fir on the bluff were putting out bouquets of leaves on their upper branches. When the wind was right you could smell sap and resin on the warm air. There was even a stray daffodil, or maybe it was a jonquil—I could never tell the difference—that somehow had taken root in a sunny spot near the top, a flickering of yellow light among matted tufts of grass. On that morning there was a bit of leftover winter in the breeze coming off the water. I was brewing a pot of tea after breakfast when I heard a knock on the door but nobody opened the door. Everyone I knew tapped once or twice, waited a few seconds and walked in. I said to come in and he opened the door and stood in the doorway. I felt a cool draught. He was lean, his face bronze. He wore a plaid work shirt and a mackinaw jacket, blue jeans and buff-coloured boots. Eyes absorbed me like a blotter, inspection and judgement in one glance. He could see I knew she sent him.

"How is she?" I tried to sound calm.

"She has TB." He was talking to a stranger.

Everything drained out of me.

"Where is she?"

"On the reserve." His voice was toneless.

"She should be in a sanatorium. I'll get her into one. Wait till I pack. We'll go back together."

Framed by the open doorway, his presence was momentous and indifferent.

"She doesn't want you to come."

"I want to see her. Take me back with you."

Something like interest stirred in him for the pink-faced stranger. His eyes shifted to my hand, still holding the teapot.

"Drink your tea and wait. I'll bring you any messages."

And he was gone. I went to the empty doorway. He was already walking along the tracks. I shouted but he didn't stop.

I dragged one of the boats into the water and climbed in, rowed out to where the incoming tide would pull me along the shore. I took in the oars and drifted past shacks and oil refinery storage tanks on a cleared hillside and a tanker moored at the refinery dock, and the cracking plant on the point, its high thin pipe like a steel match that never burnt out. The boat turned around completely several times and I had to use the oars to keep from drifting ashore at the point. Past that I floated along a shoreline mostly of forest. I put ashore at a small island and sat on a rock, trying to let the breeze slap out of me my one thought. I'd never see her again. I was crying before I knew I was, and I heard myself, loud and alone. The sound went out over the spinning braiding waters and disappeared. When I stopped I heard gulls crying into the wind, and far off across those waters broken sounds of children shouting. I rowed back against the current, forcing myself with aching shoulders and arms, not caring if I passed out from exhaustion. When I put in again I could barely manage to drag the boat onto the sand and left its stern afloat. I forced myself up the stairs and fell onto the bed and passed out. It was dark when I woke up and when I lit the lamp I saw a rat in a corner eating from a torn bag of oats. I threw a gumboot at it. I'd left the door open. The rat flung itself out into the darkness in a swivelling lurch of balled muscle and claws. I could hear its scrambling descent, a plump hairy ugliness bouncing down the stairs and its snake tail thwacking against them. I threw the bag of oats after it and slammed the frame of boards and crosspieces shut. My arms and shoulders were sore and I was shaking so hard I had a drink from a mickey of rye somebody had left. After a while I was hungry but the eggs smelled bad, the bread was mouldy, the butter rancid and the chunk of bacon was on the floor. It had been gnawed by my intruder. I drank some more and passed out, thinking about all of it and that the only thing left was a goddam daffodil.

Years passed and nobody came with another message and I knew Josie had died. I thought about going up there but knew she had reasons for not wanting to see me. When I was certain she was dead, the feeling becoming a fact one day, I knew I would go up there sometime. It wasn't till long after I'd been told to vacate and was living downtown that I went. I was a pensioner and had a steady income, as well as some savings. I had a little trouble locating her reserve. A few visits to the library and talking with eastside aboriginals led to talks with others and finally to one who came from a band near hers.

On a Friday in the fall of 1975 I took a bus to Kamloops. I hadn't been through the interior since the mid Thirties. Not much had changed, except some of the towns I remembered had grown a bit. Compared with a boxcar, the bus was a cramped way to enjoy the scenery. I've never liked being confined. The rest stops let me enjoy the fresh air but there weren't enough to suit me. It was getting late when I arrived. I was tired of being closed in and happy to eat a restaurant meal and spent the night at a hotel. The next morning I took a bus north to the Chilcotin Plateau. To me it was part of the Cariboo, grasslands and lakes, with mountains to the east and west. If you want to split hairs, it's to the west and beside the Cariboo, which I'd seen many times from a boxcar during the Depression. My destination was Williams Lake, the town nearest to the reserves in the area. Four hours and 180 miles later I was in the office of the bus station asking about transportation to Josie's band. A secretary said it was about an hour or so away, depending upon the transportation. I got a room in a hotel, left my bag there and ate at a café before standing on the side of the highway, my thumb up. A pickup stopped and I mentioned Josie's band. The driver said he was passing it and would drop me off.

The driver, a member of another local band, could see I wasn't but didn't ask any questions. I looked at the stretches of grassland, the lakes and rivers, and to the west I could see hills and a mountain range and saw why it would've had a hold on Josie, and for her own reasons as well. I don't know what I expected but when we got there after some dusty miles along a dirt road all I saw when I got out of the truck was a sign on the other side of a ditch overgrown with vines and grass, and beyond it a stretch of grassland with groves of mixed fir and cedar. On a piece of plywood nailed to a couple of two-by-fours and painted white black letters said, "Private property, hunting, fishing, camping and hiking prohibited." A corduroy log bridge had been built over the ditch, and at the other end two tire ruts ploughed the bumpy land into the distance. I crossed the bridge and began walking along the ruts. After a few minutes I got to a small rise and could see a group of wooden bungalows and ranch houses, many with a TV antenna on the roof, a woodshed at the back and a pickup in front. To almost all of the houses smaller ruts led off in shallower tracings from the main ones. Off to the side of the houses was a stream below a bank covered in long grass gone brown during the summer. No roads or sidewalks, no blocks of housing or lampposts, but organization of its own kind and for its own purposes. These were Josie's people and I had a sudden feeling of being close to her, as if I could find her there. I could feel my heart beating and I remembered how everything ended between us. I picked out the largest ranch house and walked towards it. A dog from behind a neighboring bungalow ran out and began to bark and a voice told it to keep quiet. I knew I was being watched. I crossed the smooth footworn earth in front of the house and knocked on the screen door and the sound was noisy in the silence around me. The inner door opened and a middle-aged woman, stocky and wearing a plain dress, stared without any expression on her face. I told her I was looking for someone who knew something about Josephine Littletree, who once lived there and died about fifteen years ago. She said her husband could help me but I would have to wait till he got home. I thanked her and stood there and she studied my face for a moment before saying I was welcome to wait inside. She opened the inner door wider and she held open the screen door and I went in. I followed her into the living room and she pointed to a couch and said to sit down. She asked if I wanted a cup of coffee and I thanked her and said no I was fine and would sit and wait. She was cooking something, she told me, and I would have to wait alone. She left and I looked around at the varnished fir slats on the walls and floor, and the oval chocolate and orange rugs like wound woollen braids. Next to the couch was a table with a ceramic lamp with a base in the shape of a galloping horse. Against the opposite wall was a horsehair black leather sofa and a leather footstool, and nearby a couple of rocking chairs. I guess I expected to see headdresses of eagle feathers, beaded buckskin jackets and skirts nailed to the wall, tom-toms on the floor and peace pipes arranged like teepee poles around an earthenware ashtray in the shape of a coiled rattlesnake. There was none of that. Through a window in back of the horsehair sofa I could see the front yard. Occasionally some kids ran by, followed by jumping yelping dogs. It was Saturday and there was no school. I'd waited an hour when a pickup passed in front and parked at the side. A door slammed and another one, into the kitchen, and I could hear voices. She was telling him. He didn't seem to want to listen, his boots hammering down the hallway and through the archway. He was about fifty, all sinew and muscle, face the colour of split cedar, large pores in his cheeks, a scar on the side of his nose. He wore blue jeans, a denim jacket and red plaid shirt and a straw Stetson, the brim curled up at the sides. He stared. His eyes had that dark shade water has under a white sky. He spoke as if his voice was used to doling out impatience.

"You're on band property. Didn't you see the sign?"

"I did."

"Do you think the council put it up as a joke?"

"I'm looking for someone who can tell me something about Josephine Littletree."

"What for?"

"I knew her years ago, on the coast."

"The coast?"

His eyes weren't focused on me any more, they were looking at a film he was rerunning for himself, and he flicked his head towards the door.

"Come on."

I followed him out into the cool sunny air and across the front yard and over tire ruts and hoof prints and more ruts and past houses and grassland to a place at the top of the bank beside the stream. A path through tall grass led to an oblong mound where the grass had been cut short. Half-hidden stones bordered the mound. At the end further from the whisper of rushing water an oval cedar tablet, varnished and inscribed, "Josephine Littletree, 1920-1960." He took off his hat and looked over at me.

"The elders decided to bury her here. She was special to us."

"She was special to me."

"You were her man."

"I was her m-man." The tears came but I held them back and looked away. Dammit, dammit, not now. In front of him.

"Her grandmother knew many of the old stories of our people and told them to her, beginning when she was a child. When she grew up, Josephine went around to the different bands and collected them. She put them all in a book and told them to the adults and children. Nobody was like her. She was the best storyteller."

"She never told me."

"You weren't one of us. Too much was different. And she couldn't be like you. That's why she had the abortion."

"Abortion?"

"Back in the Forties. You wouldn't marry her."

"I didn't know."

"It's all over now."

I looked down at the swelling of earth. The wind had picked up. The air was getting chilly. Like quick shadows of running feet the wind played over the grass. All that way to come to know what I could never understand. "Josephine Littletree" on a piece of wood. That's all I would know. Littletree. All the promise of that. A tramp like Sam McLendon wouldn't get it, wouldn't see such promise.

After putting on his Stetson, he placed a hand on my shoulder.

"When you're ready come back to the house."

He turned and walked away. He walked fast. Like a man who had been forced to remember something he didn't want to, something safely buried. And I knew. It was simple. "You were her man." The hand he put on my shoulder. The Highland. The same hand. The toilet, when he pushed me to keep me down, out of the way of the knife. But for her, for the cousin he loved in a way I'd never know, as kin you die for, kill for, grieve for, and you remember always. No quarter and no shame. You live and die together. He was born into the creed and so was she and both of them understood. No questions and no regrets. If he was uncomfortable with the Highland memory now it was because her memory suffered by that, her image tarnished by brutality. On a lovely woman no shame must fall, even in death.

It got very quiet. All the irreconcilable thoughts gathered. It's hard to accept your life when you've made a mess, and harder when you see you've helped to ruin another life. I couldn't know what I was doing, except that's an excuse. You meet someone and think what's between you is what matters. And you find out there were other things long before she met you and they can matter too, even more sometimes. There isn't any way to figure these things out, they happen, and you're in the middle of something you hadn't dreamt of. Love doesn't make the difference most of the time, only fools us into thinking so. The most love can do is help people pretend they're going to beat the odds. Sooner or later most get the right idea and give up. I've heard of lucky exceptions, never met any. For her sake I'd like to think we weren't the worst failures. She never left her home. The ochre earth smelled of her, sweet and wild, the evening air came soft like her sunset hair, the falling silk a low breath in the dark. She couldn't leave because anywhere else was death quick or slow, bigots and bitches, hired beds and booze, and that was my failure, to understand my shack wasn't anything but a tramp's leaking and draughty indifference to what anyone thought.

The wind went from chilly to cold, the sky shutting down towards four o'clock. There wasn't any point in staying longer. I walked the few yards over to the edge of the bank and looked down the ten-foot slope at the stream. It was more like a creek, low that time of year but still busy. On each side were boulders bleached by the long summer, and the cracked earth paler than where the channel of water ran clear with its faraway whisper. I walked down the slope, put my hand into the water, letting its cool glove clasp it. If she was anywhere she was there and that would be her final touch. I raised a cupped palm and drank it. I didn't know how many parts per million of total dissolved solids or which mineral salts that creek water contained, but it went through me like nothing else I ever drank, a chilled freshness with an aftertaste of alkaline fizz. I said, "Thanks, Josie." Time to go, and I stood up and turned and walked up the slope and past her grave without looking back. She was inside me now.

Her cousin's name was Bill Paul. His wife's name was Betty. They invited me to stay for dinner. I told them I had to get back to my hotel, where my things were in a bag, and catch a bus south. Bill said he'd drive me in later. Betty had made venison stew and baking soda biscuits and baked some winter squash, which she said her people considered sacred food. She showed me some that were incredible, including a huge one, the rind mother of pearl and what looked like frozen sea foam on it. We ate in the kitchen at a painted wood table and they kept pushing food at me and everything was tasty. After we ate Bill said there were things of Josie's I should look at. He left and returned with a large book, a

Manila envelope, a necklace and some pictures and put them down on the cleared table. As Josie's closest living relative he got them after she died, he told me. I looked at everything with a kind of flip-flopping happy sadness, wanting to see and feeling at the same time I was an intruder. The book was a collection of her people's stories she had written down in her own hand. They didn't mean anything to me. I thumbed through one for what I considered a respectable period and put them aside. The necklace was a string of carved painted wooden beads, and they got a respectable look too before they joined the stories. A quick gander into the envelope showed lots of folded paper and small writing and needing a good light to read it. Maybe later. The pictures were the attraction for me. Some showed Josie as a child, and a few were of her in front of a log cabin in the woods. Seeing her so young made me feel I'd never met her. All were snapshots, no studio stuff. Nothing to put in a frame. Bill guessed what I was thinking.

"Take a picture for yourself. And those folded papers. She wrote all that when she was in the sanatorium. It might be interesting to you. Meant to look myself but never got around to it."

I picked a photo of Josie standing in front of a house and he said it was her grandmother's house, still standing. Probably in her late teens, she looked about three years younger than when we met. She was wearing a knitted sweater, the top light and the bottom dark, in a squared interlocking pattern where the colours joined in the middle. Her wool skirt was dark and plain and her shoes were old-fashioned high-button things probably borrowed from somebody or left behind by a relative, she probably going barefoot most of the time and having no good shoes since leaving school. Her hair was parted in the middle and drawn back until almost straight, but a few of the curls escaped, Josie's own rebellion against another lost cause. She was smiling, ready to be hurt and not caring and caring, and most of all proud and not shy about it. The European features stood out, oval face and thin nose and lips, coated with their inherited bronze, as if she was made up to play an Indian princess in front of people who wouldn't have an Indian in their home or want one marrying their son, and wouldn't want to hear about him going down to skid row and buying one to spread her legs, worrying about tainted blood when they were the mongrel product of a dozen races on the right side of light. Wipe off that makeup or the next performance will be on a squeaky mattress. There is no human being in a science lab or on an operating table, where life in capital letters is impersonal, and that goes for politics too. A leftist once called me an outsider because I never followed the party line, especially the brotherhood stuff, under which I've found a lot of sneaky racism. Behind world revolution were the old European prejudices, like the smell of boiled cabbage. They were the children of their parents, those immigrants who stepped off steamships carrying everything they owned in wicker baskets and spouting lots of fancy tales about their homeland and noble ancestry, the ones from Britain telling the biggest lies.

Betty came to Williams Lake, sitting between us in the

cab and complaining she didn't get in much and Bill saying that he took her in lots. "Once in a blue moon," she said. I was holding a bag of buttered biscuits she gave me to eat on the trip back. The truck banged over the potholes on the dirt road, bouncing us around sometimes. The asphalt came like a commercial for new tires and I saw scattered lights before the downtown cluster came into view, hovering in the distance. They dropped me off at my hotel. I thanked them for everything. The truck made a U-turn, leaving in a roar of muffler exhaust and squealing tire spin, and I stood and wondered where I'd been. A grease spot on the brown paper and the smell of melted butter reminded me. There were no buses running that late. I stayed the night and left next morning. On the trip back from Kamloops an old woman sitting beside me said in a soft leaning voice that Rosicrucians were the cause of the world's problems. Her husband knew, had been in the government once but he was dead now. She asked what I did. I said I rounded up left-handed red-haired suspects for the Gestapo and shipped them to amusement parks where they died laughing. I was SS, a "Super Snoop," on the lookout for phony dye jobs, and some left-handers were mix-handed or ambidextrous, so that could be tricky too. She moved to another seat.

First thing I did when I got back was to get the snapshot blown up and framed. It wasn't much after all the years but it was enough. Most don't have more and lots have less. After a while there isn't anything except memories. I had some good ones. As everyone knows, you tend to forget the bad ones. Where I'm living now is a lot warmer in the winter than the shack was and I don't have to collect and cut driftwood, there aren't any rats and I've got a toilet in my suite and tap water in the bathroom as well as the kitchen. As long as I pay the rent no cops are going to throw me out. The door has a lock and needs it (I never did get one for the shack and no one ever broke in or had to). Shopping and pubs are close by, and so is noisy traffic with the sooty smell of pollution coming into my place every rush-hour afternoon. As long as I'm careful at the end of the month, when pension and welfare cheques are issued, I won't get mugged. I've been forced to trade freedom for comfort. It's a minimum-security prison, the government the warden and city bulls the guards, your meals guaranteed, but you've got to watch the cons for a careless shiv. This land is too good, attracts so many, and sooner or later we'll have all those problems everyone else has because there's too many greedy bastards making money selling it down the river, thinking more is better when it never has been except for making money, which is not the first law of man. They're wood lice on a rotting log. They've got places to go, scurrying through the dark and the rain, busy begetting more of themselves and their gadgets, part of a big nothing that's too much to think about, until the last log is gone and there's only a mass of squirming lice crawling over the swollen and putrefying carcass of itself. That's what I learned from Josie, though I never told her. I had the feeling of being in myself free, of refusing to squeeze in among the others. But she taught me that you have to know what love means when it happens. It's the everything without walls. Build around it and you're lost because it won't stay trapped inside a small idea. I put Josie in my shack and it wasn't right because she lived out there in the water and among the trees. She tried to stay and didn't get marriage or freedom—a ring and a new family or a return to the old one—while I stayed free. She left before I knew enough to say I was sorry.

The intellectuals don't know any more than we do, except they've got some more words, that's all. And the bigger the words and the better they sound, the more they hide. Plain words hide nothing. But plain words can tell lies too, the kind that make the truth even harder to find.

Josephine Littletree's Manuscript

Attached by paper clip to the inside of the back cover of the seventh booklet of Sam's manuscript was a Manila envelope. It was the one given to him by Bill Paul. Inside was a large bundle of folded sheets of unlined paper, both sides filled with handwriting in faded green ink from a fountain pen. There are no margins, the writing using up all the available space. And yet it is quick and smooth, the letters clear and flowing. The nib has left tiny clots of ink, mostly in commas, periods, the dotting of an "i" or crossing of a "t." The paper is watermarked linen bond with an off-white tint and there are very few corrections or overwritings. The circumstances in which it was written suggest that it is not a fair copy but was dictated by the clarity of powerful emotions. Most of the manuscript was written in Braeburn sanatorium, on the outskirts of Kamloops. Sam had Josie admitted as a patient there.

This is not the place to document the lack of health care for First Nations peoples in British Columbia in the past except to point out it was neglectful if not intentional and that all levels of government were discriminatory and the medical establishment largely ignored indigenous peoples with tuberculosis. They weren't eligible for admission to sanatoriums or city hospitals. First Nations war veterans apparently were allowed in Braeburn but Josie doesn't mention any, and most probably would have had there been any there. One is left with the conclusion that during Dr. Moxon's tenure as head none applied or those that did were excluded. Claims by staff that some patients were admitted for reasons other than tuberculosis and money was accepted for Josie's care lie beyond the purview of this book. At this remove and without evidence these must be matters for speculation. Until the late 1960s the single exception in aboriginal care was the Methodist Residential School near Chilliwack, which at first was partially a treatment centre for tuberculosis and then became a sanatorium, eventually expanding to include two converted military hospitals in other parts of the province. By the late 1950s many tuberculosis patients were receiving home care, thanks to drugs, and sanatoriums were being phased out. By 1960 Braeburn had been turned into a mental asylum. Long after Josie's time as a patient, local hospitals accepted aboriginal patients.

A note about passes and permits mentioned in the manuscript. Beginning in 1885 First Nations peoples had to get a pass to leave their reserve and a permit to sell anything off it. These were obvious ways of controlling their movement and their income. This system was in place until 1940.

I don't know if Sam realized when he gave me the booklets that Josie's envelope was attached or it was an oversight. But Josie's words as much as Sam's are part of their story. Some readers may be surprised on reading them. It is clear to me that Sam never read them. The pages are printed here complete and unedited.

These words are for you, Grandmother. You were the only one who really loved me and the only one I loved. I thought I was in love three times. They were all failures, the last the worst because I couldn't be who I am. I didn't go whoring or die from drinking. But the white man has found another way to kill me, with his germs, as he killed my mother and sister. You told me not to hate the white in me. I've tried though it's been hard. I know I'm going to die soon and I don't care. At least the useless pain and tiredness will be over. I don't mean my body as much as my spirit. I thought once I could help our people. Now I know I won't be able to do anything. My life has been worthless. When I was a girl and you used to talk about our problems I thought I'd be able to change things. I understand it hasn't all been my fault. My spirit says, fight on until you die, and if you haven't given up you haven't lost. My spirit yearns to meet with you, Grandmother, to hold your hand and walk with you again the way we did when I was a little girl. I remember the evening you led me into a grove of trees. Later I would know them as red cedar. You took me to a cedar and put my hand on it. The bark looked like twistings of long hair and felt smooth.

"This, Josie, is red cedar, the tree we call 'long life maker.' This evening I am giving you another name. Littletree. Like this small one, you will grow to a great height. This one will serve for fire, smoking fish, carving and for building canoes and houses. As it grows, this cedar will suffer fire, windstorms, long winters and dry summers, and it must stand where it is. It will live until it is taken by us for our use. But it will never be the last tree. That is not the way with us. There will be others that live until they are very old, rising into the sky. Whole stands of them, with the sun pouring down between them in golden streams with dust floating like tiny sparkling fish. Our people take to live. We live with the land. If we lose that, we are lost. This time is dangerous for us. We are few and becoming fewer. You must do what you can to help us live as we have lived for so long. Help us remember who we are. Be a voice for your people. And take what will come. This will be your life."

Now forty years later what have I done? Where have I gone? What has my body meant? To be nothing is to be something unless someone tells you you are nothing. That is a nothing of his own making, a lie so he can be something by standing on top of you. The true nothing is like the wind, to be there and not be seen moving or breathing. You said, Grandmother, the wind has wings but you can't see them. I see them now, almost. Everything is almost to me now, always was but I didn't understand. What we see are shadows of the wind. And everything around us, things and ideas, are these shadows. The true nothing waits for us behind everything. Sometimes when they take me outside I can feel your embrace in the pure swift air and I lean back in my chair and smile. My spirit can see yours, Grandmother, in a way beyond my knowing. I write but you are these words, you are the wind across these pages. This is enough to have known. I tell my last story.

I remember that day in September when the Indian agent came. He drove up in a police car with an RCMP constable.

The agent was short and pudgy, wore a brown suit and a bowler hat. He carried a briefcase. You went outside and talked on the porch with him, Grandmother. I watched from inside the house, peeking between the curtains in the front room. The agent sounded as if he was picking up a parcel.

"We've come for the girl that lives here. Josephine MacCammon. She has to attend school. We're taking her with us."

"She's from Kamloops. She can go to school there."

"She's been living with you. She's got to attend school here."

"I'm sending her back."

"It's too late. We're taking her."

"I don't know where she is. Come back later."

"There's no use lying. I'm from the Department of Indian Affairs, which decides where Indian children go to school."

He turned to the constable.

"Search the house."

"You can't go inside my house."

The constable went to the door and you tried to stop him from opening it. He pushed your hands away. He came into the front room and picked me up and carried me outside. I was shaking.

"Where are they taking me, Grandma?"

"It's all right, Josie. I'll come for you."

I found out later that you came to the school but were refused entrance. You stood on the school grounds for two days and nights before the police took you away. I never thought you wouldn't come. But I knew the school wouldn't let you see me. Five minutes in that place told me it was a prison. St. Jerome's Mission School. Priests and nuns were our jailers. They wore black, as if they hated life and were already dead. To us kids they were like monsters ready to punish us for making mistakes. Our biggest mistake was being Indian. That meant they could do whatever they wanted to us.

We got to the school in the afternoon. My clothes were taken and I was given the same dress as the other girls. It was a sack with a big white collar cut into scallops. The nuns gave us orders but otherwise didn't speak to us. All the kids were herded into the refectory, a room with long tables and benches. We lined up and picked up a bowl and spoon and passed an older girl who threw a ladle full of watery mashed potatoes into the bowl. We sat at the tables and ate the tasteless stuff. Afterwards we were taken to dormitories, all the kids in mine being six or seven, except a four-year-old who sucked her thumb. If we said anything in our language we were slapped. We were taken to a bathroom before being ordered to get ready for bed. We undressed in silence as the nuns watched us. The lights were turned out and the nuns left but I felt there was one nearby in case we spoke or got out of bed. I lay there and could hear a girl crying and I said in a loud whisper, "We're all as miserable as you." A sharp voice said, "Quiet."

Early next morning a loud sound woke me. A nun had hit the end of my bed with a strap. She hit the end of every bed as she walked along the row, first on one side of the aisle and then the other. Your bed got the first whack and you got the next if you weren't fast enough getting out of bed and dressed. You got whacked for being slow at anything. The bathroom again, and be quick or Sister Celeste—that was her name—would use the strap on your naked bum in the toilet stall. We were herded into the refectory, bowl and spoon, and this time potatoes with peas.

That morning was the first day of school and all the grades went to the assembly hall to hear Father Mellors. He was the head and always looked serious. I never saw him smile in the time I was there. His voice was the same, no matter what he said, as if his words could hurt you.

"The government has determined you will be educated. We do our very best here to fulfil that mandate, but much depends upon you. You children should be grateful that this society cares enough to care for you. Be orderly, obey the rules, obey your teachers, learn your lessons and those tasks asked of you. Failure to comply with any of these means punishment, swift and severe.

"We do not shirk our responsibility. You must not shirk yours. Together we can make your time here memorable. You will be prepared for the life you will lead as responsible citizens after you leave. As homemakers and farmers you will be contributing to the growth and the prosperity of this nation. This will be an important time in your life because you are being forged into something new and better, ready to take your proper place in this society. For ten months a year this will be your home. As you will come to know, there's no home like St. Jerome's."

He bowed his head.

"Heavenly Father, grant each of us who are Thy servants the wisdom and strength to prepare young minds to follow Thy commandments. Let the soil be fertile. Let the seeds we plant bear good fruit. May none be unwilling, for those that are will be dealt with according to the old maxim, Spare the rod and spoil the child."

As we left the assembly hall in silence in pairs the girl next to me said "Shirk?" A nun walking beside us reached over and slapped her. I said, "Means quiet." I got slapped harder.

In that school when you weren't scared you were bored. The schoolwork was the same for all grades: arithmetic, reading and writing in English, and lots of religion, every morning and most of Sunday. The girls were taught homemaking, which meant sewing and cooking, cleaning and washing, as if our people had never done any of these things. Boys were taught to be farmers, as if we had no knowledge of the land. We weren't supposed to be anything more than domestics or labourers. Most of the teachers didn't know much. They weren't there to educate us but to break us down, turn us into little second-class Christians. We spent half a day in school and half a day working in the fields around the school, growing potatoes, peas, beets, carrots and onions. All we got to eat was potatoes, sometimes with peas. Most of the food was sold to help support St. Jerome's. But the teachers ate well, had wine, meat and fish with their fruit and vegetables.

The kids got weak because of the bad diet but the school never changed it. Many of them got sick and died from disease or hunger. The four-year-old who sucked her thumb was the first in my dormitory to die. You saw more and more empty beds when you woke up in the morning. Once I woke early and saw Sister Celeste remove the bodies with the help of other nuns. When they were finished she would bang her strap against the beds to wake us. The weaker and sicker kids couldn't move very fast and she would strap them. They would fall and she would strap them where they lay. Their cries and whimpers made her angrier and she would continue beating them until they would crawl along the cold floor. We got so used to her strapping it became a part of our lives. We heard that the dead bodies were buried in unmarked graves in a field somewhere. None of us ever found out where.

What saved me was the advice you gave me, Grandmother, when I came to live with you. "Chew your food well, Josie. You'll get more from it." I told the other girls but they were so hungry they would eat too fast. I knew I would live if I was strong and if I hated the school, not myself. I never let the teachers beat the Indian out of me. I told myself I was a prisoner, not a student. How they used God against us. They told us Hell was waiting for kids that sinned. How could we sin? By not obeying them in everything. By obeying them we were obeying God. Even in my child's mind I thought, this is for them, not for us. Supposedly saving our souls, they were destroying our bodies and stealing who we were. We were their servants, not servants of God. I have heard many lies in my life. The most arrogant is that the God of white people lets them destroy others by killing them or making them believing slaves.

The teachers. Sisters Eileen, Francoise and Dominique taught homemaking. Sister Eileen was small and wore round glasses and did only what she had to. Sister Francoise was from a farm in Quebec and could only speak a few words of English. We couldn't understand what she was saying and she thought that was our fault. Her accent would make Father Mellors frown. Sister Dominique was fat and had a mustache. She never did anything unless Father Mellors visited our classroom, and then she would order us around. She knew that would get a look of approval from him. Fathers Claude and Jean-Jacques were supposed to teach the boys farming but were more interested in hockey. Sister Claire taught reading and writing. She was smarter than the others. She never yelled and would take us on walks and tell stories. She came there in my third year, taking over from Sister Celeste, who was put in charge of our religious instruction.

Two more.

Father Hugh taught arithmetic. He smelled of wine, was always drunk. At the beginning of class he would put the lesson on the board and sit at his desk and his eyes would close very slowly. After we did our work—the lesson was usually easy—we'd talk among ourselves. A boy would crouch and listen near the door and when he heard footsteps he would run to his desk and make a noise. This would warn us and wake the teacher. Once Father Mellors came in and demanded to know what the noise was and Father Hugh said he dropped a book. Father Mellors frowned and left.

Father Jardine was feared by all of us. He was supposed to be a records clerk or a secretary to Father Mellors, but his real job was punishing kids. His hands were long and bony and his hair grew back from his forehead in a vee. He had staring eyes and his lips were always in a sneer. When he appeared in a hall or room everybody would fall silent. He would walk through that silence, kids waiting for him to pass and hoping he wouldn't speak to them because if he spoke to you you had broken some rule, maybe without even knowing it, and were to be punished. Every year some of the boys ran away. They were caught and punished in front of the whole school. They would have to pull down their underpants and bend over to be beaten. Father Jardine beat them with a bullwhip or a paddle. As he swung the whip or paddle his face would look the same as when he walked through a silent crowd of frightened children. The boys would cry out and one boy collapsed and fell onto the floor. He had to be carried away and we heard that he died and was buried with the kids who died of sickness and starvation. We heard that two boys who ran away had been found frozen to death in the snow. One morning screams came from the girls' bathroom. I ran and looked in and saw girls standing over a girl who was covered in blood. During the night she had sneaked out of bed and scratched her wrists with a bobby pin until the veins burst. Sister Celeste shoved her way past me. "Get out, all of you." She left and came back with another nun. They carried the body away. When Sister Celeste returned she ordered us to clean up the blood.

After ten months I returned to you skinny and weak, Grandmother. You fattened and cheered me up but there was always the thought lurking that I had to go back to that place. None of the kids mentioned the school during the vacation. There were sad faces among the parents whose children did not return. Later I found out it was the same in all the bands. Nobody said much and I began to understand it was expected children would die at that school. This had happened for many years. Our people had to bear it.

"How long do I have to go to that school? I hate it, Grandma."

"I have a plan but you are too young yet, Josie. In three years you will be ready."

"That long?"

"That long."

When the time came for me to begin a third year at the school, the man in the bowler hat came for Jimmy John too. From the beginning Jimmy John kept breaking the rules and getting punished. He took his anger at being there out on the other boys. He was tough, beating boys his own age and getting beaten by older ones he challenged. The school was turning him into the wild savage it was supposed to beat out of us. By his second year younger boys were doing him favours to stay on his good side. The priests and nuns gave up trying to scare or teach him. Like them, he became a bully. We hardly talked to each other. During vacation I didn't see much of him. He went off somewhere with boys from his gang at school. He wasn't afraid of you, Grandmother, because you didn't punish, only talked to him. At school he was always being slapped, strapped, whipped, or beaten with a paddle. He was proof that the school discipline ruined kids and created the need for even more discipline. I think you gave up on him the night he said to you, "You're not my mother." I could see the hurt in your face. That night you lost a grandson and I lost a brother. You were right in not ever hitting him. That would have made him worse. We never gave up loving him. That's part of being who we are.

By my fourth year I had had enough of their education. I was eleven, spent most of my time working in the fields planting and digging up potatoes. The only part of our education the school cared about were the religious lessons. We listened and we prayed, prayed for the day we could leave. As for the rest, we could barely read and write.

A cold morning in early March. I wasn't moving fast enough to the bathroom to satisfy Sister Celeste. She swung her strap and I blocked it with my arm. She began to hit me on my arms and legs and even my face. She wouldn't stop and I tried to grab the strap and she became angrier and tried to hit me even harder. She was panting, her face was red. She took me to see Father Mellors, who ignored my welts and bruises and took her side.

"You were warned about being disobedient. You will be punished by Father Jardine."

Father Jardine was busy, probably praying for more strength in his right arm, so I was to be punished the next day. That night I escaped. I took a blanket with me and walked twenty-five miles through the freezing night to the reserve. You fed me and I slept and you stayed up all night figuring out where to hide me when they came. They didn't come for two days. It was the weather. I wasn't caught that night because it was too cold for them to be bothered searching and they thought I would freeze to death, anyway. When the constable and agent came I was wrapped in blankets under the porch. I could hear their boots climbing the steps. The knock on your door, the agent's voice and yours.

"Don't think you can get away with this. We catch all runaways."

"You ought to be ashamed of yourself, chasing a little girl. Get off my porch."

"You're hiding her somewhere. You could be charged."

"I hide nobody. I protect my own."

"The law says she's got to be educated."

"Educated? You raped our women, brought smallpox and wiped out whole bands. When we defended ourselves, you wanted peace. Our leaders went unarmed to meet with you. You jailed and hanged them. White man's justice. You think we forget?"

"Shut your mouth."

"Don't touch me. White son of a bitch."

I ran out from under the porch.

"You leave my grandma alone."

I was to be whipped in the assembly hall in front of the whole school. I lay in my bed in the dormitory thinking, I will not cry, even if they kill me. I remembered the boy who had died from a whipping and the beaten boys who had trouble walking for days afterwards. During my years at St. Jerome's no girl had been beaten. Before I fell asleep I heard

Sister Celeste walking along the aisle in the darkness. She stopped at a bed across and two down from mine. It was Rachel's bed. She was seven years old, small and quiet, with scared eyes. After a while I heard the bed moving back and forth and grunts and moans and small cries all in a rush. Then it was quiet, Sister Celeste left and I fell asleep.

I had seen it all before as part of the audience. Now I was the one who was marched in and left to stand on the stage alone in front of everybody. I would have to take down my underpants and bend over the table beside me. Sister Dominique, who had marched me in, joined Father Mellors and the other teachers, who were sitting on folding wooden chairs at the back of the stage. Father Jardine was standing with a whip at the side. Eyes stared at me in the silence and my knees were shaking. Father Mellors came to the front and spoke.

"Disobedience will not be tolerated. This girl was disobedient, ran away and will be punished. This school is here for your benefit, to educate you. You must follow the rules, do as you are told. Let this be a lesson to you all."

He walked to his chair and sat down. Sister Claire stood up.

"I ask to be the one to administer the punishment."

Father Mellors frowned at her.

"Father Jardine administers the punishment in this school."

"She is the first girl to be punished in this way. Are you going to let a man whip an eleven-year-old girl?"

"This is Father Jardine's duty."

"I'm sure Father Jardine knows his duty. We've all seen

him perform. His enthusiasm is obvious. But in this instance it may result in permanent damage. If the intent is to instruct and not to injure, perhaps permanently, a woman mindful of that should be the one to administer the punishment."

I had never heard anybody talk that way to Father Mellors. He scowled.

"Enough. Sit down. Be quiet. Father Jardine will punish her."

Sister Claire walked over and stood beside me.

"I will stand between and take the punishment."

"You are making a mockery of this school and its rules."

"I am doing what I feel is right."

"You have no right to question what I say or do."

"Then I am like this girl and should be punished."

"The church authorities will hear of this."

Sister Claire, tall and erect, walked over to Father Jardine and held out her hand. He hesitated and she made a slight motion her hand and he gave her the whip. She walked back to me. I began to pull down my underpants.

"No, leave them on. Bend over the desk."

I did and she swung the whip once, letting it lightly touch my bum. She threw the whip out onto the floor of the hall. She took my hand and we walked off the stage and through the silence to the back and she pushed one of the two swinging doors open. Her habit brushed against the door as we left, and when the door closed we were alone. She spoke quietly.

"It's the end for us here. He's going to take his revenge. I'll send word. You be ready."

It was almost noon, I was in Sister Celeste's religious instruction class, and Father Hugh came and told her I was to go with him. Father Mellors wanted to see me. Father Hugh looked nervous, as he did whenever he hadn't been drinking. Sister Celeste, who had been glaring at me since the beginning of class, grinned. In the hall Father Hugh whispered Sister Claire had sent for me. We went to the rear of the school. Sister Claire was sitting in the back of a car. She opened the door and I got in and sat beside her. Father Hugh sat in front behind the wheel. I remembered Rachel. I told Sister Claire about Sister Celeste and she asked which classroom Rachel would be in and told Father Hugh to go and get her. He threw his hands in the air. "May as well be hung for a sheep as a lamb." "Two lambs, Father."

As we waited, Sister Claire told me what had happened.

"I knew Father Mellors wouldn't wait long. He's written to the church authorities about me. He's decided to get rid of Father Hugh as well, for drinking. The real reason is he's easy on the children, never punishes them. We're being transferred. We have the car to drive to the railway station. We'll take you to your reserve first."

Father Hugh hurried to the car. He was holding onto Rachel, who looked frightened. I opened the door and pulled Rachel in. I hugged her.

"We're going home."

She started to cry.

Father Hugh ground the starter motor when he turned the ignition key and he ground the transmission gears as he shifted into first and we hurtled off. I kept looking back, feeling better as the school became smaller. It was a white and wonderful day, everything covered in snow and the sky a bright blue. I looked at Sister Claire. She was smiling but it was not a happy smile. It was the smile of someone who is thinking about many things. I was curious about her.

"Where are you from?"

"Montréal. I'm French and English. My family are bankers and corporation lawyers. I have a university degree. My husband was killed in the War. It was hard for me, getting over that. I decided to join a religious order, came out two years ago hoping to help Indian children. What I've seen has shocked and angered me. The children's food, the brutality. When I asked for textbooks and readers I was told there wasn't enough money. To save chalk I was told to write on the blackboard only when necessary. There was never enough paper, pens or ink. I thought taking classes for walks would help. But nothing I could do would make that place a school."

"You're not like the other nuns."

"They're from farms and working-class families. Nuns are given a basic education to teach homemaking and some arithmetic, a little reading and writing. They're taught to obey superiors. So Father Mellors is used to dealing with submissive women. I can and will challenge him and now he knows that."

"Are you going to stay a nun?"

She smiled.

"We'll see."

We drove for a while in silence. Father Hugh was shifting

gears easier now. I put my arm through Rachel's and we leaned against each other. I thought of something. I asked Sister Claire.

"Who's going to drive the car back to the school?"

"Father Claude was supposed to drive us to the station but Father Hugh gave him some brandy and left him in a shed in the fields, so the car will be at the station until tomorrow, which gives us more time."

"That was my best stuff I gave him."

"It was in a good cause."

Father Hugh didn't answer.

"Wasn't it?"

"I can't say yes, not when it comes to drink."

"I thought it was the opposite."

I gave Father Hugh directions to the reserve. I asked Rachel and she told me which band she was from. It was much further away. I told Sister Claire, and that my grandmother was my guardian and would take care of everything.

"You must think a lot of her."

"She's the best grandma in the world."

It was mid afternoon when we reached the road into the reserve. Father Hugh stopped and looked at the hoof prints and wagon tracks in the snow.

"I don't know if we can make it into the reserve and back again on that road. We've got to get to the station."

"The police car makes it," I said.

"Drive on," Sister Claire said.

Father Hugh shrugged and entered the road, following the wheel tracks. It was a bumpy ride but the snow wasn't deep.

The wheels would spin sometimes but we didn't get stuck. I pointed to your house, Grandmother, and he stopped nearby. You stepped out onto the porch and I can still see the expression on your face as Sister Claire got out of the car. When Rachel and I got out you didn't know what to think until I ran up onto the porch and hugged you. Father Hugh stayed in the car and Sister Claire took Rachel's hand and brought her to the bottom of the porch steps. I tried to explain.

"This is Sister Claire. She stopped them from beating me and got us out. This is Rachel, Grandma. Do you know her people?"

"I think I do. After everything that happened yesterday this is too much for me. I'm grateful to you, Sister. I spent an uncomfortable night. Didn't know what to do."

"We have to catch a train. Can you hide them quickly? I don't know when the authorities are going to be notified. If they're caught, what I've done will go for nought."

"I know of a place where no one will find them. I'll send them off before sundown. Come up here, Rachel. The Sister has to go."

Rachel climbed the steps. You put a hand out and took hers. Father Hugh revved the engine. Sister Claire raised her hand.

"Goodbye."

The car disappeared into the white distance as I stared after it.

"Come inside, you two. I've got things to do."

You sent me to Jack Drew's house to fetch him, then to Mary Johnson's house to tell her about Rachel and to get word to her band. We set out immediately after you fed us, dressed us in warm clothes and said you'd come to see us soon. Rachel asked about her mother and you said she'd be told and would come and see her. Jack Drew took us to Ed George's cabin in our hunting grounds, carrying Rachel on his shoulders. "What's he like?" I asked on the way, looking up at him as Rachel held on, her arms tight around his neck. "He's a trapper and knows those woods like nobody else. He's got two hunting dogs, Pal and Person. They're harmless but they bark like hell. Can hear them miles away. They'll sniff out and spot somebody way before he can spot you."

After crossing what seemed like miles of snowy grassland we followed a narrow path between low hills, our boots scuffing dry snow. I thought about what Jack Drew said.

"Is he going to want to look after two girls?"

Jack Drew laughed.

"He'd do anything your grandmother asked. He wanted to marry her once. Many years ago. But she picked a guy who was the best trapper and hunter in this country. Raised horses too. One day he dropped dead from a stroke. There was your grandmother, a widow with a young daughter. And there was Ed George again saying he still wanted to marry her, but she said no, she'd raise her daughter herself. And she did. She sold off the horses. Planted the biggest garden in our band. Grew enough to trade all the extra for what she needed. Nobody can grow stuff like that woman. Planted saplings for an orchard. Made jam. People came from other bands to get it. She ran traplines for a while too. Did some hunting. She can handle a rifle. No, he won't kick about looking after you. He'll be happy to do her a favour."

"People that old can still like each other?"

"They're not that old. And liking somebody doesn't change. Young. Old. It's the same whether your Rachel's age or yours or mine or Ed's even."

"Rachel's only seven."

Rachel raised her head from her arm.

"I only five."

"You're seven."

"I only five."

"She should know her own age, Josie."

"I guess."

The light was fading, the sun dropping towards the horizon. Strands of cloud had turned rosy pink and the snow seemed to be blushing. The air was getting colder. I felt like sitting down in the snow. It seemed we had been walking all day. Jack Drew stopped and pointed. He was pointing at a hill that looked like so many others.

"We're there. If you look up at that hill you can see a grove of trees. Ed's cabin is in there. It'll take us another half hour or so."

We could hear something. It was the bellowing sound of hounds. We walked towards it. Rachel seemed to be sleeping.

"Those are his dogs. Don't worry, they know me."

Halfway up the hill I could see the dogs running towards us and barking. They were a muddy brown, had big muzzles and floppy ears. Jack Drew called to them and they wagged their tails, sniffing us in turn. Rachel woke up, lifted her head and felt safe where she was. They gave her a look before following us to the top. The pine and fir didn't look as dense there and we could see a log cabin and a man standing in front. His grey hair was down to his shoulders and he wore a mackinaw jacket, jeans, boots and a peaked cap with earflaps. His jeans were patched and his jacket looked as if he never took it off. He waved to Jack Drew and gave us a quick look. He spoke slowly and I knew he always spoke like that because his brain worked that way.

"Hi, Jack. What have you brought me?"

"Ruth's granddaughter, along with her young friend."

He looked at me closely, as if he was trying to see someone else.

"You've come a long way. Get inside and get warm."

After telling his dogs to stay outside, he opened the door. We followed him into a large room with log walls, a stove, some wooden chairs around a table, and a wooden couch with cushions. There was a stone fireplace with a fire going and a door to another room. There was a strong smell of fried meat. But it was wonderful to be out of the cold. He invited us to sit on the couch. Jack Drew put Rachel down and I sat beside her and Ed George inspected us. He grinned.

"So Ruth sent me guests. What goes on, Jack?"

"They escaped from St. Jerome's. They've got to stay hidden."

"I guessed as much. I don't mind doing Ruth a good turn. I've got a storeroom in the back that'll make a good bedroom for you two. What are your names?"

"She's Rachel and I'm Josie."

"Pleased to meet you. You've already met my dogs."

Jack Drew stayed the night. It was freezing outside and he wouldn't have been able to find his way in the dark. Ed George fixed the storeroom for us. We could hear him throwing stuff around. You had packed some clothes for us, Grandmother. When the bedroom was ready, Ed George came out and we went in and changed. That was when I saw Rachel's crotch, red and swollen. She had been chewed and rubbed raw between her legs. That was why she was so tired and slept on the way. I ran into the other room.

"She's been hurt, she needs help. A nun did it at the school."

I described what I saw. Ed George rummaged around in a chest of drawers in our bedroom. He took out an earthenware jar with an elastic band around a paper cover over the mouth. He handed the jar to me.

"This'll fix her up. It's ointment made from plants. Put this on her. Not too much. Do the same tomorrow and every day till she gets better."

I smeared the ointment over the whole area and Rachel whimpered at the slightest touch. After a few minutes the ointment began to work, she perked up and we went to eat.

We ate at the table with Jack Drew. Ed George made herbal tea in a cup. He gave it to Rachel. He took a round loaf of sourdough bread out of the oven and cut slices for us. From a cupboard beside the stove he took out strips of dried venison and a bowl of dried blueberries and brewed a pot of tea. I liked everything. Rachel liked the blueberries. Ed George looked at her.

"You better put her to bed. She needs rest."

There was no bed in the cabin. Ed George slept on the couch. For our bed he had put planks over upended crates and some blankets on them. It was cold in the storeroom unless the door was open. I held Rachel's hand until she fell asleep. Afterwards I went and sat with the men. Jack Drew was talking.

"I remember that place. The beatings. Working in the fields to feed them, make money for them. All we got was potatoes. One of the bastards used to sneak off with this little kid. Take him to the boiler room. We knew what was going on but you couldn't say anything or you'd get beaten. In this goddam country you can't do a thing about it except hand over your kids to them and hate yourself. If we were the savages they called us we would have gone there and burnt the place down, with them in it. Give them a taste of their hell. We got more than a taste of it."

He looked at Ed George.

"You didn't go."

"No. My dad ran away, was the only one they didn't catch. When my time came he sent me here. Police don't bother you. Too big and wild. No Indian agent is going to come here without a Mountie. We get hold of an agent he'd be lucky to get out alive, especially that Tuck Browner."

"That tub of lard. I saw him in Williams Lake a few months ago and said to him, 'You still got nothing better to do than chase kids?'"

"What'd he say?"

"Nothing. Indian agents got power. We're supposed to

get a pass off them every time we leave the reserve and a permit to sell stuff off reserve. They handle government payments, credit and loans. Most times we don't bother with passes and we never have trouble getting a permit. He knows our people. Something might happen to him. But he goes after kids to get them in that school. The more kids he brings them, the more money they get from the government. He's getting something from the school."

"He's the one pushed my grandma," I said.

Ed George stood up, put his hands in his pockets, took them out and sat down again.

"I'll remember that."

Jack Drew glanced my way and I could see a bit of a grin. As we drank the rest of the tea, I asked him if he had ever met my mother or my father.

"I knew them both. Your mother was good-looking. Took after your grandmother. Lots of guys wanted to marry her. She hadn't made up her mind when your father showed up. Came to the reserve one day looking for a guide. He was a geologist turned prospector, wanted to explore the Cariboo. Those guys are always looking for the mother lode and I think he thought he found it when he saw your mother. Your grandmother wanted her to marry somebody from our bands. When she saw what was between them, she gave up. Before they got married he got a job in the government assay office in Kamloops. He'd decided he needed a regular income to support a family. He'd go prospecting part-time. They'd come up to live with your grandmother and he'd take off on prospecting trips. After your sister and you were born, he'd come up alone. On a trip in the backcountry in 1923 he was killed in a rockslide. Guide warned him the footing wasn't safe on that part of the mountain but he went ahead. Your mother brought you and your sister and baby brother and moved in with your grandmother and then your mother and sister got TB. It was tough on your grandmother looking after them and losing them. You and your brother were all the family she had left. She took to calling you 'my Josie.'"

"How come you know all this stuff?" Ed George said.

"None of it's secret. You've lived alone too long, that's your problem."

"Don't think I'm missing nothing but not knowing everybody's business."

"Even Ruth's?"

Jack Drew winked at me. Ed George didn't see.

"I don't mind you telling me about her, if that's what you want to know."

"I was talking to Josie."

"I couldn't help hearing, now could I?"

That night Rachel had nightmares, crying out in her sleep. I held onto her, telling her everything was all right. After a while she was quiet and I fell asleep. Next morning I put more ointment on her. She was healing but it was still hard to look. Jack Drew left after breakfast. He said he would tell you everything, Grandmother. Ed George made herbal tea. Rachel drank it and felt better. She and I put our coats on and went outside and played with the dogs. Ed George had told me he'd kept them out of the cabin on purpose the night before because he didn't want them bothering us. They had their own little kennel beside the cabin, anyway. Later I asked him why he'd named them Pal and Person. No reason, he said.

Rachel got better and had more energy. She had nightmares for a week. After that she talked in her sleep sometimes. Ed George would check his traplines every day, sometimes coming back with a marmot. He'd hunt deer and moose. He killed a moose and we ate fresh meat for a couple of days. He told us he was going to cure the rest. He would make sourdough bread every day and he taught me how to make it. He had sacks and bowls of dried berries from last summer and fall and we ate those. In the cupboard beside the stove was a shelf with glass jars of seeds and leaves of dried plants and herbs. If we weren't feeling well, he'd get something out of a jar and give it to us. He didn't talk much, not with us. He'd talk to his dogs, usually outside if the weather wasn't bad. You'd think they were human, but dogs had been his only company for so long. I began to understand why he called them Pal and Person. But he still seemed odd. I said so one day.

"You know something, Ed George? You're peculiar."

"Is that good?"

"Don't think so."

"Guess it goes along with my life. You put a word to it, that's all."

"Don't feel bad. Everybody is a bit peculiar. You more than most. If you weren't, me and Rachel wouldn't have a place to hide out."

"Guess you're right. Putting it that way."

I looked at Rachel.

"You like Ed George, don't you?"

She nodded.

"Like me too, don't you?"

She shook her head from side to side.

"I only five."

"I made a mistake. You like me though, don't you?"

She grinned.

Two weeks after we arrived, Grandmother, you came up with Rachel's mother and father. She ran to meet her mother, who picked her up and hugged and kissed her. Later Rachel cried when her mother told her she couldn't go back with them. When she heard that she would be put back in St. Jerome's if she returned to her band, her eyes looked scared. You brought beeswax candles and jars of honey for Ed George and teased him.

"You taking good care of these girls?"

"Don't they look all right to you?"

"Hm."

"A guy does what he can and it's still not enough. I'm going outside and talk to my dogs."

You told me the Indian agent had come to your house.

"He threatened me with jail if I didn't tell him where you were and I said, 'Threaten all you want, won't do you any good.' Seems the school is upset because you two are the only runaways who haven't been caught in more than twenty years. The last was Ed's father. They might send someone up here. I'll warn Ed."

You stayed two days and spent most of the time cleaning up the cabin. Ed George said he wouldn't be able to find anything any more. You made a wonderful stew with mushrooms and leaves you picked in the forest. We ate it with sourdough and a little dried venison. You told Ed George to change our diet.

"More berries and less meat. And fresh berries as soon as they appear. Catch some fish. Don't fry it. Steam it with a little water. I've brought some parsley seeds you can plant. We don't want these girls to end up looking like you."

The night before you left you talked with him in a corner and I knew it was about the Indian agent. Your voices were low and at the end he nodded. The next morning Rachel stopped looking sad when her mother promised to visit again soon. She and I stood in front of the cabin watching as the three of you rode down the path and disappeared into the forest. I took her for a walk so she'd feel better.

The next couple of days were warmer. I cleared the snow, weeds and twigs from a sunny patch of ground near some pines, where I planned on planting the parsley seeds. Ed George spent a lot of time away from the cabin, always taking his rifle with him. The dogs were put outside every night. He built a shelter fifty yards away from the cabin. He told me it was a hiding place for Rachel and me if anybody showed up. It looked like a pile of old logs but there was a space inside. The entrance was big enough for Rachel and me to squeeze through.

A few days after you left, Grandmother, I was digging around in the soil in that sunny patch, welcoming early spring weather, and saw Ed George hurrying up the path and waving his arms and shouting for Rachel and me to get into the shelter. We ran and got inside and I told her to keep quiet, everything would be all right. I peeked through a space between the logs. I could hear the dogs barking nonstop. Ed George was standing outside the cabin. He called the dogs to him and said 'Be quiet' in a sharp voice. After a while I could see the Indian agent approaching the cabin. An RCMP constable was walking a little behind him. He raised a gloved hand, said hi to Ed George. Ed George raised his hand. He called him Constable Wavell. The Indian agent seemed irritated at this, got down to business.

"I'm Tuck Browner, with the Department of Indian Affairs, looking for two runaways from St. Jerome's school. You seen or heard anything of them?"

Ed George shook his head. The agent looked at the cabin door. It was shut. He spoke to the constable.

"We'll take a look inside."

Ed George didn't move or say anything. The constable didn't move and the agent pointed at the door.

"We're going inside."

The constable looked at Ed George.

"You mind, Ed?"

Ed George shook his head and stood aside. The constable opened the door and went inside, followed by the agent. I could hear things being thrown around. This lasted for a few minutes. When the agent and constable returned, the agent was holding a hairpin with a tortoiseshell heart attached. It was Rachel's. The agent held the hairpin up in front of Ed George, close to his eyes.

"What have we here? Don't tell me this is yours?"

Ed George didn't answer.

"I think we've found them. Where you hiding them?"

The constable stepped in front of the agent.

"Have you seen them, Ed?"

Ed George shook his head.

The constable looked at the agent.

"That's good enough for me."

The agent made a fist around the hairpin.

"He hasn't said a damn word."

The constable walked partway down the path before turning around.

"We've spent two days up here. I've got my duties back at Williams Lake. As far as I'm concerned, it's over. My report will say investigation discontinued after a thorough search, whereabouts and fate of the runaways unknown."

"You're letting them go."

"I'm walking down the trail, getting on my horse and riding back to Williams Lake. Do what you want."

"I've got my job."

"I've got mine."

The constable walked down the path. The agent stared at Ed George.

"You're not getting away with this."

He tossed the hairpin at Ed George and followed the constable down the path. I kept holding onto Rachel. Ed George didn't move for a long time. Finally he walked down the path with the dogs and disappeared for a few minutes. When he returned he came over and peeked into the shelter.

"You can come out."

We followed him back to the cabin. I picked up Rachel's hairpin and cleaned it with snow at the side of the cabin and handed it to her. We went inside and I helped straighten out the mess. A jar of honey had been smashed. A beeswax candle was missing. We finished, everything looking as before, and Ed George scooped up the honey from the broken jar. He inspected it for bits of glass and we ate it with sourdough and tea. All this time Ed George had been thinking, and he spoke as he chewed on a chunk of sourdough spread with honey, honey making his lips slick.

"You girls stay inside for the next couple of days. The dogs will be outside day and night. There'll be plenty of warning. I've got things to do. Don't worry, I'll be around. When they visited, they brought some clothes up for you. Give me something you worn, like a sock or a scarf. Something you won't miss if you don't get it back."

I handed over an old scarf and Rachel a pair of woollen socks with holes in them. She had gotten new ones for her birthday. It was the day after her mother and father came. We gave Rachel a party. Ed George looked at our stuff and seemed to be satisfied. He put the dogs outside and we went to bed. Next morning he left the dogs and disappeared. He came back late and we ate dinner. Next day he disappeared, returning in the afternoon. He sat us down at the table. He told us what he'd been doing.

"I knew that agent would come back looking for your hiding place. I put your scarf and socks where somebody would see them if he was searching for somebody. Almost hidden, sort of lost by accident. There's a trail leading off the main one. I wouldn't advise nobody to take that trail. It leads to a den. There's nothing meaner than a mother grizzly that's got cubs. He took the bait and walked right in on her. She made short work of that agent. I saw the remains. She tore out his liver. What else, I won't tell you girls. It'll help her make milk. That fat carcass will end up helping feed her cubs. Put it to some use after all."

He remembered something and went outside, returned wearing a bowler hat.

"I picked this up as a souvenir. How does it look?"

"Throw it away."

"Brand new."

"Get rid of it. I'll tell my grandma."

"All right."

Rachel giggled.

"Funny man, Ed George."

He looked at me.

"What does she mean?"

"She means, like peculiar. More different than most people. She's learning from me. She's only five."

"I only six."

Ed George dropped the bowler hat on the floor and sat down.

"How you girls going to learn anything, stuck up here?"

"I didn't learn much at that school. But I can read and write a little and do some arithmetic. My grandma has some books left by my father and she'll bring them up. I'll teach Rachel."

"Your grandmother be coming up regular?"

"Rachel's mother will be coming too."

"I don't know if I like so many people around."

"You don't want to see my grandma?"

"I didn't say I didn't, did I?"

"Maybe I could teach you a few things, Ed George."

"I don't need none of that, thank you."

Next time you came up, Grandmother, you told me there was a new Indian agent. When Tuck Browner didn't show up after a week, a search party went looking but found nothing. The police figured he'd been killed by an animal or had gotten lost and starved to death. Jimmy John had run away from the school and been caught and was beaten by Father Jardine. You said you weren't going to hide him with us when vacation came because he wouldn't obey Ed George and might give away our location. You didn't know where to hide Jimmy John, but you didn't have to because when vacation came he took off without telling you where he was going. That was the beginning of years of not knowing where he was or what he was doing. He would show up sometimes, wanting money, looking a lot older and drinking too much.

For the next few years Rachel and I lived in that cabin. From my father's books I learned science and arithmetic and history and taught myself to write much better and I taught Rachel. We felt safe except when Ed George would leave, sometimes for days, to check his traplines or to go off hunting with the dogs. He said nobody would come around, we'd be all right. There were two bars we put across the door at night and the window was too small for anything or anybody to crawl through. It was a solidly built cabin, the logs a foot wide and well put together, and not a whisper of wind could get inside. I knew no animal, even a wolf or a bear, could get to us. But when the two of us were alone, it would take me a while to fall asleep. One night I heard whispering. I got up and walked barefoot to the door and put my ear to it. From the sound of the voices I knew two white men were outside.

"Kick the door in."

"Suppose they got a gun?"

"We got one."

"It's a six-shooter. They probably got a rifle."

"We'll get in fast. We'll surprise 'em."

"Suppose we don't."

"More 'n' likely there's nobody here or we'd have heard dogs. All we have to do is break in and clean 'em out."

"Maybe they're keeping the dogs quiet so we'll think there's nobody."

"They didn't know we're coming. Any dogs would've started barking long time ago. It's quiet. We're all right."

I ran back into the bedroom and woke Rachel, putting a hand over her mouth.

"Be quiet, there's somebody outside."

Ed George would always take his rifle when he left. But he had an old revolver, which he said he was going to teach me to shoot. It was in the chest of drawers in our bedroom. I got it and on tiptoe went to the window. The window was four feet to the left of the door. It was a square hole covered by a piece of wood on hinges and with a latch. I pulled a chair over to the window, stepped up on the chair and undid the latch and opened the window. As I poked the gun out, holding it with both hands, fingers grabbed the barrel. As I pulled back I pulled the trigger and there was a loud noise. I heard a yell. I dropped the gun and it fell on the floor.

"I think I'm blinded."

The other man didn't answer.

"He's run off. Left me. Help me. I'll die."

I closed the window and fastened the latch. The man kept hollering. I climbed down from the chair, my hands trembling as I felt around in the darkness for the gun, finding it under the chair. Rachel had come to the bedroom doorway.

"Is the man hurt, Josie?"

The hollering stopped and the man's voice changed.

"Help me, little girls. Oh please, help me."

There was a knock on the door. I went to Rachel and held her.

"Be quiet. The man's not hurt. I've got a gun. We're safe."

The knock became a banging and the voice changed again.

"Open up or we'll get you."

I found the matchbox, beside the stove, and took out a match. I lit a candle that was in a saucer on the table and went back into the bedroom, taking Rachel with me, holding onto her hand. I checked the gun. Five shots left. I looked in the chest of drawers and found a box of cartridges. I opened it. It was half full. The banging on the door began again, harder. The door sounded solid. There was no give to it.

"Open up. We'll burn the place down."

I took Rachel back into the front room and sat her on the couch. I had the box of cartridges with me.

"Stay here."

I put the saucer with the candle on the arm of the couch and pulled the chair back to the window. I climbed up on it and waited. There were hard knocks on the wood covering the window and it began to give way, the hinges loosened and the latch sprang open. I held the gun with both hands directly in front of me. When the wood swung back I fired. There was another yell, this time more like a scream. A burning branch came through the window, falling on the floor. I jumped down and threw a couch cushion over it and pounded on the cushion. Another flaming branch was thrown in and I did the same. I climbed onto the chair. When I saw a burning branch approaching the window I fired and could hear cursing. The branch disappeared and I got closer and fired again. Another curse and silence. There was a lot of smoke in the cabin and we were coughing. I ran into the bedroom and soaked our scarves in our water jug, gave Rachel hers and told her to hold it over her face. I did the same and sat with her and we waited. Hours later we could see light coming through the window in a pale shaft.

"Are they gone, Josie?"

"We have to wait."

"I'm sleepy."

"You sleep. I'll stay awake."

Rachel nodded and was asleep. I nodded but didn't go to sleep. After a couple of hours I went to the window. I got up on tiptoe and peeked from the side. I couldn't see anything. But I wasn't going to go outside. I went back and sat beside Rachel and before I knew it I was asleep. A loud knock made me jump and I was wide awake.

"Open up, I'm back."

It wasn't Ed George's voice.

"I got presents for you."

I picked up the gun and took out the empty shells and filled the chambers. Rachel was still sleeping.

"Come out and have a look."

Did he think I was as stupid as he was?

"Come on, open up. You going to keep me waiting all day?"

And all night too. Ed George wouldn't be coming back until the next day.

"I'm getting mad out here. You going to open up?"

Why do stupid people think saying the same thing over and over again is going to get them what they want? That only works with other stupid people. A loud bang on the door and silence. The door was too solid. The walls were too strong. They would have to cut lots of brush, pile it against the cabin and burn it down. They sounded too lazy to do that, but they must have been desperate to still be there. Probably starving, which meant they were weak. They would be thirsty. The weather had been hot. The rain barrel was empty. We'd had to get water from a spring. The second yell had sounded real, so one of them was hurt. If I bribed them with food and water to get rid of them, that would make them stronger and more likely to cut brush. The only way out was to kill them.

I went to the cupboard with the jars of herbs. Ed George collected all kinds of things. He'd warned me not to open certain jars on the highest shelf. Two contained plants and a third one mushrooms, all poisonous. He'd told me you'd warned him about them, Grandmother, and had given him specimens to remind him. "I forget things," he said. I took down the three jars. The stuff looked harmless to me. I knew Ed George was peculiar and I wondered if he had made everything up. But he wouldn't lie about you. Not taking any chances, I took out something from each jar, grinding it all together. I put the powder in the water jug, added water from our water bucket and stirred everything and tied a piece of twine around the jug handle. I went to the window and slowly edged the jug off the windowsill, holding onto the end of the twine. I could feel the jug sliding around the outside of the logs. It was tin and made a scraping noise. I coughed to make sure. The jug was snatched away, the string pulled from my hands.

I never did ask Ed George what was in those jars. He probably didn't know, took your word so I took his. That's tradition. After a while their groans woke Rachel. Her eyes got scared. Rachel never said much. Her eyes spoke for her. I sat with her.

"It'll be over soon."

I didn't go outside. I wanted Ed George to see them first. He got back the next afternoon. We could hear the dogs barking. I looked out the window to make sure before taking the bars off the door. I went outside and saw them curled up and clutching their bellies. They were scrawny, had beards and their hands didn't look as if they had done much work. Probably greenhorn prospectors down on their luck and lost or escaped convicts. I could see a marmot paw sticking out of the bulging canvas sack Ed George had slung over his right shoulder. His rifle was slung by a woven cord over his left one. The dogs were barking at and sniffing the bodies.

"What are those guys doing there?"

"Why don't you ask them?"

"What happened?"

"We invited them to a party and they didn't like the cake. What do you think happened? They sneaked up and tried to break in night before last. I fed them stuff from those jars on the high shelf."

"How did you do that?"

"Ground it up and put it in the water jug. They were thirsty."

"You hand them the jug? You said they were trying to break in."

"No, through the window after I shot one of them."

"They drank the water after that?"

"I told you. They were thirsty."

He laughed.

"They're not thirsty now."

"We need one of your dogs."

"Hey now, I need my dogs."

"Then get us a dog from a reserve before you take off next time. Leave the dogs here while you're gone."

"They'll miss me."

"No, they won't. You can take us with you and we'll pick out a dog."

"Guess they won't miss me much. Much."

I pointed at the men.

"You going to bury them, or something?"

"Guess so. They'll start to stink in this weather. Sooner the better. Put this stuff away first."

He put the bodies on a travois and dragged them off, harness around his shoulders. At dinner he told us he'd dropped them off a cliff half a mile away.

"Coyotes 'll pick 'em clean soon enough."

Two weeks later we got our dog, a malamute called Strike. He'd been a sled dog in the Yukon. He was big, white and grey and had a wolf snarl that made Pal and Person stay out of his way. Ed George got him for nothing because the owner had too many dogs and wanted to keep only his hunting dogs. Rachel and I liked him and he seemed to know he was there for us. The top of one ear was missing, probably lost in a fight. I would've bet he didn't lose the fight. He was gentle and quiet but very intense around feeding time. We'd fry his meat rare when there was a fresh kill, liver being his favourite. He would howl outside sometimes on cold nights. It was a wild, mournful sound, as if he was thinking of a faraway place.

Ed George taught me how to shoot the revolver and the rifle. He'd put a block of wood on a log and I'd try to knock it off, beginning at fifty feet and then further off. The rifle had a kick to it. The revolver was easier but pulled to the right and the sight was off, so I had to adjust for that. Ed George said I was good but I think he was trying to save ammunition. He never offered to take me hunting. I didn't want to go. There was one rifle, and what could I hunt with a six-shooter, and besides, Rachel couldn't come and couldn't be left alone. All I wanted was to feel safe when he left us. I told Ed George the box of cartridges was almost empty and he said he had to get some for his rifle. I took the hint and next time you came up, Grandmother, I told you. You said you'd get Jack Drew to bring some for me. Ed George mentioned his rifle.

"You've been using up a lot of ammunition lately, Ed."

"Josie's learning to shoot."

"Josie shot a bad man," Rachel said.

So the story came out. I wasn't going to say anything because I knew what would happen. I didn't want Ed George to get into trouble with you. And we had a dog.

"That's why Josie wanted a dog. You always leave them alone for two nights?"

"I got to trap and hunt or how can I live? I'm not a babysitter."

"That's clear. Guess I better look for somebody else to take care of them. I was wrong about you. I'll take them with me."

"Now wait. Don't get all upset. I don't mind them being here, not really. When have I ever said no to helping?"

"It's the first time you've been asked."

"All right, but you going to hold this one thing against me? How was I to know? That was the first time. And I been up here fifty years."

"They could've been murdered."

Ed George got up and walked around the cabin, scratching his chin.

"I won't leave 'em again, not on purpose. But sometimes if I can't get back the one night, even if I try, it's one night."

"That dog looks as if he'll take better care of them. We'll let it stand for now, but if I ever hear different."

Ed George kept walking around the cabin but his step was lighter. You made dinner, Grandmother. It was the best we had since your last visit. You told Rachel her mother would visit with Jack Drew when he brought the cartridges. Ed George reminded you not to forget his. You looked at me and shook your head. I had to grin.

Ed George never left us alone even for a night after that, except once when there was a sudden heavy snowfall. The next morning he was back at dawn, saying he'd almost been buried alive the snow had been coming down so fast.

I walked with Strike across grasslands and around lakes and over streams and up hills and mountains. We stayed away from bears and they left us alone. Ed George showed me how to fish. He'd built a seventy-foot pier at a nearby lake years ago. I fished off the end of it most times, and always if we were short of food. But sometimes I sat on the grass at the edge of the lake and tried my luck. There was a rowboat without oars on the shore near the pier. I took it out once, using a pole to move and guide it, but it took on water so fast I was too busy bailing to fish. Ed George said he was going to patch the leaks and make some oars but never did. I tried other lakes but that was my favourite because it wasn't far from the cabin, was large, deep and there were lots of fish. Ed George called it Mystery Lake and I asked him why. He said somebody called it that once and the name stuck. It didn't look mysterious. I had a hunch Ed George called it that for some reason. What the reason could be I left as another mystery.

I'd carry my catch on my back in a wicker basket and fry or poach it and the three of us would have a feast. Rachel wasn't much for roaming around or fishing. She liked to embroider and do beadwork. She was good at it. She began to carve beads. No school but we had the books you brought up, Grandmother, and I read and kept teaching Rachel reading and writing. Jack Drew told us the new Indian agent began to get complaints from all the bands about the treatment of the kids at St. Jerome's. Some didn't return after vacation. They were sent to our hunting grounds to hide them. That's how I met Joe Bob. He was from a different band and I hadn't met him before and I didn't remember seeing him at St. Jerome's.

We met when I was fishing. I hadn't caught anything yet that day. He walked onto the pier and I heard his steps and turned and saw him. His hands were in his pockets.

"Catch anything?"

"Does it look like it?"

He walked to the shore, picked up a rock and threw it into the water and left.

"Thanks for scaring the fish."

A week later he was back. He had a fishing pole and cast

his line and sat on the side of the pier. I hadn't caught anything. We sat a few feet apart. He spoke first.

"I remember seeing you at St. Jerome's."

"I don't remember seeing you."

"You probably did. I'm Joe Bob."

"I don't remember that name. There were lots of boys."

"As tall as me?"

"One or two, maybe. I didn't look."

"How long you been up here?"

"About two years."

"I came last month. My father said I didn't have to go back."

After a while he stuck the end of the pole into a space between two planks and lay back on the deck.

"Fishing's stupid. I'd rather go hunting."

"You don't eat fish?"

"Sure."

"Somebody else has to catch it for you."

"Do you eat meat?"

"Yeah."

"Do you hunt?"

"No."

"Somebody else has to kill it for you."

We looked directly at each other for the first time. He was still lying on the deck. His line tightened and the pole was pulled from between the planks and dragged into the water. He jumped up.

"I got a bite."

He dove into the water. He swam after them but the line

and pole were out somewhere in the middle of the lake. He swam back and stood knee deep in water near the shore. He splashed the water around with his hands.

"Want to go swimming?"

"I'd have to take off my clothes."

"Go ahead, I won't look."

"You'll look later on."

"I won't."

"Go chase the fish."

My line tightened and I stood up, pulling back on the rod.

"Look if you want."

I caught four rainbow trout that afternoon. He watched and said nothing. I put them in the basket and headed for the cabin. He offered to carry the rod and basket. I said I was used to carrying them. Would I be fishing again next week? Maybe. We said goodbye at the bottom of the path that led to the cabin.

Next time I took Strike. Joe Bob was already there, pole stuck between the planks. Strike growled. I told him to be quiet and I cast my line.

"Somebody said you live with Ed George."

"Yeah. So?"

"So nothing. Rachel is from my band."

"So?"

"So nothing. That your dog?"

"Follows me around. Like some boys."

"You're stuck up."

He tore a sliver off a plank and was going to throw it into

the water but tossed it behind him and Strike growled.

"Come here, boy."

Strike snarled.

"He obeys me."

"Poor dog."

I caught three char and a rainbow by noon and decided to leave early. He stood up as I slung the wicker basket over my shoulder and picked up my rod.

"You going to follow me?"

"No."

But he did.

"Think I'll go see Rachel."

"You don't know her."

"Don't have to."

As we neared the cabin, Pal and Person began barking. Ed George shushed them and frowned at our unwelcome guest.

"You come around with the idea of chasing girls, you got to deal with me."

"I came to see Rachel. We're from the same band."

We went inside and Joe Bob said hello and introduced himself. Rachel looked up from beadwork she was putting on a sweater. Rachel's eyes always said everything. Her eyes were blank.

"I don't remember you."

I shook my head.

"Looks like nobody knows you."

"You people are real friendly. Good thing I'm not starving."

"We'd feed a stray dog."

He turned around and walked out and down the path. I went to the doorway and shouted.

"Since you're here, you can stay for dinner."

He stopped but didn't turn. His hands were fists. I called Strike to me. We walked down and I stood in front of Joe Bob. I could see tears in his eyes. We were both thirteen. God, what a world when you're a kid.

"His name is Strike. He was a sled dog. You can pet him. Good dog."

I held Strike by his collar and Joe Bob put his hand on Strike's head. He crouched down and stroked his head and Strike wagged his tail.

"Now I'll never be able to turn him on you."

"You're different."

"As long as you remember that."

At dinner Joe Bob said he was living with some boys in a cabin ten miles away. Ed George said he knew the owner.

"That was Shorty Moosehead's cabin years ago. He was killed in a snowslide."

"Why Moosehead?" Rachel said.

"He had a head like a moose. Nobody would marry him."

"That why he came up here?"

"Guess so."

"That why you're here? You don't have a head like a moose."

"Guess there's another reason."

Ed George looked uncomfortable. You can't make a woman love you and he knew that.

Joe Bob grinned.

"Short and head like a moose. Guess I'm lucky."

Rachel studied him.

"Your head is more like a dog's."

"Shut up."

"You shut up. Know who my dad is?"

Joe Bob thought for a while and remembered.

"I didn't mean nothing."

Ed George told a story about Shorty Moosehead.

"Shorty had people up north. Visited them once. Went with this hunting party over to Jasper. Somebody said they're in Alberta. Shorty looked around, scratched his head.

"'Where's the line? We didn't cross the line.'

"'What line?' somebody said.

"'Where Alberta is.'

"'There's no line.'

"'Sure there is. I seen it on a map. Different colours too. How come Alberta's the same colour?'"

Rachel giggled.

"That's why he couldn't get married."

I put in my two cents' worth.

"Shorty believed what he saw. He thought maps were real. We know they're not but we act as if they are. We play a trick on ourselves because it's played on us. Whites drew lines around us and called them reserves so they could take the rest of the land, reserve it for themselves. They behaved as if they were doing us a favour. They did themselves the favour. They see our colour so they can draw another line between us and them. Schools draw more lines around us, telling us what we can think and can say and even lines around our languages. There's lines everywhere, like ropes tying us up. Maybe Shorty wasn't far wrong."

Rachel's eyes stared.

"You're real smart, Josie, but you're scary."

Ed George put his fork down and pushed his plate away.

"Too much thinking is bad for you. Stupid is better. That's why I like talking to my dogs. They don't have no questions and I don't have no answers."

I looked at Joe Bob. His mouth was full.

"I liked the fish. The way you cooked it with water. Never had it that way. What's the green stuff?"

"Parsley."

"Can't say I like it."

Ed George asked Joe Bob how he knew about us.

"Everybody knows about you. All the bands. No agent's going to come here now after that last one never came back. Not only that. It's bad at the school. The teachers and everything. And young boys picked on by older boys. They tried doing things to me when I was younger. But I could always fight and was bigger than most. I got some of the younger ones together in a gang but it was tough. I got bigger but I was sick of all of it. I told my father and he said, 'You're not going back.'"

I looked at Rachel. She was remembering. As usual, we were sitting beside each other. I put my arm around her and she looked up at me. Her eyes were big but they weren't scared.

"You guys got enough to eat?" Ed George asked Joe Bob.

"There's five of us. We got two rifles. I'm a good shot. The others aren't bad."

"Oh boy, best at everything," Rachel said, herself once again.

Joe Bob had seen me put my arm around Rachel and figured it was about St. Jerome's.

"I shot a deer last week and a moose two weeks before. We been eating good."

"You run short, come over," Ed George said. "I got stuff put by. You want to pick some berries and dry 'em for winter. You know about curing meat?"

"My father told me."

"You fish?"

Joe Bob looked at me.

"No."

"Josie's a good fisher. We cure some for the winter and it's there if you want it."

Joe Bob nodded and looked at the open window, saw the light beginning to fade.

"I better start back. I don't want to lose the light."

I gave him a loaf of sourdough to take with him.

Joe Bob didn't show up for two weeks. I heard the dogs barking and went outside. He was sitting bareback on a big horse. It was brown, had a black mane and tail, a blaze on its forehead and white hair almost covered its hooves.

"Where did you get him?"

"My father bought him in Williams Lake. He's a farm horse. Handy if you want to bring in supplies. Or pull anything on a travois, like a dead moose."

"I'll remember that if I ever have a dead moose."

Ed George came out of the cabin.

"He's not going to take you anywhere quick, is he? You're going to have to cut lots of grass to feed him this winter. He's a hay burner. Course, if you get snowed in, he'll feed your bunch for a couple of months."

"Don't plan on that happening."

"Most don't. That's what separates the hunter from the hunted."

Ed George left and Joe Bob looked down at me.

"Climb up. Take you for a ride."

"No. I'm busy."

"Doing what?"

"Too much to waste my time telling you."

"Go do it, then. So long."

He turned the horse and they rode off like it was a one-horse parade.

"Don't go to sleep and fall off."

That fall I picked blueberries, currants, cranberries and huckleberries and Rachel and I gorged on them. I dried some for the winter, and parsley too, which I'd been growing all summer. Ed George cured venison, moose and fish for the winter. He gave some to Joe Bob, and I offered berries, fresh and dried, but he wasn't interested. I didn't mention parsley.

Joe Bob usually visited alone. We would talk in the cabin or among the nearby pines or go fishing, and sometimes I would let him carry the basket back. I was careful because I didn't know my own heart. I liked him but I was barely fourteen. My mother and you, Grandmother, had taken your time in picking a husband and you both had been happy until they died. I wanted to do the same and not be rushed. And I had to think of Rachel. She would have to spend many years in the hunting grounds before she was past school age. Ed George couldn't look after her. I was Rachel's big sister.

There was something else. Joe Bob had a mean streak. He never showed it to me or to Ed George. And no matter how much Rachel teased him, he ignored her after that first time. But I could see something was bothering him. He never talked about what happened to him at St. Jerome's and I never asked. I thought about Jimmy John. He had a gang and had escaped too but drank too much and disappeared for much of the time, nobody knew where. I first saw the other side of Joe Bob when he brought Len Spurgeon to visit. Len had brown hair and grey eyes and lighter skin than any of us. He was shorter than Joe Bob and not as tough. Nobody was. Joe Bob ordered him around and no matter what he did it wasn't good enough. Joe Bob called him White Boy.

The three of us were sitting among the pines near the cabin the first time Len Spurgeon visited, and Joe Bob began throwing pine cones at him.

"Cut it out," Len said.

"Think you can make me?"

He threw another cone and it hit Len in the eye. Len cried out and rubbed his eye.

"Look at the little crybaby."

"Stop it," I said.

"Aw, feeling sorry for the little crybaby."

"Keep this up and you're not welcome. What's wrong with you? Why are you picking on him? Because he could pass for white?"

Joe Bob dropped a cone he was holding. He lay back on the grass and closed his eyes. Len went inside the cabin and talked with Rachel and Ed George. I stayed with Joe Bob. After a while he sat up and picked a blade of grass and chewed on it.

"I'm sorry you got mad."

"Why don't you go tell Len you're sorry for what you said?"

"No."

Joe Bob brought all of the boys he was living with to the cabin. He'd bring one or two at a time, not everybody. He'd be all right for a while. You never knew when he would turn on them but you knew he would. He'd pick on them in front of us but he knew what I thought, so he'd try to control himself. I could imagine what it was like living with him. I could tell the other boys would have liked to move in with us. But we didn't have the room, and you couldn't put young guys and girls together without having trouble of some kind. Rachel was too young. I had enough trouble dealing with Joe Bob. I'd heard of boys sneaking into the girls' dormitory at night at St. Jerome's and helping them run off so they could fool around. The girls had always been caught. School policy was to try and marry us at graduation so we'd be proper Christians, no matter what we got up to. It was their way of saying, we've done our best and at least they're lawfully married and their brats aren't heathen bastards.

In our religious instruction we'd been told we had to be strong and control our desires because the flesh is weak. The flesh isn't weak. It's too strong for most people. Joe Bob gave in willingly at thirteen, if I'm guessing right. I didn't give in till I was sixteen. By then he was pestering me every time we met. My first time was in the woods. It was over before I knew what happened, and Joe Bob was lying beside me and grinning.

"How do you feel?"

"All right."

"Let's do it again."

"All right. But this time don't do it as if you're late for something. The ground is too lumpy. I've got to have something under my bum."

"My jacket. We'll bring a blanket next time."

"When's that?"

"Next time I come over. Tomorrow."

"I've got to dry berries and parsley and some herbs Ed George picked the last few days. He's going to teach me about herbs. And I've got to help him cure stuff. My grandma said the signs say the winter is going to be long and cold. Better come over next week."

"That long?"

"You take the meat he offers you, don't you, and herbs are good for sickness."

"You're not like Sally Heems."

"Who's she?"

"This widow in my band."

"You've been with her?"

"Last year. I went back. Went to Kamloops for a while too. My father hid me. I met her. She invited me over. That's why I didn't come around for months. She wore me out. Wanted it all the time. My thing got sore. When it was sore, she showed me some other ways to make her happy."

"Maybe you should go back to her."

"She's fat. You look sexy."

"You're saying that to get what you want."

"You want it too. I could tell at the end."

"We're wasting time talking. Hurry up and do it. But don't hurry too much, like I said. Finish outside me from now on. I don't want to get pregnant."

"What?"

"I'm sixteen. I don't want a baby. So pull out. Come on my belly or my bum."

"What if I can't?"

"You can if you want. Or I'll be busy drying more herbs."

Joe Bob tried to pull out most times. The rest was luck.

Everything was good for a year. But there was something on his mind. I knew it had to do with his mean streak. I didn't ask. I felt he would tell me when he was ready. We fished a lot that fall. I fished. He was there for sex. We would lie in the grass by the lake afterwards. He said it quietly.

"I killed somebody."

"Who?"

"A boy at the school. It was after you ran away. He was older. He wanted to fuck me. I didn't want to. He and his gang would try to get me alone. I stole a knife at dinner and sharpened it and kept it on me. I was pretty tall and strong and I'd had fights and won them all. But they were too many. I had to watch out at night in the dormitory, keeping the knife handy. Some nights I couldn't sleep. I decided to go after him. I waited till one night he was in the bathroom alone. I sneaked in but he saw me. We were same height but he was heavier. I had the knife up my sleeve but I didn't want to use it. Thought I could handle him with my fists. He was washing up. He threw soapy water in my eyes and I couldn't see and he began pounding on me. I pulled out the knife and stabbed without seeing and he let go of me. I could hear him groaning and I rubbed my eyes. He was on the floor and the knife was sticking out of his pants. He looked scared and said, 'Help me.' I bent down and ripped out the knife, slitting his belly open. He grabbed his belly and rolled over on the floor. I went to the sink to get the blood off my hands. It was still full and when I dropped the knife in the water blood came off the blade like red smoke."

I looked at Joe Bob. His eyes were closed tight.

"I ran away that night. His gang would find out who did it. Maybe they'd be scared and lay off me. But I didn't want to wait around to find out."

"It wasn't your fault. It was the school. Putting the younger and older boys together. Taking us away from our people, our ways."

"Know what I remember? Ripping the knife out, slitting him apart. I liked it. It was like being drunk."

"So that's why you pick on Len and the others."

"Why?"

"You like feeling big. Tough. You got lucky, Joe Bob. If you hadn't got the knife out in time, he would have killed you."

"Yeah, but I did. That's all that matters."

"I would have helped him."

"He wanted to kill me."

"I still would have."

"You're a girl, for sure."

"You don't have to be a girl to want to help somebody."

"Helps though."

"No sense talking to you."

"You never been in a spot like that. It's you or the other guy and you want him dead, you don't care how."

He opened his eyes and looked at me.

"You don't believe that religious stuff they told us, do you? Only thing I did in that class was stare at Sister Celeste. She's got such big tits they stick out like torpedoes. She's got a nice bum. I saw her bend over. I'd like to be alone with her. Teach her a few things."

"She wouldn't be interested."

"How do you know?"

"Ask Rachel."

He closed his eyes and lay back. I stared up at the open blue sky.

"I don't think that religions are bad. It's some people who belong to them. But to me their rules at St. Jerome's were like a prison to test people, to see if they could stand not having any fun. They wanted us to think like them and they punished us if we didn't. I couldn't see any reason for it except following rules. Who made up their rules? How does suffering help anybody? They said Christ suffered for our sins. If He suffered for us, we should be free to enjoy ourselves. Their rules make them think it's bad to enjoy themselves unless they enjoy suffering. But they ate and drank better than we did and didn't work in the fields, we did. If you want to suffer, go right ahead, but don't tell a bunch of kids they've got to suffer more than you because it's good for them."

"You think too much."

"Better than not thinking at all."

"I think about having fun."

"That's all you think about."

"Been thinking about something else. Want to go to Kamloops? We're past school age. We can leave here."

"I can't leave Rachel. She's eleven."

"She's got Ed George."

"Why do you want to go to Kamloops?"

"I'm tired of this place. Want to go places, see things, do things."

"How are we going to live there?"

"My father knows people."

"How would they help us?"

"Don't ask so many questions. We'll do all right."

"We haven't got any money."

"I'll get some."

"Come up with some real plans. Maybe I'll listen."

The following spring Joe Bob said his father had given him the address of his aunt and uncle in Kamloops and they were expecting us in May. He told me his father had given him some money. We'd get a lift from a band member travelling there who had a wagon. What did his uncle do? Worked in a grain and feed store. What did Joe Bob plan on doing? Getting a job in that store. I couldn't come up with any excuses and said yes but first had to talk with Rachel. I didn't like leaving her. Her mother came up every few months, sometimes with her father, but if I left she'd have Ed George for company most of the time. And Ed George couldn't be a father or fatherly if he tried. I decided I'd stay if she showed any fear at my leaving. One afternoon before dinner I sat beside her on the couch. We were alone and she was embroidering a shirt, working the needle and thread in that unhurried patient way she had.

"Joe Bob wants to leave the Cariboo and go to Kamloops. We're past school age. We don't have to stay here any more. I don't know if I want to go."

"You're thinking about me. I'll be all right."

"You're eleven."

"You were eleven when you came here. Guess you think I'm not like you."

"You don't go fishing or pick berries."

"Could if I had to. I let you go because you like fishing and picking and you and Joe Bob can meet."

"You'd be alone except for Ed George. Who you going to talk to?"

"To Strike."

We laughed.

"You'll end up like Ed George. Peculiar."

"There's others up here. They'll come by. We're pretty

well known. You might come back to visit or stay. I got beadwork and embroidery."

"That enough?"

"When Father Hugh came to the classroom for me that day, I thought he was going to take me to be punished. He didn't say anything. We went outside and I could see Sister Claire in the back seat of that big car. I thought, is she like the other one? Is she going to take me some place and hurt me? But she was always nice to the kids. Took us on walks. She wouldn't punish you that morning. She walked away with you. I didn't know what to think. I saw the top of your head and you opened the door and pulled me in and said, 'We're going home.' I was all alone, the youngest kid in the school, and you remembered me. You go wherever you want and do whatever you want. Don't worry about me."

The day we left Joe Bob rode over on the farm horse. We'd be joining the wagon in Williams Lake. Rachel and I hugged, parting for the first time in five years. Ed George kept busy until the last minute and came over and we said goodbye. He handed me a package of dried venison. I gave it to Joe Bob, along with a bag of my stuff and grabbed his hand and he pulled me up and I sat behind him. I looked back once and saw them standing there, getting smaller in the morning light.

That morning I felt leaving the Cariboo was leaving best part of my life. Joe Bob was impatient with that plodding horse. He kept goading him with his heels. I jabbed Joe Bob in the back with a finger.

"He's not a race horse. He's used to pulling a plough or wagon."

"Can't wait to get out of this place."

"It's only Kamloops."

"You've never been there."

"I was born there. Left when I was three."

"That's not like being there."

"The world isn't waiting for you, Mr. Remarkable."

When we got to Williams Lake, we couldn't find the wagon. It wasn't where Joe Bob said it would be, so we spent half an hour looking and found it on the other side of town. The driver had a frown. He was a big man, with huge hands and wide fingers.

"Took your time getting here. Tie your horse to the back and climb up and let's go."

He made room for us on the seat. Joe Bob climbed up but I didn't.

"I got to pee."

The driver slapped his thigh.

"Shit. Over there behind them bushes."

Two minutes later we were on our way. Joe Bob didn't speak to the driver and the driver acted as if he didn't know him. I got the idea that he wasn't from Joe Bob's band and probably hadn't even met him before we showed up. That was the first of many surprises.

Because the skies had been clear for days and the weather warm, the road was dry and we made good time. We turned south at 150 Mile House. A couple of hours later the driver fed and rested the team. He rested them twice more. It was dark when we reached an inn. The driver said he was going to stable the team. He looked at Joe Bob, who seemed uncertain.

"What about your horse?"

"I got no money."

"How you going to pay me?"

"My uncle is going to pay you when we get to Kamloops."

"You don't think I'm dumb enough to fall for that? Unless I see some money fast, I'm dropping you two here and taking that horse as payment."

Joe Bob turned to me.

"You got any money?"

"I got a dollar my grandma gave me for my birthday."

"Shit," the driver said.

Joe Bob turned back to the driver.

"How about the horse, the dollar and my uncle pays the rest? He's good for it."

"Shit."

"His name is Billy Bighead."

The driver scratched his stubble.

"Shit. Gimme the dollar."

I took the dollar from my bag and held it out. He snatched it out of my hand.

"What are you two going to do for grub and a bed?"

Joe Bob sounded cheerful.

"We got food. We'll sleep in the wagon."

After the driver left I found out what I had let myself in for.

"What about the money your father gave you?"

"He didn't give me any."

"Your uncle's name isn't Billy Bighead, is it?"

"No."

"You lied about everything to get me to go with you. You have an uncle in Kamloops?"

"Yeah."

"Does he know we're coming?"

"No, but he'll treat us good."

"What about the job you're supposed to get?"

"I'll get it."

"What about the driver?"

"I'll take care of him. Don't worry."

"One of us has to."

"I'm hungry. Let's eat."

"I hope it's not cold tonight."

"We'll keep each other warm."

"If you got any ideas about doing it in the back of the wagon, you keep them to yourself, Joe Bob. I'm not in the mood."

We ate the dried venison. I tried to think but gave up. Later on Joe Bob tried to snuggle up and my elbow warned him off. I didn't get much sleep. Joe Bob snored. Another rude awakening. First night together.

The next day nobody said anything and that night our driver stayed at an inn at 100 Mile House and we slept in the wagon. Three more nights, same thing. The following evening I was glad to see the outskirts of Kamloops. After the first night we didn't talk about paying the driver. Part of me was hoping everything would fall apart and we'd end up back in the Cariboo. But I'd no memory of having seen a big town. So another part of me was hoping that somehow Joe Bob would get things right, at least enough for us to stay for a while. I knew things would clear up one way or another before the night was over. There was a feeling of adventure about the whole thing. That didn't last long.

I'd never seen so many cars, some honking at us to get that lumbering wagon with its iron-shod wooden spoke wheels out of the way. Joe Bob kept looking around as if the tall buildings, storefronts, signs, paved streets and crowded sidewalks were on display for him. A couple of hicks from the sticks, that's what we were. We weren't the right colour either, not to some of those glancing our way. The driver stopped on a street that wasn't busy and pulled back on the long wheel brake.

"Where's your uncle live?"

"On the other side of town. Want to get a beer?"

"You trying to pull something?"

"It's warm and I'm thirsty."

"You don't have money to buy beer or any goddam thing else."

"My uncle does. He sells feed and grain and buys horses. He'll buy the one you got from me. Give you a good price. Tell you something. He bootlegs. We go to his place and drink the first round free. No bullshit. What do you say?"

"Where is it?"

"Not far from here. Turn left at the next street. Unless you got something against a good time. Girls too. It's in the old part of town."

"If you're lying—."

"You'll find out."

The driver turned the corner and we entered the

waterfront area. Dingy streets, sooty buildings sharing walls and vacant lots, murky lights behind torn window curtains. Stray cats prowling garbage cans. After a while Joe Bob pointed.

"That's the place over there."

He looked at me.

"You stay out here. You'll be all right."

It was completely dark now. They climbed down and went into a narrow building with lights behind shutters on the second floor. I was alone for twenty minutes. Joe Bob hurried out and untied the farm horse and mounted.

"Get up behind me."

He gave me his hand and pulled me up and we set off as fast as that old horse could go.

"What happened?"

"Don't know your Joe Bob. I been here before. Slipped him a Mickey Finn. He's out. We'll go see my uncle."

"I won't believe you've got an uncle till I see him."

Joe Bob's uncle lived in a shack behind a street bordering the river, three blocks from where we left the driver. There was an unlit dirt path from the street to the shack. We got off the horse and walked down the path. A smell of sewage came off the river. There were movements in the darkness, probably rats. Next to the shack were a wagon and a shed. A cart horse stamped its big hooves in the shed. Joe Bob tied ours to the wagon and knocked on the door of the shack. Nothing happened. He knocked harder, still nothing. He pounded on it with his fist. A groggy voice boomed.

"What the fuck ya want?"

"It's Joe Bob."

"Who?"

"Joe Bob."

"Wait a minute."

The door opened and a man holding a kerosene lantern brought it close to Joe Bob's face.

"You again. Where's my money?"

"You'll get it. Takes a while."

"Takes forever with you."

He brought the lantern close to my face.

"Who's she?"

"This is Josie. My girlfriend."

"Guess ya wanna come in."

He turned away and we followed him in. The air stank of rotten fish and sweat and rancid oil. One sniff and I knew Joe Bob didn't have an aunt. Not in Kamloops. No woman would've put up with that stink. I looked at Joe Bob but he was looking around the shack. His uncle put the lantern on a table with a top the size of a serving tray. It was the only table. There was a folding chair beside the table, a hammock hanging from hooks across a corner of the room and a trunk without a top. The rest of the shack was filled with crates of empty bottles. I picked up the smell of sour wine in the stink.

"Make yourselves comfortable."

Joe Bob emptied and turned over a couple of crates for us to sit on. After shutting the door, his uncle sat on the folding chair, which looked as if it was about to completely unfold permanently.

"What brings ya?"

"I wanted to see you."

"That so? Don't want money?"

"No."

"That's good. Got none."

"How's the junk business?"

"Didn't I tell ya I got no money? How long ya staying?"

"Long enough so's I can get on my own feet."

"That sounds like a fucking long time."

"I got some ideas."

"Keep 'em to yourself."

"You're missing out on a good thing."

"Don't sling me the bull."

He looked at me.

"I don't have no place for a girl to sleep. Joe Bob makes some room and sleeps on the floor."

"It's warm outside tonight. I'll sleep in your wagon."

"Suit yourself."

Joe Bob's uncle offered a blanket but it stank and I said no, we'd use our jackets. The back of the wagon was empty except for some rusty cans. The stars were out and it was warm. I lay back on the lumpy clothes, Joe Bob beside me, and we talked.

"You go ahead and do things without thinking. This is going to end in a bunch of trouble. There's nothing for us here. Let's go back."

"What's back there?"

"What's your father do?"

"Grows potatoes, peas, squash, lots of stuff."

"We could do that."

"Not me."

"We're sleeping in the back of a wagon. What's our future?"

"We only got here. Can't expect things to happen right away."

"They won't happen. Nothing's ahead but this."

"I need some money, that's all."

"Where you going to get it?"

"You'll see."

"What're you going to do with it?"

"You're always asking questions."

"I'm supposed to shut up and let you decide everything."

"Everything's going to work out. You'll see."

It wasn't that I didn't want to stay. But I had no confidence in Joe Bob. I knew he couldn't do what he said. It was all a dream. But I couldn't desert him. We were together, no matter what, and I knew that part of his problem wasn't his doing, it was the white world being against us. I looked up at the stars and wanted to be far away.

Joe Bob's uncle banged his fist on the side of the wagon at dawn.

"I got to get going."

We jumped down and he brought his horse from the shed and hitched it to the wagon. He climbed up to the seat and grabbed the reins and Joe Bob untied our horse. In the morning light I could see his uncle clearly. Short and stocky, he was wearing cracked leather boots, stained overalls, a faded plaid shirt, a wrinkled leather vest and on his bald head was a beret. He put a thumb against one side of his nose and blew and black snot flew out.

"Don't give your horse none of my feed. I'll know if you do. Don't take nothing from the shack neither. Everything in there's mine."

He flicked the reins and the wagon creaked up the dirt path to the street. I shook my head.

"I can't believe he belongs to our people. What's his name?"

"Calls himself Louis Legrande. My father told me his real name is Zato Zlaff."

"What kind of a name is Zato Zlaff?"

"All I know is that's his name."

Joe Bob went into the shed and came back with a feedbag half full of oats and slipped it carefully onto the horse's head.

"He won't catch on. He's fucking stupid."

He went into the shack and came out with dried venison wrapped in brown paper. He brought crates for us to sit on.

"Pretended I was asleep once. Saw him pull up a floorboard and take out stuff."

"What else do you know about him?"

"My father said his father was a trapper. Couldn't catch nothing. Bad shot too. Couldn't hunt. So he married a widow in our band. She was real desperate. Know how he died? Stepped in one of his own traps. Had to wait for somebody to come by. Kept firing his rifle. Ran out of bullets. Two days later somebody found him. Leg got infected by then. Had it taken off but died anyway. This guy's as dumb as his father."

Joe Bob pointed at the shed.

"No time like the present."

"Where did you hear that?"

"Movie."

"Bet your uncle never cleans it."

"It's clean. Go have a look."

The door was open and I peeked in. The shed was cleaner than the shack and smelled better. That's not saying much. But there was nowhere else. We laid our jackets on a pile of straw and went at each other like we'd been apart for a year. We were in there a long time. Something about horses and ploughs and furrows. Or not knowing what was ahead for us. Or that dried venison. We hadn't said we loved each other and never did. When you think you do, you don't say. You don't have to. Being young had something to do with it. And if it wasn't the purest love, it would have to do for me. And about Joe Bob that morning I had no complaints.

"You're like a wildcat, Josie."

"You're not tired already, are you?"

"I could go all day."

"Go as slow as you can next time."

"Pretty well have to."

"Kiss my tits too. Suck the nipples."

"That's for babies."

"It'll get me going. Get me excited."

"You get excited."

"This will be better."

"How do you know?"

"I know, Joe Bob."

We didn't go anywhere that day but when Joe Bob's uncle got back late that afternoon he thought we had been out.

"You look tired."

"I been looking for work."

"She looks tired."

"She's been looking."

"Find anything?"

"Not yet."

"Keep looking."

"We will."

Joe Bob was right. His uncle never noticed the missing oats. We'd eaten again and Joe Bob had put the package of dried venison back under the floorboard. His uncle didn't offer us anything to eat. He ate a slab of stale bread with lard on it. He drank wine from a jug. After singing something in a language I'd never heard, he passed out and started farting and we got out of the shack.

We lay in the wagon and looked up at the stars. At least I did. Joe Bob was picking his teeth with a piece of straw. He turned his head to face me.

"He's got some money. I know where it is."

"You mean you haven't stolen it?"

"Been waiting. I figure now's the time."

"Can't take his money."

"It's not his. It's my father's. He sold stuff for him in Williams Lake and didn't give him the money. He never came back. I showed up last year and didn't say nothing and he figured we forgot."

"What stuff of your father's?"

"Potatoes, squash. Ten bucks worth."

"He says you owe him money."

"He bootlegs wine. For this guy in the Okanagan. I sold some for him. Says I kept the money. He's lying."

"Doesn't he sell junk?"

"That's so the cops won't catch on. Makes more from the wine."

"Who's he sell it to?"

"Winos. Alkies who run out on the weekend and got to have something. They're the only ones who can drink it besides him. It's bad shit. But those kind of guys will do anything to get it. He's been robbed and beaten up. Takes a pipe wrench with him. Keeps it under the seat."

"Thought it was for tightening wheels."

"You're funny."

After his uncle left the next morning Joe Bob went into the shack and returned with a bunch of bills and coins. It looked like too much.

"That's more than ten bucks."

"He won't miss it. There's lots left."

"Now two guys in Kamloops will be looking for us. And we got a horse that's slower than a mud turtle."

We ate the rest of the dried venison before we left. Joe Bob folded the brown paper and put it back. We fed the horse and took a bag of oats with us. As we were leaving, there was a noise behind the shack. Joe Bob went to see and I followed. A rat had been caught in a trap. It was large, with sleek black hairs. The end of its tail stuck out of the trap. Joe Bob touched it. The rat whirled and lunged, gripping the wire mesh with its incisors. Joe Bob jabbed a piece of straw into the rat's nose and it gnawed on the straw and shredded it to bits.

"Let's give him a surprise."

He lifted the trap by the ring on the top and carried it to the front of the shack and opened the door enough to put the trap on the floor, lifted the entrance and poked the rat with a straw and it scurried into the shack. He kicked the wire cage inside, shut the door and grinned, chewing on the straw.

"He traps and eats 'em. Have to catch this one all over again."

"You didn't eat any?"

"You been here two days and you still don't know he gives nobody nothing."

"You wouldn't though, would you? They're full of disease."

"How come he isn't dead?"

"It's probably the wine. Kills germs."

We got on the horse and rode up the dirt path onto the street. Joe Bob went to the same building he had taken our driver. This time I went inside with him. We walked up a flight of narrow stairs to the second floor. Joe Bob knocked and a woman answered. He told her who he was and she opened the door and smirked at him. She was wearing a pink dressing gown that was tight on her, with fuzzy white fur like candyfloss around the collar. Her heels stuck out from the back of her pink slippers. Their fur balls had gone brown. She had a towel wrapped around her hair.

"You're back. What in hell's the time?"

"After twelve. Guess we're kind of early."

Joe Bob grinned at me.

"This is Opal Schultz. She was my first woman."

"First for a lot of guys. Cure your virginity in a fucking hurry, if you'll pardon my language."

As she talked I could see she had large teeth with a gap between the front ones. There was phlegm in her throat and as she spoke it came into her mouth and she looked around for a place to spit. She closed the door halfway. She gagged on gobs of mucous as she coughed them up, spitting and spewing. The door opened again.

"Come on in."

We entered a large room with tables and chairs and a bar with a row of bottles on a shelf behind it. The place smelled of cigarette and cigar smoke and stale beer. Her rump swung as she walked between the tables, stopping once to rearrange some chairs. She swayed, a hand on the back of a chair to steady herself.

"I got to get me some rest. Start work at six (sex?). Have a seat, you two. You can tell her."

She yawned and left. We sat down.

"Tell me what?"

"Opal's in a spot. She needs somebody. I told her about you. That you would help."

I slapped him across the face as hard as I could. The slap knocked his head sideways.

"You dirty liar. Dirty rotten liar. You been lying ever since we left. Now you want to turn me into her."

I ran out and down the steps and he followed. I heard him trip and fall and I kept running. I ran to the horse and unhitched it and was mounting when I felt him grab me from behind and pull me down. He turned me and I could see his face was bloody.

"I'd kill any man who touched you, Josie."

"Liar."

"Listen to me. She wants somebody to clean the place and cook for her. The woman she had quit on her. She told me the other night. When I brought the driver. The girls got no time to do it. I'm going to be the bouncer. It's only for a while."

"You want me to work in a whorehouse. That's your big plan, is it? We stayed at your pig of an uncle's so you could steal off him. Now you bring me here."

"It's not so bad. We make some money and have a place to stay and I can look around for something."

"Where do we stay?"

"Upstairs. There's a room."

"Where the girls work. We'll have to hear that. That's going to be something. Get you excited."

"It's down at the end of the hall. You won't hear nothing."

"You saw the room?"

"Yeah."

"You mean that about killing any man?"

He squeezed me and kissed me and I could taste the blood on his face. Joe Bob wasn't a kisser. Even when it counted. So this was different.

"It's one thing I'd never lie about, Josie."

"I'm not wiping up her spit. Or anybody else's."

"I'll do it."

He never did. She didn't spit on the floor again. She would use a hanky until it was caked with snot or soaked in slime. I would pick them up with two fingers and throw them into a laundry bag. All bedding and clothes went to a laundry. Not Opal. She went to bed or slept in a tub of hot water. To the customers and the girls she was Mrs. Spring. She probably thought of it after having spent so much time on a mattress. One-track mind. I asked Joe Bob how he knew her real name. He said the first time he was there she was drunk and talked about being a kid back in Fort William. As the madam she picked her customers, usually young guys. Anybody else wanted her paid more. Nobody did.

The girls were far from. Girls and Kamloops. It was a business to them, or at least they behaved as if it was. ("Somebody has to fuck these dopey guys. May as well make some money from it.") I didn't see them as martyrs or wanted to know if they had been abused or abandoned. I had my own problems. I didn't feel any link with them. The way I saw it they were for hire by the hour to anybody. If they didn't act as if it bothered them, it wasn't going to bother me. I wasn't popular. I didn't try to be.

Maybelle from Mississippi. "I do declare, you look like a Chickasaw." ("Keep your legs open, Maybelle, there's a wasp in the room.") Lisette from Montréal. "Men are such pigs here." ("We'd get you better but they wouldn't pay.") Bettina from Timmins. "Jesus Christ, I'm tired. I got to lie down." ("You're in the right business.")

It was the whorehouse on the waterfront. The regulars

were easiest. Some had a favourite, would show up regularly on a certain night. It was like having a mistress but you shared her. Some customers didn't behave, and that's where Joe Bob came in. The previous bouncer had found religion. Strange things happen in country towns. The drunks were bad, would argue about anything and stagger all over the place and end up puking on the floor. My job. We didn't get mean guys that want to hurt a woman. They'll pick up a streetwalker and take her to an isolated spot. Twice we had trouble. One night screams came from Lisette's room. Joe Bob rushed up with a sap. Opal followed with a club. The guy was beaten until he passed out. He'd gone berserk when Lisette laughed, said he was tiny and should find a mouse. That's one time Lisette's snottiness got the better of her. She said that she was tired and forgot to be her usual charming self. Opal called this monster she knew whenever she had trouble. He was built like a mountain, with a face like a cliff. He dragged the guy away. The other time it was a maniac wanting Maybelle to eat his dried turd in a bag he'd taped between his ass. Her southern background alerted her. "No Southerner would stick his hand back there and dig around in front of a lady, and I presumed no decent Northerner would neither." The monster was called. I wouldn't have been surprised if there was extra sewage floating in the Thompson River that night.

Virtue has a price. Mopping floors, emptying ashtrays, throwing out liquor bottles, changing bedding, sending out the laundry, cleaning toilets, cooking. Opal and the girls weren't fussy. I usually made toast and boiled eggs for breakfast, fried steak and chips for dinner and made sure there were plenty of chocolates on hand. The food was delivered by a local grocery. The grocer was a regular, so Opal got good deals. The law didn't bother her. A guy would visit late on Saturday nights and she'd take him into her room. She always answered the door at that time. He wore a hat low on his forehead. There were a couple of other evening visitors who pulled their hat brims down or put their collars up or both. In a big city they'd have walked in without all that secrecy but Kamloops was a country town and they may have been churchgoers. Speaking of which, I didn't see any moral reformers around the waterfront. The air wouldn't have been good for them. Better to write us off.

Joe Bob and I went to the movies a lot, especially the Saturday matinee at the Star. It was convenient because that was before the girls started work. The Star showed mostly westerns, cowboys and Indians. All the good guys were white. All the bad guys were white. The Indians were savages, authentic Hollywood background like the pintos and sagebrush. Smoke signals and teepees and braves streaked with paint going on war parties, noses like rusty knife blades and mouths jagged lids of open tin cans whooping and riding across the plains after the poor settlers in their wagon trains. Those blonde women and girls in their sunbonnets and calico dresses had to be saved, and here comes the US cavalry in blue, riding in a perfect line, sabres drawn and trumpets blaring from the soundtrack and our people all died for the umpteenth time and we sat there eating the rancid-smelling popcorn. I didn't mind all that as much as when we played noble savages helping the invaders of our land to clean up their own mess of thieves and murderers and land speculators and whisky salesmen so these invaders could set up ranches and farms and we could retire to reserves and die slowly of alcoholism and poverty. I hated most the princesses with their pale skins darkened with makeup and hair in a braid and a feather in their beaded headbands and wearing tailored fringed dresses and boots of calfskin, and you could see their painted fingernails.

One Saturday it was so bad. The actress looked like a white girl in a school play. Joe Bob and I were laughing. I told him I would go up on stage and take my clothes off. He dared me so I got up and ran down the aisle and climbed onto the stage in front of the screen—big death scene, she can't marry the paleface fur trapper and army scout because she's dying from an arrow meant for him by a renegade brave (renegade according to the palfaces, and how convenient)—and I pulled off my sweater and unzipped my skirt and undid my bra and pulled down my panties. The movie stopped, the lights went up. "Look at a real Indian," I said. The adults started laughing or booing and some kids threw popcorn. They wanted the movie and thought I was crazy or showing off. Even our people in the audience didn't see why I did it. Everybody started talking about me and getting upset. Everything became personal and I felt embarrassed standing there naked in front of them. Somebody said, "Get off." It sounded loud because there wasn't much noise any more. They were staring now, inspecting me, seeing me but not in the way I wanted. "You'll remember," I said, not knowing exactly what I meant but wanting to impress them and to save my dignity too. I saw the manager come running down the aisle and I grabbed my clothes and jumped off and ran for the exit. I pushed it open and ran through the back alley. He stood outside the exit and yelled, "Don't ever come back here again, you—." "You." I knew what he wanted to say.

We went to the Rex and everyone was white and most were older and stared at us in the line outside. The movies were for whites. The woman in the booth pushed the tickets in our direction as if we had a disease. The ticket taker frowned, the usher was sarcastic. People in the seats kept giving us looks. In some of the movies the actors wore tuxedos and the actresses wore gowns and furs and tiaras and everybody used cigarette holders and drank champagne and talked with foreign accents at parties in mansions they had driven to in limousines. Joe Bob was bored. He blamed me for not being able to go to the Star any more. I said, you can go, and you can take Marie MacDonald. That shut him up for the rest of the movie. Marie MacDonald was from Joe Bob's band. They had grown up together. She was living with her sister in Kamloops. Her sister had married a white guy, a truck driver. We'd met the sisters at a matinee at the Star and I could see she liked him. They started flirting a bit, talking about when they were kids. I warned him later.

"If I smell her on you, we're finished. She can clean up the shit in the whorehouse because I'll be heading back to the Cariboo. You put me in the shit. She'll get me out of it."

I could see he didn't believe me. I pointed at him.

"Try me and see. And I'll be able to smell her, no matter how hard you try to scrub it off."

I didn't have too much trouble with him after that. But I kept an eye open.

Some days, even weeks, were so boring I began to think I was working in a crummy hotel with hourly patrons. After four months I wanted to quit. I asked Joe Bob when and he said to hold on, he needed more time. I could see he wasn't in any hurry. He liked seeing that whites guys behaved and throwing them out if they didn't. It all changed one night. A party of drunken guys barged in and demanded action. Opal was good at handling men, especially the young ones. But these were vicious, throwing around furniture and insulting the girls. She couldn't call the police, only Joe Bob, and four guys were a lot to handle, so she called the monster too. I was in the kitchen cleaning up. One of them saw me.

"Hey, what have we here? Hi, cutie."

I ignored him. He staggered into the kitchen and put a hand on my shoulder.

"I said hi."

Joe Bob had come downstairs and seen him. He pushed him away.

"Hands off her."

"Fuck off, squawman."

He took a wild swing at Joe Bob, who knocked him down and out with one punch. The others were on their way in but Opal had a supply of clubs and had handed them out to the girls. All-out attack on the troublemakers. When the monster arrived four bodies were stretched out beside the entrance door, bruised, groaning and swearing. The one Joe Bob had knocked out came to and looked up at him. He sneered.

"I'll get you. You fucking Indian."

"Any time, powder puff. Name the place."

The sight of the monster silenced our guests and he dragged them out and down the stairs, two in each hand. When he returned he said he had put them in their car and they had driven away. Opal offered him a beer and he drank it and another before leaving and the rest of us put back the furniture. I mopped the floor later. That night I talked things over with Joe Bob in our bedroom.

"I don't like that guy. He's a mean bastard."

"I can handle him if he shows up."

"Suppose he has a gang with him? You can't handle them."

"Don't worry about him."

"We been here too long. Something's bound to go wrong sooner or later in this place."

"Everything worked out, didn't it?"

"It only takes one time for it not to, Joe Bob."

"You worry too much, that's your problem."

A few days later I was returning from our grocer's with a special order. Maybelle had a craving for something special—cactus pears, persimmons or pomegranates. All he had were Anjou pears and I bought some. It was early morning and I was sleepy and not watching as carefully as I usually did. On my way back a hand darted out of a doorway, grabbing my arm and squeezing it. A shape came out of the shadows. It was the driver who had brought us down from Williams Lake. I felt strangely relieved it wasn't the guy who caused the trouble at Opal's.

"You're not getting away this time. Where's Joe Bob?"

"At Opal's."

"Come on."

He pulled me by the arm the two blocks to the building and pushed me up the stairs ahead of him. He banged on the door. Opal opened it. She wasn't in a good mood. It had been a busy night.

"I wanna see Joe Bob. He owes me for the ride I give him and this girl down here from Williams Lake."

Opal smiled. Bad sign.

"You get a free ride with one of the girls."

"Don't try none of your tricks with me like last time. I want my money."

"That's what comes of being generous. Joe Bob is going to give you a free ride down those stairs and if you ever show up here again, I'll get the monster after you."

"What're you talking about?"

"You saw him last time. He takes care of troublemakers. Your choice, mister. You want to float face up or face down in the Thompson? Get him out of here."

Joe Bob put one arm around the driver's neck and with the other twisted the driver's arm behind his back. A quick exit.

About this time Joe Bob started to drink. He never got drunk in the whorehouse but before or after work. And he'd get into fights around the waterfront. He'd fight for any reason. Every now and then he would explode and start punching somebody. White guys would try to beat him up but he won every fight he ever got into. Except the last one. The four drunks returned two months later and with an extra guy. We were going through an alley downtown. They blocked our way. They wanted him bad and Joe Bob knew and wasn't afraid. Fighting to him had become like breathing. He would feel suffocated and have to get some air by beating somebody up. It was drizzling and the asphalt in the alley was slippery. The guy he'd knocked out stood in front of the others.

"Hey, chief, I see you got your nice-looking pussy with you."

I was scared and looked around to see if there was another way out. I saw lots of garbage cans and the rear exits of hotels and cafés, and a roll-down metal blind where deliveries were made, and everything was shut. Joe Bob didn't stop walking and he didn't slow down. He didn't say anything. I knew he was going to walk right through them. I decided, if this is it this is it, and kept walking beside him. My throat was dry and my body seemed to be made of fire and air. I hated them and wanted to kill them. Joe Bob turned eighteen a month earlier and was tall and lean and his big hands and their bony knuckles were a blur when he was fighting. I'd never seen anybody he fought last more than a minute. Those five were heavier, and two were taller. Not one would have stood after a minute alone with him. I thought, it's been the same from the beginning, always going against bad odds. I was so proud of Joe Bob I felt like crying and thought, let the end come, let Joe Bob and me die fighting. It was me they touched first, and it was that bastard with the sneer. "Here, pussy." Fingers like cold snakes on my bare arm. But dirty like no snake is. I pulled my arm away. The fingers came again. I slapped them away. Before I knew it Joe Bob was swinging at him and he yelled and went down, mouth bleeding and nose smashed. The others jumped in and their weight was too much and he began to stagger. I jumped on the back of one, clawing at his eyes, fingernails digging deep into the sockets. He screamed. He fell back and I could feel blood and something squishy on my hands. An elbow hit me on the back of my head and I fell onto the asphalt, my hands feeling the slick wetness and oily grit. I felt woozy, my head hurt, but I could hear thudding punches and grunting and swearing and shoes scraping against stones. I tried to get up and felt dizzy. I remember thinking the drizzle felt cool on my face. I got onto my hands and knees and saw boots kicking a bundle of something. I wondered what they were kicking and then I screamed. They stopped and ran, two of them dragged away by the others, leaving a trail of blood. I crawled over and his face was so swollen and bloody I didn't recognize it. There was a tear in his scalp, a flap of loose skin hanging from it. His upper lip was partly torn away. One of his hands had been trampled on and squashed. I hollered for help. Somebody finally came and went to phone for an ambulance and I rode to the hospital with him and a doctor stitched him up. He spent the night there and I went back to the whorehouse and told them what happened.

Joe Bob took months to heal and never could close his

right hand completely again. The doctor did a bad job stitching his face and there were lumps and thick scars that made him look deformed. I kept working and the monster became the bouncer and Opal waited. But all Joe Bob could think of was getting so drunk he would pass out. Finally Opal had to let him go. She wanted me to keep working but I had to look after Joe Bob. I'd find him lying in ditches and alleyways. When he came to he'd try to get rid of me. I knew he thought I didn't want him any more. No matter what I said to him, he pushed me away. One day—he was only nineteen—he sat on the tracks and a train ran over him. I don't know if he was too drunk to know what he was doing. It hurt me that I couldn't make him see I wanted to be with him. Joe Bob and me together, in all the alleys wherever they go.

Grandmother, you told me that men sometimes come in pairs to a woman, one complementing the other. Fred Edwards was easygoing and would fight only if he had to. He had stayed at Joe Bob's cabin after Joe Bob and I left for Kamloops. Len told him about me. I had come back to the reserve to recover from what happened. He came to your house to see me. He had a friendly face and walked in a loose way that suited him. He nodded when he spoke, as if he was convincing himself as well as you. He didn't get mad and didn't swear. I never heard him complain about anything. He wasn't sour on white people. He was all for copying them.

"You got to be like them before they'll respect you."

This seemed so wrong it could be right. After losing Joe Bob I wanted to believe in something and someone. When we got together and stayed in your house I found out about one of his habits. Sex came second to sudden ideas.

"Where you going?"

"Thought of something. Got to write it down or I'll forget."

"Not now. We haven't finished."

"I'll be back."

Ten minutes later he was.

"You're not getting in here, Fred."

"Why?"

"You leave in the middle of everything. Leave when I'm ready. For some stupid idea. Sleep on the floor."

"It's a million dollar idea."

"Not another one?"

"This one is really good. An ad for a line of moccasins: 'Tread lightly on me.'"

"Sounds dumb, as if you're stepping on something dangerous, like a snake. The water moccasin."

"No, you're walking lightly on the sole of the moccasin. Gives people the idea of comfort and getting places fast."

"They'll think fangs are going to bite them when they put their feet inside."

"How about, tread lightly in me?"

"That's a warning."

"Tread lightly with me?"

"Sounds like tires."

"Step lightly with me?"

"Sounds like dancing."

"Got to be positive, Josie. Can I get back in?"

"No."

Two weeks later he left our bed in such a hurry he woke me up. I thought he'd gone to pee. When he returned he was excited. He shook me fully awake.

"This is really something. I thought of a contest, like a pageant, among the women in the bands. The contestants would be named after a lake here, like Miss Alexis Lake, Miss Anahim Lake, Miss Tatla Lake, Miss Chilko Lake. They'd be judged on embroidery, beadwork, making moccasins, stuff like that."

"What's the point?"

"It would make us proud of our women."

"Do we need a contest?"

"This is where it gets brilliant. The winner will be given the title of Miss Cariboo. We'll take her to Kamloops. Get her story in the Sentinel, with pictures. It'll be good publicity for the bands."

"Miss Cariboo?"

"What's wrong?"

"If you have to ask, you'll never understand."

"And you know what's going to top it? We'll have one-piece bathing suits made of buckskin, with fringes around the breasts and hips, for all the contestants to wear. The Sentinel will send up a photographer, you can bet on that. Advance publicity. Get them ready there to receive the winner."

"Now I know you're nuts. Our women aren't going to wear bathing suits."

"That's where you come in. Tell them it's good for our people."

"It'll make us look pathetic, imitating white people."

"Got to think big, Josie. Think ahead. White people run things. You want us to be behind the times? Sitting around campfires telling old stories when there's magazines, newspapers, radio and movies?"

"Are we supposed to be second-rate white people?"

"No. Didn't I mention embroidery, beadwork and making moccasins? I'm trying to add a little glamour, that's all. Sex appeal. What's so bad about that?"

One thing I learned about dealing with Fred. He got so many ideas that he'd forget the last one when he came up with another. All I had to do was wait. After a while I tried not to listen. But I felt that was wrong. He believed his ideas would benefit our people. He wanted to make money and he thought all of us would if we listened to him. After a while I began to think of him as a man with a puppet show who thinks his puppets are real. In Fred's case they were real, and he never understood that. He was the biggest dreamer I ever met but all of his dreams were a white man's dreams. There was hardly room in them for any of us, including him. But he never stopped trying to figure a way in.

To him Indian agents and the Department of Indian Affairs were nothing. Neither were the Catholic Church or St. Jerome's. "I'll manage things," he'd say. I asked about his experience at the school.

"I told the priests and nuns I had visions of heavenly light. One every night and it blinded me. They couldn't decide if I was phony or crazy or was blessed. Father Mellors asked me questions to see if I was a phony. I went into a trance, mumbled and drooled. They didn't want to take a chance punishing me in case they were wrong. So they left me alone. The other kids figured I was crazy. Nobody bothered with me. The only thing were those lousy potatoes every day and the cold dormitory, but I figured if I kicked they'd catch on I wasn't blessed. Saintly people aren't bothered by such things. I got tired of the whole thing. Being blessed isn't easy. You got to have a certain look all the time. If a nun caught me looking at her in an unsaintly way, I'd be finished. So I didn't go back one fall. I heard about the cabin where Joe Bob had stayed, and that Len and the others were still around, so I went up there, knew that after Tuck Browner disappeared when you escaped nobody was going to come looking for me."

It was when Fred told me about his early life that I could begin to understand him. His mother had died in childbirth and his father, from a well-off family in Kamloops, didn't want anything to do with him. He was sent up to his mother's band. From the beginning he was busy trying to make money. Selling bags of hazelnuts and pails of berries in Williams Lake when he was ten. He was full of ideas. He wanted to set up a hunting and fishing lodge on our land and fly in wealthy businessmen from the coast. The lodge was going to be at a lake and a seaplane would land there. For rich tourists during the summer there was going to be a souvenir shop to sell things like bear claw necklaces and miniature totem poles. "We don't carve totem poles," I said.

"That doesn't matter," he said. "What do they know?" We were going to put on native dances, buffalo hunts and smoke peace pipes. "There's never been buffalo here," I said. "We'll get some, it's only a show anyway," he said. I said I'd never seen a peace pipe. "Don't get technical," he said. "And when you're choreographing the native dances make them like those musicals at the show. You know, a line of maidens in buckskin tops and shorts kicking up their moccasins." He was way ahead of his time. He wanted to have a "working museum" explaining the potlatch and showing the making of clay pots, adobe huts, wigwams, sweat lodges, dugouts and birch bark canoes. And customers would be shown how to make their own sand paintings. "You're getting all the nations mixed up," I told him. "Blame Hollywood," he said. I asked him where the money was coming from for the building supplies and that other stuff. "A syndicate that can see the vast future returns on their capital investment in such a venture." "What future?—the country's on relief, nobody's got any money, least of all for us."

I reminded him we were under the jurisdiction of the federal government. Indian Affairs officials would have to approve everything. And we'd be competing with white resorts and hunting and fishing lodges. Did he think whites, those that didn't think we were too stupid to run our own businesses, were going to stand by and see us make money?

"That's where I got it figured. Our partners will be white and they'll have connections to the government. Indian Affairs takes its orders from politicians and politicians take them from the big boys. We've got nothing to worry about."

The beginning was supposed to be a truck, any kind of old truck, so he could travel and sell his ideas. But he hadn't enough money to buy one. He had fifteen dollars in worn creased bills in his back pocket. Selling fish and wild game and "guaranteed genuine tribal relics" and Tread Lightly moccasins made by reserve women and jugs of hard cider didn't bring in enough. He liked western shirts of embroidered satin, string ties with silver horseshoe clasps, cowboy boots decorated with designs and ten-gallon hats made of felt. He'd get a dressmaker to put fancy stitching on the pockets of his blue jeans. "You belong on a dude ranch or in a Wild West show," I said. But I liked him because after Joe Bob I was tired, needed not to think. Fred did the thinking for both of us, and the dreaming. I didn't believe in any of it but that never bothered him. He'd grin and wink. I was nineteen and he was twenty-two.

Fred was quiet for a few days. No plans, no waking me up in the middle of the night. I knew he was hatching something. He told me one morning after breakfast.

"We'll go to Kamloops. See my father's family. They'll loan me money for a truck. We can get started."

"Can you drive?"

"I gave this Hindu a good price on a pair of moccasins. He drives a dump truck. Delivers wood. Let me drive his truck, showed me everything. Told me there's a guy in the Kamloops motor vehicle office, where you go for the test. You slip him a couple of dollars and he passes you. I'll use my aunt and uncle's address there. Same last name."

"What about your father? Where does he live?"

He shook his head.

"Somewhere else. They're looking after him."

"Who?"

"People."

"Is he sick?"

"Kind of."

"What's he got?"

"Something."

"Tell me, Fred."

"He gets funny sometimes. He doesn't know who he is, thinks he's somebody else."

"Who?"

"I don't know. People I never heard of."

"Do you go see him?"

"Couple of years ago. He didn't know me. I said, 'Hi, Dad, how are you?' He stared at me like I was the crazy one."

"What makes you think his family will give you money?"

"They won't say no when I tell them about my ideas. I'm asking for enough to buy a truck, that's all. They're rich. Wait till you see the mansion."

"They got rid of you. Why would they suddenly turn around and give you money?"

"Maybe they'll feel guilty. I sort of get along with Uncle Ernie and Aunt Lettie."

"You see them much?"

"When I saw my father that time, and years ago when I wanted to see the family. I told Father Mellors I had this vision of the Thompson River flooding and Kamloops under water. I said a voice told me to go down there and it wouldn't happen. Tuck Browner took me. Called me a smart little bastard."

"They've never asked to see you."

"No, but last time after I told him some of my ideas Uncle Ernie said, 'Fred Edwards, you could sell cow shit in a barn.'"

"Maybe he meant should."

"You got him wrong."

"You go by yourself. You don't need me."

"I need you to get Aunt Lettie on my side. When she sees that you're backing me up, she'll agree to give me the money."

Fred was right. The house was a mansion. The siding was white and the trim blue. There were three floors, lots of gables, a tower-shaped room at the top of one front corner, and a deep verandah with round posts. Next to the front door was what looked like a key in a lock. He turned it a few times and a bell rang inside. A couple of minutes later the door was opened by a pale grey-haired woman dressed all in white, with a pointed nose and disapproving lips. On seeing Fred she raised her eyebrows. She looked me up and down as if she'd been forced to smell something bad. You could've distilled her voice and sold it as bottled snob.

"Fred? What are you doing here?"

"I've come for a visit, Aunt Lettie, and I brought my girlfriend."

"I suppose you had better come in for a while."

Fred walked in as if he visited every day and I followed. His aunt looked at my shoes.

"Wipe your feet. You can wait in the drawing room. Don't touch anything. I'll see to things."

She waited until I had wiped my shoes on the inside doormat. I followed Fred into a small room with a view of the front lawn. White gauzy curtains gathered into pleats and tied with sashes framed the sides of the window and there were red tulips in stained glass along the top. We sat on a beige sofa with white lace on the back and arms. The room was full of framed photographs on tables and desks. Wedding pictures, pictures of children, and two of men in uniform. The hardwood floor was shiny and a strip of carpet ran down the middle. A small fireplace of dark red tile had a flower screen in front of it.

Fred's aunt returned after a few minutes and sat on a couch across from us. Her eyes narrowed, focusing on me.

"Don't leave any smudges on the lace. So, Fred, what brings you down here again from the land of the noble savage?"

"Money."

Her face froze.

"Have to see your uncle about that. He's out in the garden. Spends Sunday out there. I told him you're here."

She looked at me.

"Some of us have to work even on the Lord's Day. We can't afford to take life easy, as some do."

"I didn't know you worked, Aunt Lettie."

"Who do you think keeps this house spic and span, Fred? And tends the flowers?"

"Oh yeah."

She eyed me again.

"Don't press down too hard on the cushions. They're expensive."

I grinned.

"Would you like a list of the places my bum has sat today? So you can decide if you approve?"

Fred squirmed beside me.

"Mind if I go see Uncle Ernie? He's out in the garden, is he? I'll leave you two alone to get to know each other. By the way, this is Josephine Littletree."

He almost ran out of the room. His aunt studied me.

"You don't look altogether Indian."

I didn't trust myself to answer.

"Do you know how to use a knife and fork?"

"A spoon too."

"How nice. Fred's mother was a disappointment when it came to the social graces. A regular savage. Met her once. That was enough. Could hardly speak English. Fred's father isn't all there. You can see it in Fred. Full of the most idiotic ideas. We really didn't know what to do with him, what with him not being one of us. We decided it would be best if he was raised on a reservation by his own people. By that time his father had been put in the asylum. We couldn't look after him. Wandering around the estate in his underwear. That's how he met her. He simply vanished, left Kamloops one day and got lost up there, was wandering through the bushes when he saw her. She was washing clothes in a creek. Very primitive. Insisted on marrying her. They got married up there, thank God. He was still in his right mind enough to find a church. So it was a Christian ceremony, no bones through the nose or whatever they do, trade so many cows or horses for somebody's daughter. Though for her a dog would have been more than enough. She wasn't on the scene very long. Ruptured something giving birth to Fred, we heard. Sad. Do you take tea?"

"I've never tasted it."

"No surprise, I guess. It's part of civilized life. Is Littletree your real name? You can at least tell me that."

"My father's surname was MacCammon."

"A Scot. I knew you looked faintly British somehow. So you and Fred are half-breeds. I suppose that's why you're attracted to each other. The British connection. I don't approve of mixing the races. There are fewer of us than the others and those whites who mix with nonwhites are helping to destroy the white race. We'll end up mongrels, and no different from inferior strains. Civilization is a product of the white race. We're more intelligent and industrious. And better looking too."

She noticed I had begun staring up at the ceiling.

"Who gave you the name 'Littletree'?"

"I don't want to talk about that."

Fred returned with his uncle, a bulky man with no hair on the top of his head but a bushy white clump growing out of each side. He was wearing a checked shirt, a tie, and his overalls had grass stains at the knees. He was holding a pair of garden gloves. Fred's aunt noticed.

"Change your pants, dear. And get rid of those gloves. You don't want to be dirtying the carpet. Don't forget your hands. We're having tea."

"All in good time. So this is your princess, is it, Fred? How are you, my dear? If you'll forgive the word."

I nodded.

"A quiet one. We must get you to speak."

"Dear?"

"I'm going, dear."

His uncle left and Fred sat down and his aunt stood up.

"I'll make the tea."

Alone we whispered.

"They're racist. You think they're going to give you money?"

"We'll work on them."

"They've already been worked on."

"Trust me."

"Let's get out of here. I don't like being insulted, do you?"

Fred's uncle brought in a table. His aunt followed with a tray. On it were a teapot, cups and saucers, a creamer and a sugar bowl. On her second trip she returned with a lemon and a knife. She poured. He served. I turned down everything but the tea. In a different setting I might have enjoyed it but in that house I could hardly swallow. Everybody had a second cup but me. Fred's uncle smacked his lips.

"I like my tea strong."

Fred's aunt frowned at the lip smacking. She looked at the pictures of the men in uniform.

"Next Friday is the anniversary of the death of our son, Tom. He was killed at Vimy Ridge."

Fred nodded.

"Too bad. Got to watch it when you're driving in the country. Those back roads can be rough. We came down in a wagon."

"He was killed in France."

"What was he doing driving over there?"

"He was in the army. He was killed in battle."

"Oh, I see. Guess he had no choice."

"He died for his country. That's some comfort."

"How could he die fighting for his country over there?"

"We supported Britain in the War. You fight for the mother country. It's like fighting for your own. You wouldn't understand. The man in the naval uniform is my brother, Bill. He died last year. In London."

"Is there another war there?"

"He was killed in a traffic accident in London, Ontario."

"Well, that goes to show you, doesn't it, Aunt Lettie?"

"Show me what?"

"They're both dead. Doesn't matter how."

"One was an accident. The other wasn't."

"Yeah, but some guys don't get killed in a war, do they? So it's like an accident who does."

"My son was a brave man who died with other brave men."

"Wasn't your brother brave?"

"What's that got to do with it?"

"If they were both brave, it doesn't matter how they died."

"My son died bravely. My brother was knocked down by a car. He didn't know he was going to be knocked down. My son knew he was risking his life."

"Yeah, but every time you walk across a street there's a chance you'll be killed. And same goes for driving a car."

"You ever had to wear a gas mask? Has anybody ever taken a shot at you? Has a bomb or an artillery shell fallen on you? Or anybody tried to cut your throat or strangle you? Beat your stupid head in with a shovel?"

"Not yet."

"Have you been to see your father lately?" Fred's uncle said.

"No. He doesn't know me."

"He should."

With darting hands Fred's aunt gathered up the cups and saucers and carried away the tray, her face a stone carving. His uncle didn't seem bothered.

"Where are you staying?"

"Nowhere."

"Where are your bags?"

"We left them at the stable where the driver fed and rested his team. I've come down to talk with you about an idea I've got. To get going I need a hundred dollars for a truck. I'll pay you back."

"Afraid you'll have to talk to the wife about money. She holds the purse strings."

"She told me to see you."

"Nope. She's the money manager."

"We're kind of in a jam. We were hoping to stay for a couple of days."

"Have to see the wife about that."

He left. We whispered.

"They're giving us the run around."

"How about you're pregnant?"

"We're not married. She'll throw me out as a slut."

"You're getting money. We're waiting for it."

"From who? I'm a half-breed. That's what she called us. And you had to go make her mad."

"You're sick. You got to rest."

"Didn't you hear? She's freaky about dirt. Thinks we're filthy. She'll clean this sofa soon as we're gone."

"Tell her you're a medium. You can contact her dead son."

"Why is it me has to be something? What about you coming up with something you can fake?"

"We got no money, no place to go."

"What about the idea you're going to talk with him about?"

"I made that up."

"Great, Fred. We're stuck in Kamloops with no money."

"He's coming back. Think of something."

"All right. I'm a medium."

"Thanks, Josie."

His uncle's frowning face appeared.

"Before you say anything, Uncle Ernie, Josie would like to speak with Aunt Lettie. It's important."

He returned with her and two sourpusses stared at me.

"The business Fred was going to speak to you about concerns me. Some Indians have psychic powers as mediums for messages from the beyond. From when I was a girl it was recognized by my tribe (ugh) that I had an unusual gift for receiving and transmitting such messages. I've held séances, but only in my tribe, and the results have been very good, and sometimes even surprised me. Fred thinks I should set up in business here in Kamloops as Madame Josephine. We don't really need money for a truck. We need it for rent and to buy newspaper advertising and things like a crystal ball, turban and silk cape with stars. A hundred dollars will start us off. You'll get your money back. And if you want, I will hold a free séance here in this house and try to contact anybody you wish. Anybody in the Edwards family."

Fred's uncle wasn't impressed.

"That stuff is phony. I don't believe in it."

"Most mediums are fakes. I've never made any money with my powers. But Fred's a businessman and thinks I can. He's attended my séances."

"She's really good, Aunt Lettie. Making contact with the spirits. Sending messages back and forth like Western Union. She gets so tired she collapses after."

"Fred thinks I can do anything. It doesn't always work but I can try."

Aunt Lettie's frown didn't change.

"I wouldn't dirty my son's memory by doing such a thing. I think you should leave."

I turned to Fred.

"I knew they wouldn't be interested. You have to respect the memory of someone who won the DSO at Vimy Ridge."

"How did you know Tom won the DSO?"

"It flashed through my mind. When you're a medium, things like that happen to you."

After his aunt agreed to the séance, Fred asked me in our

attic room how I knew about the DSO.

"I wasn't lying. It came to me."

"You are psychic. We'll set up in business."

"Not a chance."

We stalled for the next couple of days, raising expectations as we rested and tried to figure out what to do. Fred told his aunt I was having my period and was a heavy bleeder. He said that would interfere with reaching the spirits because they didn't come through when there was blood being spilled, no matter what the reason. He said his aunt had a disgusted look about the blood. We weren't offered meals. While our hosts slept Fred would scout around (ugh) in the kitchen. They seemed to live on canned fruit, shortbread cookies and tea. The first night he managed to find half a loaf of stale sliced white bread and a tin of corned beef. We ate in our room. He opened the tin with the key on the side and sliced the meat with his jackknife. I found a flap of hairy ear in my sandwich and wouldn't eat any more. He went to the kitchen and brought back cookies and a can of sliced peaches, opened the can with the jackknife and fished out slices for me.

"Got any ideas, Josie?"

"Why don't you come up with one? You're supposed to be the idea man."

"You can always pretend to hear things."

"Why don't you look around and find out something about their son? Something I can work with. By the way, there's something you should know. I worked in a whorehouse."

Fred looked hurt for a while and then he grinned.

"That doesn't make any difference. You probably had a reason. You've always got a good reason. You're my girl now and that's all I care about."

I kissed him.

"I wasn't one of the girls. I cleaned the floors and changed the sheets. Joe Bob was the bouncer. When I first saw your uncle I knew I'd seen him before. Couldn't remember where. Tonight I did. He was a customer."

"He didn't recognize you."

"I worked mostly during the day, before the girls got up. Most customers never saw me. In the evening there were special customers for the madam. Important businessmen, guys in politics or on the police force. She'd answer the door when they arrived. Sometimes she answered it during the day, if the bouncer wasn't there. At night the bouncer always answered unless she had somebody coming. They'd have their collar up or hat brim pulled down. I didn't pay much attention, was usually tidying things in the kitchen. But I remember a guy with a bunch of white hair like fuzz sticking out from under the sides of his hat. It was your uncle."

"We're set. We got the money."

"He'll say it wasn't him. I can't prove it was. Opal—she's the madam—wouldn't back me up. If she did word would get out and the other big shots wouldn't trust her any more."

"What'll we do?"

"I'll figure out something about your uncle. Find anything you can about their son. Look in his old bedroom. Can you throw your voice, like ventriloquist with a dummy?"

"No."

"You'd have to be in the room with me or they wouldn't believe it's really his voice. Guess I'll have to pretend I'm hearing messages."

"You going to need a crystal ball and a turban?"

"I mentioned that stuff to impress them. Besides, I'm not a Hindu or a Gypsy. She's a tough old bitch. It depends how bad she wants to believe it's her son."

For dinner we had cookies and a can of fruit cocktail. Fred told me he found the room.

"It's on the second floor. It's his because there's all kinds of pictures of him. The door was open. She was cleaning in there. I sneaked up and peeked. I'll go tonight when they're sleeping. They go to bed early."

He went down at ten thirty and was back in five minutes.

"She's weird. She sleeps in there."

"How do you know?"

"I could hear her snoring."

"Think you could get in during the day? Does she ever leave the house?"

"I don't know. I only been here twice before this. Like I told you. That first time I remember they said they go to bed with the chickens. I was a kid and I thought it was funny. Last time she said, 'You're always in the garden' and he said, 'You're always going to church.' That's all I remember."

"You'll have to hang around and get in when she's not there. We need more time. Tell her I'm still bleeding a lot and too sick to leave the room. That I'll hold the séance in a couple of days."

Next morning Fred told her.

"She wasn't happy but I could see she can't wait for it. I got another can of fruit cocktail and some cookies off her. She counted out the cookies. She said, 'There's a depression going on.'"

We ate and Fred left to see if he could sneak into the bedroom. I was taking nap and there was a knock on the door before it opened. Uncle Ernie. I half expected him. Working in a whorehouse teaches you things.

"I came to see how the princess is."

"Bleeding. Want to see the napkins?"

He looked uncomfortable.

"So you're not in a receptive mood."

"Is that supposed to be a joke?"

He didn't get it. Then he did and came closer and I sat up.

"About the money. That could be managed. The wife doesn't have to know about it. I'd like something in return."

"What?"

"A smart girl like you should know what I mean. What're are you doing with a guy like Fred?"

"He's my boyfriend."

"Drop him. I could make things comfortable for you. You'd never have to worry about money. You'd have your own place."

"You're looking for a whore."

"No whore in this city would have what you'd have."

"You sure of that? You know all about whores?"

"No more than most men."

"Maybe a little more. I notice your hair sticks out quite a bit at the sides."

"When you don't have much, you grow it where you can."

"I've seen it before. You were wearing a hat with the brim turned down."

"Smart bitch. I had you figured from the beginning. Waterfront klootch. Making back money for booze."

"I worked on my knees, not my back. Kept my eyes open."

"Think this is going to get you anywhere?"

"It'll keep you from believing you can bullshit me into bed."

"Don't ever think you've got anything on me. I've got friends in this town. And forget about telling my wife. She'd never believe you."

"She thinks the only dirt on you is from the garden. As Opal says, a customer is a customer as long as he doesn't tear up the place. You're not likely to do that. Collar up, brim down, you're safe."

Fred rushed in a few minutes past noon.

"I got in there. She's having tea with him in the garden. I went through the drawers and the closet. Here's what I found. Hurry up."

He handed me a stamp album, high school report cards, birthday cards from relatives and a card from a girl, and stacks of letters from the front. I went through the letters. Stuff about muddy trenches, rations, friends wounded or killed, missing his home and family, and several references to the same girl who sent him the birthday card. Her name was Veronica. He hinted at being unhappy about something to do with her.

"Hurry, Josie."

"Wait. I'm on to something here."

When I had finished Fred took everything back, said he made sure nothing looked disturbed.

"What did you find, Josie?"

"Your aunt wanted to keep her son all to herself. She broke up a relationship between him and a girl he liked. He doesn't say how. In the last letter he says he doesn't care if he survives the war. He blames himself for not being stronger."

"You going to tell her?"

"She knows. She's read the letters."

"What are you going to do?"

"Give her a show."

I told Fred to tell his aunt I would hold the séance in the drawing room at ten minutes before eight. I said to tell her I needed more food to be strong. She counted out two more cookies than last time and we got a handful of old raisins. Fred sneaked down at night and took another tin of corned beef. I turned it down for the raisins.

"There's no ear in it, Josie."

"Don't care."

At seven thirty the next evening Fred went down and told them I was ready and they were to be in the drawing room when I arrived. Fred's uncle didn't want to go but she made him. I asked for the tea table to be put in front of the sofa. I planned to sit there. At ten to eight I entered and sat behind the table. Fred was sitting at the end of the sofa, a couple of feet from me. His aunt and uncle were sitting on the couch opposite me. The Edwards were frowning but her frown wasn't as deep. I put my hands on the table, the palms down. My voice sounded as mysterious as I could make it.

"All the lights must be out. There must be absolute silence. Don't move. I have to concentrate."

"This is ridiculous," Uncle Ernie said.

"Ssssh," Aunt Lettie said.

Fred turned out the lights. I stared into the darkness.

"Is there anyone who wishes to speak with anybody here?"

Nothing happened.

"Can you hear me, Thomas Edwards? Are you there?"

I waited and nothing. It was a flop. I would try once more. What did they expect for a few cookies?

"Can you hear me, Thomas Edwards? Are you there? Do you wish to speak with anybody? Can you hear me?"

"Ysssssssssss."

I jumped. The sound had come out of my mouth. It wasn't a word. I thought maybe I was in a trance and didn't know what I was saying.

"Tommy? Is that you? I can hear you. I miss you, dear."

The loving mother act. I didn't have to act any more.

"We can hear you. What are you saying? It's about Veronica. What about her? You're sorry. About what? Leaving her."

At that point I was listening.

"There was no other way. You had to do it. Do what? End it. How? In the assault on the enemy positions. You walked into the guns. Straight for them. Up the ridge.

Leading the way into the trenches. Waving the soldiers forward. Capturing a trench. And then another. Waving them forward. Dead enemy everywhere. Smoke, grenades exploding, machine guns rattling, yells, screams. You heard a thump. A German mortar. You saw a blinding flash, felt your body fly apart. You were floating high above the ridge, the battle below. You could see it, tiny figures swarming over the ground, the flashes from bursting shells, the slits of the trenches like scars, but no sounds any more. You felt an incredible peace. It was over. You had done it."

"Oh, my brave boy."

I could hear Aunt Lettie crying. But it wasn't over.

"What are you saying? What about the train station? Veronica was waiting there. You were supposed to meet. You were leaving with her. Your mother had a fit and collapsed, fell down and had to be driven to the hospital. At her bedside she made you promise never to leave her. She had you sit with her all day. Every time you tried to leave she held onto your hand. All the old arguments. Her family is poor. She's not one of us. You'd be ruining your life. And Veronica was waiting. You found out later she waited until it was dark, left her suitcase at the station, went home and hanged herself in her bedroom."

Aunt Lettie wasn't crying now.

"That's all a lie about the hospital. I never did that. Holding onto his hand or the rest. You're making it up. Putting lies in my son's mouth."

"I told you that stuff is fake," Uncle Ernie said. He got up and turned on the lights.

"I never met your son or Veronica. How could I know how he died or how she died?"

She stood up, her mouth twisted, and pointed at me.

"This is what comes of being generous and of trusting people. Get out of my house."

That was when it happened, a sound upstairs in her son's bedroom. Fred got up and grinned.

"I told you she was good, Aunt Lettie. She's brought a spirit into your house."

"You're as crazy as your father."

Another sound from the bedroom, this time louder. She looked at her husband.

"Go and see."

He didn't move. She threw up her hands.

"I'll go. I want you two out of here when I come back down."

We could hear the thumps of her steps on the stairs. There was a scream. Uncle Ernie rushed up and yelled. I smelled smoke.

"Let's get out of here, Josie."

I followed Fred into the kitchen. He filled a bag with food.

"You got something coming for your séance."

When we left the smell of smoke was strong and I could hear a crackling sound above. At the gate we stopped and looked back. Flames and smoke were coming out of the second floor windows, making them look like burning eyes. There was a thud, as if a floor collapsed, and a cloud of sparks and rolling smoke burst out of the open front door.

We heard a roaring sound. Flames began to come out everywhere and rise into the night sky. The house looked like a haystack on fire. Fred put the bag of food down.

"You don't have much of a chance when fire gets going in a wooden house. We couldn't have helped them."

Fred had some money. We went to a waterfront hotel. We ate in the room. He'd taken shortbread cookies, cans of pears and peaches, more of that corned beef, and packages of raisins, prunes and marshmallows. As we ate he confessed.

"I came up with my own plan if things didn't work out with the séance. I got everything together the day before. While they were waiting for you, I went up to that room. I hung a piece of rope between a bureau doorknob and the closet doorknob. Tied some string around a rock and hung it from the rope. Lit a candle and put it on a chair, moved the chair so the candle was an inch below the rope. I had to guess how long it would take the rope to burn through. Didn't know if it would work."

"You guessed pretty good. What about the second noise?"

"Don't know what that was. Guess something fell over. Could be the rope hit the chair and it took a while to fall. Candle or burning rope could've started the fire."

"How he died and that stuff about the train station wasn't in the letters."

"You made it up?"

"I couldn't make that up."

"What do you think?"

"I think I'm getting tired of cookies and canned fruit."

"These marshmallows are good with raisins and prunes."

"How can you eat that stuff with cookies and corned beef?"

The next morning Fred had a stomachache. We couldn't leave. I went down at noon and paid for another day. There was a copy of the Kamloops Sentinel on the desk. The desk clerk tapped a finger on it.

"The Edwards' mansion burnt down. Biggest news around here for a while."

I looked at the headline.

"Want to read it? Go ahead, take a chair over there."

I sat in the tiny lobby in a chair with a torn leather horsehair cushion. The story took up most of the front page, with a description of the fire and the recollections of friends of the dead couple. Badly burnt, their bodies were found at the bottom of the stairs. They had tumbled down them, Uncle Ernie on top, Aunt Lettie's hands around his throat. His shoes had climbed halfway up her body. "Bertha Smuts, an old friend said, 'They were such a devoted couple. Poor Lettie never recovered from her son's death. I think Ernie dealt with it by doing charity work, especially down around the waterfront.' Another longtime friend, Leonie Maltravers, said, 'It's tragic they died on the anniversary of their son's death, but I suppose somehow fitting in a way.'" Fred's father was mentioned as Ernie's only remaining living relative. "He is currently residing in a rest home and was not available for comment."

The next morning we picked up our bags at the stable and took them to the hotel. Fred had enough money to rent the room for three more days. He talked again about getting a truck. Where was the money?

"Don't worry, I've got a plan."

The plan turned out to be delivering wood. He would use his Hindu friend's truck in the evenings and when he took a day off. That lasted for three weeks. There wasn't enough money in it. We were living from day to day. And Fred would leave the engine running while he talked too long with customers and have to spend money on gas. The Hindu said Fred was too hard on the brakes and rode the clutch all the time. He decided to quit before he got stuck with repair bills. He couldn't get a job with delivery companies because he didn't have a driver's licence. He couldn't get one because he couldn't use the Edwards' address. The house was a heap of ashes and splintered burnt timbers. He drove me over in the truck. We got out and looked around. I found what looked like a lump of tarnished silver. It was a spoon.

"Who inherits their property?"

"I think Aunt Lettie has relatives back East, in Ontario. They'll get it. Me or my father won't get anything. That's for sure."

"Listen, Fred. You're one of those people the police say have no fixed address. Like a vagrant. Or a hobo. Let's go back to the reserve. We'll live with my grandmother. You can hatch plans there. We won't have to worry about rent."

"You still believe in me, don't you, Josie?"

"I need to go back."

"Everything will work out. Something came to me today."

"Send it back."

"You're not interested?"

"Not a bit."

"It's sure fire."

"They all are."

"What did you pick up a while ago?"

"Your aunt's good manners. Let's get out of here."

What finished everything was another big plan. He'd leave the reserve and go to Kamloops, hitching a ride if somebody was going that way. He wanted me to go with him but I said I'd had enough of life in that place for a while. He told me he went to see gangster movies at the Rex. He'd watch gangsters robbing stores, banks and warehouses. Sometimes he would forget to eat his dinner and his jaw would slowly drop as he remembered. He started saying things like "I ain't no dirty yellow rat," "that stool pigeon is gonna be wearing a cement overcoat," "gimme the gat, I'm pulling a heist," "you mugs take orders from me, if ya know what's good for ya," "fill that squealer full of lead," "they'll throw you in the clink," "I'm not gonna land in the big house," "you'll fry for this," "drop dead, copper, I ain't singin'." He talked about Alcatraz. Sing Sing. And all the time he was planning his own heist.

He didn't say anything until a few days before he did it. We were sitting on the edge of the bed and it was early morning. I'd reached the point where I was going to tell him either he stopped that crazy talk or I'd leave him. He mentioned us getting married after he made some real loot.

"I'm not going to be a sap for much longer. I already cased the joint. Did it last time I went there. A pushover."

"What are you talking about?"

"Gonna pull a stickup."

"You mean rob some place? They'll know you in those clothes."

He looked like an ad for the Great Western Garment Company.

"I've got a disguise."

From inside his shirt he took a piece of black cloth, probably cut out of some old serge or worsted suit. He spread the cloth on his knee. There were two eyeholes and a rubber band tied to each side. He put it on and his voice sounded heavier through the material.

"Nobody's going to know it's me."

"Take it off. Don't let anybody on the reserve see it."

"No one here sings. They're not squealers."

"You better not do it. You'll get caught."

"Already got the getaway planned. I'm taking it on the lam, heading into the high country, where I'll hole up."

"You need a truck."

"I got one."

"Where'd you get it?"

"Never mind."

"You stole it."

"Not yet. That's where you come in."

"I don't want anything to do with this."

"All you have to do is keep the guy busy while I hotwire the ignition."

"He'll report it stolen and the police will be looking for you."

"They won't get us because we're taking it the same day."

I didn't want to help. He said this was the one time he needed me to believe in him. He was going to do it, anyway, and I couldn't let him do it alone. I thought maybe the two of us would get away with it. We hitched a ride on a wagon. I told you, Grandmother, that I was going to help him start a business. I hated lying to you. The truck we were going to take was in a broken-down garage full of wrecks in the oldest part of Kamloops. None of them looked as if they could be started, even with a key. There were engines and transmissions on the cracked concrete floor and on benches, and stacks of bald tires in the corners. Pails were filled with black crankcase oil that looked like heavy syrup and smelled like burnt metal. A couple of trucks had no doors and were on blocks. A sign outside on the grimy red-brick building said, "Active Transfer." Beside the gas pump outside was a flatbed truck that looked a little better than the others and Fred said that was the one. I was supposed to get the mechanic into his office and keep him there while Fred started the truck and drove off. He said the guy was alone in the early morning, when we got there. He'd give me five minutes, looking in the window of the bakery around the corner, before he went to start the truck. He would be waiting a block away five minutes later. So I had ten horrible minutes to kill with Gus (the name sewn onto his filthy overalls), who stepped out of any woman's nightmare. He was ugly, dirty, smelly and had weird red eyes that stared as if he wasn't sure where he was going to begin touching me. I got Gus into his office by telling him I needed a truck and driver to take some trunks and suitcases to my aunt's house, where I was going to live for a while because I was new in town.

"Where would that be?" He chewed on his blue tongue as he spoke.

"It's a deserted area near an old sawmill."

"Un huh."

He rubbed the stubble on his chin, cracks in his fingers cobwebs of black grime. He sat behind a desk on a stool with sawed-off legs. I made up an address and he picked up a carpenter's pencil and wrote on the back of an old month torn off a calendar. He rubbed the stubble on his head, stood up and brought his stink and flattened nose and pickled breath over to me.

"Never heard of it. You wouldn't be kidding me, would you?"

"I told you, I need a truck to move my stuff."

He grabbed my left breast, squeezing it until it hurt. His mouth came closer and I twisted away but he held onto me, his fingernails beginning to dig in like knifepoints.

"I've got a disease."

"What kind?"

"Sticklers' Disease." I heard the truck start.

"What kind is that?"

"I don't know, I caught it off Sticklers."

"You're a smart one. What're you playing at, you klootch?"

He pressed me against the wall and his slimy lips and rotten teeth were on my mouth, sucking out my breath. The engine backfired as the truck drove away and he let go and swore and ran out and I ran too. I ran in the opposite direction to the meeting place, doubled back a block away and saw the truck parked behind a delivery van. Fred was gunning the engine.

"You're late."

"Get going. He's looking for us."

We nearly tipped over turning the corner and the rickety thing shook and roared. My breast hurt and I pulled at my sweater and bra to ease the pain. I felt inside and touched the lumps his fingers had left. My breast was sticky wet.

"I'm hurt."

"Bad?"

The truck was lurching and backfiring and steam began to hiss from the radiator cap.

"Pretty bad."

"All you have to do is drive me away from the bank."

"I can't drive." I felt my breast again and when I looked at my hand it was smeared with blood.

"It's easy. See this pedal my left foot is on. Press it down. Shove the gearshift lever over a bit and forward like this here, then let the pedal up and press the accelerator. Where my right foot is. The pedal in between is the brake pedal. I'll leave the motor running."

"I don't know if I can do it."

"Sure you can. Do like I said and when we get out of the city I'll take over."

We were in the business district now. He slowed down and parked in front of a bank. It was a stone building with columns on either side of the entrance and big metal doors.

I felt sick about the whole thing. My bra was hurting me. I couldn't stand it. I had to take it off. I reached behind and under my sweater and undid the hooks and eased the cups off and pulled the bra out. There were blotches of red on it and watery stains. I felt better but my wool sweater itched where it touched my breast, so I pulled the sweater away from it. I folded the cups and stuck them under the seat.

Fred put on the mask. He was wearing an old suit that was too big for him. He took out a boy's cap pistol from the inside jacket pocket. I felt better when I saw it. At least he wasn't going to be a murderer too. He opened the door, told me to move over behind the wheel. He leaned out and his jacket moved up, showing where he cut the mask.

"You cut the seat of your pants."

"The jacket covers it."

He put the cap pistol into an outside jacket pocket, keeping his hand there. He stepped down onto the sidewalk and shut the door, went around by the steaming radiator and pushed open a metal door and disappeared. I held the jittery steel-spoked wheel and put my foot on the round clutch pedal. The truck was shaking uncertainly and I hoped it wouldn't stall. A woman wearing a mink stole around her expensively dressed shoulders and lots of makeup and jewellery gave me a dirty look as she walked by, as if I had no right to sit above her or drive and I sneered and broke her stare. A couple of minutes later Fred ran out with a paper bag in his hand. He jerked open the passenger side door and fell headfirst onto the seat, sat up and slammed the door so hard the window shook.

"Hurry up, drive."

I pressed on the clutch but it wouldn't go down.

"I can't, it's too hard. You didn't tell me that."

"Try again. Hurry up."

I put both feet on it and it gave a bit. I slammed the gearshift forward and there was a grinding noise and we jerked ahead. Everything began shaking too much. The engine slowed, dying. A moment from stalling.

"Give it the gas."

I stomped on the accelerator and the engine howled and we lunged forward again and settled into a whining roar at ten miles an hour. The wheel was so stiff I could hardly turn it as we barged into traffic.

"Shift."

I looked at him and he pointed to the pedal and I put both feet on it. He pulled the gearshift back and there was a whizzing grinding of spinning metal.

"More."

I put all my weight on it. He pulled the gearshift all the way back and I let the pedal up.

"Gas."

I was quicker this time and we settled into a steady loud twenty-five, the engine still straining but not as much. He looked at the gearshift, was going to say something but didn't. We were so slow and noisy I thought the police would be waiting for us somewhere up ahead but they weren't. I coasted through intersections, not bothering about stoplights or stop signs. I stayed in the middle of the road because I didn't want to hit parked cars. Other drivers got out of the way with a lot of honking, and some of their mouths were open and moving fast. I couldn't hear what they were saying. I was glad to get out of the business district, away from those high buildings. It was like being trapped. Fred leaned over, half off the seat, and began steering and told me to crawl in back of him so he could take my place. The change was smooth, except I bumped into him and the pain got worse. I didn't say anything but he knew and after he shifted into third and we picked up speed he decided something.

"I'll let you off somewhere and get word to you."

"All right. There's that waterfront whorehouse I told you about."

The engine strained to forty in a shaking growl and the truck banged and bounced around on its squealing leaf springs. The rear axle hub hit the rim of a pothole and we careened dangerously. Traffic was light down there and we didn't hit anything. He stopped in the middle of the road and I got out. He gunned the engine and it wailed and the truck shook and lurched away, tilting on two wheels as he turned a corner and disappeared.

"Well, look what the cat dragged in," Opal said when she opened the door.

"It's a cathouse, isn't it?'

I found out later Fred had to abandon the truck an hour after he let me off. He forgot about putting water in the radiator. The radiator boiled dry and the engine seized. The police found the truck the next morning and him later on, hiding in an empty cabin on the edge of town. He lost the pistol. At his trial he said he used a cap pistol but nobody believed him. Everybody believed the eyewitnesses, who said they saw him holding a revolver. He got ten years for armed robbery. The woman wearing the stole described me pretty well for the newspapers and my bra was found. That's as near as the law got to me and I remained the "mystery accomplice." I went to see Fred in prison. Full of plans and eager as ever. He said he'd still be young when he got out and I said I'd wait for him. He said I didn't have to, though if I did it would be a good idea to start making souvenirs and relics. We'd be ready to start the store and museum when his sentence was up. A year later he was knifed to death. He was mistaken for someone else in the prison library, where he was reading books on business.

I'd begun to see I wouldn't have much luck in my life. No matter what I did it would never work out. I started thinking about what you said and though it wasn't clear yet, I knew it explained why things were going bad for me. Things were going bad for a lot of us and had been ever since the strangers came. That's how I saw them, as strangers who didn't belong to this land and would never know how to live with it. I saw that what Fred wanted to do was wrong, we shouldn't turn ourselves into a show, dead and stuffed souvenirs of a lost battle. Buffalo hides on the floor of somebody's den. There were too many of them when we saw our doom in their murder of the land. We didn't see the threat soon enough or we would have killed them all or died trying. I dreamt of one last battle, with the nations united against them and the sun going down red on our final day. Better to die a warrior than to live a slave, to make them fear the copper sun and the blood moon. Call a man a colour, you put him in a cell he can't escape from. Nothing else will matter because you have robbed him of his freedom, though he still walks around. I am not red though my blood is from the iron in it, and theirs is red for the same reason. I learned that from my father's books, and about the exploration of the continent and westward movement of the pioneers, but not about cruelty and racial murder. They couldn't take the land from us because it wasn't ours. The land is itself, it's no one's, and they waste their lives trying to own it, to buy and sell it as they buy and sell potatoes. They are children who grab something and say, it's mine, mine. I know something worse. Each man is limited by what he knows, thinking that is the way to see the world. He can't accept what he isn't because that would be denying what he is. He is blind when he sees others, as the strangers were blind about us. The same species, and every people a stranger to every other, split apart by ideas of differences. Man is tribal and man is doomed.

Poor Fred. I forgot him too quickly. But I had to. All I wanted to do was drink. During that year I would wake up on a dirty mattress and could smell my sweat, a whiff of hot tar. And the cheap wine stinking of chemicals, like paint thinner or varnish. The faces of men and women, as drunk as I was, would float in front of me, sad masks without eyes. They would mumble in the darkness and I would mumble back, feel sick and try to keep from choking on my vomit. I didn't recognize my own face any more when I saw it in a mirror. I would sit on bricks in an empty lot or in alleyways with my back against a garbage can or in a field or ditch somewhere in the night and drink from the neck of the bottle when my turn came. I'd pee my pants and pass out. I hated anyone or anything that kept me from that next drink. I never wanted to see or feel the hard world again. There were only shadows and soft moving shapes I bumped into and slurred words and my dry throat and the tilt of the sour wine into me. One day I woke up in a field and my shoes and jacket were gone. It was a cold morning and the grass was wet. I couldn't stop shivering. I began to vomit and after a while all that came out was yellow slime. It burnt my throat and my stomach hurt. I began to cry, cried all day. I went to you, Grandmother. I shivered in your arms. You put me to bed and stripped off my clothes. When I woke up you had broth ready. The smell made me sick. I could hardly swallow the first mouthful. Finally I could sip a little and keep it down. It's so easy to write this now. The slowness of the death of my craving still haunts me. All I could think was, I can't live without a drink. I'd start shaking and couldn't stop. I thought I was going crazy. You became an enemy, I hated you. I kept the hate inside. I smiled to fool you into thinking I was happy. No lying words though because you were smart. I planned to escape from your house when you were sleeping, go drinking and sober up and return before you woke up. I was even going to hide my breath with SenSen. It's all right, I told myself, she won't catch on. You said nothing as my appetite slowly returned and the craving died, because all the time you knew what would happen.

One morning I was better. On that morning you looked at me.

"What are you going to do, Josie?"

"Don't know."

"You remember what I said to you when you were a girl about helping our people?"

"How can I help anybody? My life is a wreck."

"Your life is with your people. You can read and write. You're smart. Save what we have left. Where would you look to find us?"

"Our culture."

"Go to all the bands and listen to our stories, write them down, collect them before they are lost to us. How long will it be before the white man gets us to forget them, so they will no longer be told? When I was a girl I was told that white men came here and wrote them down. They have been put in books for other whites to read. That's no good to us. We must have our own books. Keep the stories alive for ourselves. We must be our own storytellers. So we stay alive as a people. They are what we are."

"How do I start?"

"Ask the old people. They will know the stories. Some of the stories will be the same among the bands and some will be different in small or big ways. Write them all down. Your book will be the one other storytellers will look at to know everything."

"Maybe most of us want to watch movies now, Grandmother. Maybe the stories bore them."

"Do you like what you see about us in movies? Do you like what the white man says about us in books?"

"It makes me sick."

"Gather together the stories, tell them. Make your people well."

Before beginning I went to see Rachel. I had been away from the hunting grounds for more than two years and needed to return. I passed the lake where I had fished. Memories of Joe Bob returned. The rowboat was on the shore beside the pier and had been turned over. The seams had been caulked. The handles of oars stuck out from under the boat. As I walked up the path to the cabin I could hear the dogs. Strike led the others to me and I crouched down and petted and hugged him. Pal and Person wagged their tails and yapped. My escorts led the way. I saw the door had been opened to let in the fresh spring air. Rachel came to the doorway, taller, hair gathered behind her and her big eyes wide. She was wearing jeans and moccasins and a beaded sweater. She ran down the path and we hugged. The dogs make a racket. Ed George came from behind the cabin, where he had been chopping firewood. He was holding an axe. For something to do, he tapped the handle on the ground a few times to see if the blade had loosened. I waved. He nodded. That was his way. Anything else and I would have been worried about him. When Pal and Person went to him, he said something to them, probably about looking forward to having an early summer.

After dinner that night Ed George talked outside to his

dogs. Rachel and I talked on the couch. She and Ed George had heard about Joe Bob and Fred Edwards from Rachel's parents. I told her about my drinking. She was worried about me.

"You look more serious, Josie."

"You mean older?"

"I guess so. Tired too. You going to stay? That would help you."

"I don't know. My grandma thinks I should write down our stories and tell them. I wanted to see how you were first. I see Ed George finally patched the boat and made oars."

"Len did that last fall. He comes every few days to see how we're doing. He's taken me berry picking and out in the boat to fish. I haven't caught much. But I'm getting better. The last time I caught a char and a trout. I'm so glad that you're here so we can talk. I want to ask you about something that's been bothering me."

"About what happened to you at school?"

She nodded.

"Since that time I don't like anybody to touch me except you or my mom. I'd go all cold and stiff if anybody else tried. Len seems to understand. He's never tried to, even when we're alone."

"Maybe Joe Bob told him. Joe Bob could tell the first time he was here that something had happened. That's why you could tease him and he never got mad. Len must like you. And you must like him, or you wouldn't have gone anywhere with him."

"What should I do?"

"You'll be fourteen in a couple of months?"

She nodded.

"I didn't let Joe Bob touch me till I was sixteen. Start slow. If Len really likes you, he won't mind. If he minds, he's not worth it. I'll talk to Len next time he visits."

"Maybe he won't want to get serious with me because he thinks I've been ruined."

"You haven't been ruined. You're not responsible for what that bitch did. You're a victim. You don't have to stay one. And a guy who really likes you would be the best medicine. You're a fresh flower. I'm an old weed. Two dead boyfriends and had a drinking problem."

Len visited two days later. I could tell he liked Rachel a lot and she liked him. They behaved as if they were a couple of kids, and that's what they were, but there was something more between them. Ed George was checking traplines. Rachel was embroidering a shirt, probably Len's. I asked him to help me carry in some firewood. The only listener at the woodpile was Strike.

"Did Joe Bob tell you he thought something happened to Rachel at St. Jerome's?"

"Sort of."

"Something did. It was personal. She was a nun. I know of one time. There may have been others. Rachel's been trying to recover ever since. There's only two people she can stand to touch her. You're not one of them. Not yet. Do you care for her enough to try and be one?"

"Yeah, I sure do."

"Take things easy with her. You're both very young. You

got lots of time. Be careful, be slow, and you'll be happy."

Len wouldn't let me carry any wood. On the way back he stopped for a moment.

"I was sorry to hear about Joe Bob. We used to fight and he'd pick on me but he was a good guy."

"Seems all of us are victims, doesn't it?"

The next day I had a talk with Ed George. There was something I had to know. He was chopping firewood behind the cabin. I sat down on a pile of sawn logs a few feet away from the chopping block.

"I see that Len patched the rowboat and made oars."

He kept chopping.

"Where did that rowboat come from? You didn't build it."

He reached for another log.

"It wasn't left over from the Flood. (St. Jerome's had to be good for something.) You didn't build the pier either. It's Mystery Lake for a reason."

The axe came down and split the log but not in the middle this time.

"I figure you would have patched that boat and made oars if it was yours. How a rowboat even got up here must be an interesting story. And that's the mystery. There's something at the bottom of the lake, isn't there?"

He threw the split pieces onto the pile of firewood and swung the axe. It bit deep into the chopping block. He sat on the ground. He drew up his knees and rested his arms on them.

"One of them planes that lands on water."

"You mean a plane with pontoons, a seaplane?"

"Happened about ten years ago. Flew over a couple of times and left. About a month later it landed and four guys rowed in in that boat. Hid in the bushes so I could hear. They didn't speak like us or like people in Williams Lake. You might know. You been more places. They said they'd camp on the shore and throw a pier together and next time would put up a cabin. Didn't like that. This is our land for hunting and fishing. They chopped trees, sank pilings, sawed and hammered planks and flew away a week later. Empty cans all over the place. And liquor bottles too. They got drunk every night. I had to figure things out.

"Spoke to my dogs. They were pups then. You guys can't bark no more or you'll give me away, I told 'em. Anything happens to me, who's going to feed you, huh? Have to hunt groundhogs and mice. How would you like that? After getting moose and venison. They caught on. After that they went quiet. They got sense, those dogs.

"Didn't know when those guys be back. Four against one. Better to make it them against each other. I picked up some of their empty bottles. Left enough around so they wouldn't think nothing was wrong. Dug a couple of holes near where they had camped. Covered them with grass. They came back two weeks later. Brought tools to put up the cabin. Lots of grub. A case of whisky. They got drunk the first night. Never left the shore. When they were snoring I sneaked down, took some bottles out of the case and left the box flaps up a little so they'd see. Put an empty bottle in one of the holes I'd dug. Left the neck sticking out. Next morning first one up saw the case, got the others up.

"'What happened to the whisky?'

"'What the hell you talking about?' one of the others says.

"'Most of the bottles are gone.'

"'You were up first. Maybe you took 'em.'

"'Yeah, so you could blame us,' another of 'em says.

"The fourth guy goes to pee. He finds the bottle in the hole.

"'Look at this.'

"The others go over.

"'There's one of your empties,' he says to the guy who woke them up.

"'I swear I didn't touch the bottles. Who's playing tricks here?'

"'Somebody is.'

"'There's nobody else around.'

"'How do we know? This is Indian land. Maybe they don't want us up here. This could be a warning.'

"'They're on reserves, wouldn't be out here. It's one of us.'

"'They hunt and trap here. I know that for a goddam fact.'

"'He's right, they do. Fish too.'

"'It's still crown land. They don't own it.'

"'You know how far this is from any kind of town? If anything happens here, who's going to know?'

"'Like about Elsie, huh? I know about you two.'

"'Anything you heard is not true, I swear. I never had anything to do with her.'

"'You must have had a good time laughing behind my

back. I don't know why I'm up here with a son of a bitch like you.'

"'It's all in your head. You need to see a doctor, pal.'

"The one who had got the others up had a plan.

"'Cut out the arguing. Let's look around today. Check the whole area. We have to find a site for the cabin, anyway. We'll sleep in shifts tonight.'

"They decided to split up. Elsie's husband went one way with a friend and the guy who said he didn't went the other with the fourth guy. Husband had a rifle, the other guy had a shotgun. They said they would fire a shot if anything happened. They didn't trust each other. Those bottles did it, and Elsie helped too. It wouldn't be hard for them to figure the other two be laying a trap. I had my rifle. Waited till they were far enough apart and fired a shot in the direction of the pair that had the shotgun. All I had to do was wait. Pretty soon I hear shots and curses. The quiet told me it was over. Went and saw the bodies. Looked like the guy with the shotgun cut down the other two and the one with him grabbed the dead man's rifle and shot the shooter and that guy caved in his skull with the butt before he dropped dead. I rowed them all out to the plane and set fire to it. Didn't keep the rifle or the shotgun. Figured I didn't have no right to 'em. Kept their tools though, including this axe. Pretty near blinded me when I was rowing back and the gas tank went up and that plane went down like a bird on fire. Went to my dogs and told 'em they could bark again. They started in right away. Made quite a racket for a long time, but I figured they had it all stored up."

"What made you so sure things would work out that way?"

Ed George stood up and yanked the axe out of the chopping block. He ran his thumb along the edge of the blade.

"Things happen to you out in the wild if you're not used to it. Come out here from the city expecting nothing different and you find it's all different. You got to accept it, not try to change it. Or it'll get to you. You'll start hearing and seeing things, and thinking things, like those guys. All it took was a few bottles. This place is the same as my dogs. Treat it right and it'll treat you right."

"What did you do with the whisky?"

"Gave it to Shorty Moosehead. I never had much to do with liquor."

"What about the oars?"

"Gave him them too. Offered him the rowboat. He didn't want it. What're you going to do with the oars without a boat? I asked him. Said he'd clear snow off the roof of his cabin with 'em. You never cleared the snow off your roof before, I said. Course not, he says. Didn't have no oars."

Ed George picked up a log and put it on the chopping block, swung the axe and split the log clean in two, straight down the middle. It was the kind of thing you do to please yourself and nobody else. He had the right, if anybody did. He earned it.

We sing songs about birds. They can't understand them. There's a song about us we can't understand. Some of us hear it. To each it's a different song and a different singer. I hear a bird that can't sing. I hear the raven.

It was wonderful, Grandmother, listening to so many tell all the traditional stories in our language, the sounds of the words alive with memories. Raven brought light and fire to our people. He took them from those who wouldn't share. He teaches generosity through sharing. His cleverness serves us. Raven is not a god. He is not without fault. He sees what is and what should be and changes them. He is guided by a spirit within him. That makes Raven sacred to us. This is our religion, that the animals around us are sacred, have the power to change form and to play tricks, sometimes for good and sometimes selfishly. When these are for good, good results. When they aren't, the animal has tricked himself. This tells us about ourselves. We change our form, grinning and frowning, crying and laughing, cringing and threatening, fawning upon and disdaining. We play tricks, lying and pretending and flattering and praising. When a god is your master, you are taught the lessons of authority and obedience. And you inflict them on others. When an animal is your teacher, you are taught lessons about arrogance and about humility. Raven is one of us in his failings as he is above us in benevolence. Sometimes he walks among us, hungry and desperate. Other times he flies with great sweeping wings across the northern skies carrying our dreams with him.

If you look for heroes in our stories you will find none. No fearless conquerors, wars or impossible deeds. A constant theme is finding enough to eat and sharing it with those in need and being grateful to those who help. No gods step in to help but animals do, the animals of everyday life. Men seek the daughters of other men and sometimes their wives. Cheating wives are deserted or punished and faithful ones rewarded. Women teach survival, reject and desert a man they don't want and kill one who sleeps again with his first wife. There are monster people and monstrous sea creatures, overcome with trickery or a magic staff. This is storytelling that teaches the danger and magic in what is around us and how to live as a person and a member of your people. Like the animals in the stories, we can make a good or a bad job of it. Whenever any of us fail, we all do.

I have written down the stories I gathered from all the bands and put them in a book for future storytellers. When I visited a band I would ask to hear every story they knew and afterwards would ask if they had heard this or that story they hadn't told me, or a slightly different version of one they had, and if not would tell them. Most bands knew most stories but sometimes not a slightly different version. I was happy to find our people still remembered the stories. All I've done is collect them, I said when I showed it to you, Grandmother. You told me I did a good job. That made me proud because I knew you knew most versions, and some by heart. You've given us our own book, Josie, and now you must tell the stories with all the spirit you have in you. I decided to write them in both our language and English. If the schools have their way, our language will soon be extinct. We must fight to keep it, but I thought that an English version would be helpful in the future to those of us who can't speak ours. Why is the story of my little life not in our language? I live in the invader's society and our language is limited. We have no word for "movie," "truck," "constable," "seaplane," "agent," "gas," "gear" and many others. Rather than write in a combination of two languages, I have chosen the simpler path.

After I had taken down the stories I went to the cabin for a rest and told Ed George, Rachel and Len many of them. Like me before I began collecting, they hadn't heard all of them. I told the stories of Raven first. Ed George was puzzled about the story of how light came to the world.

"So one man had all the light in a box and wouldn't give it up and Raven turned himself into a fir needle and the guy's wife drank water with the needle in it and got pregnant, had a kid and that kid was Raven. And the kid played with the box, rolled it outside the man's house, turned himself back into Raven and flew away. He meets these women who're picking berries and they give Raven some in return for opening the box and there's light everywhere. I don't see how those women could've picked berries if it was dark, and how could there be berries with no light to grow 'em?"

"It's a myth, not a real story."

"Yeah, but it's supposed to be telling you about something real, like light, ain't it? And when people get tired of light all the time, how can Raven tell the light to be dark some of the time and light the rest?"

"Because Raven has magic powers."

"I seen a lot of ravens and never seen 'em do nothing but what they always do."

"In myths and legends people and animals don't behave the way they usually do."

"So what's real don't have to be real no more? I don't see no reason for that."

"Myths are old stories that explained things our people didn't understand then."

"Why bother with old stories?"

"Because they're part of our history, tell us how our people saw things once."

When I told the story of the man who married a bear, Ed George thought he could get the better of me.

"Now you got to admit this one is hard to swallow. This lady bear likes a guy, beds down with him and gives him berries. Next day another guy goes to get berries and she kills him. First guy beds down with a woman and the bear gets jealous and tears his arm off. He goes home, covers his shoulder with a blanket, nobody catches on. Am I right so far? Next time he sees the bear she's a woman with two kids and they're his. But he don't know till she puts back his missing arm. This one's full of holes. She's a bear one time and a woman next time. Why didn't his blood run out when she tore off his arm? Why didn't nobody notice his arm was gone? And don't tell me that arm wouldn't be all swelled up and stiff and useless when she put it back on. I ain't even going to mention bedding down with a lady bear. Try that and see where it gets you."

Sitting beside me on the couch, Rachel looked up from her embroidery.

"Why do you talk to your dogs?"

"'Cause they understand me."

"How can dogs understand people?"

"They can, that's all."

"That doesn't make sense."

"It does to me."

"So did those stories to our people."

A couple of months after I returned to the reserve Jimmy John showed up with a girl. Her name was Nora and she was from a reserve in Alberta. She was plain, with a flat face, and wore a long braid. She was quiet, and that's the way Jimmy John liked his women. They moved into an abandoned cabin on the edge of the reserve and Nora fixed it up. Everybody gave stuff to help them out. I took over some blankets you gave them, Grandmother. Nora said to thank you. We sat and talked, at least I did. The only thing she said was that Jimmy John was visiting. She didn't say who or where. I found out later he was visiting some bottles with friends in Williams Lake. It wouldn't have mattered who, where or what. Nora was ready to accept. Jimmy John came over to borrow money from you the next day and that's how I found out where he'd been. He didn't hide anything from me. We were talking alone on the front porch and I mentioned Nora.

"You going to get married?"

"We're good as we are."

"Suppose she gets pregnant?"

"We'll think about that if it happens."

"You mean she will."

"She can get rid of it."

"Suppose she doesn't want to?"

"She'll do what I say."

"You don't care how she feels. Same old Jimmy John. Not happy ruining your life, you got to ruin somebody else's too. Why did you come back?"

"None of your fucking business. You got no right to horn in on what I do."

"You feel free about getting money off Grandma though, don't you, so you can drink yourself stinko. Nora doesn't know what she's in for."

"Stay away from us, nosy bitch."

A week later Mary Johnson came by.

"I was passing Jimmy John's cabin. I think he's beating her up. I know it's none of my business but it sounds bad. Maybe you better go down there."

I could hear the screams from the road. I opened the door and saw her lying on the floor. He was beating her with his belt. Her face was swollen and blood was streaming from her nose. I went over and pushed him away and he tried to punch me but he was drunk and missed and fell down. I pulled the belt out of his hand and threw it away. I helped Nora over to the bed and laid her on it and soaked a towel in the water bucket and cleaned the blood off her face. Her eyes were swollen shut. There were swellings and bruises on her arms. Her right hand was torn open between her thumb and forefinger. I ran back and got ointment from you and cleaned and wrapped her hand in a strip of cloth. I sat on the edge of the bed and didn't know what to do. Nora was quiet and still. Jimmy John got to his knees and looked around.

"What's going on?"

"You beat her."

"I was drunk. How is she?"

"She's black and blue. Her hand is torn."

"Shit."

"Is that it? You beat her half to death and you say shit."

"What do you want me to say?"

"You couldn't say it, anyway."

Things didn't get any better. I'd see Nora with a black eye or a swollen jaw. She never said anything. Jimmy John came around for money but you said no because of how he was treating her. He got money, though. I heard he sold Nora to guys in beer parlours in Williams Lake and Kamloops. Nobody in the band would talk to him except for a couple of drinking pals. He came to get money one last time and saw me writing in my book of stories. He was drunk. I was sitting at my desk in the front room. He slumped onto the sofa and laughed.

"Heard about you and your fucking stories. Nothing but shit. Who you kidding? Always the smart one. Grandma's 'my Josie.' Know who you're talking to? John James MacCammon, known as Jimmy John. Know what we are? Niggers of the north. Red niggers. Been to Kamloops? Yeah, you know. Treated like shit. Don't tell me. I know all about it. Want our cunts. Nothing else. So where's your fucking raven in all this? You're part of the bullshit. Peddling a load of old stories like it was some kind of way out. There's no way out."

I put down my pen.

"You couldn't see it if there was."

"Going smart on me, like you always did. I live my own life. I don't need advice from you. Save it for the others."

"Nobody could ever tell you a thing. You never listened, not even to Grandma."

"She never had time for me, only for 'my Josie.'"

"You're blaming her for what you are. What you've always been. Selfish. No time for anybody but you and what you want. Your girlfriends are all like Nora and they put up with it because they're used to being shit on by whites and by our men like you. Grandma taught me to take pride in myself."

"You're known as a hardass bitch."

"By you and your pals, not the others, and if you've come here for money, forget it. She's already told you she won't give you any and why."

"You been talking to her."

"You really are stupid. Don't you know, nobody tells her anything. She makes her own decisions. I've been with her long enough to know her mind."

"Is that why you're fucking around with those stories, to stay close to her?"

"Go away."

"I got you figured. You're set to get everything she's got."

"She hasn't got much. It's who she is and what she stands for that's valuable. You'll never understand. You're your own worst enemy."

"I'm my own best friend."

"I feel sorry for you."

"Feel any way you fucking want because I couldn't care less."

He got up and staggered out, stomping down the stairs. I could hear him laughing as he walked away through the rain. He wasn't wearing a coat or jacket. I realized he had sat there in drenched shirt and pants, water dripping from his face, slick hair plastered to his head.

It was a rainy night a month later when Jimmy John came to the house. It was after ten and I was getting ready for bed. You were sleeping. He shook the front doorknob and hammered on the door until I opened it. He was wearing a coat and hat this time and wasn't drunk.

"You got to come. She's hurt bad."

I put on a coat and followed him to the cabin. The door was open. There was a kerosene lantern on the table near the bed. The flame flickered, throwing shadows along the walls and on the ceiling. Nora was half off the bed, her head inches from the floor, blood trickling from her nose. I felt for a pulse in her wrist and then her neck to make sure. She was dead.

"You beat her to death."

"Didn't know what I was doing."

"How did it happen?"

"I got back from drinking with the guys. She was sitting on the bed crying and I hollered at her to stop it. She wouldn't. I started hitting her and couldn't stop. She started screaming and I went crazy and when she stopped I fell down and passed out. When I woke up I saw her. I didn't mean to do it."

"Keep your excuses to yourself. You're going to help me bury her."

"You helping me?"

"Looks like it. And don't you dare say thanks."

I wrapped Nora's body in the bloody sheets and put a blanket around them. Jimmy John picked her up and slung her over his shoulder. I carried the lantern, a shovel for him and a small spade for me. We took her into the dark forest, rain dripping from the branches. We found a small clearing behind a tangle of branches on a nurse log. We dug into the soggy earth. He wanted to quit after a while but I said to dig deeper, we didn't want a coyote digging her up. I lowered Nora's body into the hole and filled it and threw a pile of brush on top and we left without saying a word.

I took the rest of the bedclothes outside and doused them with kerosene and set fire to them. I wiped the blood off the floor. Jimmy John sat slumped in a chair. I sat on the bare bed frame.

"You've got to get out of here."

"Where'll I go?"

"Far away. Vancouver. I'll go with you, so it'll look like the three of us left together. I'll leave a note for Grandma and pack some stuff. We'll go this morning. Borrow a wagon from one of your pals. Get going."

It was dawn when we set off for Williams Lake. The rain had eased off to a drizzle but the muddy roads slowed us down. We left the wagon and team at a stable in town for his pal to pick up and we hitched a ride to Kamloops. At Kamloops we climbed into a boxcar on a train headed west.

Tired, we fell asleep after the train started. When I woke up I saw a couple of hobos who had joined us at one of the stations along the way. Jimmy John was still sleeping. I nudged him and he woke up and saw the hobos. There was enough daylight coming in between the wooden slats to see them clearly. They were sitting at the opposite end from us and one of them wore a crumpled Stetson with the brim curled up. He grinned at me.

"Penny for your thoughts."

"A penny won't get you a thing."

Jimmy John broke in.

"Fuck off. Don't bother us."

"Wouldn't like to sell her, would you?"

"How much you got?"

"Dollar."

"Let's see it."

"Come on over."

"You come here."

He got up. We stood up. So did the other guy. Nobody moved. Standing up I felt the swaying of the boxcar more. One of the guys took a knife from inside his jacket. It looked like it came from a café. There were blasts from the locomotive whistle as the train slowed down. We were entering a station. Jimmy John went over and slid open the door nearer to us and I followed and we jumped onto the moving ground. We stumbled but kept our feet as the boxcars rolled by.

"You were ready to sell me, like you sold Nora."

"I was stalling. I didn't sell Nora."

"Don't lie. It's too late."

The next freight train took us to Vancouver. We got off in the yards of the CNR station and walked to Main Street. We went north to Cordova and west into skid row. Jimmy John had been there before. I had brought some money, knowing he wouldn't have any. We ate hamburgers at a café and went to a beer parlour to talk about our situation. I only had a few dollars but that figured as part of my plan. I didn't want Jimmy John arrested and tried and sent to prison or hanged. I remembered what white man's justice had done to Fred. Prejudice and mistaken identity. I would wait and see. I suppose I knew all the time what would happen. I knew he'd sold Nora without even thinking about it. But I had to know how long it would take him to get around to selling me. He wouldn't want to return to the Cariboo without another girlfriend, somebody to sell and beat up. He'd need money to live in Vancouver and look around for the next one. I could get him that.

One thing about skid row. Everybody is an outcast. Nobody feels superior enough to look down on anybody else. That makes it dangerous. There aren't any rules. What you got is up for grabs. Jimmy John knew that. We sat with our backs against the wall and he drank and I took a sip of the soapy tasting beer. My craving didn't return. I smiled to myself. Jimmy John tapped his fingers on the table. He'd finished his beer.

"We need a room. How much you got?"

"Few dollars."

"That won't last long. What are we going to do after that?"

"There's war on. Plenty of jobs around now, even for us. Look around. Can you drive?"

"Sure."

"Get a job with a bootlegger."

"We need real money."

"I'm going back in a while. I don't like it here."

"We got here today. You'll love it after a few weeks."

A couple of guys at a nearby table were looking at me over their sudsy beer glasses. Jimmy John noticed.

"You know, Josie, you're good-looking. A lot of guys would like you."

"Really?"

"Yeah, you know."

"I'm not looking for a boyfriend. Not right now. I've got things to do. Maybe later."

"Doesn't have to be a boyfriend. Lots of guys are looking for some fun."

"You mean they're looking for a fuck."

"You don't have to put it that way."

"What way would you put it?"

"You're Grandma's girl, all right."

"She taught me self-respect."

"That won't get you far."

"You think your way will?"

"It's something you should think about. Our money isn't going to last."

"Our money?"

"You going to finish that?"

I pushed my glass towards him. He drank the beer in

three gulps. He'd started working on me quicker than I thought he would. But he was used to it. I'd heard he'd pimped a string of girlfriends. Nora hadn't been the first he'd sold to strangers and strange men. She wouldn't be the last unless, and that's where I came in. The one who would even up the odds. My money ran out after three days. We spent two more nursing a glass of beer inside a beer parlour to stay warm, spending the nights huddled in alleyways under old newspapers. It was December and the weather was getting colder, with the dampness of sea air. Sleet followed cold rain and finally it snowed. Though I knew from the beginning which way it would go, I gave him one more chance. He was one of us. And maybe St. Jerome's had something to do with it. I had a handful of change, enough for a couple of glasses of beer. I showed him.

"I'm going back. You coming?"

"Back there? Listen, Josie. It's getting dark. You want to spend another night in an alley? We'll get sick out here. There's a place on Powell. The Brompton. It's a few blocks away. Bottom of Victoria Drive. Fishermen drink there. They got money. They'll pay big. Do it once, that's all. We'll get a room with the money and talk things over."

Snow was falling in large fluffy flakes. I was tired and hungry. We trudged through the empty streets alongside railway tracks, passing a pier, machine shops and a sugar refinery. The Brompton was on the northeast corner, in front of the tracks. We got a table near the back and my handful of change bought our last two glasses. He looked around, sizing up the few customers. The evening crowd was beginning to come in. A long hour later two guys entered and sat near us. They looked at me. Jimmy John invited them to sit with us. They were Slav fishermen, with broad shoulders and tough faces. They didn't hide their interest.

"You a good-looking girl."

I let Jimmy John do the talking.

"She's no squaw, she's a real princess. Her father's the big chief."

One of them laughed, showing brown horse teeth.

"No papoose?"

"She's a virgin."

"Don't believe you."

"There's a way to find out."

"How much?"

"Five dollars."

"For two of us."

"Ten for both."

"Too much. Give you seven."

"Virgins don't come cheap. When's the last time you had one?"

"She's not white. Get a white one for that much."

"That's the price."

They looked at each other. The guy with the horse teeth shrugged.

"All right."

"You pay for the room upstairs."

"What shit is this?"

"You don't expect her to do it in the snow?"

"Smart guy. Watch out, smart guy."

"You can stay with her all night. How's that?"

"You are a Jew, you know that? All right."

I sat back and smiled.

"I want ten dollars. Each. Twenty dollars. Or you get nothing."

"What the fuck is this? You two playing a game? You making suckers of us. Fucking Indians worse than Jews."

Jimmy John hit the side of my face with the back of his hand.

"I made a deal and you're going to go through with it."

"There's no deal, there never was. It's all in your head."

He grabbed my arm.

"You do what I say."

"Or what? You think I'm another Nora? I saved you, brother. And now I'm giving you up."

He shook me hard, yelling in my face.

"You do what I say."

He looked at them.

"She'll do what I say. Let's get a room."

I shook my head.

"Twenty dollars."

The fisherman looked as if he was laughing. But no sounds came out of his mouth.

"You a real smart guy. We don't like smart guys."

"I'm telling you, the bitch will do it."

The manager came over.

"You're bothering the customers. Take your argument outside."

Jimmy John headed for the rear exit, a few feet away,

dragging me along by the arm. I didn't resist, knew what was coming. They followed us out. It was a blizzard outside. There was a fence between the small space at the back of the hotel and the tracks. It happened by the fence. "Go get a room, I'll bring her in, like I told you." "We got a truck. Do it in there. No half-breed horseshit." "You think I'm going to fall for that? A room or no deal." "Fuck you, you piece of Indian shit." A knife into his neck, blood pouring out and mouth bursting with something between a cry and a moan as his shoes slipped on the snowy asphalt. I knelt down beside him and cried. I cried for Nora and the others and for all of us. At the edge of the Pacific, in my own land, I was in a city of strangers.

There's a sadness that has no bottom. You fall until you don't feel you're falling but floating nowhere. Afterwards I lived with a white man, a friendly stranger. He was the only white man who didn't want to treat me like a mare. He smelled like a pig. I made him take baths to get rid of the smell but it would come back after a couple of days. His body was like an old baby's, with pink rashes and a pot belly. I wouldn't kiss him until he had all his rotten teeth pulled. At night I would look away until he put out the lantern. Sex is like being drunk. You don't see until the morning. It's not a headache then. It's his dirty underwear and bristles and snoring. I could see that white was really lard with bits of rash. Lying beside him as he snored I thought, is this what being better is about, having skin the sun has not seen? Like worms and baby mice. Or is it believing what you are is better because it's you? Do frogs love green and snails grey, bears brown or black and snakes whatever colours they are? Too bad we're not chameleons. Or would we find another way of pretending we're superior? We use uniforms of skin to accept ourselves and do what we want with others. We live in a pale century, the sun has gone out. I don't want to see bad colours. It's like having a pale skin underneath. No matter who I love now, I must hate someone too. To love one kind means to hate all the others.

You said, Grandmother, I was a spirit child. I was one of those who from the beginning can see to the end and the beginning again, to the place where everything always is. You said I would carry the place inside and would know when something was right or wrong. How will I know the wrong? I asked. You will feel your balance is gone, that you are not walking a straight path, you said. It may only be one step but you will know. And each time you will lose something very small, too small sometimes to know but it will be gone like a part of you. If you lose much you will become sick and die inside before your body does. You have chosen the sickness, have decided not to listen to yourself. Your reason for this may be strong. It may convince you for a long time but finally you will be sick. You may live for many years but you have already killed yourself. You must choose, and your choice will save or kill you. Those who can see everything are born to know much. They cannot say, I do not want to know or I want to know only some things. Each thing is every thing. For you, my child, there is one path.

I know now, Grandmother, what you meant. You were telling me that I am apart from others and must live in myself.

They will never know what I see or how I see. I thought once love would change my life. It made my life more mixed up. I couldn't think clearly. But even as a girl I knew some were different. When I asked Ivy George why she had kept going to see a mean drunk she said, "I like his bum." "You said he beats you afterwards. Yet you still go to him." He would take her out to a rusty car abandoned at the edge of town and have her sit on him in the front seat. There was broken glass everywhere and a nest of mice somewhere in the back. They ran over her feet sometimes and squeaked as she was moving up and down on him. She was cut by the glass sometimes and she could feel the slipperiness of the blood running down her legs and between her toes and she cried and tried to get off but he held onto her and said it was better and she was tighter than ever. She went to a doctor and had her legs stitched and bandaged, saying when asked, she used a dull razor blade. When she could walk right again she went back to the car. Why? Her answer—his bum. She was barely fifteen. He was white and married. When he got tired of her his friends shared her. One night she was drunk and two policemen picked her up on the road outside Kamloops and had her in the back seat of a police car. She left for Vancouver a year later, became a prostitute and died at nineteen. Bill Paul saw her there two weeks before she died. She was drunk and sick. He remembered her sitting in a beer parlour with a guy who was being nice to her. She sneered, "You only want to fuck me, white man."

Useless, like a bird with a broken wing. When you come back, where do you go? I saw the sky, at least I tried, but saw nothing. Only days like bright spots before my eyes. The loss is gradual, a slow sickness, and you accept the weakness as charity. Taking you back, going back into something you've never seen or don't remember seeing, maybe something else. Who am I, little egg-tooth Josie pecking her way out into a vastness that gobbles her up. My body is an accident, the result of many accidents, a gathering of elements that will go somewhere else after a while. Getting sick is only a quicker way of wearing out. Goodbye, my personal universe, we've had a great meeting, and now my lungs are rotting away because the colonists are greedy for territory and can't stop reproducing. How many times can you be invaded? This must happen anyway and I am used to defeat. And my personal defeat will be theirs because their land is dying and they will die too. Bacteria can't figure things out, except to make more of themselves and wait until there is a new continent somewhere and a foul wind to carry them. Where does my spirit go? A place beyond imagining, I imagine. I won't give up my spirit, despite science. It's the me of my, the I of mine and I claim nothing for it but the entire everything inside out and outside in. If I've got to go fancyfooted and princessing about interstellar space, I think I should be free of the old mud. Wear a couple of stars for nipples (Milky Way) and a crotchload of sparklers, my midnight blueskin bare as any baby's. Soar for sore, chaste for chased. Josie will pose at the other end of your telescope. You'll have to aim it carefully with your excited hands. See that, and that, never so close before, cold as pack ice. She had a body once, soft and smooth, fluff and fur. Skintight, warm and bouncy and full of play. Those legs saucy, racing against the wind.

But what I want to say is this, that nothing hurts the way you think it will. It's a surprise you crash into, something between you and the world. A fight to keep yourself from becoming somebody different, and then nobody. There are different Josies, each one further and further apart, till I am not me any more. Each is like an old doll I've thrown into a corner. I think, were they me? The one I am now is jealous and thinks I like them too much. No, they are the dead years, the past dressed up in musty worn-out clothes, somebody's playthings once. Life pours out of the holes in them, stares with button eyes, grins a sagging faded grin. I don't have time to patch them up and hold them and say I'm sorry. There'll be another one in the corner and getting dusty. It'll be the last, and I can be happy about that. It's convenient how memories float by and you can lie and watch them and even think you could change them a little bit and sometimes a lot. Not the truth, only the parts bothering you. How fast you understood, how quickly you answered, how you looked when he surprised you and how you controlled yourself in the tight spots. And you don't need to answer to anybody except you. Everybody could use a few changes.

You didn't change much over the years, Grandmother. A step slower, a touch greyer, a little less on your plate. But you stayed you, your eyes staring out at a world wanting to be rid of us. I remember the last time. At dinner you got up without eating and came to my end of the table and placed your hand on mine. Your lips moved and I saw you shape the words, "my Josie." You walked into your bedroom and shut the door behind you. I sat at the table until morning and went to see you. You were lying on your bed, your arms at your sides and your eyes closed. I knew. I went to see Mary Johnson and we prepared everything. Word spread fast and people came from all the bands to pay their respects. You were known as the Proud One, the one who could never be outstared by the strangers. I heard many stories about you as a girl and young woman. Hiding in the hunting grounds like Rachel and me, you killed deer. You made a dugout canoe to go fishing. You made a pet of a wild dog. You fought a bear and killed it by driving a knife through its eyes. Of the men who wanted you, you picked the strongest, the best hunter and trapper. You and he were the ones who built Ed George's cabin. You told his father about the cabin and said Ed George could hide there. You were the one who filled those jars with healing herbs and poisonous plants. No wonder he held you in such awe.

Jack Drew told a story to the rest of us seated in the front room that day.

"She was a fighter. When they came to take her daughter to school the first time, she hid her under the house, behind the front steps. But the Indian agent, the one before Browner, sniffed around and got down on his hands and knees and spotted her. Ruth got a hoe and started to beat him over the head with it. The Mountie grabbed her and the agent was ready to hit her. But some of us were standing around and we started hollering and going for guns and shovels. 'You've got a war on your hands if you touch that woman,' somebody yelled. The Mountie let her go and she spit at the agent. 'We should've killed you bastards when you first came,' she said. 'You're lucky you're a woman,' the agent said. 'When has that ever stopped you rapists?' she answered him. But they took her daughter and she had to bear it. We've all had to over the years. She was speaking for us that day, as if our nation was speaking through her. Never be another like her."

[There is a break in the manuscript at this point. The bottom half of the sheet on which the above paragraph is written is blank. On the remaining sheets, undoubtedly written later, Josie's handwriting is fainter, some letters and occasionally whole words suggested by a quick stroke or mark. Words, and sometimes whole phrases, are almost indecipherable. I spent many hours working on these phantoms. In the case of words and phrases that couldn't be made out with any degree of certainty, I have put my best guess in brackets. The deterioration was quite likely the result of her illness. It must have been an effort of will to write anything at the end.]

A man with a briefcase came from Vancouver and knocked on your door, Grandmother. Miss Littletree? I'm David Lawrence, a lawyer. Sam McLendon sent me to speak with you. May I come in? We sat in the front room and he told me. Sam wants you to be admitted to the sanatorium near Kamloops. I've seen Dr. Moxon, head of the sanatorium, and he's agreed to an initial year. I understand Braeburn is the most advanced treatment centre for tuberculosis in the province. Speaking personally, I'd like to say something. I'm two years out of law school and the low man in my firm. But my time costs money. Sam's paying a lot to send me here. He's obviously worried about you.

So it was done before I was told. I could have said no. They couldn't have forced me. I thought about how many of our people in my condition would never get the chance to get into places like that. Why should I be privileged? But if I was the first, maybe I wouldn't be the last. We're stuck with this society. We had to start somewhere. If it was with me, it was worth a try. I knew what I would be facing but by that time I wasn't looking to be cured.

Quite a fuss before you arrived, Josie. Dr. Moxon was straddling the fence, as usual. It's amazing he doesn't get a picket up his behind. Nursing and administrative staff were all assembled in the conference room. It was crowded, everybody standing. He stood at the front fiddling with his glasses and touching that big mole on the side of his face, next to his nose. You've never heard his voice. If a crab could speak, it would sound like him. I've bent the rules. Natives aren't usually admitted to Braeburn, and it's against my better judgement, but I've agreed to accept one as a patient here. This will be the first and may well be the last time. I've taken into consideration that she's a woman and the application was made by a white man who has employed a lawyer as his agent. We'll look on this as a trial period. And this will be a trial for us as well. As soon as he finished some objected, saying this would establish a precedent and we'd be flooded with native patients. But Helen—she's matron here—and I spoke up for you. Some of the other patients aren't too happy. News travels fast in this place. Most of the complainers are women. I wouldn't worry about them. Some of us don't care much for them. I've heard that Moxon's taken money for your care from the man who wanted you in here. You're a Status Indian. He shouldn't take any money for your care, or he should've applied to the government to pay for you, but I guess he didn't want to lose the money if the government said no to you being here, and that would be a possibility, considering the government's attitude towards Indians. He didn't mention that to the staff, letting us believe it was his good nature that persuaded him to accept you. He's a fraud and a hypocrite. What else would you expect at Braeburn?

We've got everything to help. Rest and fresh air, dry and warm. And all the medicines. The older stuff, streptomycin and para-aminosalicylic acid—PAS—and the latest, isoniazid—INH—so Braeburn is right up to date. And besides the antimicrobial stuff, I should mention the pneumothorax procedure. Artificial pneumothorax as well, first used here. You're in the right place, if you can forget the head and a lot of the patients.

I scribble and the past comes back. This pen is a wand conjuring memories. It almost moves by itself. I can hardly see what it writes and don't care, anyway. Don't even know who left it in the drawer of the night table, and the paper and the bottles of ink. Fate. A likely story. Nobody's said anything yet, haven't even asked. Amazed the heathen writes, let alone English. Expected smoke signals, afraid I'll use the blankets and torch the place. Expected to be loco, part of being uncivilized. Refuses teatime, there's your proof. Your heathen belong in a corral, I can hear them muttering. Not fit to be among the righteous white. A wild looking thing, stares when she's able to stop coughing and spitting bloody phlegm, hacking the wee hours to pieces. Bet she's known lots of men, would want to strip naked and engage the men here if we weren't around to watch. She's not civil enough to have a conversation with, that's for sure. Today you're expected to accept everybody, regardless. Must be hard on the staff. In the past they would have refused to treat her. We know who's spreading these diseases around, living in abominable conditions. The only one who has anything to do with that thing is Miss Menzies. She does fuss over her, even though she is a nurse. Have you noticed how dark her hair is? Really black, isn't it? I noticed that right away when I first came here. I thought she was French or Eye-talian. Not with a name like Menzies. That's Scottish. Scots can have black hair. I have a distant cousin with black hair. I think this one could be a half-breed. I'll bet that's why she pays so much attention to her. It takes one to like one, I suppose. And ask yourself this? Why do they get along so good? Changes her pillow all the time. Always asking her how she is. Plain as the nose on your face. Half-breed. Wonder how she got to be a nurse? Maybe she's not a nurse. Maybe she's a nurse's aide. I notice Matron Fairfax is cool to that other one. Polite and cool. She is a nurse. It's her job. Isn't she beautiful? Isn't she? When she puts those blue eyes on you you'd think you were looking at a real angel. And such a sweet face. Such beautiful hair. Like pale honey. She must get a permanent. Not like, you know. I'll bet she doesn't even comb that frizzy mop of hers. Sometimes I think she's a witch. I wouldn't doubt it. You can't change them. All they want to do is get pie-eyed and have [scads] of little papooses. We had a grocery store, Earl and me. They'd stagger in and start picking at stuff and eating it. Right in the store. Free as you please. The RCMP said there was nothing we could do about it but keep things out of their reach. We had to put all the fruit and candy on the counter. I suppose they thought we were in business for our health. And you know they don't work. Lie around filthy on those reserves and live off government money. Know what the sergeant told me? There's a cliff outside of Kamloops, near the river, and every Monday one of the junior officers has to go to the bottom and collect the bodies. They get pie-eyed and jump off every weekend. That's nothing, listen to this. I heard there was a swing bridge somewhere and it opened to let a boat through and a bunch of cars were waiting for it to close. A carload of them pulled out of the lineup and went straight down the oncoming lane and off into the river. Every last one of them drowned. They probably thought it was a shortcut to The Happy Hunting Ground. My husband used to say, don't mix alcohol and Indians or you'll get mixed-up Indians. They love getting drunk and fooling around. That one's had the Devil up her skirts. She's collected a few scalps. You can see it in her face. They have that look. You know. I know.

I remember this place back in the Thirties, when my mother and I used to come out to visit my father. He was a war veteran and had gotten TB over there. Most patients were soldiers. There were more than 300 of them. Elizabeth Mannering was the matron. I can still see her in that spotless white uniform, with her cap high up on her upswept hair and always tilted forward like a little sailboat. She would stop by and talk to us. She told us the sanatorium was built near Kamloops because of the dry climate and fresh air. Patients needed to be outdoors as much as possible to take advantage of that dry fresh air. City air was too polluted and most other places were too wet. She told us about the diet of the patients, why eggs and milk and butter were important. Of course, now there's drugs. She headed a contingent of volunteer nurses that went to France when the War started. And she won medals. She didn't tell us that, one of the nurses did. The Mons Star, the Victory Medal, and the Royal Red Cross Medal. She said Matron was most proud of the Royal Red Cross Medal. It was the oldest, given to military nurses for exceptional services. Florence Nightingale was first to receive it. I asked if I could see it. The next time we came up the nurse showed us. It was in a small case on purple velvet, a gold cross with flared arms forming a square and enamelled in red. In the centre was a gold medallion with an outline of the old king's head. On the top arm was inscribed "Faith," and on the left and right arms "Hope" and "Charity," and on the bottom arm "1883." Elizabeth

Mannering retired in the Forties or the early Fifties. I was going to be a nurse but I got married instead. It's serving in another way though, isn't it?

I remember when the King and Queen came through in '39. Stopped right here in Kamloops. That was a red-letter day. May 20—something. The whole town was at the railway station. Including a bunch from City Hall. The family went, the neighbours. I was standing beside my mother. It was about 9:30 in the evening. The station lights were blazing. We could see the train approaching and people started waving flags. My mother had a Union Jack. She'd come over in 1910. The Royal Hudson came in slowly, a strip of Tuscan red with cream numbers on the side and the Royal coat of arms in front. The headlight was on, the bell was ringing. As it came to a stop the cheering began and the conductor got off the parlour car at the end. They came out, standing under the awning, and the cheering got louder. The flags looked like a field of flowers in a high wind. The mayor was there with his wife, standing on the platform. They stepped down, the Queen helped by a railway official. Later I went and stood in the same place she had stood. The mayor made a speech and handed them something and they climbed back up. The whole thing was over in fifteen minutes. Had to be on their way to Vancouver. As the train pulled out, everybody waving goodbye, they waved back. Such an elegant wave, like the neck of a dying swan. You'd expect that of them, wouldn't you?

Near the end, as the train was leaving the station, we could hear this voice behind us. He wasn't talking to anybody but he knew people could hear.

"What's the holdup? Who's the dumpy broad and the goof? And that fat-faced clown? The circus come to town? I got to get across the tracks, be on my way."

It was a hobo a few feet away. He was wearing a cheap coat and carrying a small cardboard suitcase that bulged. He didn't have a beard but wasn't close-shaven like a decent man. My mother waved her flag in his face.

"You shut your mouth, you dirty bum. You're talking about our king and queen."

"Is that what they're supposed to be? Camelot, huh? Arthur and Guinevere. Who's Lancelot? That fat-faced politician?"

"Show respect for your betters."

"They're not my betters. Go back to the slum you came from."

"If I was a man, I'd teach you a lesson. I bet you were a shirker, didn't serve your country."

"I was in the trenches. Wallace Andrew Begg, serving King and country. All present and accounted for. I saw men gassed, puking their lungs out and gasping for air. I saw them blown apart. You couldn't find a chunk of them larger than a fifty-cent piece. I saw them machine-gunned and hanging on barbed wire, bleeding to death. I heard them screaming in pain in no man's land. I saw a man fall off a duckboard and drown in mud, begging a pal for a bullet in the brain as he went under. I've seen enough for a thousand nightmares. That's the price of surviving."

"You must have been wounded in the head."

"Don't you know what's behind this? There's going to

be a war. They're here to review the troops. Get you colonials all hopped up. Your jackass of a prime minister is hoping you fall for it, take the heat off him."

"You're a traitor, that's what you are."

"I stopped trying to be British years ago. I don't kiss Royal ass, like most of my fellow citizens. What's the betting those two don't shake a hand that's not British, except a couple of politicians in Quebec and maybe a savage out west. Don't worry, they use a hanky afterwards in the limo."

You couldn't get through to him. He was obviously crazy. A Mountie had been standing nearby. I spoke with him.

"That man's a vagrant. He should be arrested."

He came and spoke to the man.

"Where are you going, sir?"

"Vancouver. Once I get across the tracks and hop a freight. There's a jungle close by. If I can't make a freight, I'll spend the night there and be gone tomorrow."

"See that you are, sir."

"Aren't you going to arrest him, officer?"

"He'll be out of town by tomorrow."

That was misplaced leniency, if you ask me. People like that never learn, do they? He'd probably spent lots of nights behind bars at public expense. A night in jail wouldn't have taught him to curb his tongue in front of decent people.

Did I tell you my mother had collected stuff about the Royal family for decades? Started when she was a girl in England. She had magazines commemorating jubilees. Weddings, too. Anything to do with the monarchy, she had pictures of it. After she died we took it all to the library. The man at the desk wasn't interested. He said it had to do with a foreign country. Can you believe it? I went and saw the librarian, a friend of mine, Violet Junkin. Nice woman, soft-spoken, like all librarians are. You have to be quiet in a library because they're doing all that reading. She never got married. Married to books, I guess. Somebody has to look after that stuff or else we wouldn't have a history. We came out of her office and I gave the man at the desk a dirty look. Violet crouched down and went through the boxes.

"It's archival material, quite extensive. We'll take it."

I sneered at that man and thanked Violet. Imagine saying England was a foreign country? Beyond belief. He didn't look English, more like some kind of European. They're letting in anything now.

Hi. Haven't seen you around before. I'll empty this wastebasket and you can move your wheelchair back. At least you don't have to worry about wet floors when I do the mopping. I'm head custodian here. Art Kuby. Care for a stick of Juicy Fruit? Don't know what you're missing. I always carry a pack. Keep spares in my locker. I'm a two-stick man. Three packs a day. Sometimes four. Got me so I could get off cigarettes. Spend as much now on gum as I did on smokes. Better for you, though. Still got yellow fingers from the nicotine. Takes a while, I guess. The craving's gone, though. You know, you're the prettiest one here. Sure are. I'm sharp-eyed when it comes to women's looks. Say, listen, I'll bet you're tired of being cooped up. You need a change. Sitting out on a balcony and in a garden has got to be boring. You look like you could use some fun. I got a Caddy. Got it brand new. Can't even feel the road, it rides so soft, like you're on a cloud. Be a treat for you. There's ways of getting out if you want. Nobody has to know. Back in no time. Nobody know you're gone. Even the goddam snoops. I know all the best places around here. Pop the chair in the back seat. Put you up in front. Put some cold ones in the ice chest I got. Nothing beats a spin, especially after this place. I only work here and I can't wait till quitting time. The nurses are always bitching about wet floors. I can't help it if they don't watch where they walk. They want the areas I mop roped off, then they want to get through. I'm supposed to read their minds all the goddam time. Maybe a fall on their asses would do them some good. I only got one helper and he's got the shakes from booze most times and stays in the boiler room sleeping it off, goddam useless. And I can't get more help because of the goddam budget. The floor wax isn't beeswax. The closest a bee ever got to it was fly over it. It's some kind of cheap petroleum shit. No shine, I keep hearing. It's impossible to shine a floor with this stuff, I tell them. My dust mops are worn down to the wood and anybody can hear the clacking they make when they hit something and how they scrape against hardwood. Try to sweep, that's a goddam laugh. And I'm supposed to fix anything that's broken. Windows, doors, locks, radiators, furniture. They think I can turn into any kind of tradesman. Can't get a raise, can't take my holidays during the summer.

Hello, dear. Have you accepted the Lord? Jesus loves you, you know. Open your heart and accept His love. If you do that, you experience the joy all sinners do when they have accepted their Saviour. It's as easy as saying, come into my heart, Jesus. Fill me with your love, that I may walk with the righteous and may know true peace. Leave the ways of wickedness. Repent of your sins. The love of the Almighty is all-forgiving. Do not be afraid of His love. It is a bright light shining on the evil blackness of sins. You look troubled, dear. I've seen that look on the faces of so many. Heavens above, I certainly have. And mercy sakes, it's disappeared on repentance. Bless my soul, it has. I've been so moved I wanted to shout out, [heave me into the Red Sea, Atlantic Ocean]. Only last week at the tabernacle I saw a woman like you who unburdened herself of sin and began crying and screaming with joy. She ran up and down the aisles flinging her arms here and there and in her ecstasy gave a couple of our slower members an awful black eye and a bloody nose and stepped on the toes of some others. We had to grab her and hold her down before she hurt herself or someone else bad or burst a blood vessel. I'm going to leave this with you. Study the parable and it'll point the way. Next time we'll have a nice long chat about it. I'll answer your questions and we'll pray together.

Hi. Art (practising the low art of getting her into bed by impressing her with chewing gum). I got some Chiclets here. Hard candy coating. And Dentyne. Use both myself sometimes. Don't know what you're missing. Think about that trip? Do you good. Get out, see the country. Did I say my Caddy was a convertible? Great in weather like this. Put the top down. Wind in your hair. Blow away the cobwebs. Pack a couple of sandwiches. Have a picnic. Sound good? Maybe I could bring you some Life Savers. Eat them myself sometimes. Orange and cherry flavours. I like to put my tongue into the hole and suck. Melts all around. Say, look. Getting kind of late. It's cold out here. I could wheel you in, take you down to the custodian's room. That's where I keep my Juicy Fruit. A few cold ones too. Against the rules. But what they don't know—. Nobody ever goes down there. It's private. Nice and warm. Got a cot. My helper's always sleeping it off in the boiler room, so don't worry about him. Be a change for you. Chew on a stick. Get you in the mood. All right, I'm coming. Goddam bitches again (sotto voce—where did that come from?). Always complaining about something. Won't leave a guy alone. I got a bum finger too. Stuck it in a knothole, fixing splinters in a floor. Try to get first aid around here. "It's swollen, Mr. Kuby. It'll go down." I'll get lockjaw. Won't be able to chew. Or maybe gangrene will set in. That'd be great. They'll lop off my hand. They'll fire me, say it was my fault. Compensation Board will back them up. Won't get a pension. I'll be selling pencils on the street. I got to go.

He said so many things. Kittens played in my stomach. I thought maybe there is a white man who understands. Maybe he means it. I had my friend, the pink man. Trying to please and never understanding me. This one was different. Thin and serious. Looked into my eyes. Long hands, thin fingers. He didn't like me too much. That got me. I liked him. I don't like to think so now. He seemed to talk for me, even though the words were strange. The others used those words too but they sounded different coming from his mouth. His voice was different. Quick, soft and knowing. As if the sounds were so many parts of a machine and he was the man who could put them all together and make sense of them. It all sounds strange now. Downtrodden masses, fat capitalists, sweated labor, oppressed workers, dialectical materialism, dictatorship of the proletariat, the Politburo, the Comintern—the Third International. I listened, pretending I was interested. Watching his eyes watching mine. He was trying to impress me, not the way he tried to impress the others. He was careful. He knew I was smarter than them. And a woman. I hated his kind of revolutionary talk. He knew that. So he talked one way to the rest and another to me. Not changing his ideas or opinions but pretending they were mine already and he was saying what I would say if I thought about them. He probably enjoyed thinking he was outwitting poor little Josie, a sucker for any kind of talk about solving Indian problems. Forget the Comintern. She wants something more personal to bring out the Pocahontas in her. A flame-skinned Joan of Arc, Saint Joan of the aboriginals. Political, not religious. I can hear him, the soft excited voice. The coming worldwide revolt of the dark underraces, who will throw out the usurpers wherever they are found and restore the true life of the soul, the ancient heritage of the primitive peoples and threatened with extinction everywhere by the ravages of a perverted industrialism-cum-colonialism. I can remember him getting excited on those mornings, those Saturdays and Sundays when he used to come by before the others showed up, leaning forward on the couch and holding his cup between his hands to warm them, turning it in his palms, his fingers spread out in a web and the striped brown pants of his suit too short when he was sitting down and showing thin hairy legs below the frayed cuffs. His knees bulged out, a pair of knobs.

"I take a broad view of the struggle. It's not only the workingman and workingwoman, it's the oppressed peoples around the world. Capitalism is an outmoded system. What will replace it will be more sensitive to native societies corrupted by capitalism and its lackeys. They can't be denied their true historical individuality. That's repeating the mistakes of the past. We've got to be flexible enough to accommodate—within true socialist principles—the ancient tribes and customs. Otherwise, proletarian government will be an oppressor too. We can talk about the workers' struggle, Sam. What's that to Josie? She's got her own fight. We can't blame her for telling us off for spouting socialist principles. Indians have been oppressed since the arrival of the fur traders. Supplying beaver pelts for hats for fashionable bourgeois. Trading posts were capitalist outposts peddling religion and stealing native goods and land and using their women in return for cheap trinkets and bad whisky. Early European capitalists, that's what they really were, exploiting colonial subjects. Imperialist hirelings of aristocratic masters."

"I suppose Neanderthal man was a capitalist when he conked a fellow Neanderthal on the head and took his joint of meat and dragged off his woman."

"All right, Sam, I'm cutting history out of the whole

cloth. But the roots are there. Factor, factories. Industry, industrial. Share, shares. Stock, stocks. Dialectical materialism on the march to socialism."

"You forgot prophet, profit. Nothing surprises about the human animal. But don't go hog wild. There's more to it than working stiffs punching a time clock."

"The trouble with you is you won't stand shoulder to shoulder with your fellow workers."

"I don't believe in anything except the sunrise. Somebody telling me in a bunch of doubletalk he's got history boiled down to making out your own paycheque couldn't convince me of anything except his arrogance."

"You're a real cynic."

"The best way to be until the truth comes along, if it ever does."

Sometimes afterwards we'd be alone for a while and he'd grin, meaning that's Sam. I'd grin, not knowing what to say. It went on like that, grins and looks that meant you can't do anything about Sam, and then they meant something else, or maybe they always did. At those times he'd talk to me in a softer voice, asking me questions about my life. I knew he was getting closer and sometimes I wanted him to and other times I didn't know what I wanted. I thought his ideas and feelings were the same thing, that he liked me in two ways and they were really one. Me as a woman and me as a victim of oppression. I knew his idea of oppression wasn't as real as mine. He talked it but I'd felt it. But I liked him trying to please me and wanted to believe together we could do something. When the two of us were alone he said I should become an activist so I could do something about Indian problems. He said we could work together, his know-how and my passionate feelings. I asked how he knew I was passionate. He said my hair was the banner of my soul. Once he came and sat beside me on the bed and held my hand and said he loved me and wanted to show his love. I already saw it in his pants. After so much serious talking in that soft voice he looked ridiculous. I laughed. He grabbed my wrist, tried to kiss me. I let him, turning my cheek. My wrist hurt, so I pulled it out of his hand. He pushed me back onto the bed and pulled up my skirt but I rolled away, another Indian giver, tricky Josie. He stood up, tried to look dignified, his pants flat again. I had stopped laughing.

"He'll be back soon."

"He went up the tracks."

"He's gone to get some water. He told me before you came."

"Why didn't you tell me?"

"Didn't know you were going to jump me."

"I'm leaving."

"You knocked over Sam's table. Give me a hand to put things back before he gets here."

"I'm going."

"Give me a hand. I can hear him crossing the tracks."

"You clean up. I'll keep him outside."

"Is that all you're good for, talking?"

"Give me a chance. I'll show you something else I'm good at."

"What's that, bragging?"

"Wait and see."

"I've seen already. You're no surprise."

Make Josie do the cleaning. Why didn't that warn me? Sam returned and didn't ask why he'd gone before the others had showed up. None of the later arrivals asked for him. That was a clue, too.

Hi. Brought you some breath mints. Says they sweeten your breath. Not that your breath smells or anything. You didn't want any of that other stuff. You wouldn't go for bubble gum. That stuff's for kids. So I thought these would be all right. Even if your breath don't stink, they're good. I don't need them because my breath always smells of Juicy Fruit. Excuse me a second. I got to get rid of this wad. I never throw them on the floor like some do, or stick them on chairs and things. You get careful about messes when you have to clean them up. Your mess is my mess. I save the wrappers and put my wads in them. Put them in my pocket. At the end of the day I empty all my pockets into the trash bin. That way everything's neat. Excuse me while I fill up again. Like I told you, I'm a two-stick man. Guess you're wondering why I don't get tired of the same flavour. Every few months I switch to something else for a week. Dentyne and Doublemint are good for a change. But all they do is get me so I'm ready for Juicy Fruit again. There was a guy who used to work here who always had a big bunch of bubble gum in his mouth. Could blow a bubble bigger than his head. He'd seal it with his tongue and stick it somewhere flat. Looked like a pink balloon. Took a while for it to shrink. That's pretty much showing off, I think. There's something wrong when a grown-up man does that kind of thing. Especially on the job. I heard his whole family was off. His sister was put away. One of the nurses told me. Told me not to tell anybody. Who would I tell? You're the first one, and he's gone, anyway. He's a night watchman at a porno warehouse. Said he could get me all the safes I want. Any colour. Some have little rubber knobs on them, for when a woman isn't tight any more or a guy is kind of small. You don't mind me talking this way? Some women would, the stuck-up kind. They got here a special way. The old man and old lady did it by long distance messenger. No sweat, no fun. There's a few of them in this place. I feel like telling them, what's that thing between your legs for, a stocking stuffer? Keep your millions in there, do you? You'd think I had the plague the way they treat me. A lot of them aren't really sick. Alkies taking a rest cure. When your job is on the line, you keep your mouth shut. But you still see what's going on and they can't hide everything. They never wanted you here. I heard some of the staff. Those broads taking the rest cure are against you too. Goddam phonies. Praying Mary is all right. Don't let her get on your nerves. She's been coming around since before I started, trying to get everybody to Heaven. I got stacks of those religious pamphlets she hands out. I told her she was wasting her time with me. I'm a born sinner. She held up her Bible. No one is lost, no one who will believe, she said. Your phonies put on the religious act when she shows up, stop knifing each other and pray. They don't read the stuff she hands out. And they make fun of her being hard of hearing. They look at each other every time she says,

"What did you say, dear?" She's not out the door before they're saying how dowdy she looks and that she's been wearing the same clothes for years. She's a joke to them and she doesn't know it. I got to go, got work to do. My assistant got the job because his uncle's in politics. I can't get rid of the bastard. Uncle owns a chain of drugstores. He's on the board here. Nice. Supplies drugs and medical equipment. So I got no chance. Try the mints, they're good. Don't use the stuff myself.

He never tried that again. Those times we were alone he'd go on about working together on native problems. I liked him for that. I hadn't rejected him, anyway. But I didn't want him too soon. I enjoyed listening to him. I didn't think he'd say all that only to impress me. I wanted to believe it wasn't hopeless for us to do something. A partnership. That's how he put it. Me and him against the entrenched interests. Fighting prejudice and leading the progressive forces of mankind to victory. An uphill fight, banners flying. No mercy for the enemy, the bloated plutocrats. Brothers and sisters of the working class, lift yourself out of ignorance and exploitation, break your chains and march with us. Your choice is clear. Wage slavery or freedom, bigotry or racial equality. It seems impossible to me now that I listened so hopefully, but on those weekend mornings in the shack his words did sound thrilling. To me that whole time is not real any more. It's a dream that hurts now because it makes fun of the old feelings. It makes the years seem empty.

He said to me one day, "Josie, how attached are you to Sam?"

"I've been with him for two years."

"Do you want to stay with him?"

"I don't know. I never thought about it."

"Would you leave with me?"

"Why?"

"I already told you. I love you."

"Yeah. You showed it."

"That was wrong. I'm talking about the two of us as equal partners doing something about the way those like you are being treated, putting an end to it by organizing, establishing liaisons between the unions and the reserves to effect political change."

"You don't understand us. We're many nations, each with its own traditions and language, like the nations of Europe. We're smaller, that's all. Each nation is made up of many bands, and each band has its own council, its elders. Bands don't get involved in politics. Each band and nation lives by its own ways, some members working and living off reserve, but we don't pay attention to anything unless it affects us. The bands won't listen to your kind of talk about overthrowing capitalism. What's that got to do with them?"

"Your traditional ways have been destroyed by government regulations and restrictions. You're wards of the government, on relief. That's why I need you. I could train you so you could go to them and explain the significance of our program. The coming collapse will involve them whether they like it or not. You could explain why. You could make them one nation."

"That's squawk talk from Europe. It's different with us. The land is our home. We move over it the way you walk through the rooms of a house. We don't destroy it and call it civilization. We don't crowd it and call it government. We have a government and it's our treaty with the land."

"What about our treaty?"

I had to grin. The revolutionist being personal. I still liked him, though he was trying to get around me. And I was in a frisky mood.

"I haven't broken it."

He came and sat beside me on the bed but this time he only talked. This was more exciting to me than if he'd tried anything. His voice was calm too. This was new coming from a man.

"Don't deny your heritage and your feelings."

"What do you know about my feelings?"

"I know you like me. Or you'd have ignored me."

"Maybe I'm bored here or maybe I like to hear you talk."

"That's another way of saying you like me."

"Don't kid me. You think I'm an untamed woman who'll give anyone a good time. Then so long. You think because I live down here in these shacks I'm an easy lay. A few big words and I'm yours."

"Don't cheapen yourself. I believe in you. Whether you like me or not. I want to bring out and nurture the special gift you have for helping others. Because I know you have it. You've been kept down by a racist society. All I want to do is give you a chance. You owe it to others. They're waiting for your leadership."

He put his hand on mine and it felt softly warm and so did I. Little things got busy inside of me. They tickled and burned and bubbled and yearned and there was something else too. Trickier, deeper. A whirlpool. I was afraid of it. It meant no more kidding, ever, or until the end of everything with this man who sold himself through his political words. I slid my hand from underneath his and felt free as my fingers slipped away one by one and returned to me. I've never understood love or the something it pretends to be. I've tried both the fleshy and emotional kinds and what's in between, and love somehow disappears, goes somewhere when nobody's looking. There's no kind with any guarantee, no matter who's doing the promising. I'd given up, almost, and didn't want to believe a revolutionary who'd become all hearts and flowers.

"Don't touch me. Not yet. I'll go with you but I'll say when. You'll have to give me some time."

He got up and left without saying anything. I couldn't read his face. He was good at hiding feelings. I was looking with clouded eyes.

Hey, a special present. It's Christmas, I'm splurging. A box of Ganong's. Now these are chocolates. I buy the best. I got them gift-wrapped at the store. A bow and everything. Now you got to like these, right? I've never known a woman to say no to chocolates. Eat them myself sometimes. I had to try these. Had a couple. Hope you don't mind. I put the bow and ribbon back. Eat a Ganong's and you won't be able to stop yourself. I see you had visitors for Christmas. A whole slew of them. Brought you lots of stuff. Thanks for sending that cake down to me. Going to take me a while to finish it off. I can taste the bit of dark rum. That won't bother me. Not that I'm a boozer. A nip of the hard stuff during the holidays and only beer the rest of the year. I count the bottles. Two is my limit. I used to drink a lot more. Fell down drunk a few times—out cold don't know how long. No way to live. Wake up in the middle of the day with the shakes and the sun in your face. Mouth full of fur. Some broad passed out beside you. Room stinking of both of you. She wants more money. Afterwards you're by yourself. Wondering if you picked up some disease. I did once. Went to the doctor. Gave me something. It cleared up. I know you should wear a safe if she's a chippie, and some of this loose stuff on the fly is chancy. But a guy likes to ride bareback. Catch a loose caboose and the last thing you're thinking of is wrapping it in sheep's gut, or whatever that crap is. Like stuffing and unpeeling a wiener. You think sex is good sense? Not to me. You've got to have it, and after you've had it you're sick of it for a while. I was almost married once. Engaged for two years. By that time I was fed up with her playing around with my balls all the time. With those moods of hers. Yes, no, yes, no. Need it now. Don't feel like it. You did it before when I wanted to. I don't now. Why not? I don't, that's all. I'd fish around and find the reason was something else. Sometimes there wasn't any reason I could find. Imagine being married to her? Don't know what I was thinking of. I've bagged some beaver in my time. Could hang the pelts and fill a wall. They were all chippies. Every one of them. I wasn't first and wouldn't be the last. Didn't bother me much at the time. Bothers me a bit now. Seems a waste. Like some kind of exercise, but you're supposed to feel tired out after from conquering the world. I didn't conquer anything. Bent a lot of dirty mattresses. The broads took off. Sometimes I thought if I could get a nice one. But there wasn't a nice one for me. I'll tell you something. Guys are afraid of women. What you got between your legs is a mystery to them. So they make a big deal out of screwing you. Most guys aren't necessary. All women need are a few brainy ones for the fathers of their kids. The rest of us are donkeys, limp dicks or walking hard-ons trying to be important. Donkeys do the pick and shovel work, limp dicks are stuck in offices and hard-ons become politicians. Who builds statues to guys and puts up monuments to them? Guys. No woman thinks that much of a guy, he's what you call a provider. She's thinking of her kids. She doesn't care what size dick he's got as long as he knows how to use it. Guys run around measuring their dicks and worrying, boasting about how many broads they've screwed, and they lie like crazy about it. A woman doesn't care about numbers, she's looking for a suitable guy. What about your harems? All those women for one lousy dick. A lot of unsatisfied women. Should be the other way around. I think women let guys get away with that kind of stuff because guys would use their muscle to push them around anyway, so why fight it? And they figure, as long as they get a kid out of it let the rooster crow. Troubles in the world. Guys trying to make themselves important. Guys are still hunting meat, only it's themselves. Armies standing at attention like a lot of stiff pricks. All those artillery pieces and gun barrels sticking up in the air. No woman wastes her time reviewing troops unless she has to. No thrill for her. Tries to keep from yawning. A woman fights little wars, family stuff, protecting her kids, getting food, changing husbands. Sometimes it's bitch versus bitch. Bombs don't fall, no rapes. A woman is sensible compared to most guys because she's got the mystery inside like a secret. A guy never makes a woman, she makes a guy a copy of himself. I think nature gave him something to do so she'd have somebody there to protect her baby. The biggest liars are men. I don't say best, I say biggest. Comes natural to them. Don't have any other way to parade in front of a woman, who's trying to see over the highest pile of bullshit in the whole damn universe. That's where sex comes in. Hurries things along and no thinking. Makes everything easy as pie à la mode.

He didn't ask me again. He came every weekend as usual, always before the others, and sat on the couch. When I was alone with him he didn't ever hint about me leaving with him. He never came and sat on the bed. He talked about the wartime news with us. When alone with me he talked about the problems of Indians in this country, and of native peoples everywhere and how to help them. When the others showed up he would stay long enough to show them how smart he was. Always the first to go, he would leave the lesser lights to argue among themselves. That class conflict stuff was boring. I'd heard so much of it. I'd leave the shack and wander up the beach, dig for clams or talk to anyone interesting. A lot of kids played there when they weren't in school. I liked playing with them. I used to walk barefoot. Once I cut my foot on a barnacle and a boy helped me back to the shack. He was a little guy and was so serious about my injury. I had to stoop down so I could lean on his shoulder. I gave him some cookies. He looked sad as he walked out. I wanted to go after him and say, what's wrong? And I realized I was the one who was sad. I sat on the bed and let my foot dangle over the edge and bleed as a roomful of men argued about the class struggle. Finally somebody noticed and they all got concerned about me. I hobbled over to the stove, heated some water and cleaned and dressed the cut with cloth torn from an old shirt I'd washed the day before. They went back to what really interested them. I'd interrupted serious work. They were busy solving the problems of the world on weak tea and stale crusts of bread.

It was crowded on weekends. They sat on the couch and a couple of old chairs and on orange crates. I sat on the bed. That was my place right from the beginning. Most came in the afternoon and stayed till ten during the summer. When the weather was bad during the winter hardly anybody showed up. There were a couple of dozen visitors over the years but I remember the regulars. The one always eating sunflower seeds would sneak peeks at me, at my breasts and up my dress when I wore one. His hands reminded me of a rabbit's front paws, with their quick nervous fingers. When I caught him staring he'd blink and look away. I wore a low-cut silk blouse once and I thought he was going to have a fit. He swallowed a seed without cracking the shell and gagged. After that I went back to sweaters. The old Scotsman used to kid me. The Englishman was stiff. Checkers was always sociable. The other union organizer didn't say much to me. He was busy spouting. There was one who always brought a book with him. He'd stop reading to get into the conversation. They would fill a mug from a big brown teapot and pass around a package of cookies. I never served and they didn't ask me. I guess it was my pride and their talk about equality. I would leave in the afternoon if the weather wasn't too bad and get back around five and cook myself something. After seven I'd turn my back on them and go to sleep. I've always been a good sleeper, noise doesn't bother me. They would mention me once in a while, finding a way to make me part of their political stuff, and try to outdo each other.

"The day of the dark races is coming. We whites are going to be ground down. The way we've ground them down for centuries. There'll be a reckoning."

"Josie'll come to our rescue, won't ye, Josie? Like the fair lassie, ye are. Ye'll save us whites. Yur wee heart's too kind."

"More 'n' likely she'll scalp us. I wouldn't blame her."

"She wouldn't get much off you, would she?"

"I still got some left."

"Bloody little."

"At least what's there is good. Not like what you've got."

"What's wrong with mine?"

"Nothing, if you like fuzz."

"I've got fine hair, that's all."

"I can almost see it between the bald spots."

"I've got a high forehead."

"And it goes right to your neck."

"It means a high intelligence."

"Why can't you win a game of checkers?"

"Because that's a different kind of intelligence. Games."

"Brains are brains, aren't they?"

"No, they're not. People have different talents. Like a painter. Or a scientist. A musician. An actor. Nobody's good at everything. It's impossible."

"What does your forehead mean you're good at?"

"It means he's good at thinking he's good."

"I'll bet Josie's a good dancer, huh, Josie? I'd like to see her rain dance."

"You want more rain? We need a sun dance."

"Another pot, Sam. If you don't mind. Whose turn was it to bring cookies? Do we have to have bread with our tea today? I need a sweet taste."

"Be glad you've got bread. There's millions dying of hunger around the world now. And millions dying in the Soviet Union fighting the fascists. Come the revolution there won't be any more hunger or fascists. Until then, make do."

"Bloody right. I'm reminded of what's written down in the last chapter of—."

"Forget it. I can't take one of your quotes now."

"There's nothing wrong with a little party doctrine."

"That's right. You make us wonder about you, Leo. Your commitment to the movement. How deep it is."

"I don't carry a party card but I'm for the working class."

"How far does that go?"

"I was in Spain. Saw action there. Don't tell me what to

think or hear. I'm a socialist and not a party hack like you. I think and say what I please."

"Party hack? I know how to obey."

"You follow the party line. So did Bukharin, Rykov, Kamenev, Zinoviev and Tuchashevski."

"I'm loyal, which is more than they were. They were all traitors, subversives that deserved to be liquidated."

"No wonder we lost in Spain. The gutless democracies betrayed us and we were betrayed by our own. We killed more of each other than the fascists did. All those summary trials and firing squads. It was hopeless, we were told to leave. I marched in the farewell parade of the international brigades in Barcelona. Women threw flowers at us from balconies. Some had tears in their eyes. Part of me died that day. We left them at the mercy of those fascist bastards. At the end lots of our comrades couldn't make it over the Pyrenees into France. So don't tell me. Don't give me the party line. You son of a bitch. Viva la Republica!"

"Revisionism and sentimentality."

"Grab him. Take it easy, Leo. Sit down. He didn't mean anything. We're all friends."

"Get Leo a towel. He spilled his tea."

"That's enough. In my shack everyone's got right to yak and be heard. But keep the bickering down. Or don't come here."

"Checkers, anybody?"

"After I get some tea."

"The tea, Sam, where is the tea?"

"And darker, please. As dark as the lassie's bonny black eyes."

"Josie's eyes are hazel."

"Sugar, please."

"Look into my mug and make it extra sweet, Josie."

"Nobody could make that mug of yours look sweet, not even Josie."

"Silly outmoded romantic capitalist nonsense. Socialist realism's done away with all that."

"Here we go, love me, love my tractor. How many tons of coal have we dug together today, Olga, my comrade in arms?"

"You're making fun of our comrades and allies."

"Have you heard this?"

Olga on the Volga
Wore the shortest toga
And when she bent ovah
You could see the cliffs of Dovah
And when she had to pee
Squatted on her potty
Looking so very cheeky
And made the Yellow Sea.

"Hey, my family is Russian."

"So is mine."

"Drink up, you guys, and have an oatmeal cookie, and with raisins no less. Josie baked them this morning."

"See what I'm saying about the dark races? They're going to rule over us some day. They'll do everything better. Even bake a better cookie."

None of that interested me. The arguments, the joking.

I didn't understand what they were talking about and didn't want to. All those problems were somewhere else, safely far away, had nothing to do with what bothered me. He would argue quietly. He played peacemaker to show how stupid the rest were. But he never openly made fun of anyone. And he didn't seem to do it to please me. It seemed to be his natural way. If he's a phony he's the smartest one I've met, I thought. But maybe he's so phony he doesn't even know it. He's only being himself. Snakes don't know they're snakes. They have to be that because that's what they are. No choice in the matter. Can't be expected to please their dinner. Pardon me, but you're on my menu, lady. There was a tingle of danger about the whole thing, which made the little crazies inside of me want to do crazier things sometimes. Because I knew I was going away with him and we would be face to face alone. You grab a garter snake by the tail and snap it to break its spine and blood oozes from its mouth like a melted ruby. You wear it around your thigh. A thong tight around your thigh. Before you kill it you can let it slither between your breasts, dry quick rasp. Let it escape over your belly and flex between your legs, let it furrow among the grassy hair split for a smooth trail deeper, tighter. The life of a thing squirming for water and earth, and a whiff of blood.

You try the Ganongs? I told you they were good. You got any left? Mind if I have one? Thanks. I'll get you another box. Hey, maybe for Valentine's. Somebody slipped on a floor upstairs. Bitches tried to blame it on me. A bad waxing job.

Told them I haven't waxed it for months because I haven't been able to get any wax and they said that made it dangerous. Can't win, can I? I need another Ganongs. That Matron Fairfax is the worst. Bet she's a miss. Bean up her ass. Walks like it. I think she was born wearing that uniform. Don't socialize with the patients, Mr. Kuby. They're tired, Mr. Kuby. She means you. I told her you enjoy my company. She's too nice to tell you she's tired, Mr. Kuby. I'm sure that you've got lots to do. I don't like the way she says "Mr. Kuby," like I'm slime. Too low to speak to. I'm not educated. Didn't come from England, like her. I don't have an accent you could polish your nails with. In this country nobody's supposed to be better than anybody else. Don't believe it. There's plenty of that. Why are there private schools and private clubs? The rich marry each other. Praying Mary told me we're all equal. In the eyes of God. Nice woman. No matter what He thinks, a lot of Christians don't act like it, I said. Not that I'm against money. And I got mine. Made it on stocks. I read the financial page each day. Stock quotations, latest news. I go to the library and read up on all the companies. Their histories, current situations. I look at the weekly financial paper from back East. I didn't want to pay for it myself so I got the library to get it in. They said there wasn't much call for it. I thought we were living in a capitalist country, I said. Are you against a free market economy? They got it in. Some other stuff too. They still don't have as much as those big city libraries but I manage. I got a broker out on the coast. A couple of years ago I invested in Crown Sugar. I'd been watching them. Good earnings, top management. I figure, attractive for somebody.

They amalgamated, there was a new stock issue and a three for one split. I made $210,000. Atlas-Advance Pulp and Paper this last year. New plant equipment needed, solid management, potential. Somebody's going to have their eye on them, I'm thinking. Successful takeover bid, smoke clears. Two for one split. I got $85,000. You know, when I was walking to the bank with that cheque for $210,000 I couldn't believe it was in my hands. I kept looking at it. They wouldn't accept it. They thought it was phony. Because I'm a janitor. I wasn't wearing a suit. This is honest money, check with my broker, I said. I gave them his number. After they phoned, the manager comes out and says hi and slobbers all over me. I thought about changing banks but I figured they're all the same. So I haven't done bad. I'm worth, house and car and everything, over $550,000. I know guys on the coast who live in rented rooms and drive old cars. They play the market, make enough to live on, and have about a hundred grand they've saved. They're waiting to make the big strike. They're always at the exchange. Drinking coffee and smoking. Staring up at the board. Every time I go out there I've got to listen to the same old stuff. Mining claims, assay results. Turns out to be a swindle, or some crazy old prospector's been talking too long to trees. Those guys won't make it. They want it all in one bundle. They don't read up on the companies like I do. Find out what's what. They don't buy and sell the right way. They wait too long. When a stock goes up you tell yourself at what price you're going to sell. If you keep waiting to make the last nickel, it'll start to go down. Same thing when you buy. You tell yourself the price. If you wait for the stock to keep going down, you'll be waiting when it goes up. Last time I was there we all went out to dinner. I took a look at their cars in the parking lot. A broken-down LaSalle, a rusty Nash, a beat-up Hudson Hornet and a Kaiser—that's right, a Kaiser. And right there alongside them, my new Caddy. You should've seen the looks it got. They couldn't take their eyes off it. In a few years you guys will be able to start a car museum, I told them. We go inside and they order burgers. I got a T-bone steak, French fries on the side, a green salad and apple pie à la mode for dessert. They're talking about gold mines and silver mines, ore samples, rich veins, placer this and placer that. Some of it was to impress me, the hick from the sticks. They didn't like the idea of the T-bone, and especially after seeing the convertible. I looked at them. The cuffs of their suits were frayed, their ties had food stains, old tight knots. Shirt collars were curled up. They started smoking while I was still eating. Since I quit I can't stand the smell of cigarette smoke. I told myself, this is the last time I eat with these hard-luck artists. Ash on my French fries. Could hardly finish dessert. They ordered more coffee and talked about emerald mines in Columbia. Diamond mines in South Africa. Rubies and sapphires in India and Burma. Gold in Australia, Siberia. They even got around to the Klondike and sunken Spanish galleons. When I left they were still talking. They were high on caffeine and buried treasure. Like I said, they wait too long.

I picked a time and told him. He said to meet him that Sunday at the beer parlour near the tracks. There was an argument when I packed up and left but no one could have stopped me. I walked up the tracks and told myself I was glad to get away. I didn't know what was going to happen. I didn't care. I was leaving. A change. I had to do something. That's what I thought. Do something. You're dying here doing nothing. If you want to change anything you've got to start. The shopping bags got heavier as I walked. Mostly clothes. I thought about those I'd be meeting. They would be strangers. Except one. I didn't trust him. But I liked him. Because. It's always because. That's a way of saying you have to. I was trying. That was important. Get going and don't think. That's exciting. Not knowing what's going to happen. Everything going funny in my tummy. That's not my word. Where did I get it from? Nurse. Tracks snaking ahead in steel curves. He was standing there, outside. Didn't offer to take one of the bags. Oh, I knew him. Cigarette cough. He rolled his own. Tight suit mission handout. Half-soled brogues with taps on the heels for longer wear. Scabs on his chin and jaw from shaving. Rubbed an overused double-edged safety razor blade around the inside of a glass to keep it honed. I'd seen Sam do that. Rented a furnished room with hotplate, toilet down the hall. I'd spent a night in a room like that with Jimmy John. Probably a mantelpiece radio, his own, for the war news. Caffeine and nicotine had kept him going, had helped to kill the hunger during the hard years. And those resharpened slogans he'd shouted in union halls, on the picket line and at rallies and repeated quietly at cell meetings.

We stood and waited for a streetcar and he didn't say

anything. He grinned at me. It was a Sunday in July, only noon and very warm already. When the streetcar came he got on ahead of me and paid our fares. I followed him to a bench seat facing towards the middle and sat down, still nothing said. I can be silent. It's part of the heritage. Along the way other passengers got on and when there were no more seats later passengers held onto straps or stanchions. One of them was an older woman, plump and red-faced and with a big plastic purse scrunched permanently in the middle of each side like an accordion. He got up and offered his seat to her and she sat beside me, careful to avoid touching me, as if I was dirty. I could smell face powder under the rouge and perfume. Part of the heritage too. Underneath everything a middle-aged woman's fear of not being enough or being too much. A bead of sweat glistened on her forehead like a watery pimple. It must have been a relief to forget and feel superior. She kept her high-heeled shoes away from my bags, her knees together and shifted away from me. She frowned as if her shoulder was being invisibly touched. She'd have been more comfortable standing up. He hadn't done her a favour, after all. My subtle sense, I have one, hinted he did it to have a laugh. Usually I ignore my subtle sense, it's troublesome. When she stood up to get off the heel of her shoe kicked my bags over and a coat fell out. She stepped on it and the heel caught in the collar and dragged it. She stopped, lifted her shoe and left without a word or looking back, clumping down the steps. It was a silent Lord's Day in the big city. At Granville and Georgia he said something and moved towards the exit and I followed. There was a cigar store on the corner. He said he wanted to buy some tobacco for cigarettes. We went inside and I saw a wooden Indian near the door. Blocky, arms folded, feather in the headband, flared nostrils, the cedar grain weather-beaten wrinkles along the varnished face staring out at traffic. I'd never seen one. I knew it had to do with tobacco. But there were no statues of Frenchmen at perfume counters or carved Russians where caviar was sold. And I could imagine the trouble if the stuffed and painted figure of an Englishman appeared next to a display of tea and crumpets. Was I being too sensitive? Should I have laughed at myself, or had somebody already laughed? But I could laugh. These invaders had taken our peaceful sundried smoke and turned it into sugar-cured lung cancer. Revenge, tobacco for whisky and broken treaties. Wasn't enough. I'd become wood too, the kind whites carved their initials into. He took a paper out of a packet he'd bought, dropped shredded tobacco into the vee, tucked and rolled, licked the sticky edge and tapered the ends. He'd probably done that thousands of times. What he did next was new, was intentional. He took a match and casually struck it across the cheek of the Indian. I heard the gritty scrape, smelled the rotten egg stink of sulphur and saw the lickbite of flame scorch the wood. He lit the cigarette and inhaled and I waited, caught a whiff of smoke, almost cool on a hot day inside a cool store. Leaves turned into ashes. He puffed a few times and breathed out the smoke in long gauzy spears. I breathed them in, the sharp fumes. I watched the glow at the lit end, a ruby eye getting larger and smaller. Ash fell onto the floor between us. A small ceremony of no significance to anybody except us. I ran a finger along the bulge of the cheek, the smooth varnish where it had been scorched, felt a tiny scar. He watched as if not watching, gauging me.

A woman's voice behind me, young and sensible and eager.

"You're here. I thought I was early."

The last thing I expected. I felt sick, dizzy with surprise. I turned. She was in her early twenties, thin, pretty, with polite eyes and long sandy hair pulled around her ears and gathered at the back. She wore a light cotton blouse and skirt, both the colour of vanilla ice cream. Nothing bad had come close to her or probably ever would. She had the decency of those who've had a decent life. It happened too fast for me to do anything but hide my feelings behind a quick smile. She held out her hand. It felt softly warm. Too soft for holding anything except a pen or cup. And she was going to be friendly, no matter what.

"I'm Margaret Tavistock. And you must be Josie. Happy to meet you. Don's told me all about you. We'll have plenty of time to chat. Car's outside. Let me help you with those bags."

She picked both of them up and walked outside and we followed and he grinned, young and impulsive, what can you expect? So I was his worldly woman now. Oh, I knew him. There was a long cream-coloured sedan parked at the curb. She opened a back door and put the bags on the seat, went around and opened a front door and sat behind the steering wheel. He got in beside her and they both looked at me, standing on the sidewalk, the back door still wide open. There would have been room on the front seat for me but I was expected to sit with my shopping bags. I got in and didn't slam the door. It swung closed with a firm heaviness that said comfort. She started the engine. There was a low vibrating sound and I sank into the light brown plaid and watched their backs as she turned the big steering wheel. They spoke low and I couldn't hear them. It was a short drive back the way we had come, to the downtown eastside, a street between the business district and the edge of skid row. We could have met her there instead of uptown but he had a reason. She parked beside an old stone building which fitted in between a corner store with apartments above and a large apartment block. It was a hall and a notice on a board near the entrance said there would be a public lecture that evening at seven. It wasn't even two yet. I picked up the bags—she didn't offer this time—and followed them into a big room filled with chairs, with an aisle between them. There were some men standing in a corner near a table with a hot plate with a coffee pot on it. More were at the front near a stand like a pulpit. They went to the front and began talking with them and I put the bags down and sat in a chair. I had had enough. I didn't know what he was up to and didn't care. No more following like a bitch in heat. After a while she came over and asked if I wanted a cup of coffee. She got one for herself too and sat next to me. With bubbles in her voice she told me why we'd gone there.

"My father's going to give a lecture tonight. He's an economics professor at the university. Classical theory, supply and demand. He's been coming down (the way she said it) for years to speak to workingmen. During the Depression this place was packed when profs gave lectures. Because of the War the audience has gone to practically nothing. I don't think these lectures are going to go on much longer. They're talking at the university of going to a more structured form, extramural courses for extension students. Dad has always gotten a kick out of coming here. He'll miss it when it's finally over. Last couple of years I came along out of curiosity. Graduated last year, thinking of doing postgrad in economics or political science. Anyway, I met Don here. About a year ago we had what is known as a heated discussion, good-natured though. He asked me out. I'm trying to get him to enroll at varsity, but he says his life is union politics. My father could get him some kind of scholarship and I think he'd make a wonderful teacher."

Not one question about me. That's how I knew she was worried. He'd gotten her to pick us up so we'd meet each other. He was going to play one against the other and wasn't even careful about it. Guilt I didn't expect from him, sneakiness yes. I knew I was the extra woman, the one who'd finally be thrown away. She was too good a catch, ivy growing all over her. White virgin for sacrifice, cheap only at the right price. I was there to show how sympathetic he was to Indian problems, especially female ones. She could take it either way, kindness or crotch, and that's where love comes in. And she was the jealous type. I was the bait she was supposed to replace with herself. He was hurrying her along in case a varsity grad got to her first. The white man was after me again. I was supposed to play princess yearning to be his squaw, help him get the real sucker. He hadn't pestered me to leave the shack because he had set up the real target already. He hadn't been patient with me, he was arrogant, and my new life as a political bride was to help snag the professor's daughter.

About four she had to leave to pick up Dad. And eat too, but that would have meant an invitation. Better not take a chance. The savage might say yes. Claws into the food. Duck quacks into the seat. Idiot grin. Ha ha. He came over but didn't mention her. I said I was hungry. He said there were free doughnuts by the coffee pot. He didn't offer to get me one or another cup of coffee. The lecture was a joke to him. He tossed a live butt onto the floor.

"Old Alec's been delivering the message to this heathen since before I came out here. He feels good about helping the uneducated. Talking textbook economics to workingmen. He thinks he's teaching them something. They come in to get warm and grab a bite."

I held out my cup.

"Get me a doughnut and a refill."

He tried to ignore me. I shook the cup.

"I'm tired."

He could take that any way he wanted. He didn't like it but he took the cup and left. Princesses don't come cheap. Not this Pocahontas, anyway. I put my feet up on another chair. There were plenty of empty ones around. That's when the seed man came over, spitting hulls between his words. He looked at the bags.

"What are you doing here?"

"Learning."

"I see Don's here. Sam couldn't make it, I guess."

He took my silence to mean he could sit down. He reached into a dirty jacket pocket for more seeds. The flap was torn. Bits of hull like crushed cockroaches were stuck to that side of the jacket.

"Sam used to come in the old days, before you knew him. All the guys did. Somewhere to go, have a gab, grab a coffee an'. Not like now, with the War."

He came back and handed me the cup and a doughnut. It was round and glazed, with a hole in the middle. (Where else, Josie? You're getting tired.)

"Hello, Don, I've been talking to Josie. You're helping her improve her education on the finer points of economics, I see."

"We were talking, if you don't mind."

"Sure, I was going. Nice to see you."

He got up, reaching into his pocket as he walked away.

"Why did you talk to him that way?"

"He runs errands. Useful at times."

"Somebody to look down on."

"I didn't make him stupid."

"You like it, though."

"Forget it. Listen, I've got to go somewhere. I'll be back in time for the talk. You'll be all right."

He was gone before I could say anything. I leaned back and shut my eyes. No one was going to bother me there. The place was all about dead words. I fell asleep thinking about him. The way he had of assuming he could do anything he wanted. I dreamt about the shack, it was on fire and I was running with a pail of water and couldn't get there. Something kept holding onto me. It was a hand on my shoulder. She was leaning over me, full of kindness like sugar candy.

"Sorry to wake you but the lecture is going to begin."

I looked around the hall. Less than twenty seats occupied. Seated behind the stand was a man with lots of snowy hair. He was wearing a tweed jacket with leather patches on the elbows. His shirt had a faint checked pattern and he wore a green tartan wool tie. His face had the same look as his daughter's, as if he had never seen real trouble. I remembered missionaries that came to the school to speak about spreading the Word of the Lord. They were on their way to China. They thought we were Christians. You knew that anything you could say wouldn't make a bit of difference to them because their minds were made up. They saw the world one way. It was somebody else's they had taken up and now wouldn't let go for anything. His eyes had the same confidence. Their look said that he had always gotten what he expected because what he expected was right. And if he didn't get it, it was someone else's fault. He'd never look at himself except to prove he couldn't make a mistake, not a deliberate one. He could only be mistaken. He would be kind as long as it was easy. When it was hard he would blame others. He could never understand anything except what he had been taught. He passed on other people's ideas, having none of his own.

He arrived when the lecture began and sat next to her in

the front row. They didn't touch or even look at each other, but that was worse than if I'd seen them together in bed naked. He hadn't got her that far yet. Probably only smooching in the back seat and maybe a hand where she said it didn't belong, at least not yet. What had he told her about me? Missionary work among the savages? Where did she think I was going to sleep, in a teepee? And what had he planned for me? She'd been so well educated she was bound to be stupid about important things. I was an Indian, expected to sleep anywhere and with anybody. I decided to live up to my reputation, left my feet on the chair. Not that anybody noticed. The place was almost empty. Some had already fallen asleep or were nodding. One guy had to be poked to get him to stop snoring, another got up to leave. The professor looked at his watch, put his pipe in a side pocket of his jacket, stood up and walked over to the stand. He took sheets of paper out of a briefcase on the floor beside it. He placed them on the stand and looked around the room. There was a rumble from one of the chairs, a smothered foghorn. The professor looked down. Did his eyebrows twitch?

"My talk tonight will be about the current wartime economy. A few years ago the American and Canadian governments were criticized in some quarters for what was seen as meddling in a free market economy. The public sector had been limited to such areas as defence, diplomacy, federal crime and Indian affairs. The worldwide collapse in October of Twenty-nine changed all that. Millions of unemployed finally couldn't be ignored. Something had gone wrong with the laws that govern the marketplace, and conventional monetary and fiscal policy were temporarily at least to be found wanting. The answer to many was more government involvement in the public sector with respect to implementing programs that would correct the worst effects of widespread unemployment. So by the early Thirties we got welfare, relief camps and public works projects. Except to extreme conservatives, that traditional and honoured measure of fiscal responsibility, a balanced budget, was no longer seen as sacrosanct. Men had gone back to work largely due to government getting involved in the marketplace, which didn't worsen or solve the crisis. Armageddon came not financially but militarily, here in Thirty-nine, and in Forty-one in the United States, when governments were forced to engage in deficit spending. War bonds were to finance the conflict, and for that future generations would be saddled with a national debt beyond anything ever envisioned in peacetime. No one said anything because our democracies were in grave peril. Tonight I want to consider the future ramifications of these greatly increased levels of public spending."

He considered for an hour, after which there was a question period. I looked at the front row. From what I could see from near the back, they didn't seem to have moved. Two seated statues, arms folded. I was in a bad mood. I don't like glazed doughnuts, especially on an empty stomach. The professor had taken out his pipe and was filling it, waiting for questions. A man in a ragged coat that looked as if he slept in it asked whether it might be a good idea if ration coupons were used for everything from now on so everybody got the same amount of everything and there wouldn't be any rich or poor.

"That would be an extreme measure, and I think unwarranted. Supplementary monetary payments are a better way of redistributing income because they do it indirectly, don't interfere with natural market forces. The other would lead to bartering, and that's a crude mechanism compared with the market, which uses sophisticated financial instruments to move goods and services. Government is there to help, not to control the economy. Otherwise it becomes an instrument of government policy. To a certain extent state control has always been a factor, if we think of ancient Rome, or later on mercantilism, where national policy dictated economic goals. But that's different from unlimited state interference."

"They're doing all right in the Soviet Union, aren't they?"

"They still use a currency, together with wage and price controls. But the market is hamstrung by what the communist party determines as national goals. State-owned companies restrict consumer choice. They have to use gold internationally, where balance of payments is involved. Gold is no longer the hallowed way of backing a currency, as it was before Britain went off the gold standard in the Thirties. But you need a medium of exchange internationally. Gold serves that purpose."

"If everybody was communist, we wouldn't need gold any more."

The professor lit his pipe and took a few puffs, letting out the smoke in a leisurely trail before he continued.

"Political science is not my field, but I think it's safe to say those who seek perfection in government usually end up showing the imperfection in themselves. The Soviet Union is a good example. A whole class of peasant farmers, the kulaks, was wiped out because it wouldn't adopt the government policy of forced collectivization. Other examples of coercion resulting in draconian measures come to mind."

"They're fighting on our side, aren't they?"

"Britain found an ally in the Soviet Union after it was invaded, but until then the Soviet government abided by the Nazi-Soviet Nonaggression Pact."

"Because they didn't trust the West. That's why they signed it."

"And perhaps the West had reason not to trust a regime whose stated aim is the overthrow of capitalism by any means."

"They say they don't want international revolution now. And they're for the worker."

"Yes, that's the propaganda."

"If it wasn't for them, western governments wouldn't have been forced to do something for the workingman."

"I think farsighted noncommunists who advocated a new social policy were not motivated by that. Though some extreme conservatives would find that hard to believe."

The man in the ragged coat stood up. He hadn't shaved in days. His bony hands looked grimy. I wasn't near him but I knew he'd have a bad smell. He'd been seated on the aisle in the second row, twenty feet from the professor, but the space between them looked a lot further.

"Answer one more question."

"If I can." Puff puff.

"Where am I going to sleep tonight?"

The only answer was, find a park bench if you can't get into a mission. But that wasn't an answer. The professor knew that but he stopped puffing, showing he was sympathetic. The homeless man walked out through the silence, taking his time. I could see his shoes were handouts and too big for him. As he passed me he wiped his nose with the back of his hand and there was something pathetic about that. I thought the professor had it all his own way so far. Someone had to ask a question he couldn't use to show how smart he was.

"I have a question." Stand up, Josie.

"Yes?" Puff puff again.

"What are you doing here?"

"I don't understand." Puff.

"There's no one here who wants to listen to you."

"That's not for you to determine, young lady."

"I'm not that young and I'm not a lady, especially to you. Everyone here is here for a reason that has nothing to do with what you're talking about."

The professor was a gentleman and he knew I was on the warpath (ugh, but I had to use it) but didn't know why. So he didn't answer me. He looked around the room as if it was full of students. It was full of memories.

"I'll take another question."

"You haven't answered mine."

The professor got very professorial.

"I would ask you to show some respect for the rest of the audience."

"I am. You're the one who's not showing respect. We don't want to hear about things we can't do anything about. Don't try to fool us into thinking we're important enough to do something about them. That makes you seem important. But you're as small as the rest of us, only you don't know it. You're one of the preachers of education, who say that knowing more is better. You offer truth for free but you're lying. It's not truth, it's obedience training to accept our lives. We've heard it in school. All the stuff you're talking about is no more than what the pieman said to Simple Simon, 'If you haven't got a penny, you don't get any.'"

Puff puff puff puff puff.

They all expected me to leave like that tramp, wander off and find some place to sleep. It didn't matter if I was right or wrong, they were used to everything in the right place and all in order. The professor wasn't there to be asked hard questions, he was there to make everybody feel better. I was a troublemaker. Didn't I understand that nobody could do anything about these things? I should listen and keep my mouth shut. Once I left, once they had gotten rid of me, things would go back to their usual routine, as daring as a turtle's next step. It was consideration they wanted, him coming there to speak. His educated words were not spoken by them and his ideas were knowledge shared under special conditions and never really understood because they belonged to the educated. His audience had to believe this because it made sense of everything. Somebody must know the answers. To know that was enough. It was an agreement that would be broken when truth had become a fact instead of an idea and the truth-teller couldn't deny it. Then they could know a more terrible truth. One day they might have to kill him for telling lies.

The professor smacked the bowl of his pipe quickly against the flat of his hand a few times and ashes fell to the floor. We were finished with each other, but one thing was left. I walked to the front and looked down at them. She turned her face away but he didn't. I had to get him out of me, get all of him outside so I could say there was nothing left. I didn't want to carry anything back except my bags. I didn't care about him any more. It was pride and I had to be able to say to myself, you weren't a fool, not finally, you told him off without tears. I had liked him because I wanted what he offered about helping my people, all the nations. I'd wanted to believe him because it was a way of getting the pain out, the pain I'd known since I was a girl. That made me not see he was a small man who lied like he breathed, to live. He had to think everybody else was a fool to be tricked. That made him the biggest of all fools. The professor lived in a dream that the world could be understood the way a scientist understands by cutting up or putting things into a test tube, but the man I was looking at now hated dreams as much as he hated what the world made him be. We walk among shadows. A dream is a way through. It is necessary for as long as we need it. When we forget what a dream is, we see shadows. When we mistake a shadow for a dream, the nightmare begins. He could only see shadows. He had been born that way. He laughed at those who believed in more. I knew that and thought I could live with it. But he was a born hater, I wasn't. My hate was a disease I was trying to cure, his was his life.

He stared back at me, as if to say, you're nothing but another sucker. I hated his grin. Nobody had ever tricked me like this, making me ashamed of myself, turning my deepest feelings into another dirty Indian joke. The one chance I had to do something had been thrown back at me. I knew there wouldn't be any more. The rest of my life would be spent retelling and compiling the old stories. I could have done more if someone had helped me. I could see now that no one was going to help. The only thing was to leave these invaders, and leave nothing. And so I waved to the back a beckoning hand (from some old book). I was playing to an educated audience.

"Seeds." He came rushing up to the front, brushing his jacket.

"Do you know this man?"

"Sure. He's Don Richards."

"Where have you seen him?"

"Sam's place. On the inlet."

"What does he do there?"

"You know. Talk politics."

"What kind?"

"Communism, inside stuff. He knows more than anybody. More than the head of the party. If you want to know what Moscow's thinking, ask Don. Among us guys he's what's known as a hard-liner, a party member. He's been to the Kremlin. He was head of the Young Communists here."

He sputtered, the words came so fast. A blob of sunflower spit paste landed on my nose. I wore it as a battle scar. No one was grinning, especially the hard-liner. The varsity pair was being very varsity, trying to ignore what the dog did on the living room carpet in front of the dinner guests. The professor put his pipe into his pocket and his notes into his briefcase stiffly. His daughter's face was baked meringue, her eyes two flakes of granite. They left. He got up, smirking. I turned my back on him and he grabbed my arm. I pulled it away. He swore. He was anatomically correct, the closest he got to me (oh, Josie, what a showoff you are). I looked at Seeds, who was reaching into his pocket.

"Seeds, get my bags."

We walked out and into a hot evening full of strangers. Everybody was busy driving or walking somewhere, and some talking, laughing. Sometimes under a big truth there are a lot of small ones. Out there was the big truth, everyday life. What I'd said was smaller. It always happens when words are used. The doing, the living of anything is what makes it true. Words are ghosts speaking about what they have done or what they can never do. There's an unhappiness behind arguments, the feeling you'll never get anywhere. Words going to war, killing each other and not caring who's right but who's alive. I was alive but most of the words were already forgotten and there was no one to say, you were right, you told them off. Did you show them up. What a great job. You against all that education and double-crossing opportunism. After all those words there I was, where they didn't mean anything.

I thanked Seeds and he offered to carry my bags to where I could get a streetcar. I said I didn't have the fare and he said he'd pay. A loan, I said. All right, he said, pay me back when you're rich. Don't mention anything to Sam about tonight. He shrugged. Don't worry. Let's get going, I said, the sooner I get back the better. Yeah, he said, it's dark along the tracks, even in summer, and dangerous too. Never know when a fast freight will come around the bend. Guys have been run over walking in the middle of the tracks. I knew a guy named Wee Geordie. Big son of a gun. An eastbound freight ran over him one night, cut him in two. Myself, I don't drink.

I saw their car, still at the curb. As we walked by I could hear the professor's voice coming from an open window. It sounded different. He was off duty.

"Can we give you a lift?"

"I'm getting a streetcar."

"Where are you going?"

"Victoria Drive."

"We'll take you there."

It was in the opposite direction to where they were going. The professor wanted to do something for me now, and that made me feel important. I couldn't admit that to myself. But I told myself I was tired, the streetcar was slow. I didn't accept right away. I was still arguing with him, he was still an enemy. But to him the argument was over. It wasn't personal. It was though. Or he wouldn't have asked.

"That's all right. I'll take the streetcar."

"It's no trouble. You'll have to wait a long time for a streetcar this late."

He was playing the same game I was. We were on the same level. We're all on that level when trying for what we're after. I didn't want to overdo it. Because finally you've got to say yes or no or it starts to look like a game. I accepted and said goodnight to Seeds and thanked him. He was disappointed because when the professor invited him too the invitation was meant to be refused and Seeds knew it. A helper's a helper, after all. He vanished into the fading light with the others coming out of the lecture. The professor got out. He put my bags on the rear seat and made room for me in front. His daughter was driving. She hadn't said a word. It was different, sitting there beside them. I didn't think I'd been accepted. It was a ride. But I had impressed them. She drove slowly along Hastings. He'd probably told her to when he got out of the car. Hastings looked different from a car, as if you owned it but it wasn't so important a thing to own now, anyway. After he introduced himself and her, he asked my name.

"You know, Josie, you cut me to the quick tonight. What you said reminded me of the men who used to come to my lectures in the Thirties, unemployed radicals who'd argue like the blazes with me. The way you did. Not like my bored students, who don't know the world at all. Sometimes I think I'm a babysitter, with ivy around the rattle."

He shook his head.

"I didn't know that he was one of the zigzaggers. That's what the other leftists call them. They zig and zag, following the Moscow line, whatever it is and no matter how it changes. An enemy today is a friend tomorrow, and vice versa. He's the smartest I've met. We had him out to dinner a few weeks ago. He'd taken Margaret to a union picnic and a rally in support of organizing something. He said he was raised on the prairies and believed in the farm co-op movement. Talked about national health care. I thought he was a Sunday school socialist. He even made fun of some of the communists he knows. A guy who can quote whole passages verbatim from important communist works. I don't mind being told my own business by a firebrand (a quick look at me) but I can't stand a phony. I guess (a quick look at her) . . . ."

Her fingers squeezed the wheel. When she changed gears she swatted the shift lever on the steering column as if she was slapping it back and forth. As we came to Victoria Drive he asked where I was going. I said down the hill to Powell and along the tracks. He told her to turn and drive down. He asked how far along the tracks I lived and I said about a couple of miles. He told her to park on Powell.

"That's too far, especially this time of night. Isn't there another way?"

"There's a path through the bush, but that's across the city boundary. It's a long drive."

"That's all right, we'll take you there. Give Margaret the directions."

I gave her directions and she drove without saying a word.

The sky was almost completely dark by now. From behind the windshield the rows of streetlights on the hills seemed looping strands of yellow-white pearls on a blue velvet cushion. Those hills were once a thick forest under the stars of a green evening. The paths of hunters would be vanishing among the trees. The shore would be moon-splashed rocks and sand and the water a sheet spread deep and everlasting, the stunned moment on a silver plate. And through the silence the last song of a lost bird. There was nothing left but a few notes.

When we got to the end of the street where the path began, all I could see were the black clumps of bushes and trees. I knew there was a wire fence there, built by an oil refinery around its storage tanks, and the path ran down alongside the fence. I'd taken it a couple of times. We'd usually walk along the tracks to reach paths on the other side of the city line or all the way to the beer parlour on Powell. But this was closer to the shack. That night there was no moon and after staring for a while I could make out some strands of barbed wire along the top of the fence. Carrying the bags down would be tricky in the dark. The professor reached over and opened the glove compartment and took out a flashlight. He thought about handing it to me before remembering I'd be carrying my bags. Maybe he realized I was not much older than his daughter.

"It's too dark for you to go alone. I'll go with you."

"You're going to leave me here?" she said.

The nearest light was on the refinery side of the fence, a bulb under a green shade hanging from a pole a couple of hundred feet away.

"Stay here and lock the doors or come with us," he said.

She thought about being brave (ugh) for a moment before joining us. I took a couple of steps towards the fence and saw the path, a footprint wide and almost covered by bushes. I didn't need the light. Heritage. But it was more fun this way. Different heritage. He handed me a bag and kept the other and switched on the flashlight. We walked single file, he led the way, I followed and she brought up the rear (that doesn't sound right but she deserved it). A few feet in something scampered or scurried (one of those words) off the path and she bumped up against me. I thought, he deserved you, though you didn't deserve him. I was becoming charitable, a very becoming thing. It was probably hunger or maybe the smell of water (no, I won't say it). As we went slowly, pushing the branches away from our faces I let a branch go, timed to hit her when she didn't expect it. Petty, small-minded, bitchy, peevish, revengeful. Our scout/outrider kept a steady pace (where's my old pinto/paint?). Into the redman's land on a treacherous trail, the professor's girl breathing down my neck, fearing some savage will snatch her panties (or pant on her snatch). Natch. All those quivering arrows want a quiver. Stand and deliver the male. Of his offal burden, the dirty thing. I'll save her slit. Princess for target practice, cheap. Sweaty whiff of ripe banana. Soft fig, ooze plump. Split salmon, belly up. Who's spoiled rotten, huh? Fishy. Maggot feast, squirming sperm. Shredded cow draped over a boxcar coupling, suck-knuckle and drawbar, sunburnt taint of beef. Raunchy haunches. Only flies need apply. Klootches have rubber lips. Stick it in any hole, she doesn't care. She's crazy for it. Sore between tit and tailbone. We have a special on. And it came to pass the privateers went in unto her and she delivereth of sundry happenstances a babe of many colours, and they saw and were much displeased at the place of peaceful waters where they builded them cities where hosed annas rose from broady houses, or called bored ellos, to the unnovitiated. And there the breeds bed unwed and gave head and bred and bled and dead. Let's be clear about this. I claim this land for the crown, to be held in promiscuity by its hairs. In the name of the greatwhiteoldbroad over the big water who pisses at the spa and wipes herself with treepaper from her colonies, hitches up her crinolines after pulling at a pantysnatch between plug thighs' pinkmottled crease and maybe farts eggstink before granting an audience to the ambassador of some Meadowgeranium nothingcountry. And is he Empressed, oh my, by her hair bun and rummyniscences about whatwehaveincommon as they suck a lemon together in their weepy tea. In the name of lineages so long they go back to piles of mouldy caveturd and earthmothers squatting to deliver on a promissory note. Not good enough, too common, and besides there's tint taint, the old skin excuse. She is not one of ours, she is something else. She's the witch who can see dead fetuses in jug wine, end of a race to extinction. The cloudy hours to years, wine sour piss running out along the sidewalk, somebody digging your grave. Garbage in a gunny sack. Not even our own names. Select your own place to die, if there's a free spot left. There may only be timber wolves howling into the wilderness. Nothing is something when you're staring into eternity.

[The rest of this page is blank.]

All I could see ahead of me was the flick of a light beam on the trail. There was a cosy mystery about the whole thing, stepping between two strangers down the dark incline, down to the water I could smell and almost hear. They were my guests in the leafy darkness brushing against our cheeks. I was taking them out of their lives, into an invisibility none of us understood. And I felt the whole thing was planned.

"Ow." She fell against me and into the bushes. She was a nuisance. He stopped and turned his flashlight on us. I could see her through some overhanging leaves, lying on her side. Her skirt was bunched up around her thighs. When the light moved up I could see her teeth holding her lower lip. Her teeth were small and even and glazed like creamy porcelain in the light.

"You all right, Margaret?"

"I tripped on something. My ankle hurts."

"She probably caught a shoe on a root," I said.

He handed me the flashlight. It was the colour of nickel, felt heavy and somehow was comforting. He kneeled down to look at her. I shone the light on her right ankle. It was swollen and a little pinker than the other one. He touched it. She groaned. He patted her leg softly.

"Can you walk?"

"I don't know. I'll try."

"You can use my shoulder for support."

He looked up at me.

"How far are we along?"

"Almost the middle. The steps are a few minutes away."

"Have to take Margaret back. She can't make it."

There it was. I left the bags and guided them back. When we got to the car he said he was sorry and I should take the flashlight. I said I couldn't hold it and carry the bags too, could make it without a light. I didn't mention heritage. I keep that to myself. He said goodbye, I said goodbye, she didn't. Probably in too much pain. As I came to the end of the trail (ugh) and started to walk down the steps, I felt I'd been cheated. In your life and out. Glimpse of something and gone. Crossing the tracks again and to nothing.

As I crossed I heard the professor's voice behind me. He had followed me down the trail after taking care of his lame daughter. He was at the top of the steps, a flashlight beam. I went to the bottom.

"How would you like to give a talk at the university?"

"About what?"

"Native problems, customs. Anything you want."

"I've never spoken in public."

"Judging by your performance tonight, I'd say you'd do quite well. You'd be speaking about a subject you know. That should help. I could arrange something in a couple of weeks and pick you up here, right at the top of the trail. Let's say two weeks from this coming Wednesday, at five o'clock?"

I agreed and the flashlight beam turned away and disappeared. I recrossed the tracks in a better mood. When

I pushed the door open he was sitting on the bed and staring at the floor. He looked up and I could see he'd been crying. I felt sorry for him, always had. I put the bags in a corner and sat on the bed. He looked at the bags. I sighed. I'm a pretty good sigher when I want to be. Breathless intake, slow breath out almost silent (very important), an air of unspeakable sorrow. It broke his mood.

"Why?"

"It was a bust. Made a mistake."

"If you ever do that again, Josie."

"Get me something. I'm starving."

After I ate I told him about the professor's offer.

"So you've ditched one phony for another."

"He's not a phony. I told you, he's an economics professor at the university."

"What's in it for him?"

"Nothing."

I knew he was jealous. That wasn't my problem. As I thought about my talk over the next two weeks, he would make comments. I tried to ignore them.

"Preparing for your debut as a professional Indian? What's next, a Wild West show? You can hit the lecture circuit, wearing buckskin. The prof can be your manager. 'Josie, performing half-breed, dances rain or shine, does striptease, feathers and all.' Next stop the movies. You can play a princess saving the great white hunter."

I only hit him over the head with the frying pan once.

I decided to speak about our stories, to give the audience, which I expected to be mostly students, some idea of our spiritual tradition. I told the professor when he picked me up, minus his daughter (didn't say, I didn't ask).

"Good idea. I've reserved Brooke Hall for you. You should have a big audience. I put a notice in the campus newspaper and had handbills posted on bulletin boards. How do you feel?"

"A little nervous."

"That's natural. Have you had dinner?"

"I ate at noon."

"We'll get something in the cafeteria there. We should be at the campus by six. Your talk's scheduled for seven. Did you make notes?"

"No. Ours is an oral tradition."

"Yes."

Brooke Hall was a two-storey white stucco building. Most of the ground floor was a large room for lectures. There was an anteroom at each end and a door led to a cafeteria. It was almost six when we got there. Many of the dinner crowd of students and faculty were leaving. Part of my audience was heading for the lecture room. We got trays and cutlery and I chose a roast beef sandwich from the offerings. He poured himself a cup of coffee and selected a small package of digestive biscuits. He paid for my sandwich. We sat in the half empty cafeteria, the serving women busy taking away platters and tubs of food from the counter. Sounds of washing up, clanging pans and clinking spoons and clacking piles of plates came from behind the door to the kitchen. He opened the package of biscuits, took a bite and had a sip of coffee. He was chewing the same biscuit when I finished the sandwich. As the professor had another sip, I wondered why I had come. What consideration would be given to what I had to say by people with busy lives in the middle of a war? But I knew that after the war was over, my little war would still be going on. It was a war in my country, not halfway around the world.

There was a wall clock in the cafeteria. At ten to seven we headed for the lecture room. There was a platform at one end, about a foot higher than the main floor. On it were a speaker's stand, which he called a lectern, and two chairs. The room was more than half full and people were still coming in and I got a case of the wobblies but it passed. We sat and waited. The professor consulted his watch, waiting a couple of minutes past seven to let in latecomers before walking to the lectern.

"Tonight's speaker is Josephine Littletree, who will be talking about her people's tribal myths. A couple of points before she begins. Miss Littletree hasn't had the benefit of a university education. I don't know if that's a good or a bad thing, or maybe irrelevant. Delivering a talk to a campus audience is new to her. And remember that she will be speaking about what is to most British Columbians, including I daresay to any anthropology students present, an unfamiliar culture. This will be a learning experience both for her and us. I ask you to please welcome her to Brooke Hall."

There was polite applause from the now almost full room. I walked to the lectern and he gave me an encouraging grin and sat down. There I was in front of my audience. The room went quiet. I put my hands on the sides of the lectern. How do you begin? So much needed to be said, to be made public. But I couldn't do it all at once. I had to work with the audience, see what I could get them to understand. Being there was an accomplishment, I told myself.

"Thank you, Professor Tavistock, for giving me this opportunity to speak. No, I have not been to university. People like me don't get to places like this, and most of us don't know they exist. Our world is different, partly by choice and partly because we have to be what the government says we must be. There is no Department of English or Welsh, Scottish, Irish or French Affairs but there is a Department of Indian Affairs. But you didn't come to listen to that. So I will not disappoint you any longer.

"I'm here to tell you about my people, who live in the Cariboo area or more correctly west of it, if you're a geographer and like maps. I've collected our stories from the different bands. They're an important part of our culture. We have traditions, we have a culture. We're not uncivilized, as anthropologists, the churches and governments have said.

"We have an oral tradition. We tell stories that reflect our beliefs. These have been passed down for centuries. In one of them, Raven, a special animal to my nation, gives people fire. Fire is kept by one man, who won't share it. Raven ties wood shavings to his hair, dances in the man's house for two days, until the man gets tired of guarding his fire and falls asleep. Raven puts his head near the fire, the shavings light and he sets fires around the country. The man tries to get his fire back but it's burning everywhere. The forest catches fire and the fire remains in the wood. And that's why you can start a fire by rubbing sticks together."

A smirking guy directly in front of me in the first row spoke up.

"That's like a fairy tale for children."

"Are you a Christian?"

"Yes."

"You believe the stories in the Bible?"

"Yes."

"In the story of Noah's Ark, your god causes a great flood and all the animals are gathered together in a boat until land reappears."

The smirk got wider.

"I don't take that story literally, if that's what you're getting at. The Flood was to punish people for their sins, a rather drastic sign from God. It's an allegory, if you know what that word means. It's to teach the masses in terms they would understand."

"Maybe you can explain something. Three times Noah sent out a dove to see if the waters had subsided, the second one returning with an olive leaf. A dove has a special meaning for Christians as a symbol of peace and purity. The dove with an olive branch symbolizes the Holy Spirit. Is a dove superior to a raven, or is that too allegorical for you?"

He was sneering now.

"You don't read the Bible very carefully, but I'm not surprised. Before Noah sent out the doves, he sent out a raven. The raven didn't return. St. Jerome, whom you may have heard of—he's the one who wrote the Vulgate, the

Catholic Bible—calls the raven 'the foul bird of wickedness.' The raven is a scavenger that feeds on dead flesh. Biblical scholars guess that the raven was busy feeding on all the dead bodies floating on the waters of the Flood. His blackness is symbolic of darkness, sin, all that stuff. Not quite the dove as a symbol of the Holy Spirit, would you say?"

"I know about St. Jerome. The school I attended was named after him. Jerome also wrote a life of St. Paul the Hermit. He mentions Paul was visited by a bird. Every day it brought him half a loaf of bread. Otherwise he would have starved. Do you know what kind of bird?"

No response.

"It was a raven."

He got upset, the poor man.

"You're not going to get away with that. Pagan myths are not on the same level as the Bible and other Christian writings. They teach moral lessons. What does your tribal stuff teach except believing that animals can have magical powers?"

"The story I told teaches generosity, sharing. Yours teaches obedience through drastic punishment. Everybody drowns but the righteous. Sounds familiar. Never seems to work though, does it?"

Some in the audience laughed.

"The truth is, you Indians aren't capable of understanding Western ideas or art or culture."

"When I was a girl I was forced to attend a Catholic residential school. I received daily religious instruction, along with beatings, semi-starvation, planting and digging up potatoes half a day every day except Sunday, and long separations from my people. I was taught nothing of Western ideas, art or culture except what could be used against me. I was taught to hate myself by people who told me their god was merciful and just. They weren't merciful and just to their prisoners. Don't expect a convict who's been condemned for a crime she didn't commit to love her jailers. And don't ever say 'you Indians' to me again or I may show you how much of a savage I am."

Boos from the audience.

"You know nothing of me or my people. And when I try to explain I'm called 'you Indians' and when I defend my right to be a person I'm booed. I didn't come here expecting much sympathy. But I thought you'd at least act civilized to fool me."

Mixed laughter and boos.

The man with the smirk wasn't finished. He played to the audience.

"There's a war going on and it's not in this country. We have to focus our energies on winning that war and not on righting so-called wrongs against those who've got a soft life on reserves."

"Ever been to a reserve? Seen the poverty? The disease? Know the rate of tuberculosis? It's twenty times higher than the rest of the population."

"I'm getting a little tired of hearing that everything is our fault. You're repeating the same old line. You're like a rusty gate. I hear your hinges."

"You weren't asked here. You invaded land occupied for

thousands of years by independent nations. They stood in your way. And you pushed them aside as if they were worthless. It's easier to steal if you're stealing from those you consider inferior. You're thieves without the honesty to admit it. I know how you think. I learned it in school. Your school. As to the war, you're fighting your own kind, that grab and take, and that's why wars among you never end but get worse. We've cared for this land and we've taken care of it, and of the animals. You've won with guns, deceit, but you'll lose the land and we'll be lost along with you. You've betrayed yourselves as well as us and don't even know it. You're the worst disease you've inflicted on us."

There were loud boos and he got personal.

"You don't even really look all that Indian."

"What's that got to do with what I've been saying? In this country you're an Indian if you have any Indian blood at all. My people accept me as one of them. The rest of this country won't accept me."

"How do you know?"

"Darken your face with makeup and ride a bus or streetcar in this city. And don't pretend you don't know what I'm talking about. People judge by skin colour and not intelligence or character. If they did, you'd be showing off to the other monkeys in the zoo."

A frown replaced the smirk. Someone hollered, "Go back to the reserve." The audience began to leave. The professor rushed up to the lectern.

"I would like to thank Miss Littletree for her enlightening explanation of native myths. I'm sure we all learned something tonight."

The hall was emptying fast. He turned to me.

"Our little experiment didn't go quite as planned, did it?"

Our? He knew less about the real world than Ed George. I felt sorry for him. As sorry as you could feel for a man who lives in a cocoon.

On the drive back to the inlet trail we didn't say much. When we parted he wished me good luck. As I walked down the trail I could smell the salt water and felt sad and happy. Sam saw by my face it had been a flop.

"Told you he was a phony."

"He's not phony. His country is. He's too dumb to know it. Education made him stupid."

"Shouldn't have gone. Waste of time."

"They'll remember me. I told them off."

"Made the bastards uncomfortable, did you? Won't make any difference."

"Does to me."

Did you see? I saw. Who does she think she is, anyway, refusing to eat the food? Nothing wrong with the hash. Some nice bits of ham in it. There's too many here that cater to her. That janitor for one. Big goon. Him and his Ganong's. You'd think she was my lady fair. Well, I think he's weird. Chasing after sick women. Always trying to stare down their blouses or up, you know. Remember, Nancy Mears complained about him, and Gail Stenner did. Nancy told me—keep this to yourself—that he'd rub up against her chair while he was talking and this funny look would come over his face. She could smell something. She had to call for the nurse. He got his finger jammed into her cushion, had bored a hole into it and couldn't get it out until they picked her up. She couldn't get rid of him, then her mother complained and he stayed away. She's dead now, poor girl. Matron Fairfax has got his number, though. She'd like to get rid of him. I had to laugh once. He was supposed to be hosing out the men's washroom on the main floor. He left the hose on and water leaked from under the door and flooded the hall and reached the reception desk. Somebody slipped and that's when they noticed. Everybody was looking for him. Know where he was? In a cubicle in the ladies' washroom. He was standing on the seat, said he was fixing the toilet. There was no sign outside warning women he was in there. He had no tools. Gladys Porter, who works in the kitchen, found him, said his zipper was undone. She told me everything. She's the one with a bit of a limp whose husband died in the War. Her son sold model airplanes, built them himself out of balsa wood and put engines in them. Flew them on a line, like a kite. Once a plane went out of control and hit him in the head and drove him out of his mind, but he probably always was. A grown man who does that has to be a bit off. Anyway, Gladys found him like that, standing there. He'd been crouching on the seat when she pushed the door open. It wasn't locked but could be jammed shut. The lock was broken. Something else he was supposed to fix. He straightened up and offered her some gum. It needs a new float and trap, he told her, and the ballcock leaks. She could hardly believe what she saw, though she managed to tell him what happened. Someone must have turned it on, he said. Can't turn my back. They're looking for an excuse to fire me. As if there weren't enough reasons already to fire him. I notice Miss Menzies always smiles when he's mentioned or criticized. Doesn't really care, does she? Slack about everything she does. Except, of course, catering to her royal highness.

[The following speaker is one of the nurses. She seems in a supervisory position, which would indicate Fairfax, as would her comment on her accent.]

How are you this morning? You're losing too much weight. I'll have the doctor look at you later. You should try to eat something. Boiled eggs, or some grilled liver. The stuff's not that horrid. You can't live on fresh air. You shouldn't be out now. The weather is not suitable. The last thing you need is moist air in your lungs. There'll be plenty of time to be outside when it gets warm next spring. Do have some bananas. You smile every time I say that word, and tomatoes. At least I can raise your spirits sometimes. Here's something else that may do the trick, a letter for you. I was in the main office and the secretary found I was coming to see you and gave it to me. Your first since you've been here.

[The letter is from Sam and is attached by a pin to this page. It is dated May 3, 1957, more than two years before Josie died. It is written on two pages torn from an exercise book. As usual, the handwriting is large and slanted backwards. And although some of the words are scrawled there are no erasures. This would seem to indicate at least one earlier draft. The inclusion of the letter here grants it some significance. But what that significance is must always remain with Josie.]

Dear Josie

I know you don't want me to come and see you. The man who told me you had TB told me that. He said he'd bring me any messages. He never came back. It hasn't been easy staying here and worrying about you. I wish you'd let me visit you, even for a few minutes. The foreman at the cannery is a good guy and would give me compassionate leave any time. I promise not to bother you about anything. If it has to be one visit I'll accept that and leave you alone afterwards. I don't know why you've turned against me. We used to get along. There were troubles but nothing broke us up. I wish I could do some things over. I should have fed you better before you got sick. Maybe I should have taken you away from the dampness. These shacks aren't the best for that. There's always the wet getting into your bones. Fog and mist and raw wind and four-day rains and everything icy to touch in the morning. I tried to build this one better but I guess nothing would keep out moisture down here. Not even good joists and beams or tarpaper under the shiplap. It's too late now, anyway. I'm sorry you got tied up with a guy who couldn't do a lot better for you. I'm only a hobo whose boxcar grew stilts and who has barnacles on his bottom. Captain Billy says hi.

Your

Sam McLendon

Is she gone? Know what the dirty bitch said? Don't take her out in this weather again, Mr. Kuby, or I'll report you to Dr. Moxon. He'll go to the board of directors. I said, she wants to go out. She may but as a member of this staff you're supposed to let others look after the patients and stick to your own work. And if I see you bring her any more gums or those revolting confections I'll confiscate them. Don't the floors need sweeping? Know what I said? I think you'd make a good matron in a women's prison. She went pink. I must give up expecting civility from you besides accepting your usual disregard of rules. Let me make it plain. Any more flouting of the rules, any more trespassing into what is none of your business, and Dr. Moxon will get rid of you. Your purpose here is to clean up messes, not make them. I said, hey, I'm not going to be pushed around. I've had this job for ten years and I've only been off sick once. Keep interfering the way you are and your record will not protect you. You're not competent to decide what is good for the patients. Miss Littletree is not the first you've openly fraternized with, and I daresay she won't be the last before you will go too far. Miss Mears and Miss Stenner complained about you two years ago. The complaints are on file and can be brought forward and used against you. So that's it. I can't take you out any more or I'm canned. So they can give the rotten job to my assistant. It's all politics. I don't know why you want to go out, anyway. It's cold and wet. And you're coughing and spitting up blood. I hear you talking to yourself when I go to sneak you back in. It sounds like humming. Hey, if you don't want to tell me, that's all right. I'm not the kind of guy who pries. Not like these bitches here who spread stuff about me. You'd think I was some kind of pervert. I do my job. No help. And the thanks I get is to get talked about. You can't be friendly these days without getting called a weirdo. Your lilywhites aren't so pure. I could say a few things if I was a blabbermouth. I know what they're sneaking in. Can smell it on them. But nobody says anything because they've got connections. Miss Beanupherass would lose her job. Wouldn't that be a goddam shame? That bastard supposed to be helping me, he's got a floozie. Sneaks her in sometimes. He made a bed on top of the lockers, where there's room. Put blankets up there. Had to watch I didn't go in when they were at it. You could hear them from outside the door. She makes that kind of a grunting moan at not getting somewhere but never wanting to quit. I had to wait outside if I had business or go away till it was quiet and cough before going in. I got a sore throat once I coughed so loud. I told him to take her to the boiler room. He said the custodian's room was private. She didn't like all those pipes and gauges over there and it was too warm for her. Too warm for her? You spend all the rest of your time over there, I said. Sleeping it off, I should have told him. He said this was a nice change. I got fed up after a few weeks and told him to take her there or I'd throw their blankets out onto the basement floor. I don't care about his connections, I got rights too. He knew I meant it. Skinny little bastard. I could bounce him off the walls. The broad's not bad. Got an ass that wiggles and tits like smooth cantaloupes. And you know how some women look like they want it and that's all they ever want. He told me her husband's his uncle's bookkeeper. Who's keeping her books, huh? He's getting skinnier and skinnier. Pretty soon she'll be able to put him in her pencil sharpener. The lazy bastard never did any work. After she's finished with him he won't be doing anything, period. Not a bad way to go, though. But me, I got this job with yappy bitches who want a couple of dozen tradesmen for the price of a janitor. And expect to order me around like I'm a slave. I think we're all here for a reason, some to suffer and some to make others suffer. And the sufferers know they've got to take it, it's what their life's about. You can see it in religious paintings, the look on those faces. I'm not religious, except I can see they're looking to something else that's more important. To explain the suffering. Who am I to say they're wrong? Except I'm one of those who think those responsible should suffer too. The quicker they're made to suffer the better.

What are you doing out here, Josie? Helen would be furious if she found out. It wasn't Mr. Kuby, was it? He was warned. You've got almost nothing on, you're shivering. I'm not surprised, in this wind. And it's been raining, you're wet. Let's get you in. It's a good thing for you she has the night off. I'll get you to your room before anyone sees us. These handles are freezing cold. I think those who are up and about are in the common room watching television. I'll dry you off. We'll get some flannel pyjamas on you and get you into bed. Oh, hello Mrs. Oliphant, Mrs. Camberwell. Yes, more rain, definitely winter now. Yes, wasn't it short, though? Have to bundle up. Avoiding them is like trying to get wet hairs off your fingers. The worst gossips in the place. That's saying something. I almost laughed. I remembered you call them Elephant and Camel. They look it. A good thing they didn't see you outside. Wonder if they noticed your arms are wet? They have eyes like vultures. Circling over the dead and dying. Sorry. Besides, you needn't die unless you want to. We'll get you around this last corner. If it wasn't Mr. Kuby, I don't understand how you did it. Unless you're a lot stronger than I thought. Those doors are heavy. You're a canny one. If she finds out she'll lock you in. No, I won't tell. But don't think I'm going to let you commit suicide. All right, all right. It's not that. Something else. What is it, a ritual of some kind? Keep it to yourself then. It's Liverwurst, right in front of the door too, in her wheelchair. Hello, Mrs. Livermore. Nothing on television, I guess. No, I don't like this weather either. I'm taking her to bed. The poor dear is tired. If you'll move I'll wheel her into the room so I can change her. Get her ready for bed. Thank you so much. I have to shut the door now. Don't want her in a draught. Goodnight. I wouldn't be surprised if she waits outside for me. Pesters me about everything. Unlike you, she takes advantage of the staff. She's lonely. Her daughter put her here to be rid of her. Won't even visit. Nothing wrong with her except old age. Supposed to have high serum cholesterol and angina, but her daughter's the one with the bad heart, if you want my opinion. Her story isn't unusual. You would be surprised if I told you some things. Let's get you up. Those are soaked through. Here. You can rub yourself dry while I get your pyjamas. Those who can afford it drop their excuses off in this place. Lighter in the wallet and in the conscience. Whoever pays buys silence. We're as private as you could want without being anonymous. Sometimes I hate it. Then someone like you comes along who doesn't fit, shouldn't be here. And I think, this is the way it should be, everybody together instead of apart. You know what my crazy idea is? That the patient should be the doctor and the doctor the patient. We should learn from you what is wrong with us and you should charge us for it. Every case is different and learning about differences makes you realize that medical advice is too general. It divides us into groups according to symptoms. But symptoms don't always have the same cause. So you've got to look at each person and see what's different. And the more you see, the more you see yourself what's right and wrong. Crazy, huh? Didn't I tell you? There. All finished.

The meaning of the parable is that Jesus is the good shepherd and we are his flock. He is the light of the world. Meant to show us the way. His sacrifice was more painful because he was the child of woman and the Son of God. In Gethsemane he prayed, "O my Father, if it be possible, let this cup pass from me." He prayed twice more, accepting his ordeal: "O my Father, if this cup may not pass away from me, except I drink it, Thy will be done." But he sweated, an angel had to strengthen him, and remember what he said to Judas: "That thou doest, do quickly." Think of what it must have been like to be crucified. Think of those flat-edged iron nails being chiselled into wrists and feet. Think of the tearing pain of being hoisted up on the cross. Think of slumping there, slowly suffocating. Think of the laughter and tears below him, of being offered vinegar to drink. Think of Jesus crying out, "My God, my God, why has Thou forsaken me?" The agony of doubt in the man, knowing that he had been entrusted with a divine message: "I am the resurrection and the life. He that believeth in me, though he were dead, shall he live. And whosoever liveth and believeth in me shall never die." What a message of hope he gave to the multitudes that came to see and hear him: "All things are possible to him that believeth." And to his disciples: "Ask, and it shall be given you." And then on the cross his final words, the words of a suffering man, "It is finished." I can never read or think of those words without a tear. Have you ever wondered why there are four gospels, dear? Each tells the same story about the life and teachings of Christ, the miracles and the passion. I love them all, have no favourite because they have taught me that no two people tell the same story, even when inspired by God. People see different things. What is important is they tell the truth. Truth is different to each and each tells it differently, so every story tells you about the teller as well. In these differences Jesus becomes human and through them we see his human face, and through it the Son of God, the other face.

Someone said to me that if a certain Roman emperor hadn't seen a vision in the sky before a battle he won there wouldn't be Christians, that if he lost or his eyesight was bad or a pagan sign had appeared we'd all be followers of another religion. Some things are too great to be chancy, I said. Nothing depends on a day or on only one man's sight. Big things happen and they will be. No emperor, or any other human leader, can tell people after a victory to worship suddenly what they don't want to. You can't even tell people not to drink. They'll get it somewhere. Or not to commit adultery. They'll find a time and a place. You have to persuade them it's not right. And you know, it's harder to persuade them to do something than not do it. They could get sick and tired of something they're already doing. But to do something they don't want to, that's moving mountains and without faith, impossible. They were ready to be Christians when it was made the religion of Rome. Otherwise they'd have stuck to their worn-out truckload of gods and goddesses. Some were stolen from the Greeks and who knows where else? From what I've seen of those ancient religions, it's a lot of half-naked men and women running around chasing each other and throwing tantrums. Sex in the clouds and arguing about jurisdiction over this and that part of humans. No reason for any of it except a big case of boredom. Who needs a load of that type? Personally I can't see the fuss about Venus. I guess it's because I'm a woman. She'd have been run out of my old hometown lickety-split with the other harlots. Some of the men would have been disappointed. You can't change human nature. Temptation: "The spirit is indeed willing, but the flesh is weak." But you can always try to make sure it's as far away as possible. "Get thee behind me, Satan." So you'll always walk in the way of the righteous, the one, the true path. Are you tired, dear? Because of all my talking, I guess. I'm sorry but I'm after saving your soul. I'm a shepherd in a small way, helping to gather the flock. One of the disciples by descent of faith. I'll leave you with the parable about heaven, the man who found idle men all day to work in his vineyard and at the end of the day paid everybody the same, even though some wanted more money for working longer. They'd had more opportunity to work, that's all. Doesn't matter what you've got here, everybody will be treated the same when it comes to judgement. "So the last shall be first, and the first last: for many be called, but few chosen." I'm going now, dear. You'll be able to get some sleep. I've found the best thing for sleep is to say what I say every single night: "The Lord is my shepherd. . . ."

They're getting rid of me. Don't know if I'll be here past Friday. I've got to see Moxon tomorrow morning. He's already seen the board. It'll be a formality. Moxon can't stand up to them. He kisses their asses. Head like a skunk. They picked him to look after their alkie wives and drug-loony daughters, put the well-off moms and dads and aunts and uncles on a rest cure. So their money is easy pickings. Sanatorium—ha. This place should be called "we store and bury them." I wouldn't put my parents here. They're still around. I live with them. My mom's in her eighties. My dad's over ninety. Lazy bastard. Never had a job. Except during the War, when everybody was working. My mom told him to get one in the shipyards. Soon as the War ended and the shipyards closed he stopped working and we moved up here. Better for his lungs, he said. Houses were cheap. When I got older I went back to the coast and worked at a refinery. My eyes went bad. That's why I wear these dark glasses. My cousin told me about this job and I came back. I should have stayed at the refinery. I moved in with them and I'm renting out my house. I buy the groceries. I bought some bologna for him a few weeks ago and he choked on it. He's got false teeth and tried to chew it without them. Had to pull it out of his mouth. Big wad of it, bread too. He sat there afterwards and kept opening his mouth like a fish. Makes you think. About what you're doing. I'm fifty-five now. Nothing ahead, but I got my money no matter what happens. Moxon was called in, told to use whatever he could on me. It was my assistant and his uncle. I know too much. The broad, other things. His uncle was getting him ready all the goddam time to replace me, anyway. They'll get a new assistant and make him do all the work. This asshole will be back on top of the lockers again. That's how it works. Shitty world, huh? I'll get severance pay. Moxon is going to say he'll give me a good recommendation and forget the complaints. I'll end up a night watchman. Maybe at that porno warehouse. That guy's going to quit. Wants to go into business and sell it. Be different watching over a bunch of girlie magazines and dirty movies. Wonder if they've got a projector there I could use on the sly sometimes? For a laugh. She's coming. I got to go. Habit, I guess. I've been working too long at Braeburn. I should've seen his plan, the bastard. Take care of yourself. Won't see you again. Stay inside. Better for you. She's right. Too cold out there. Where'd I leave my goddam mop? If somebody fell on my last day here. . . .

You look terrible, Josie. You're losing colour. Coughing and wheezing. You brought it on yourself. Somebody squealed on you. No, it wasn't me. Helen's left orders for you to be watched. She's thinking about force-feeding you if you don't start eating. I told her I could get you to eat something. It's beef broth. Have a spoonful. Another, come on. It won't kill you. We're going to finish the bowl, aren't we? Or I won't tell you about Mr. Kuby. And we're going to eat these crackers too. I know it's blackmail. I'm not going to say anything until you've finished it all. All, I said. Every morsel. That's what my mother used to say when she wanted me to finish my porridge. I hated it. It'll build your bones, she would say. The only way I could get it down was to pour cream and brown sugar over it. You'll get cavities from all that sugar. It's the only way I can eat it, Mom, honest. No treats for you, then. I was going to make fudge brownies. That's not fair. Every morsel or no brownies. Every morning it would go on like that. And now I'm getting someone to eat something she doesn't want to. By the way, she put more sugar in the fudge than I ever put on the porridge. One more. Every time he sees me he sneaks peeks while sweeping or mopping. You know how men stare as if you don't know. We look too but we're smarter about it. Our one second is worth a million of their gawks and glances. Once he was staring so hard he didn't see his pail and tripped over it. Dirty water went all over the floor. He pretended it didn't happen. The way he always pretends he doesn't know what you're talking about when you tell him something. He thinks you're trying to pick on him. He gets his back up and tells you all his troubles. And you're looking at those dark glasses of his and wondering what he's seeing. I don't think it's the world we're seeing. I get this creepy feeling about him. I think he can see through clothes. Makes you want to get away from him. Those huge fingers like fried pork sausages that have split their casing in places. I'll bet he knows women think he's weird. He's got to know. You're the only one who talks to him. Listens, I should say. The staff stay away unless we've got to speak to him. He's the resident freak, and that's saying a lot when I think about this place. I know I'm taking a long time. And you're almost finished.

Mr. Kuby looked unsteady with his broom this morning when I saw him in the upper hall, and I heard him mumbling to himself. I think he's drinking. I felt sorry for him. Everybody knows he's going to be let go. Because of what those two girls said about him a couple of years ago. And slackness. He spends more time in the parking lot polishing his car than polishing the floors. He doesn't pay any attention to the heating system, to maintenance or needed repairs. And there's always a problem with the boiler. He doesn't call the serviceman. We're freezing in January and overheated in July. Something goes wrong with the ducts or pipes or there's no hot water and we have to go looking for him and can't find him. He leaves buckets and mops everywhere, can't replace a lock or a pane of glass. Some of us have a theory about where all the soap and wax go instead of in the washrooms and on floors. That slogan he's got on his car bumper, "A free market and a free man," he applies literally to himself I guess. But Helen's fair, whatever he may have said about her. She would never ask for his dismissal unless you complained about him or he kept taking you outside, and neither is likely. As for him being a victim of nepotism, I doubt that. I heard Ladner is a pain in the neck to his uncle, who'd like to forget him. He's done nothing but fool around and get drunk ever since he got out of high school. And he's gotten into so many accidents his insurance premiums are bankrupting the family. They put him here to hide him so they can go back to making money. I know he's lazy but it doesn't help to have two incompetents sloughing off and the rest of us covering for them. I have to get a stepladder and change light bulbs sometimes. You ask and ask and it's never done. They're paid to do it and I haven't got the time. I've had to go to the storeroom for bulbs and fluorescent tubes. It's in the basement, right next to the custodian's room. Helen has a duplicate key. One of the nurses or someone from the kitchen helps me with the ladder. You've never been to the custodian's room. It smells as if a rat died there in a pile of its own droppings. I've had to go looking for him a few times. He opens the door and stares at you without saying anything as you look at the light reflected off his glasses. Sometimes I think there's nothing behind them but empty eye sockets. You get the feeling he's going to grab you and haul you inside into that stink that comes from behind him and you won't see daylight again. I always start backing away before the end of my first sentence, hoping he won't come after me along the corridor. Silly, except when I think of those glasses. If you went down there you'd know what I mean. There are some men you can't get away from fast enough.

You lone. Don't care. I says to Moccasin, you fughin' ass-hole, who do you think you are, you cacksicker, dismissin' me? I bin heer mos' 'leven years and dun dun 'sclent work. Yur treatin' me like shit for cleanin' up yur shit.

You're drunk, Mr. Kuby.

Yur fughin' right I'm drunk. Good and pissed. Pisstoff too. With the whole goddam bunch. 'Cludin' yur dainties, cunts Menses and Fairfux.

I don't have to listen to this.

You'll listen. I'll pick up yur chair with you in it and throw you through the window. Hidin' behin' yur desk. I clear my throat and spit out better things than you. You pusher. Think I don't know? Shootin' up half the sickos in heer. Mainlinin' the biggies. While holdin' their hans. More pricks in heer than a whorehouse. Hey, and yur pills. Sedatives, ha. Ass kissin' yur pal, the drugstore fart.

Mr. . . .

All my life I bin puttin' up with assholes like you. Ejacashun. I got more money 'n you'll ever see. And I know plenty. Not book stuff. Yur sheepskin shit. Go 'round impressin' the cunts in heer. Know somethin', Moccasin. I don't think yur man enough to get it up one of the bishes. Can't do it. And I don't want yur ref-rence. Stick yur ref-rence. Wouldn't wipe my ass with it. Think I'm so fughin' dumb I can't see why you're doin' this?

I assure you, I have no ulterior motive. I've attempted to explain once again the reason to you. Considering the condition you're in, I shouldn't have bothered trying. When we had our little chat this morning, you were sober.

Lil' chat. That's the way the fughin' cacksicker talks. Sprays perfume on a string of farts. Sits on a pile of bullshit and pretens it don't smell. I'm standin' there listenin' and wonderin' how far I can throw the asslickin' prick 'fore he'll land.

What did he say? I saw him lurching towards the service elevator a few minutes ago, after he talked to you. He's probably in the basement. I think the office is going to call the police. Some of the staff are worried. He's made threats. He's gone crazy. He thinks they're getting rid of him because he knows too much. That's a laugh. It's because he does too little. This is his last day. They didn't want to give him notice. He's getting severance pay, and Helen says they're being generous. They're being fair. He couldn't expect more than that after being so slack. I've got to see to some others. I'll get back to you.

Don't you touch me.

Touch you? I wouldn't lay a fughin' finger on you. You're not worth shit. You heer that? Shit. You bishes think yur better 'n that woman. Talkin' behin' her back. I heer you. You Scotchlimeywhateverthefuckyouare. I'll bet yur cunts are made of cork. Yur tongues are the only things that work. You went and tol' Fairfux I was takin' her outside. None of yur fughin' business. You yappy cunts.

You've got no right to speak to us that way. You'd better get out of here.

Leave us alone. We'll get the police after you. Hope they put you in jail. Foreigner.

Maybe I should do somethin' bad.

You'll be sorry if you do. What kind of a man are you, picking on women in wheelchairs?

I've got a bad heart. If anything happens to me. . . .

Nuthin's happened to you for years. Yur husban's probly bin layin' some young piece of ass ever since he dumped you in heer. This place is a garbage can and yur the garbage. You couldn't give it away on skid row.

Some men get courage from a bottle.

That so? It takes guts to look at you two. All the years you bin sneerin' at me, thinkin' yur so 'sperior. You think I don't know you got those girls to say things 'bout me?

We had nothing to do with that. They complained to the nurses.

It was all their idea. They told us what you did.

I didn't do anything.

They said you did those things to them.

I didn't.

They were such nice girls from good families. One of them is dead.

Like it's my fault. Load of bullshit. You got yur brakes on. Good. If you don't mind, I got to take a leak.

Don't you dare. You dirty pig. Ohhhh. Euww.

Get yur hans 'way. Now you.

Help.

Isn't it terrible what happened to them? Why are you laughing, Josie? He's in the basement again. In the custodian's room. He won't come out. They've called the police. He's smashed windows all over the place, thrown fire extinguishers through them. Axes, pails of sand. He turned on that fire hose on the ground floor. The whole floor is flooded. They can't get to the hose to shut it off and they don't know where the shutoff valve is on the main water line. There's smoke coming from the boiler room. They've called the fire department. Fire and flood, he's done it all. I trust he's happy with what he's putting everybody through. We've got to evacuate the building right away. All right, Josie, let's go, you're first.

It's cold out here. The police went down to the custodian's room. Can you see anything? Look, he's on the roof. How did he get up there? He's waving his arms. Yelling something. We're so far away I can't hear what he's saying. There's so much noise. They're still bringing out patients. He's making his way down to the edge of the roof. Lots of snow up there. The tiles must be slippery. The fire department is putting up an extension ladder to get him. Wait till they get hold of him. He'll be in trouble. A policeman is out there. Behind him. See? Crouching. He could slip too. He's seen him and he's moving away. He can't get away. At the corner now. He's yelling again, saying something—I can't hear. No one can hear him this far away. I can see the vapour coming out of his mouth. His arms are stretched out. He's waving or signalling at someone or something, I can't tell. Fireman is climbing the ladder. The policeman has stopped. It's too slippery, I guess. Still shouting. Raving away like a maniac. It proves he is crazy, doesn't it? Who can hear in all this noise? Starting to snow again. He won't be able to see anything. Everything is beginning to fade behind the snow. There's only an outline now. My God, he's not there.

It was terrible, constable. He was a filthy pervert. A foreigner of some kind. They come to this country and they can't fit in. You'd think the government would keep them out. We warned about him years ago. Patients complained he molested them. But nobody would listen. And that woman egged him on. I hope she's satisfied with all the trouble she's caused.

She doesn't really belong here, you know. She's only been here a year and look what's happened. This was a nice quiet place before she got here. Nothing like this ever happened.

Goes to show, doesn't it? You can't bring her kind in without having something like this happen. Looking for an excuse to disrupt things. They're never satisfied till they've caused trouble. She's the worst I've seen. Puts on airs like she's something so special. You can smell the reserve on her. They never wash, you know. Their personal habits are filthy. My husband—he's dead now, poor man—went to a reserve once. The stories he told. You wouldn't believe it. They live like animals. You probably know more about them than we do, having to deal with them all the time for breaking the law.

I think she should be charged with something, as an accessory after the fact. That's how you say it, isn't it? For the damage he caused. Of course, her kind never have any money to pay for what they break. Too busy drinking it away.

Miss Littletree? I'm Constable Laidlaw of the local detachment. We found this note on the body. It's addressed to you. I've talked to staff and other patients here. Some of them think you could tell me more than they could about him. I'd like a statement from you for the coroner's inquest.

[The note, unsigned, is pinned to this page. It was printed on the back of a bill of lading for janitorial supplies with a leaky ballpoint pen and the printing is shaky and quite large.]

Josie

I got nothing left. I don't know what it's all about. Money, sex. All I know is I never called you by your name. You always listened to me. I never told you how much it meant. You smiled too, and that's the last thing I'll be thinking about. Shouldn't have started drinking again. Should've stuck to Juicy Fruit. Didn't know I'd take it so hard. But I can see now part of the reason you kept wanting me to take you outside. When life is something to get rid of, it's better to do it quick. You got your reasons, I got mine. Yours are complicated, mine are mixed up. Remember I said I wasn't meant to meet a nice woman? What do you know, I met one. It didn't last and it wasn't what I thought it would be like, but it was more than I ever got from anyone else.

"Come in, Rosalind, and have a seat. I've asked you and Helen here to tell you that the executive board and I have agreed Miss Littletree should no longer be a patient at Braeburn. We admitted her a year ago because an agent for a friend of hers made an application, convincing me to waive our policy of not accepting natives. The experiment, if I may term it that, hasn't worked out. She has rejected all attempts to treat her, and of late has even refused food unless you talk her into eating. She even persuaded Mr. Kuby to take her outside on a kind of suicide mission. His death is not unlinked to his unorthodox relationship with her. I should have discharged him when those complaints were made. I was too lenient, despite the urgings of members of the board and some of the patients. After what's happened the board has unanimously agreed that she should no longer be a patient here."

"You can't blame her for Mr. Kuby's death."

"I think it's fair to say their relationship at least helped to induce his mentally unbalanced state."

"It wasn't her fault. She can't be held responsible for the sanity of someone she happens to talk to."

"The fact is, he worked here for eleven years without smashing anything or jumping off the roof."

"You fired him, and maybe that's what made him jump."

"Employees are discharged all the time but they don't go jumping off roofs after breaking windows and setting fire to a building. I had to let him go because of his lax attitude, which you as a hard-working member of this staff can personally attest to. I must share part of the blame for not acting more promptly. But Miss Littletree shouldn't have fraternized with him or used him."

"How do you know what she said to him, Dr. Moxon? Maybe he was ready to have a breakdown."

"I don't think anyone but a qualified psychiatrist can assess that."

"I agree. And I think she shouldn't be blamed for what none of us can judge."

"Nonetheless, the board's decision is final and I fully concur with it. I should add that some members and patients have wondered why you took Miss Littletree out first when the order to evacuate was given."

"Because I was with her at the time. I didn't realize there was a caste system staff had to observe whenever evacuations occurred. I'd like a leave of absence to attend her elsewhere. She's dying and you're throwing her out. The least I can do is nurse her until she dies."

"I think it's her wish to die. As to your getting a leave of absence, that's impossible."

"Then you have my resignation, effective immediately. Helen can take care of the paperwork and anything else."

"If that's your wish. It will leave us short of staff. You won't, of course, expect a recommendation from me when you apply for another position. Your resignation is sudden and without good cause."

"I don't need a recommendation. I'm a registered nurse and unlike doctors and administrators we work cheap and there's always a demand for good cheap labour."

"I'm truly sorry, Miss Menzies, that Miss Littletree has ended your association with Braeburn."

"She hasn't done anything. You're using Mr. Kuby's death to get her out because you and others don't want her here."

"That's not quite the way I and those others you refer to see it."

"That's the honest way to see it.

"So Braeburn and I are quits, Josie. It's been coming for a while. You're going back to the reserve and I'm going with you. Your cousin told me when he visited you at Christmas that your grandmother left you her house. We'll stay there, and whoever's living there now won't mind leaving or being quarantined. All I need is somewhere to put my feet up. I've talked with Helen. She'll help us with anything we need, medicine and such. She'd like you to stay but she can't say anything without jeopardizing her position here. There's too many against you. I'll contact your cousin about our arrival. I've told the office we won't be leaving for a few days. That will give him time to get the house ready. Your meal tonight is roast beef, mashed potatoes, peas and carrots. We're going to eat it all, aren't we? Shut up about me. My family will understand when I tell them. I'm ornery when I get my back up. I'll be glad to go. I'm taking a shortwave radio along with us in the car. I'll be able to talk with Helen. I'm a bit of a ham, you know."

Hello, Helen? I don't know what to do with her. She won't eat any more. I can hardly get some broth into her. She's getting weaker. I know. She was all right for the first couple of weeks up here. Seeing her relatives again all the time. And the Pauls have been wonderful, done everything they could. But they seem to know what she's doing. They accept it. They see things differently. From us, anyway. I thought I knew her but I guess I don't. All she wants to do is write. We brought her paper and ink with us. She sits in her chair on the front porch and scribbles away and gets so tired her head sinks down like she's asleep, or resting. I can't tell. Her coughing fits come and go. She doesn't cough up much blood. I don't know where she gets her strength. I know. She insists on going outside. The weather has been warm for March. We're going to have an early spring. I want her to live to see it. Maybe it'll revive her. I've been out for walks. There's a grove on the edge of the reserve, behind vines and tall grass. It's lovely down there. On the way over I saw blueberry bushes, or maybe they're bilberry or huckleberry. I'm not very good at spotting plants. I'd like to take her down there but the ground in that part of the reserve is too bumpy for a wheelchair. It's too far anyway. I couldn't push it all that distance. And she can't ride a horse any more. I'd probably be able to get her there in the car but the ride would be very rough and I don't want her sicker than she is. I go there now whenever I'm feeling low. Sit with my back against a tree and close my eyes, listen to the wind. Everything goes out of me and something else comes in. I don't know what. It's like leaving your body for a while and drifting away. Sometimes I think I'm a bird circling over the grove and can even see the creek off to one side of it. A trickle, almost lost among the overhanging grass, but I can see it. Sometimes I'm the wind rubbing up against rough bark or slipping up a curving blade of grass and skimming along that fluted vee and off the point and the grass is springy with my weight though my weight is air. Or I'm the creek slipping velvet smooth between banks and bottom, which is my bottom. Or I'm a bud ready to burst and the bursting's inside and my petals are the sky. It'll hurt, it'll hurt so much and I'll love it terribly. I keep telling myself, you're a nurse, Roz, wake up, you're not supposed to feel this way. I'm also a Scot. So maybe that explains it. By the way, I haven't told her any of this. I don't want to give our girl any encouragement. Not that she needs it. Quite single-minded, she is. I've got to sign off. Her relatives may drop in and hear.

[There is a break in the manuscript at this point.]

Helen? Thank God I've got you to talk to. This woman is crazy. She looks at me in a different way now, as if I'm an enemy. I know, you're right. You told me not to come here. But I felt sorry for her because of the way she was treated there. I thought this place would revive her. It's been the opposite. She wants more than ever to die. The weather's turned cool lately and she still wants to stay out all hours on the porch. I went to get her yesterday when it was getting dark. She was out of the wheelchair and moving like a sleepwalker across the front yard. There was a mist, terrible for her lungs. I ran out to bring her back. Her face was wet, covered with a fine spray that made her skin shine. I asked her where she was going.

Leave me alone. Go away.

You've got to come inside.

You're always watching me.

I'm trying to help you.

Go away. I don't want your help.

I'm a nurse.

Nurse.

She laughed and punched me. It took all her strength.

But I'd had enough. I dragged her across the yard and up onto the porch like a sack of potatoes, threw her into the wheelchair and wheeled mademoiselle inside. I've got a black eye, a real shiner. Makeup covers most of it. You can still see a bit near the corner, that purple-yellow colour. I thought about telling her cousin and the others but it wouldn't do any good. They've accepted her death already. I know. I should get out. She's going to die soon if she keeps this up. Most times now I get the silent treatment from everybody. They're polite. I'm an outsider, that's all. Listen, I've got to whisper. I don't want her to hear this. I'm going to transfer her. Should be in a hospital. They can watch her better than I can. Phone General about admitting her. Convalescent care, extended care, wherever they'll put her. Tell them she's a public health risk, I'm leaving, there'll be no one to care for her. I know they don't care about the reserves. Say there's a danger of contact with outside persons. Get them to send a car here. I'll radio tomorrow and you can tell me.

Helen. I've only got a few minutes. She found out about the hospital. Must have heard me. She's got incredible hearing and sight. She was in the living room. It was dark. I couldn't see. I'd left the light on. She switched it off. I tripped on something heavy. I was on my hands and knees and something grazed my head. I crawled away and felt it hit my hip, then it nipped at my foot. I could hear heavy wheezing.

Get out.

I'm going.

Do you know what a nurse log is?

No.

It's rotting trunk feeds a new tree. Do you understand that death can feed life?

Yes?

That death becomes life?

Yes.

That death and life at some point are the same thing?

I guess so.

You think they're at opposite ends of reality, life on a one-way street to death.

Maybe.

You think I'm crazy.

I think you should be in a hospital.

I know what you think before you do.

I know that you can hear me talking on the radio.

I was still on my hands and knees. I didn't know what she was holding that had hit me. I could see her in the middle of the room, a darker hump against the darkness, leaning towards me in her wheelchair. I thought, was she waiting for me to move so she could hit me again? She hadn't hurt me. But the fall onto the floor had hurt my kneecaps and I'd twisted a knee. She'd put an object where I'd be certain to trip over it in the dark. I started to crawl again. The thing came through the air with a hissing sound and stung my calf. I was worried. She'd said to get out and when I tried she'd stopped me. I didn't know what she was thinking. We were alone in the house and if I yelled I didn't know if anybody would hear or would bother to come. I thought about rushing her and knocking her over but my knee was hurting enough for me to wonder whether I could move fast or stand easily. Come on, Roz, I told myself, think, you've got to get out of this. You're the nurse and she's the patient. Some patient she is. She turned on the table lamp and when I got used to the glare I could see that she was holding a whip and that the front of her sweater was soaked in blood she had coughed up while waiting. There was a smear of blood where she had wiped her chin. I felt anger and pity. I knew she wouldn't want the pity. And I needed the anger so I wouldn't feel too sorry. She had finished talking. I doubt if she could have said anything if she tried. I got up and managed to limp away. I can't stay in this house tonight. I won't ask anybody here for help. The rain has stopped. My knees aren't too bad, maybe a torn muscle in one. I'll get it looked at when I get back. There's my bag to pack, with my things. I'm leaving the medicine, for what's it's worth. No, Helen, don't drive up. It's too far for you. You wouldn't get here until tomorrow. And you're needed at the sanatorium. I can still drive. I'll stay overnight in Williams Lake. Be in Kamloops by tomorrow. These past four months seem like four years.

[The rest of this page is blank. The final paragraph is on a separate page.]

Finally it's me, Grandmother. My own ending, coughing into silence. I have to get rid of myself, not be little Josie any more, let the atoms start floating away to something else. Is that so bad? Who's so important she can't say goodbye? It's another way of saying hello. What's going to take me away is so big I can only say yes. I can be afraid or curious. What we know limits us as much as what we don't know. Everything I've done well I've done as naturally as breathing. I can do this as long as I don't think about it. What will be left? The stories. They aren't mine, they're everybody's. It's all one story, the same for everyone. The way it's told is the important thing, as if it belongs to anyone who hears it. They were given to me and I pass them on, one pair of hands to another I'll never see, a voice I'll never hear. But I know her as well as I know myself. She is one with us, Grandmother. She was when she was a baby and somebody lifted her up high and she spread her arms wide and knew if she fell she would fall into the one embrace that is all beginnings and endings of our dreams. And now I go to meet you on the wind of that embrace, into the cold nothing I won't ever feel. How can we be apart if we share one mind? I am not Josie, I never was. I am raven and she-bear, I am falcon and orca maiden, using words of the two-footed invaders. Root to branch, red cedar rising.

Letters

The last item in Josie's envelope is a letter from Sam. The letter had not been read, the envelope flap still sealed with scotch tape. It is off-white and almost square, the kind generally used for Christmas cards, and the letter was written on eight pages from one of his exercise books. Dated May 11, 1960, it was most likely written a couple of months after Josie's death and was undoubtedly forwarded from the sanatorium. The envelope has a Saltspring Island postmark, which would suggest Sam visited Captain Billy after the inlet shacks had been demolished.

Dear Josie

I dreamt last night you had died. The dream woke me up and I couldn't get back to sleep. I had to write this. It's about the first time I took you out in a rowboat on Burrard Inlet. We'd been together four months. It was Easter Sunday. A warm day in the middle of April. The water was as calm as it ever gets there, with no tide running. I rowed out and we drifted and you wanted to go over to the other side. We came ashore near a sawmill. While I pulled the boat up onto the beach you began dancing on logs floating loose in the pond in front of the loading chute. I walked up and watched you tapping and turning barefooted, stepping from log to log. You had the whole place to yourself. The men on the green chain had the day off. Those circular saws weren't screaming their jag-tooth crescendos. There were no tugs offshore with tire-nosed snouts bobbing in the swells and butting logs together, no guys with gaffs and hobnail boots hopping around the booms. The mountain of sawdust at the mill end of the pond was yesterday's souvenir. I was on the point of being magnanimous in forgiving their trespasses against the forest, when I remembered that my shack and boats were made of wood. The logs sank a bit at the light pressure of your weight. But one of them was splintered at one end, though above the water it was round and looked to be full size. It sank out of sight when you stepped on it and you went under. I hopped across on the logs and dived in at the spot where you disappeared. The water was brown and sunlight made a crisscross pattern of lime bars where the logs separated on the surface, letting me see into the brown murk. You had sunk to the bottom and I grabbed hold of you and pulled. When we came to the surface I banged my shoulder against a log but I didn't feel anything at the time. It could have been a twig instead of a log for all I felt. All I thought was, I don't want to lose her. I put you on your stomach at the muddy edge of the pond and pumped out the water you had swallowed. There wasn't much because you started yelling I was hurting you. We found a sandy place close by and I went to the boat and brought back a blanket and some rags. You took off your clothes and dried yourself with the rags and lay down on the blanket. You spread your arms and let the sun warm you. I took off my boots, shirt and pants but kept on the long johns, unbuttoned to the waist and pulled up to my knees. You smiled, your hair fluffed out, making you look so young.

"You look silly."

"I'd look sillier if I took them off."

"It's not important."

It is to some, I thought, looking down at you.

"Are you ashamed of me?" you said.

"Ashamed? What do you mean?"

"I'm an Indian."

"I don't think of you as an Indian."

"What am I to you?"

"A woman. A goddam beautiful one too."

"Don't you wish my skin was lighter?"

"Looks fine to me."

"You mean right now with no clothes on."

"No. Ever since I met you."

"You were lonely."

"I was lonely. I got lucky."

"I was better than nobody."

"You were better than anybody. You're the best."

I rowed us back under the stars, two dark shapes facing each other and talking and hearing our voices in the vast silence around us. I stopped rowing in the middle and it seemed the black silhouette of the shore was moving instead of the boat on the slow current. The sky looked painted with powdered sapphires dissolved in acid, a shining pearl up high and for background sprinkled crushed ice. The breeze brought the smell of trees, of new leaf and resin, and the hooting of an owl drifted out to us. When I began to row again the oars made invisible small splashings into the moon-glinting inky fathoms and the oarlocks creaked.

"Are you shivering?" I said.

"A little."

"I'll take off my jacket and put it over your shoulders."

"Why aren't you shivering?"

"Long johns."

"I know what's better. I'll come and sit between your legs and put my arms inside your jacket."

"I wouldn't be able to row very well."

"All right. Hand it over. Don't want to be out here any longer than I have to. I'm getting cold."

I took off my jacket and passed it to you and you draped it over your shoulders.

"Maybe you shouldn't have kept your clothes off for so long and lain naked like that. They dried in a couple of hours over the fire I made."

"You don't understand anything. I had to. It made me feel free. That's why I danced on the logs."

"I had to save you."

"I could've gotten out."

"You can't swim. That place is dangerous."

"How do you know I can't swim? I can swim better than

you. I could've come up and grabbed something. I didn't want to come back. Your shoulder still stiff?"

"It'll be all right."

"Don't blame the log."

"Why would I do that? Hope I've got more sense than that."

"If you had any real sense you'd have left me under there."

"You don't know what you're saying."

You stood up and the boat began to rock slowly. I stopped rowing and looked up at you. The stars framed your silhouette, feet on a thwart and braced against the gunwales, hands on hips. We had the whole inlet to ourselves. Your voice came from everywhere at once.

"If I was the one who had been murdered that night, would you have offered my brother a place to stay? I want the truth or I'll jump overboard. You won't find me this time. Would you have helped my brother?"

"No."

"So you're no different from those men who wanted to buy me. You didn't offer to pay, that's all. You weren't thinking of my colour because you were busy thinking of something else. I've been forced to think of it ever since I was a girl and now I can't think any other way."

You sat down and neither of us spoke the rest of the way in. I thought, tell me off but don't leave, tell me anything except you're leaving.

There's a feeling that has no name. It makes everything seem important, floods the world and makes light immortal.

All the small things become treasures and you know nobody can ever tell you different. All reasons are excuses for that feeling or denials of it, and when you've known it you've had the most any of us can have. When I was a young boy I used to fish in a lake near town. Once I was walking home from the lake with some other kids and we passed two teenagers on the trail, a guy and a girl. I could see he had been trying to get her to go into the bushes with him and she didn't want to. He pulled at her coat sleeve a couple of times and she pulled it away. I told my friends I had to tie my shoelaces and would catch up with them later. I wanted to stay and help her if she needed it. I didn't care that the guy was much older and bigger and could have pounded me into the ground with one fist. At that moment it seemed the most important thing in the world that she should be able to do what she wanted. After a while he said something, took the ends of the scarf she wore around her neck and tied them into a tight knot and walked away. I never forgot his smug look. She seemed to know why I was there. She called me over and leaned down and asked me to untie the knot but I couldn't. I couldn't keep my hands still and my clumsy fingers kept slipping as I tried to loosen that strangled silk, tried to forget the smell of her flowery perfume, how close she was, how soft and warm her throat felt. I told her I couldn't and she said it was all right. We walked together along the trail for a bit before she took a branch that led off somewhere else. We said goodbye and as I walked on alone kicking pebbles I thought if I'd been able to undo that knot I'd have done something incredibly important because of what it had meant to each of us at the moment. In a way neither understood she was my first woman and I was a too young and rather pathetic if earnest version of the man she wanted. I felt ashamed at my failure but honoured at being chosen. We narrow love down and it escapes through our fingers out into a universe of bursting stars. We're too afraid of the explosions inside. I've tried to untie that knot all my life and never did. I'm still the boy who's ashamed of himself but nobody can tell me I should stop trying. I've been at it too long, and the world can ask or give no more.

Your
Sam McLendon

The following letter completes Josie's story. A note regarding the reference in the first paragraph to her manuscript: the originals, hers and Sam's, have been deposited in the university archives. Negotiations with her people about making hers available on loan on a regular basis or as a permanent loan or ultimately transferring it to them are underway. Although because of the personal link and for the sake of academic study the manuscripts belong together, her people's claim to hers is obviously a valid one. Good intentions on both sides promise a solution satisfactory to everyone.

April 27, 2014

Dear Professor Kendrick:

Thank you for sending a photocopy of Josephine Littletree's manuscript and of your forthcoming book. Copies of her manuscript will be made available in the Williams Lake library, along with the book when it is published. Both will be important teaching aids for me, as well as of great personal significance. Your letter to the band council was passed on to me because it was thought I could best answer your questions.

About Ed George nothing is known. Nobody I talked with in any of the bands knows what happened to him. I can tell you that for many years now non-aboriginal hunters and fishers in the Cariboo have reported seeing a man with two dogs. Two years ago I talked with a party of American hunters. They said a man appeared on the other side of the lake from where they stood, about a hundred yards away, and stared at them. He had a rifle, and two dogs accompanied him. The hunters waved and shouted at him but he didn't answer. He seemed to fade back into the forest. They assured me they were sober and had not heard the stories about him. It was their first trip up here.

You refer to the book of stories mentioned in Sam McLendon's manuscript. After graduating from university I started teaching school here and was given the book by Bill

Paul. There are notes in the margins, where Josephine has made comments on the stories and the variations. She always respects the meaning and intent of each story. Older people in the bands who heard her say that her storytelling was hypnotic. She made a story seem as if it was happening in front of your eyes. I teach the stories to my pupils and give talks on them at the library. I usually end up talking about her because I think her own story, after all, is the best she ever told.

Your guess about the beads mentioned in Sam McLendon's manuscript is correct. Rachel made them for Josephine. Rachel, as you know from Josephine's manuscript, does wonderful beadwork and embroidery. She is also highly regarded among our people for carving beads. Each bead in the necklace is of one of our sacred animals. The largest is of Raven. They are on display at the library, together with Josephine's original book of stories.

Rachel and Len did get married. They're my mother and father. My father died in 1998. My mother is still alive, active despite rheumatism and clearheaded as ever. She remembers much, and some of it is painful yet, especially memories of St. Jerome's. "It never leaves, you carry it with you," she says. My father was a great support to her. They had a loving relationship. When I think of them together I always see them holding hands. Of course, Josephine was the other great support in her life. She always talks about her. She hasn't read Josephine's manuscript because she couldn't bear to read the last part. There's something Josephine doesn't mention. When my mother heard she had returned to the reserve to die, she went to see her. She wanted to talk her out of it. She told me what happened. I've heard her account often enough that I can remember it almost word for word.

My father drove her over from our reserve to Bill Paul's house and waited there when she went to see her. She could see she had changed. It was more than the result of tuberculosis. There was a nurse attending her, Ms Menzies. She was concerned about her. She had tried to do what she could for her but her efforts were rejected or evaded. She had almost given up. When my mother arrived at Josephine's grandmother's house, Josephine was out in the back in a wheelchair. It was ten o'clock in the morning and there were patches of fog drifting through the garden. She could see blood on Josephine's sweater. My mother got a chair and sat beside her and they talked about all sorts of things. My mother's wedding three years earlier, before Josephine had gotten sick, and my parents visiting her at the sanatorium at Christmas. She wheezed as she talked and my mother wondered whether that was the tuberculosis or she was also suffering from pneumonia. It hurt her to see Josephine so sick but she kept control of her emotions. When Josephine said she was getting rid of her nurse that day, it was obvious nobody could change her mind about dying. When it came time to say goodbye my mother broke down. Josephine embraced her.

"Don't cry, Rachel. I'm getting out. Like St. Jerome's. They haven't beaten me. I'm leaving. I won't play the victim. I won't be their sick Indian. They win if we hate ourselves and lose if we don't. Be proud and nobody can touch you. Go tell our stories."

When she returned to Bill Paul's house, my mother told him to check on Josephine's condition daily and Bill said the people in her band were honouring her wish by letting her die but he would go every day to see her. The next day the house was empty. There's a grove of red cedar a quarter of a mile from Josephine's grandmother's house. He found her there. She had reached the grove without her wheelchair, probably crawling much of the way. She was dead, sprawled at the foot of the smallest tree. My mother's beads were around her neck. On her hand was her mother's wedding ring.

I hope I've answered your questions. If there's anything else, please feel free to write or email.

Yours in friendship,
Josephine Littletree Spurgeon

www.ingramcontent.com/pod-product-compliance
Lightning Source LLC
LaVergne TN
LVHW050920080826
845145LV00001B/153

* 9 7 8 0 9 9 5 2 6 7 1 6 9 *